VOTED MOST LIKELY

VOTED

Most Likely

NICOLE ADAIR

Published by Validation Press, LLC

This novel is a work of fiction. Names, characters, organizations, places, events, and incidents are products of the author's imagination or are used fictitiously. Any resemblance to actual events, locales, organizations, or persons living or dead is entirely coincidental.

Cover designed and illustrated by Paige Poppe

To my mom
who's read every version of this story
and who's loved every version of me

"I HATE HIM. I hate him, I hate him, I hate him."
I slammed my locker shut, but it didn't have the effect I'd been hoping for. The hallway didn't break in half or crumble along its edges, everyone running and screaming as the world swallowed them whole. The metallic clang of my locker door rang in my ears, drowning out the laughter and whispers and noisy gossip of my fellow peers. The ringing in my ears matched the buzzing in my head. Good, more noise. More to distract me.

But it wasn't enough.

"He nearly screwed up my presentation!" I slung my backpack roughly over my shoulders before reaching up to tighten my ponytail.

"And here we go." Cat checked her makeup one last time in her tiny mirror—so covered in stickers, I wondered if she could actually see her reflection—then shut her own locker (much less forcefully) and put on her Patient Face.

"The way he was asking all those questions, trying to trip me up..." I pointlessly tightened my hairband again, gripping the long dark strands as I turned to Cat.

She made a sympathetic noise and slipped the straps of her backpack on. "He did. He totally did. You have every right to be mad. But if you make that ponytail any tighter, I'm afraid your face is going to freeze like that and that's not the expression you want immortalized on your face forever. Trust me." She swatted my hands away from my hair. "Just relax; maybe try those breathing exercises my mom recommended?"

"Now is not the moment to backseat psychoanalyze me, Dr. Lee. I'm not in the mood."

Cat raised one black eyebrow at me. "Are you ever?" she mumbled under her breath with a laugh that changed into a cough when she saw my face.

I scowled before grabbing her arm and pulling her into a run down the nearly empty hallway. "Come on, we're going to be late for chem."

I would never admit it to my best friend Catherine, but those stupid breathing exercises her psychiatrist mother gently suggested I try out ("I've just noticed you're a little tense, darling") *do* help. But sometimes not even the deepest breathing in the world can keep me from wanting to light the entire school on fire at the sight of He Who Must Not Be Named's face.

No, not Voldemort. His second in command.

Aiden Christopher Mitchell III.

The bell rang shrilly the moment we slid into the chemistry classroom, the door clicking shut softly behind us.

"You need to cut back on your primping time," I hissed to Cat. "We were almost late."

"You need to cut back on your ranting time," she hissed back before smiling serenely at me. "Think about how much time you would gain; you could pick up a new hobby."

The door flew open again as a boy with a mop of golden blond hair darted in, his backpack swinging casually off his letterman jacket-clad shoulders. His face was flushed from running to class, which served him right; it's the beginning of October in West Texas. Who did he think he was wearing a stuffy jacket at this time of year?

He came to an abrupt stop when he saw me standing at the back of the classroom and sighed, tapping at an imaginary watch on his wrist. "Almost late, Jo. Now, what would your perfect attendance record have to say about that?"

Just the sound of his voice sent my blood boiling. "Josephine," I corrected, even though he already knew that. Of course he knew my full name and that I hate every single variation of abbreviated nickname in existence. "And I'm not late. *You* are."

Aiden sauntered past me before stopping directly in front of the path to my seat. He's tall, but so am I. We are almost the exact same height, but he's got me beat by an inch or two.

Point to Mitchell, grudgingly given.

Cat sidestepped us with a whispered, "Inhale peace, exhale your troubles…" She swallowed a laugh when I glared down at her, but it's been a long time since Cat was intimidated by me. If she ever was in the first place, that is.

I glanced over at Mr. Langston's desk hoping he would admonish Aiden Christopher Mitchell III for lurking in the back of the class-room and blocking me from getting to my seat. I also hoped he would throw in a few added insults about his intelligence while waving my last exam in the air with its bright red A+ on it.

A girl can dream.

But Mr. Langston was staring at his computer with the stupor of someone who's barely hanging onto consciousness, his shoulders slumping over his cluttered desk. I could see the reflection of his online poker game in his glasses.

He's in a room full of hyperactive AP Chem kids; we're exhaust-ing, I know. But still, 10 a.m. poker?

Aiden finally turned to let me pass, gesturing me through with a stack of small red flyers in his hand that I hadn't noticed earlier.

"Student council business," he said when he caught me eyeing them. His lips twitched like a bad omen.

"Excuse me? *What* business?"

"For the blood drive."

My stomach dropped. "*What* blood drive?"

"Our school's hosting a blood drive on Thursday. Keep up." He sighed and shook his head. "Maybe if you'd been at the last meet-ing—"

"*What* meeting? We're co-presidents; how did you have a meeting without me?"

His mouth tucked into that private frown he always reserved for me, but his hazel eyes lit up with suppressed laughter. "Didn't you get the email I sent?" He scratched the back of his head and squinted like he was trying to remember something. "I must've forgotten to add you. Or maybe I typed in your email address wrong. My bad." He shrugged with a sheepish look that was 100% unnecessary and unconvincing. "We met yesterday afternoon and we voted. It was unanimous: we're having a blood drive."

He fanned himself with his obnoxiously red flyers as I stared at him with open-mouthed indignation. For the past two weeks we'd been stuck in a stalemate over what to do for our school-wide service project. He knew I didn't want to do a blood drive, that I'd adamantly opposed it every time he'd brought it up. He knew it, and he'd held a secret meeting without me, waiting for the only afternoon I wasn't at school until the sun went down to have the vote.

"But there's no way we'll have enough time to get everything set up for Thursday, that's only two days away," I said, wishing my voice didn't sound so desperate. I snatched one of the flyers out of his hands and quickly scanned over the details listed on the crimson paper. My mind was going a million miles a minute as I tried to think of a solution that tipped the odds back in my favor.

"Don't worry about it. Everything's already taken care of."

He watched me smugly as I silently opened and closed my mouth in vain. I'd forgotten that his mom was a nurse who worked at the county hospital, and he was such an over-eager over-achiever that of course he already had the whole thing organized and ready to go for Thursday. I would've wondered how he'd pulled this off, but, apparently, Golden Boys can pull off anything. And I have more important things to think about than the logistics of his asinine behavior.

Point to Mitchell.

"I believe this is the part where you say, 'thank you, Aiden,'" he said as he plucked the flyer out of my grip.

If looks could kill, Aiden Christopher Mitchell III and his blond head of hair would've been wiped off the face of the earth a long, long time ago.

I pursed my lips and stalked through the aisle without another word. My jaw was clenched so tightly my head was aching. It was going to be a miracle if I made it through our senior year without cracking a tooth. The last time I got my teeth cleaned, the hygienist sat back and frowned before carefully asking me if I'd ever considered wearing a night guard.

I didn't bother explaining that teeth grinding at night wasn't my issue.

Mr. Langston chose that moment to click out of his online gambling and rose from his chair in a flurry of motion, as if he'd only just realized the bell had rung all of five minutes ago.

"Might as well stay standing, Miss Crew. You got the top score again." He tipped an imaginary hat at me (this man seriously believed he was in Vegas or something) and motioned for the class to join in his applause.

My classmates gave up a collective sigh as they slowly clapped along, looking unimpressed. *Josephine Crew getting the top grade in class.* Someone wake them up when something actually exciting happened.

But I didn't care. The familiar rush of achievement smothered the flames of my anger and replaced them with that warm glow I felt every time I won. I glanced over my shoulder to see Aiden still standing there with his arms crossed over his chest. He wasn't applauding and I knew why.

I never applauded when he won either.

You don't cheer when your rival wins. Ever. That's the sacred rule of competition and Aiden and I had been locked in an unending one since the first day we met in the sixth grade.

Point to me.

"You were a close second, Mr. Mitchell!" Mr. Langston called out brightly, pointing to Aiden. He noted the flyers gripped in Aiden's hand and motioned him forward. "What can I do you for, my good sir?"

You were a close second, Mr. Mitchell.

Forget meditation. I just needed to record Mr. Langston singing out those words like the wannabe lounge singer he was and listen to it on repeat whenever I felt stressed. Literal music to my ears.

Aiden didn't look at me as he passed by on the opposite aisle and stood at the front of the classroom where he turned to face everyone. He hit them with his smug, mega-watt smile, and they were putty in his hands. But I guess they didn't see him as smug. They saw his grin as conspiratorial, funny, winsome. They saw him as a friend.

I rolled my eyes at the way even Mr. Langston stood up straighter. Like he was the one who needed to win Aiden's approval and not the other way around. It wasn't a secret that most of our teachers liked

Aiden a little bit more than me, a fact that annoyed me endlessly. It wasn't for lack of trying on my part. I did extra credit; I always stayed to help clean up after events; I did everything but put a shiny red apple on their desks. But it wasn't enough. Aiden smiled and laughed at their jokes and the entire faculty and student body fell for it every time.

Somehow over-achiever looks better on him than it does on me. They like the gleam of his shiny gold stars, but they always complain that mine are too blinding. The double standard is enough to make me actually consider wearing a night guard.

"Our school's hosting a community blood drive, and we need volunteers," I said loudly, forcing my voice not to waver. I was still on my feet, so it was easy for me to march to the front of the room and stand next to my mutinous co-president. Well, slightly in front of him, with my elbow jabbing into his side. Aiden looked semi-surprised at my hijacking of his announcement but recovered quickly.

Cat had been doodling absently on her notebook but jerked her head up in alarm at the words "blood drive." I could feel her probing gaze on me, brimming with humiliating concern.

"Jo is handling volunteer sign-ups," Aiden said without looking at me as he elbowed me back just as roughly. I cringed at the nickname, but he ignored me. "She's passing around the schedule, so coordinate with her." He clapped a large hand on my shoulder, shaking me slightly. "See her after class if you have any questions. She's more than happy to handle any of your concerns." I shrugged him off and swallowed the frustrated noise crawling up my throat, begging to get out. I didn't have time for this.

I didn't have time for anything.

Point to Mitchell. A stupid, immature point, but a point nonetheless.

Mr. Langston looked nervously back and forth between us as if he was afraid we were about to start brawling right in the middle of his classroom. In his fretful state, he dropped his whiteboard marker on the floor where it rolled over to Aiden's feet, bumping into his scuffed sneaker.

Aiden darted his hand down to pick it up, tossing it back with another one of his easy smiles. Mr. Langston flinched and barely caught it before it smacked him in the face.

"Nice catch, Mr. Langston."

Mr. Langston actually had the nerve to look pleased by the off-hand compliment. "High praise coming from you, Mr. Mitchell." He flashed him another imaginary hat tip.

Aiden grinned at the class again until his eyes landed on me, and his grin melted into a smirk. "Let me know how many time slots we fill, Jo," he said, sliding into his seat.

"Josephine," I hissed under my breath as I shoved myself into my own seat and yanked my backpack open, the zipper screaming loudly in protest.

But I think he heard me anyway, because his head twisted back one last time and he looked like the freaking Cheshire Cat.

I'm not sure who got that point.

Two

M Y MIND IS like an unending scorecard, folded over so many times I lose track of exactly how long it is when I fling it open each day. It's worn and torn in a few places, but the ink is crisp and stark against the imaginary page.

I know exactly where I stand.

The first day I met Aiden Christopher Mitchell III was the second week of school on a Wednesday after lunch. I don't know why I remember those seemingly insignificant details, but I do.

Maybe because his entire existence feels like a rude interruption.

"Class, we have a new student."

Everyone started quietly buzzing as the new kid rounded the corner of Mrs. Crabtree's overstuffed desk. He accidentally knocked one of her porcelain cat figurines over but caught it with a nimble hand before it hit the floor. "Sorry about that, ma'am," he said, handing the cat back to Mrs. Crabtree. He was polite and tucked in, his smile small and his striped t-shirt clean and wrinkle-free.

The boys in the class sniggered at his courtesy, unimpressed. The girls fluttered in their seats, clearly feeling the opposite. Cat's wiggling caught my eye, her black bob swishing around her face in excitement from where she sat in the aisle next to mine. I sat perfectly still with my hands folded on my desk. I wasn't sure what to think. He looked nice enough, with his buttery blond hair curling behind his ears. He needed a haircut, but that was the only unruly thing about him.

Mrs. Crabtree gently set the porcelain cat back in its rightful place before taking the boy by the shoulders, pinning him in place for all of us to continue ogling at him. "This is Aiden—" she announced in a voice any gameshow host would envy.

"—Christopher Mitchell III," he piped in, raising his finger to cut her off. She blinked a few times before smiling and nodding as if it were totally normal for a kid with that long of a name to remind you that he was, indeed, The Third, like he was some kind of prince.

Red flag number one.

"And he just moved here from across the state!" She said that like he'd flown in from Europe, like it was exotic, and far, far away. And to us, I guess it was. Everyone oohed and ahhed. Our town is embarrassingly small, so any new kid in school was very noticeable and very worth talking about. We'd all known each other since before kindergarten.

Aiden took a deep breath and held it as he stared back at us. And when he finally exhaled, the whole room lit up with him. His smile stretched wide as he looked at each person individually for a long time, scanning the crowd of classmates for potential new friends.

I felt my back straighten without making the conscious decision to do so. I found myself smoothing down my hair, even though it was pulled back into the tight ponytail I always wore. I wondered what he thought of me. I wondered why I cared.

"So tell us, Aiden. What brings your family to Pearson?" Mrs. Crabtree asked, finally releasing his shoulders but still refusing to let him sit down.

For the first time since he walked in through our classroom door, the new boy seemed nervous. He looked down and bit his lip, fiddling with the straps on his backpack until he said, "My parents wanted a fresh start." When he looked back up, his face was bright and calm, his momentary hesitancy completely vanished.

"Well, there's no better place than Pearson for a fresh start," Mrs. Crabtree said proudly. I barely resisted the urge to raise my hand and correct her. Pearson wasn't a place to start anything. The whole town felt like the end of the most boring story ever told. "Go on and pick a seat," she continued, gently pushing Aiden forward, "there are a few available." Then she turned her back on the class and began sketching out a timeline on the whiteboard.

Aiden tugged on the straps of his backpack and made a beeline for the empty seat directly in front of me. I leaned back, stunned. No one ever sat there, and for a good reason. But he was new, so how was he supposed to know?

Carter leaned across the aisle and pointed to the seat next to him, and a few of the other boys did the same, all vying for the new kid's attention. Apparently, they'd decided he was worth knowing.

But Aiden swung his backpack over the back of his chair and slid down into the seat in front of mine. "Bad move, man," Carter whispered with a quick glance at me. I resisted the urge to stick my tongue out at him. That certainly wasn't going to help (even though it might make me feel better).

Mrs. Crabtree twirled to face us, her hip jostling her cat figurines as she bumped into her desk. She was older than my great-grandmother and I was pretty sure she'd rather die at her desk than retire. But she was nice and always snuck me extra books from the school library when I was past my checkout limit. I liked her.

She peered over her small round glasses and made direct eye contact with me as she asked the question, "Now who can remember where the last battle of the Civil War took place? It was in your reading last night."

My hand was up before the question was out of her mouth. But my hand wasn't the only one. Aiden Christopher Mitchell III was sitting straight in his seat with his hand waving in the air, just about blocking mine from view.

I leaned forward and jabbed my hand up higher, nearly knocking into the new kid's head, and the class started to twitter. Cat audibly gasped. This was why no one ever wanted to sit in front of me—my enthusiasm was a bit violent. Unintentionally violent, I should add.

But that wasn't the only reason the class was humming, rustling in their seats to get a better look. Mrs. Crabtree's smile faltered as she looked back and forth between Aiden and me. Our hands had gone up at the exact same moment, both of us stretched tall.

Everyone wanted to see what I would do; everyone was waiting to see if my violence was going to turn intentional. No one ever beat me when it came to hand-raising. And no one ever tried.

Mrs. Crabtree patted her silver hair and cleared her throat noisily as if to buy herself some time. "Mr. Mitchell! What do you think?" she finally asked, avoiding my eyes and gaping mouth.

Aiden slowly lowered his hand and said, "What is Palmito Ranch, May 12, 1865?"

He answered the question like he was a contestant on *Jeopardy.*

Red flag number two.

Mrs. Crabtree beamed. "Correct! Now, who can tell me—" My hand was up before she even asked the question, but I wasn't worried; I was totally confident I would know the right answer.

"Did you have a question, Josephine?" My face flamed as I sputtered, trying to explain that I was ready and willing to share my wealth of knowledge on the Civil War. "No?" she said. "Then let's continue."

Aiden and I battled for the rest of the lesson. He never turned around to look at me, but I couldn't stop imagining his self-satisfied smile growing wider and wider. A quiet hush fell over the rest of the class as if they were watching a nail-biter of a tennis match, their wide eyes bobbing back and forth between us. I could feel a trickle of sweat dripping down my back as my prickling panic wrestled with my shock over someone so blatantly trying to outdo me.

I'd never felt like this before.

After a while, I started blurting out answers without raising my hand, and that pushed Mrs. Crabtree over the edge. Like my great-grandmother, she preferred orderly conduct, and, well, I'd basically thrown all orderly conduct out the window.

By the time the bell rang at the end of the day, I was on the verge of tears, and that made me madder than anything. I carefully slid my books into my backpack and stood, bracing myself to face this new kid who obviously did not understand how things worked in this classroom. Aiden was hunched over his own desk, haphazardly tossing his new books into his backpack.

But before I could say a word, Mrs. Crabtree's voice rang out over the clamor of her students packing up and racing each other out the door. "Miss Crew?" She crooked her finger, gesturing for me to join her at her desk.

My heart was about to beat out of my chest. I squared my shoulders and shoved my hands into the pockets of my shorts as I began my slow march to the front of the classroom, the rest of my classmates streaming past me in their eagerness to go home. Aiden briefly paused at the door and glanced over his shoulder, eyeing me curiously before he turned and walked out too. Cat was still hovering at her desk, packing up her stuff in slow motion, clearly stalling for time.

"See yourself out, Miss Lee. Josephine will join you in a moment," Mrs. Crabtree said with the final dregs of her patience before she sank heavily into her chair. Cat's jelly shoes clacked against the scarred linoleum floor as she ran to the door and motioned that she'd meet me outside.

I swallowed and tried not to squirm under my teacher's shrewd gaze, but my hands wouldn't stop fidgeting with the hem of my t-shirt. "Now Josephine, really. Would it kill you to let someone else answer a question every once in a while?" She frowned and tapped her pen against her chin as she studied me.

I squeaked out a noise when I saw her knotted hand reaching for the small pink pad on which she wrote her lunch detention slips. Mrs. Crabtree sighed and shook her head sadly. I felt like I was going to be sick all over her doily-covered desk.

In a single afternoon, my life had been completely upended. Aiden Christopher Mitchell III had waltzed in and ruined everything, turning my beloved teacher against me and landing me in detention too, which was the cherry on top. I swallowed my hurt and surprise, pushing it down until it rose again as something else, something sharp and scalding.

But Mrs. Crabtree wasn't finished with me yet. She scribbled on the notepad, tore it off, and handed it to me with her weathered hand like she was doing me a favor. "Your behavior today was… unbecoming." Her expression soured, like bad behavior smelled rotten. "But I think this new boy could be good for you. A little healthy competition is a boost to the spirit."

"Whatever you say, Mrs. Crabtree," I said mechanically, even though my anger was bubbling like a pot on a stove, steaming and threatening to spill over. "Sorry for disturbing the class," I added, because I am who I am, and I am a teacher's pet.

She patted me on the head and scooted me out the door. I walked through the empty halls on rubbery legs, exhaling a hot and heavy breath once the school doors swung shut behind me. I slumped against them and closed my eyes, feeling shaky. After all, I was only twelve and this was probably the biggest burst of feeling I'd had in my life, possibly ever.

"You're good with history," said a voice from my right. There, leaning against the school's chain-link fence and squinting in the bright afternoon sun was the new kid. He rubbed a hand through his hair as if trying to tousle it further and walked up to me. He stuck his other hand out and grinned his cheeky grin. "I'm Aiden—"

"—Christopher Mitchell III. I *know*." My hands stayed clenched into fists inside my pockets. After a long moment, he dropped his hand, letting it swing back and forth by his side.

What twelve-year-old tries to shake another kid's hand?

Red flag number three.

I pulled out the pink slip that was still clutched in my fist and waved it in his face like it was my very own scarlet letter (which I'd just finished reading the night before). "You landed me in lunch detention, thanks a lot."

His brow puckered over his hazel eyes. "What did I do?"

"You wouldn't let me answer a single question—"

"That's not true, you answered plenty—"

"But I could've answered *more*," I finished, crossing my arms tightly over my chest.

He backed up a step and looked me over, his eyes sweeping up and down once. I stuck my chin up and glared at him right back.

"You're good with history," he said again. I straightened my shoulders, ready to tell him about all the other subjects I was good at too, but before I could, he added, "But you should know that I'm better, Jo." He laughed once and turned to walk out the gate where a group of kids was waiting to walk home with him, including Cat.

"It's Josephine!" I yelled back, too angry to think of another retort.

"That's kind of a mouthful. Plus, you look like a Jo."

"Like *your* name isn't a mouthful? It's like you have three first names!"

He ignored me and untucked his shirt, then swung his backpack from over his shoulder and pulled out a football. "Anyone want to play?"

I groaned and tipped my face into my hands. A football. I should've known.

Red flags numbers four through ten.

We live in West Texas, and he just pulled out a football.

Nobody likes a know-it-all. Unless they're a Golden Boy and they can throw a perfect spiral.

I met Cat where she was still waiting for me by the gate. She didn't suggest that we walk with the boys even though I knew she wanted to. And she didn't ask what Mrs. Crabtree had said to me either. Instead, she linked her arm through mine as we started to walk and said, "Who is Josephine Crew?"

"What?"

"The smartest person I know," Cat said with a smile that scrunched up her entire face.

I stared at her blankly before surprised laughter bubbled out of me. "Did you just answer your own *Jeopardy* question?"

She nodded and added her high-pitched giggle to mine. I rolled my eyes but squeezed her arm tightly against mine, grateful for her reassurance, however ridiculous it was.

Then I muttered about Aiden the whole way home.

I'd gotten the last word in, but why didn't it feel like I'd won?

Three

F IRST, I ABUSED my locker, then my sack lunch. I slammed it down with enough force to shake the table and yanked the chair out with equal aggression before sliding into it with a sigh, spilling over the edges of the seat like a wrung-out washcloth. Like those two motions had taken all the energy I had left.

Cat didn't even look up from the notebook she was doodling in; she was used to my huffiness. I think I was her form of white noise. "How was calc?" Her flower design sprawled across the page in sweeping motions, vibrant but quiet. Just like Cat.

Honestly, I don't know how she tolerates me.

"Fine," I answered tersely, sitting up and ripping open my brown paper sack. I dug around until I found the peanut butter and banana sandwich I was searching for. Cat knows me well enough to wait me out, so after one long look at me, she went back to her doodling, occasionally forking some of the cafeteria mac 'n' cheese in her mouth without a word.

Another chair at our table screeched loudly across the beat-up floor as my sister Rose sat down next to me.

"I think I failed my vocab quiz," she said nonchalantly, flicking her auburn hair over her shoulder.

I whipped my head up so quickly, my neck cracked. "*Failed*? How? I quizzed you for like two hours last night."

Rose shrugged and rolled out her own brown paper bag, complete with matching sandwich. "Ooh, I like that design, Cat. You should do one on my binder."

"Rose, don't change the subject. You can't be failing things! You're a junior! This year—"

"*Matters*, I know. You remind me every thirty seconds, how could I ever forget." She snorted and took another bite of her sandwich. "It's just a quiz," she said through her mouthful. "I'll be fine. Guess what," she said in that rapid-fire way of hers; she changed thoughts like she was jumping from train to train. "Jordan asked me to go to homecoming with him this weekend." She waggled her eyebrows up and down as she and Cat burst into a fit of giggles.

The right side of my mouth curled into a smile—I couldn't help myself. Rose was infectious like that. She was the sweet to my sour, the sugar to my spice—or whatever other weird cooking metaphor you want to pick. She was nice and people liked her. She was fun and funny and kind. I adored her. We were only eighteen months apart and I couldn't remember a day without her.

Honestly, I don't know how she tolerates me either.

I've always felt like the watered-down version of Rose. It's like I'm leeched of all her color—her vibrant auburn hair turned to a dark muddy brown on me, her bright blue eyes reduced to my sharp steel gray. I may be the firstborn, but somehow I've always felt like I was in second place—only I'm better at spelling, which isn't much to brag about.

But that doesn't stop me from bragging anyway.

"Jordan, hmm? You mean after three desperate weeks of staring at you in biology, he finally made a move?" I stole one of her chips out of her bag and tossed it into my mouth. "Took him long enough. He's cutting it a little close to the dance though—it's only four days away," I said in disapproval.

Cat slammed her notebook shut (apparently this news was worthy of putting her pen down), her big golden hoops swaying as she leaned in across the table. "Are your parents going to let you go?"

Rose stiffened for the briefest moment, but I saw it. She laughed and smacked my hand away before I could steal another chip. "Who says they have to know?"

Cat and I shared a look. Rose was fun and funny and kind, but sometimes she was so naive it caused me physical pain. "I'll cover for you," I said before she could ask.

Of course I would. That was my job.

"Really? Oh, you're the best. I love you and I'll unload the dishwasher for you every day for a month!"

"The dreaded dishwasher duty? You must really like this guy." I grabbed another chip, and this time Rose didn't try to stop me.

"Have you seen him? He's gorgeous and—"

"Probably failing biology because he hasn't been paying attention for three weeks," I mumbled under my breath.

Rose's mouth puckered. "I was going to say he's *nice*. He's a nice guy."

Boring, I quipped in my mind. He sounded boring.

"We'll see." I scanned the cafeteria, looking for this so-called nice guy, Jordan Hernandez. It didn't take me long. He was at least a head taller than most of the boys at our school. He played varsity basketball (because of course he did) and he had dark hair that swooped across his forehead and big brown eyes that I'm sure made Rose all sorts of swoony. He caught us watching him and stumbled over his feet, nearly dropping his cafeteria tray. Rose sighed contentedly and waved. Jordan smiled shyly back at her, his cheeks flushed and pink.

He did seem nice.

"Are you sure you don't want to come with us?" Cat pleaded, folding her hands like she was saying a prayer. "It'll be fun—"

"Fifth-wheeling it at homecoming with you and my sister? Hardly."

"You could take someone," she offered. "Ethan could ask one of his friends..."

"I don't need your boyfriend to find me a pity date. And I don't want to. Homecoming is stupid and a waste of time."

"Not that most precious commodity that is 'time,'" Cat said with air quotes. "How dare we waste it."

Rose sniggered into her drink as they waited for me to say something.

I tried not to rise to the bait, I really did. I bit my tongue and held my breath, but before I knew it the words were rolling out of me. "You know, we could spend that time working on our applications."

Cat cheered and held out her hand to Rose. "Told you."

Rose muttered something under her breath before slapping a five-dollar bill in Cat's hand.

I waved my sandwich at the two of them. "What's this all about?"

Cat pocketed her newfound cash with a grin at me. "I bet Rose you couldn't make it through one whole lunch hour without bringing up our college applications." Rose glared at me like *I* was the one being annoying in this situation. Cat shook her head, looking a little disappointed even though she'd won. "You're obsessed, Josephine."

"As I should be! And so should you. It's our only way—"

"Out of here," they both finished before I could.

"Exactly," I said, narrowing my eyes at Cat. "I thought you wanted to see the world, to do something besides being another born and raised and lived and died Pearson citizen."

Cat stirred her congealed macaroni absently. "Of course I do. But this is home. I don't have to hate it here to want to leave, you know."

That was a foreign concept I couldn't comment on, so instead I took a giant bite out of my sandwich. My mouth was glued together with peanut butter, but it didn't matter. Rose and Cat had started chatting about dress shopping, so I tuned them out and tried to swallow my food, waiting until the subject returned to something that actually interested me.

"Aiden looks tired." Rose's voice pulled me back to the present.

Cat ran a hand through her short dark hair, further tousling her messy waves before tugging at her face in mock horror. "Why, oh why, did you mention You Know Who? I'm already tapped out on that subject and it's only noon."

Rose frowned and looked at me. "Why? What happened?"

"Nothing," I said, though the reminder of his existence had immediately set my insides writhing.

"It's never nothing with you two."

"Don't say it like that."

"Like what?" Rose asked, her perfectly plucked brows rising.

"Don't say 'you two' like we're… like we're together in any way. I don't like it."

Rose bit her lip, clearly trying not to laugh. "Well, that's kind of impossible. 'You two' are together constantly; you're basically in charge of every extracurricular on campus. Every club, every AP class, you're co-presidents…"

"Ugh, don't remind me," I groaned, flopping my head onto her shoulder. "It's not my fault this stupid school is so small."

I scanned the cafeteria to find Aiden holding court at his usual table full of admiring fans, all of them fawning over him. And he just sat there eating it up like that's what they'd served for hot lunch today. His letterman jacket was slung over the back of his seat, but he still had a Pearson High football t-shirt on as if he was afraid we'd forget he was the star running back if he didn't have it plastered all over his chest.

But under the horribly unflattering florescent lighting, there was an edge of weariness about him. He was slumped in his seat like it took too much effort to hold himself up and leaning on his elbow as he bantered with his football friends and flirted with the entire dance line.

"He *does* look tired," I said, sitting up quickly, my long ponytail swishing behind me. "Where does he find the energy to torment me like this if he's so exhausted?" I added, thinking of his crimes against me today (and it was only lunchtime): AP English and his rudeness during my presentation, chem and the secret blood drive, calculus and the missing brackets around my answer that he'd taken upon himself to bring up to the entire class.

Cat snorted into her soda. "I'm sure he finds it wherever you find the energy to one-up him."

I primly poked at the remains of my lunch and sniffed. "There's no way he's drinking that poisonous Kool-Aid—few can stomach it."

"Wait, is it poison or is it Kool-Aid?" Rose asked, pausing mid-bite.

"Maybe he'll crack soon," I said, ignoring her.

"Try not to sound so gleeful about it. It's… *unbecoming*." Cat smirked at me as she dredged up that timeless insult from our sixth-grade teacher, Mrs. Crabtree. "Maybe he's actually a vampire. Edward always had dark circles under his eyes too." She widened her respective eyes at us. "Once, I even saw Aiden glittering in the sun."

"That was from the back-to-school parade when all the cheerleaders dumped a vat of glitter on him and the rest of the team. You can still see traces of it everywhere." I rolled my eyes, remembering the gritty feel of the glitter in my mouth, the way I'd had to spit it out for the rest of the parade. The marching band had been assembling right in their line of fire, and you'd better believe I was in the front—I am first chair flute and section leader, after all.

First chair, first to swallow a mouthful of glitter. What a prize.

"And he did lobby for the blood drive," I said, turning to Cat conspiratorially.

"Yep, an undead giveaway. Definitely a vampire." She laughed, but then her laugh transformed into a scoff. She frowned at her plate. "Is there glitter in the mac 'n' cheese?"

"Told you. It's everywhere."

Just like Aiden.

As soon as I'd had the thought, his eyes snapped up to meet mine. Cold, calculating. Maybe he really was a vampire. I knew how much studying it took to maintain our grade point averages, and it's no secret that we're both vying for valedictorian. I knew how much time it required to manage all these clubs, the service projects, the hours of practice, not to mention the truckload of reading we had to get through each day.

I barely slept as it was.

Maybe he thinks I'm a vampire too.

His sharp gaze twitched off mine and skirted around the cafeteria like he was looking for something or someone. His fingers rubbed across his forehead agitatedly before he pulled out a book and flipped it open, then spent the rest of lunch half-listening to his giant teammates joking around and half-reading his calculus book. I smiled to myself, feeling smug. Looks like Golden Boy isn't quite as confident in his calc ability as he led us to believe.

Right as I finished my lunch, I glanced back to see him reach into his pocket and pull out a small canister. He hunched over and poured something into his hand, then tossed whatever it was into his mouth and swallowed. I squinted to see the tiny container clenched in his fist. It wasn't a normal prescription bottle, neon orange with a label on the side. This one was smaller, its shiny metal surface winking under the dull overhead lights. It was chrome and clinical; it looked like it came from outer space.

"Josephine, you've got your crazy face on." Rose flicked a grape at me. "Quit imagining strangling The Third and rein it in. Save it for your rounds today."

When I blinked, Aiden's hand was empty and he'd turned his back on me, angling his chair toward Angela Barlow, a member of the dance line and one of his many admirers. Rose was right, I needed to save my spite. Speech and Debate practice was after school today. That thought made me smile in earnest; there's nothing like a good floor-wiping to put a girl in a good mood.

"And what's this about a blood drive?" Rose asked, turning to Cat.

"Apparently, Aiden staged a coup and voted on a school-wide blood drive for this semester's service project," she answered in an exaggerated whisper.

Rose gasped. "But Josephine's terrified of needles!" She gripped my arm tightly. "Did you tell him?"

"Wow, calm down. And no, of course I didn't tell him." I swallowed roughly, trying to push down the wave of nausea I felt anytime I even heard the word "needles." "Why would I tell my mortal enemy my one fatal flaw?"

"One? Really?" Rose quipped, her hand sliding off my arm; she was obviously over any anxiety she'd felt on my behalf. "You should just tell him and do the nursing home activity like you wanted to."

"I shall not admit defeat, nor concede any weakness."

"Shall," Cat mouthed at Rose. "Nor." The two of them descended into another fit of giggles.

"Honestly, why do I tolerate either of you," I muttered, crumpling up my sack lunch and tossing it into the trash behind me.

That only made them laugh harder.

Four

O N TUESDAYS AND Thursdays the ringing of the final bell meant one thing and one thing only: it's time to debate.

As captain of the Pearson High Debate Team (please hold your applause), I was the leader in wins and, let's be honest, the only reason our team made it to state last year. Some might say that Aiden was a contributor, but I've never been one to jump on a bandwagon.

When Aiden showed up to the first day of debate practice our freshman year, I'd wanted to lie down on the filthy auditorium floor and wallow. I'd made the foolish mistake of thinking this was the one place he wouldn't be after school since he now had football practice to occupy him every day. But I should've known. In a school as small as ours, he was completely inescapable.

He marched in (late, of course) and informed the bemused debate coach that football practice had been moved back an hour to accommodate Aiden's other extracurriculars. I sat frozen in the front row, clutching the clipboard for event sign ups so hard I nearly snapped it in half. I couldn't believe that a lowly freshman player had so much sway over the team, but I guess when you're promoted to varsity at the ripe old age of fourteen allowances are made.

At least in Pearson, anyway.

Aiden slid into the seat next to mine and grabbed the clipboard out of my hands. He then proceeded to add insult to injury by scrawling his name under mine and signing up for the same event as me: the Lincoln-Douglas debate. He tossed the clipboard back in my lap without a word.

I stared at his messy signature on the sign-up sheet—the sharp, dark shape of the letters like a harbinger of our assured mutual destruction—until his name was a lingering afterimage when I closed my eyes. I'd endured all of junior high with Aiden closely tailing behind, always lurking in my shadow (okay fine, I will admit—sometimes I was the one in *his* shadow), why did I think high school was going to be any different? Why did I think I could finally have something that was just mine?

I sank lower in my seat and fumed. But what started as furious irritation gradually blossomed into a twisted version of delight. I decided right then and there that Aiden Christopher Mitchell III would never beat me in a debate. So I sat up straight and pasted on my most winning smile before passing the clipboard down the aisle as I mentally crossed my heart and hoped to die before he ever bested me in this auditorium or any other.

Our new battle lines had been drawn. We spent the next three years debating individually and clinging to our pristine records. And even though we were preparing for the same topics and the same tournaments, we never shared notes or sources. Instead, we each staked out our own side of the auditorium or the library and greedily hoarded over our material, shooting dirty looks at each other from behind our fortresses made of books and research and mutual loathing.

But we still had to work together. As the top two debaters on the team, we were forced to pair off at almost every practice. Things always escalated quickly and were usually forced to end just as swiftly, both of us red in the face and glaring. Plus, we only had one podium, and that always started things off on the wrong foot. You'd think the school would pay to get another one just to save themselves the trouble of listening to us argue over whose turn it was to use it.

Mr. Yeager, our old debate coach, retired early at the end of last year because, as he put it bluntly, "Life's too short to be stuck in a room with the likes of you two." This year's replacement was Ms. Torrence, a young and idealistic new teacher, still fresh-faced about the molding of young minds.

Our season was already underway with our first district tournament this upcoming Saturday. I was ready. I'd been prepping for weeks ever since the topic was announced, gathering arguments and evidence for every possible angle. Whether I was affirmative or negative, I would win.

For the past week I'd made Cat and Rose sit through multiple presentations, during which they'd graciously tried not to fall asleep, but once I was finished, neither one of them could decide which of my arguments had won. I was persuasive, I was succinct; in short, I was going to completely demolish the topic. Resolved: In a democracy, voting should be compulsory.

I walked into the school auditorium with a flourish, letting the doors swing shut behind me with a *bang*. Perhaps I was being a bit theatrical, but the spotlights were on and after the day I'd had I was ready to flex a little. It was time to remind Aiden who was still in the lead. Sometimes when I couldn't fall asleep at night, I pictured him on his knees, crying at my feet as the judges handed out the trophies, his head hanging low, his blond waves tumbling and tear-soaked.

Those are always the nights I get my best sleep.

I was the last one to show up to practice, hence the dramatic entrance. I'd been stuck in the hallway handling blood drive sign-ups, thanks to Aiden pawning that responsibility off on me. As I marched down the aisle toward the stage and the single podium at its center, I heard scattered whispers trailing in my wake, and when I stopped and scanned the not-so-impressive crowd, nobody would meet my eyes. Everyone looked nervous, scared even.

Except for Aiden. He was draped casually over his seat and staring right at me, his expression unreadable. I turned my attention to Ms. Torrence in the front row. She smiled at me like she was trying to put me at ease, to make me feel comfortable.

Which instantly made me uncomfortable.

"Did I miss something? What's going on?" I asked, my voice ringing out through the stillness of the cavernous auditorium.

Ms. Torrence smoothed back her already tidy pixie cut before standing and squaring her shoulders, but her agitation was obvious in the way she was gripping her clipboard with one hand and worrying her necklace with the other. "Josephine, we've discussed the upcoming tournament, and the rest of the team, myself included," she paused to gesture around the room as if I didn't know who my teammates were, "think that you and Aiden should compete in the policy debate." She said the last words in a rush, blending them together in a nearly incomprehensible blob of sound as she fanned herself with her clipboard, her eyes flicking rapidly between Aiden and me.

I barked out a laugh and she nearly jumped. "I'm sorry, I thought you said Aiden and I should compete. *Together*. In the policy debate." I clutched the back of the seat closest to me as I gasped for air between more bouts of laughter. "Hilarious, Ms. Torrence, truly. I didn't know you were such a crack up."

No one joined in with my laughter. The seven other kids on the team (like I said, not impressive) shrank down in their seats and busied themselves with their notebooks or their phones.

Ms. Torrence seemed to finally remember that she's the teacher and I'm the student as she stood a little taller and crossed her arms over her chest. "We think you could go all the way, Josephine. To nationals. That would be an incredible opportunity for our school and for the two of you. I know you're both looking to get full-ride scholarships—"

I coughed loudly, effectively cutting her off. "I think I can manage that on my own, thank you."

"But you haven't yet, have you?" she asked boldly, blinking at me from behind her glasses.

It took everything in me not to flinch. I stuck out my chin and said, "No, Ms. Torrence. I haven't made it to nationals... *yet*. But this year will be different—"

"Exactly. And the difference will be you and Aiden working together." She pointed behind her to the small crowd of simpering "teammates," a.k.a. traitors. "We voted. It's decided. It's what's best for the team."

"I can work with someone else," I said desperately. "Brandon? Want to team up?" I fixed my gaze on Brandon Lopez in the second row because he was the only one who would meet my eyes. I tried to silently communicate that he should nobly offer himself up to take Aiden's place, but Brandon didn't seem to be getting my messages because he squirmed in his seat before glancing over his shoulder at Aiden nervously.

"But Aiden's a better debater," he said sheepishly. "Sorry," he mouthed at me with a little shrug.

I could feel Aiden's eyes on me, but I refused to turn and acknowledge him even though it was our partnership we were discussing. Instead, I glared at Ms. Torrence with my hands clenched at my sides, as if that simple act could keep me from reaching out and scrambling for whatever tentative control I used to have. "What if I refuse?"

Aiden stood up and everyone turned as one to look at him, holding their breath. Slowly, I turned on my heel to face him. His gaze was steady and unblinking. I held my ground and stared right back. "I'll do it," he said.

My mouth popped open in surprise as the auditorium broke out in another wave of whispers.

He'll do it? What's that supposed to mean? What game was he playing now? One corner of his mouth twitched as he looked me up and down expectantly, as if he was just biding his time, like it was inevitable that I was about to explode. He even tapped his foot while he waited.

I took a deep breath in through my nose. *Inhale peace, exhale your troubles,* whispered Cat's lilting voice in my head. Fine. As much as I didn't want to do this (I was screaming internally), I also refused to throw a fit if he wasn't going to. I exhaled heavily and mentally rewarded myself a point for being so mature and reasonable.

"Fine. I'll do it. For the team." I gave them a thumbs up, but it still came off as extremely snarky. Only Brandon offered me a half-hearted thumbs up in return. I tried to smile, but it felt like a grimace on my lips. Aiden's face didn't change, he just sank back down in his seat to pull out his laptop and collection of notebooks that was nearly as impressive as mine.

The room was filled with a flurry of motion as my teammates unpacked their backpacks and set up their easels, all of them chatting animatedly with each other now that the worst of the standoff was over and the crisis had been averted. I stood rooted to the spot as reality caught back up with me in a sudden burst. *What did I just get myself into?* One by one, each person went off to their individual stations to work on their speeches or argue at a blank wall. Everyone, except our overly-ambitious debate coach and my new partner, Aiden.

Ms. Torrence looked pleased with herself, like she was about to literally start patting herself on the back. She was one of the only teachers left at Pearson High that would've pulled that stunt. Most of the older staff had given up on trying to make Aiden and me play nice. Our English teacher actually cried the last time he paired us in a group project together.

Hey, I'm not proud of it.

But like I said, Ms. Torrence is young, and therefore naive to the ways of the world and our cutthroat natures. She clapped her hands together, no longer looking nervous, and beamed. "All right! Let's get started."

Aiden and I both sprinted up the stairs to the stage, our backpacks jostling noisily behind us. I arrived at the podium first and plopped my pile of stuff right in the middle of its surface before turning and smiling widely at him.

"You're hogging the whole thing," he said, rolling his eyes. He reached over to nudge my notebooks to the side and his hand brushed against mine.

I jerked back. "Trust me, Aiden Christopher Mitchell III—you're going to need my notes."

"I seriously doubt you found any evidence that I didn't already find," he spat back, tucking his hands into his pockets. We stood shoulder to shoulder at the narrow podium with only a tiny sliver of space between us. If he took a step forward, I followed. If I shifted to the right, he did too. Neither of us could relax with the other one standing there trying to elbow their way onto higher ground.

I could feel Ms. Torrence's hopefulness fizzling out of her, like the tail end of a firecracker, but she didn't insert herself into the conversation or try to referee. "Do you want to practice affirmative or negative first?" she asked us hesitantly.

"Doesn't matter. I'm prepared either way. I'll let Aiden pick." I tried to sound gracious, humble even, but my voice came out so syrupy and sweet that I nearly choked on it.

"Affirmative," he said dismissively. We both snapped open our laptops, balancing them on our respective edges of the podium as we pulled out our stopwatches. "I'll take the opening—"

I snorted. "Oh, *of course,* you'd say that, without even reading what I've prepared—"

"—and you'll take the second affirmative." He didn't look up from his computer as he clicked open a screen filled with his notes, read it for about thirty seconds, then closed his laptop with a soft *click* before sliding it back into his backpack.

"What, you don't need your notes?" I asked, surprised.

"Nope. It's all up here." He tapped his forehead, right under his unruly blond hair. He still needed a haircut.

"Hmm, if you say so," I said, chewing on my lip and scanning my own open laptop. I was elated. There wasn't a chance he could remember every fact or figure he needed for his arguments off the top of his head. Not a chance.

"Let's begin!" Ms. Torrence called out as she sank into her chair. She clicked on her stopwatch, but she didn't need to. Aiden and I had already beat her to it.

He closed his eyes, took a deep breath, and then he was off. After quoting Thomas Jefferson verbatim (I would know; I had the quote memorized too), he went through each of his opening arguments, line by line without pausing once, as he laid out his framework for why the United States should require its citizens to vote, until stopping at precisely the eight-minute mark. He clicked his stopwatch at the same moment I did and turned to me expectantly. I just stood there, gaping at him like an idiot.

Aiden was a good debater—I'm not too proud to admit that. He's good, just not as good as me. But today he was on another level. He was persuasive, he was succinct, and I was the open-mouthed fool standing next to him. He smirked and gave me what looked like the hint of a wink.

Ms. Torrence cleared her throat. "Aiden, are you ready for the cross?"

"Absolutely, Ms. Torrence. Take it away." She started asking him questions, low-balls about voter turnout that were annoyingly easy to answer, and not at all helpful for actually sharpening our argument. But I barely noticed. My mind was still stewing over the fact that

Aiden had hit all the main points I would've hit myself, and that he'd done it so well.

Ugh, just thinking that thought made me feel nauseous.

When it was my turn give the next portion of our case, I tried to look at my computer as little as possible, but I stumbled a few times over the wording, and nearly forgot a few of the sources I was citing. Aiden shifted on his feet, his shrewd gaze bouncing between me and his stopwatch. I picked up the cadence of my speech to squeeze in the last phrase I wanted to close with before we each clicked our stop-watches off.

Ms. Torrence went straight into my cross-examination, lobbing more ridiculously easy questions on the nature of civic duty and the noble cause of democracy. But even though her questions were simple enough, my hands were frantic on my computer as I scrolled through my notes. I wasn't used to working with someone, and I didn't want to give Aiden the satisfaction of repeating something he'd already said.

I'd never hear the end of it.

When the three minutes were up, I was breathing heavily, which was embarrassing. I felt like I'd just run a mile at a full-out sprint. I was pretty sure I'd sweat through my shirt too, but I'd blame it on the heat from the spotlights if anyone dared to say anything about it.

"Very nice!" Ms. Torrence sang out from the front row. She sounded too relieved that her plan was working. I turned to Aiden, swallowing the compliment that kept rising up in my throat. It was obvious he'd prepared thoroughly.

"Decent work, Crew," Aiden said, leaning against the podium. "But you need to work on your flow; you were all over the place. And your words per minute pace could be taken up a notch. You were lagging."

My compliment died in my mouth. "All over the place? Taken up a notch?" I sounded breathless. "What about..." I fumbled, trying to think of something he'd done wrong, some way in which he tripped up, but my mind was blank.

Aiden grinned. "You were saying?"

I stumbled back a step. Aiden rarely smiled at me like that. Sure, he turned that mega-watt grin on the rest of the student body, but for me? He reserved his best scowls and grimaces, all narrowed eyes and puckered mouth.

He had a dimple on his left cheek.

My throat was suddenly too dry to retort. So, I did what any sane person would do in that scenario and I chugged my entire water bottle without breaking eye contact with him. When I was finished, I wiped my mouth with the back of my hand. "It's just your whole…" I waved in his direction, "attitude, your persona. We're never going to win if you don't get a new personality ASAP."

He clutched a hand over his chest and pretended to whimper. "Ouch, Josie, you've wounded me."

"Josephine," I bit out, seething.

"Sure thing. I see we're still bitter over the blood drive? Why else would you be so hostile toward me when I just gave you such a flawless debate performance?" He sighed and shook his head as he looked at me with mock compassion. "It's okay if you're jealous."

"*Jealous*? Of you? Please." An angry buzzing filled my head like a swarm of violent bees. That's when I noticed that our teammates had wandered over to watch, all of them gawking and whispering. That's when I noticed how closely we were standing together.

My face flamed as I stepped back and waved at Aiden with shaking jazz hands. "Ladies and gentlemen, Aiden Christopher Mitchell III—the boy so extra they had to name him thrice."

There were a few sniggers in the audience but other than that, it was quiet. Tough crowd.

I sighed. "Well, that's a wrap."

Aiden's brow furrowed. "But we're not finished yet, we still need to—"

"I don't know if this is going to work, Ms. Torrence," I said, cutting him off. I grabbed my laptop and notebooks and threw them into my backpack before practically running off the stage. This time, I tried to close the doors quietly behind me, but they still slammed shut, their hinges squealing noisily.

Dramatic entrance, dramatic exit. I'm nothing if not consistent.

Five

"**I**T WAS AWFUL. Horrible. I can't believe Ms. Torrence or my team. *My* team!" I was sprawled across Rose's bed, hanging upside down with my feet resting against an old One Direction poster pinned to her lilac walls. "I'm the captain, did they all forget that interesting tidbit?"

"I'm sure it was terrible," Cat crooned sympathetically from the floor where she was painting her toenails bubblegum pink.

"Are you even listening to me?" I wailed, throwing my arm over my face. "Partners!" I spat out the word like it was a curse. "Debate was supposed to be my safe zone, my sanctuary; the place I always bested him."

"Of course I'm listening. I'm multi-tasking." Cat waved a hand over her drying toes and met my eyes. "You know I'm always Team Josephine."

"Ooh, we should make shirts!" Rose clapped from her spot next to me on the bed where she was sitting cross-legged and "doing her algebra homework." By that I mean she was alternating between texting Jordan about their homecoming plans for this Saturday and browsing online for dress inspiration. "What do you think of these, Cat?" Rose held up her phone to reveal her Pinterest feed covered in '70s-style miniskirts and brightly-colored florals that hurt my eyes.

I rolled over and tried to pry the phone out of her hands, but she dodged me. "Josephine, I swear if you don't blow off some steam soon, I'm going to murder you."

Sitting up, I swung my legs over the side of her bed and folded my arms across my chest. "What's that supposed to mean?"

"She just means you're wound a little tight, babe. That's all," Cat said, screwing the lid of her nail polish back on.

"I'd say 'extremely,' not 'a little,'" amended Rose. She tossed her phone on the bed and drew her arm around my shoulder, tucking me into her like she was the older sister and I was the one who needed coddling. "Seriously though. Either you take up yoga or you go make out with someone. Otherwise, we'll be forced to lock you in your room and never let you out again."

I tried to scowl but a laugh bubbled up instead. "Well, I guess yoga it is since I have no one to make out with—"

I was interrupted by a tapping on the window followed by the appearance of the grinning freckled face of Ethan Anderson, Cat's longtime boyfriend. Rose leaned over to slide the window open and he climbed in, unfolding his angular body with the agility of someone practiced in the art of window sneaking.

"Ethan!" Cat squealed as she hobbled over on her heels with her still-drying toenails turned up in the air. She threw her arms around him and he buried his face in her hair, holding her tightly to his chest. She looked even tinier when they stood together like that, like he was about to completely engulf her. It made me feel claustrophobic just watching them. They were acting like they hadn't seen each other in days even though I knew they'd been together just a few hours ago because he always drives Cat home from school.

Cat swears she's in love, and Ethan looks at her like she hung the moon. Rose thinks they're precious. I think they're kind of hard to be around. But still, I like the guy. And I like seeing Cat so happy.

"Perfect timing, Ethan, as always," Rose said, sliding down to the floor to sit across from Ethan, where Cat was now perched on his lap. "We were just discussing who Josephine should make out with."

"Whoa, go Josephine," Ethan drawled. "Who's the lucky guy? Mitchell?"

Both Rose and Cat groaned and buried their heads in their hands.

"Yes, Ethan," I said gravely. "I've just realized I've been in love with Aiden this whole time, only I've been too blind and stubborn to see it clearly. Tomorrow, in front of the whole school, I'm going to go up to him and profess my undying love, and then we will make out. Also in front of everyone."

"Really?"

"No, Ethan. Not really," I deadpanned.

Cat rolled off Ethan's lap and landed in a discarded pile of Rose's clothes, she was laughing so hard. "Can you even imagine?" she asked as she gasped for air.

"Then I wouldn't know which team to support," Rose said, plucking at the hem of her shirt like it was an imaginary Team Josephine t-shirt.

"Well, then I won't make out with Aiden, problem solved," I said as I stood up. "I'm grabbing food, and by the time I get back I need a reasonable and *realistic* list of boys I can coerce into making out with me." I paused at the door and added, "For my sister's sanity."

I walked out the door to the sound of their laughter, but without them there to see me, my smile faded off my face.

Why does this part have to be so hard?

I see Cat and Ethan together, the way they lean into each other like they're two parts of the same whole. How they need each other, want each other, and are just fine with all that needing and wanting. The thought of needing anyone or anything that badly makes my stomach twist into painful knots. But feeling left out makes my stomach twist too.

Maybe I'm just destined to have a permanent stomachache.

And more than anything, it irritates me that I don't understand it the way my friends or classmates seem to. They just *get* it. They hang out, joking together, sharing parts of themselves freely with each other—they relax into those easy feelings of familiarity. I don't know how to have that with anyone besides my sister and Cat, and even then sometimes I have to force myself into their level of casualness.

I padded down the hall in my socks, shuffling along the carpet in desperate need of replacing. Like every other inch of our rundown house. The kitchen was dark, lit only by the glow of the small television where my dad sat parked in front of it. He didn't say anything when I flicked on the light or when I started rooting around the fridge for some leftover pizza to heat up.

My mom chose that moment to come bustling down the hall, stopping short when she saw me. Her perfectly-lined bright blue eyes narrowed as she X-rayed me with her gaze. "Quit slouching, Josephine. Your breasts aren't going to thank you for that."

I turned back to the fridge to grimace, not wanting her commentary on my ever-deepening frown lines too. But my spine stiffened without me consciously deciding to, straightening my posture to a ramrod straight line. I slammed the fridge shut and leaned against it while the microwave hummed noisily through the silence. Mom had already moved on; she stood at the counter digging through her purse until she raised her gold tube of lipstick triumphantly.

Don't say it, I cautioned myself, biting my lip in an effort to keep my mouth sealed shut. *Don't do it, don't try, don't—*

"I got the top grade on my chemistry exam today," I blurted out, totally against my better judgment.

Mom didn't look up from her handheld mirror as she finished applying her blood-red lipstick with a steady hand. She snapped the compact shut and slid it back into her purse before slinging it over her shoulder. "What was that, Josie? You got another good grade on your English paper? How nice."

I didn't bother correcting her about the nickname. If she hadn't picked up on my hatred of it over the last seventeen years, she certainly wasn't going to now.

"Chemistry exam, Mom," I repeated, banging my head against the fridge.

She smiled wanly at me but was instantly distracted by her reflection in the microwave's chrome surface, patting her shining red hair and smoothing it behind her shoulders. "Hmm, that's what I said." She went back to digging through her purse and ignoring me.

Why do you even try? You know she doesn't care, my ever-loving brain reminded me in a sing-song voice. I closed my eyes and sighed. I knew not to tell her about what had happened at debate practice today. Every time she heard me mention debate, she wrinkled her nose and made a pointed comment about how I didn't need to practice arguing, I was already a certified professional.

She'd never seen me debate, never been to a single tournament. She'd never even asked once, so neither had I.

I'd stopped inviting her to watch my events back in grade school because she never showed up. She'd either forget or already have something planned, like a lunch date with the girls she just couldn't reschedule. I got tired of seeing the empty folding chair in the audience and feeling the hot tears pricking at the corners of my eyes, so I quit asking and let go of that hope like a child letting go of a balloon.

"Have you thought any more about what we talked about the other night?" my mom asked as she plucked imaginary lint from her form-fitting dress.

A roaring noise filled my ears as I stared at her and wondered for the millionth time how Jennifer Crew and I could possibly share DNA. "If you're referring to your not-so-subtle hints that I should compete in the pageant circuit, then no. I haven't thought about it because I don't need to. Not happening."

Now she turned her full focus on me, her red lips pursing into a pout. "Really, Josephine. You don't need to be so unpleasant." She stalked over, her tall heels giving her a good three inches on me. Reaching her hand out, she held me by the chin and turned my face this way and that under the glow of the kitchen lights. "Hon, you've been blessed with my bone structure." She patted me on the cheek, but it felt more like a tiny slap. "I just don't know *why* you refuse to do anything with such a nice face." She dropped her hand and flicked a dismissive wave at me. "You'd rather waste it by shoving it in all those books. Why, when I was crowned Miss—"

"Wait, you were Miss Carl County? Well, I'll be!" I swooned across our yellowing linoleum floor and fanned myself, but she didn't laugh. Her hand gripped the strap of her purse, and all the thick southern honey was out of her voice when she said, "Honestly, Josephine. Must you be such a thorn in my side."

It wasn't a question. It was a statement. One that she'd been repeating to me since the day I was born. Since the moment she found out she was pregnant two months out of high school, ruining her chances to compete in the Miss Texas pageant.

Josephine. Such a thorn in her pretty, perfectly trim side.

She didn't say another word after that. She and her fancy purse and her big head of hair sashayed out the door, leaving only a cloud of perfume in her wake.

The microwave dinged, but I wasn't that hungry anymore.

The smell of the pizza alerted my dad to my existence. "Josephine!

Bring me a slice of that, would you please." I sighed and flopped one of the rubbery pieces onto a paper plate and walked it over to him. His eyes barely twitched from the game he was glued to. "Thank you, darling. Was that your mother I heard back there? Where'd she run off to now?"

"How should I know," I mumbled. "Book Club, Wine Club, Mothers Who Hate Their Daughters Club—"

"Well, make sure you and your sister eat something."

I blinked at him sitting there in his giant stuffed chair, his attention already turned back to the glowing TV. That was Bradley Crew. He was young and fairly fit, just a little soft around the edges, and he still had a head full of gleaming blond hair. But he acted like a man twice his age—world-weary and over it.

That's what happens to Golden Boys when apathy sneaks in and chokes out all their ambition. He was living his life like he'd already passed his expiration date. And his greatest disappointment was that he got saddled with a house full of girls and not a single boy to carry on his name or his love of the game.

But still, he was nicer to me than my mom was. So, I patted him once on the shoulder (he made a gruff noise of acknowledgment) and I left him to his football. That's what happens to star players after they graduate and the Friday night lights no longer shine down reverently upon their heads. After the shotgun wedding to the prom queen and the babies that came too soon.

I carried the rest of the pizza back to Rose's room where madness had fully descended. Rose, Cat, and Ethan were huddled around a large whiteboard hanging on the wall, and when I walked back into the room, Cat lunged to cover it up.

"Before you say anything, we need you to promise to keep an open mind!"

Apparently, they'd taken the duty of compiling me a list of make-out buddies very seriously (I, on the other hand, had not).

I flopped on the bed and bit into a slice of pizza that was both too hot and too cold at the same time. "If Caleb is on the list, then I'm out," I said through my mouthful.

"Fair enough," Rose said sagely. "Caleb is creepy and should be avoided at all costs."

"And if Liam is *not* on the list, then I'm definitely out," I added.

"Liam? Do we know any Liams?" Ethan asked, his brow furrowing.

"Liam Hemsworth," Cat laughed.

I saluted her with my slice of pizza. "Carry on."

Cat and Rose parted like the Red Sea to reveal the whiteboard behind them where a handful of names were written in Cat's tidy handwriting. I was secretly relieved to see that all of the boys they'd selected were reasonably attractive and somewhat interesting. Brandon Lopez from debate had made the list, so had Kyle from marching band, and Ray from French Club.

"Hmm," I said noncommittally, my face revealing nothing. But my mind was whirling, already busy ranking them by their GPAs, band status, or fluency in French. I didn't share my findings out loud; I think that would've pushed Cat and Rose over the edge.

"Oh, come on! This is a good list," Rose said in a pleading voice. "Just pick someone!"

"Yeah, because it's just that easy."

I flicked my crust at her. She caught it and took a bite before saying, "It is that easy. You're gorgeous! You're brilliant! You're sometimes hilarious! And you always look nice because you let me dress you."

"All of that is true, except I am *always* hilarious. My sense of humor is impeccable."

That made them laugh. Rose did have a point. Objectively, I knew I was decent looking. I had nice hair (or at least I would if I ever took it out of my trusty ponytail) and according to my mother, my bone structure was to die for. And Rose had great style, so I trusted her. At the beginning of each school year, I let her pick out a few simple outfits for me, usually all in neutrals (mostly black) so I didn't have to think about patterns or matching or anything else I was sure I didn't know how to do. But they were "well-made" and "on-trend staples," so I at least knew no one was gasping in horror when I walked into a room. I left the vintage hodgepodge to Rose.

Objectively, I added up.

I deflated onto her pillow and tried to swallow the lump rising in my throat. I blinked at the sudden moisture in my eyes and hated myself for it. "It's just that easy," I repeated. But my voice made it sound like the opposite.

Ethan cleared his throat and rubbed a hand along his scruffy jaw. "I know for a fact that all of these guys think you're hot." Cat scoffed and he blushed. "Beautiful, I mean. They all think you're pretty." Cat patted him on the back, obviously pleased with his adjustment of adjectives. "But I also know they're all scared of you."

I groaned into the pillow before dragging myself up to a sitting position. "Tell me something I don't know."

"They're intimidated by you! You're like a literal genius and you're good at everything. It's just… a lot…" he trailed off awkwardly.

My face burned and my eyes pricked dangerously. "So I'm supposed to lower myself, to not be the best I can be, so these boys will find me a little easier to handle? Be more convenient? Because I won't. I refuse to be less than I am."

I glanced down, surprised to see that I was standing, my hands perched stiffly on my hips.

Ethan looked at Cat with a pleading expression, clearly begging for her to save him. But she only had eyes for me. So did Rose. They both swelled with pride over my outburst, obviously feeling some kind of Girl Power Moment I had unintentionally created.

But I'd be lying if I said I didn't see just a shade of disappointment there too. They wanted me to fit in. They didn't want me to be lonely, even if I'd never admitted that I was.

I tried to laugh to lighten the mood and to save Ethan from looking like he was in a den of female tigers, but it came out wrong. It sounded like a sigh. "Well, time to hit the books. Gotta keep my intimidation factor up." I slugged Ethan on his shoulder and he flinched—the poor guy had sweat through his t-shirt. "I'll see you guys tomorrow."

I crossed the hall to my room and shut the door behind me, exhaling heavily into the sudden stillness. My room of white walls and tidy rows of books felt like a tranquil spa after spending so much time in Rose's cluttered chaos. When I sat down at my little white desk and flipped on my lamp, the soft light illuminated the crowded and covered surface. Normally, this was the best part of my day. Just me and my books. No incomprehensible rules to follow, no people to impress.

Nothing to prove.

But I didn't crack open a single book or pick up my pen. I didn't log on to any of the college websites or scroll through my always-open applications.

A tear rolled down my cheek and landed on the blank page of my open notebook. I sniffed and wiped it away with my finger before anyone could see the evidence even though I was alone. I wiped it away before the realization could fully sink in—that maybe I was going about this thing all wrong.

This thing called being a teenage girl.

Maybe this would be the first thing I failed.

I WOKE UP early the next morning, fully recovered from last night's pity party, table of one, and completed my homework from the day before, plus got in some flute practice.

Rose burst into my room without knocking, her robe halfway falling off and sleep still in her eyes. "Sometimes I really hate you," she mumbled, glaring at me and my flute.

"I know," I said brightly. "Now go take a shower. You look like you could use one." She drowned out the sound of my scales by slamming the door roughly behind her.

All was forgiven by the time she was shined and polished with caffeine clutched in her hand. "You look nice today," she said, giving me a once over from behind the kitchen counter.

"What, don't I usually look nice?"

"Not this nice," she said suspiciously, eyeing my black dress and ankle boots.

I scoffed and continued pouring my bowl of cereal. I didn't tell her that I'd spent an embarrassing amount of time staring at my closet today, trying to pick something out that was a little different than usual. Well, different for me. I didn't tell her because I knew she would ask me why, and I didn't really have an answer. All I had was this uncomfortable restlessness that made my skin feel like it was stretched too tight.

Dad came into the kitchen, humming to himself as he sidestepped me to open the fridge. He was always happy in the morning because that meant he was on his way to work at the only sporting goods store in town where he was the manager, and where he would be noticed for wearing his state championship ring that was always gleaming on his finger.

Mom followed closely behind him, her arms full of flyers for her latest open house, her red hair curled and bouncing on her shoulders. She was one of the only real estate agents in Pearson. It's a job that didn't give her much to do—hardly anyone moves here, and nobody ever leaves. But if any potential home buyers happened to show an interest in Pearson, Jennifer Crew liked to give them the Royal Welcome. And no, I'm not just saying that; it's the actual slogan on her business cards (purple and orange, the horrific color combo of Pearson High). She trussed up any available house on the market, making it look as appealing as possible, then came home to the shabby single-story, too-small house she neglected, the daughters that confused her, and the husband that mostly preferred his television set over her.

Rose and I finished our breakfasts as we watched our parents race out the door in a flurry of movement, neither of them saying goodbye to each other or to us. Mom only paused to yell out, "Rose, those pants are horribly unflattering. Maybe change before school, sweetie. Wear a skirt! This is the best your legs are ever gonna look!"

Rose rolled her eyes and twirled around in her bright yellow highwaisted sailor pants as the screen door swung shut behind them. "What does Jenny know. These pants are amazing."

"Definitely amazing," I mumbled. I wouldn't be caught dead wearing those pants, but I felt defensive for Rose all the same. Every time our mother implied that this was it, that high school was going to be the peak of our existence because it was the peak of hers, I had to swallow down the urge to vomit.

Rose grabbed the keys to our beat-up station wagon the two of us shared and shook them at me, her mouth flattened into a stern line. "Seriously! Who are you trying to impress? Ray? Ooh, or maybe Brandon?" She raised an eyebrow at me and smirked. "Looks like our list got you thinking."

"Thinking about how annoying you all are."

"If that's what you need to tell yourself, by all means, go for it." She looked smug as she sped through the drive to school and sang along to the country station our radio dial was permanently stuck on.

I spent the drive telling her to slow down (she drove like a maniac) and sighing at the ever-depressing view out the window. Pearson was extremely boring; even its landscape was unimaginative with its flat stretches of land only broken up by more flat stretches of land.

I craved skyscrapers and paved roads, bustling commuters and public transportation. Somehow, I knew that I'd feel less claustrophobic in a towering city where the buildings blocked the sun than I did in the wide-open plains of nothingness that Pearson offered me. I wanted something beyond churches and cotton crops, high school football and homecoming parades. I wanted to go somewhere where people didn't think they knew everything about you the moment they heard your last name.

Rose pestered me about the list all the way through the parking lot and into the school. "I expect a full report at lunch," she whispered as she dug through her locker for her seldom-used books.

But before I could snort and tell her that I'd have absolutely nothing to report on, she had locked eyes with Jordan who'd just come through the locker room doors, his dark hair wet from a recent shower. She grinned and waltzed off with a flick of her auburn hair, her hips swaying as she sauntered down the hall. I sighed and shook my head, shutting her hastily abandoned locker. Rose must've been speeding like a demon to catch Jordan after his morning basketball practice, since we were ridiculously early for class.

I was the first one to English. I had zero desire to fraternize in the hallway if Rose and Cat were nowhere to be found, so if I was early, I usually set up camp at my desk with whatever book I was in the middle of and called it good. Today was Neil Gaiman's *An Ocean at the End of the Lane*, and it was deliciously weird. I was so engrossed, I didn't notice that someone else was in the room with me until they scooted their chair back and the legs screeched against the floor.

I jumped and slammed my book shut reflexively. "Oh, it's just you," I said in a bored voice even though my heart was still hammering.

Aiden sat heavily in his chair, his eyes landing on the cover of my book. "Engaging in some light reading? *How to Make a Deal with the Devil for a Perfect GPA*?"

"I don't need to read that book, but maybe you do."

He scoffed and flipped open his own book. It was so quiet I could hear the clock ticking. "Did you practice your words per minute pace last night?" he asked a moment later, clearly intent on ruining my alone time.

I sighed but didn't shut my book this time. "I don't need to practice, but maybe you do."

His chair creaked as he turned in his seat. I could feel his eyes on me like twin spotlights. I'd been reading the same sentence over and over again for at least a full minute, but I still kept my eyes trained on the page.

"Why are you so dressed up today?"

I looked up to catch his gaze trailing down my usually unexposed legs before flicking his eyes back to meet mine. He looked genuinely curious, like I was a science experiment he was testing out.

"I'm not all 'dressed up,' I'm just dressed," I said huffily. He ran a hand through his hair and shrugged before turning back to his book. I caught a glimpse of the cover before he moved it out of my line of sight; *In Cold Blood.*

He was probably taking notes.

Silence fell between us as he continued reading, but now that my peaceful solitude had been trodden upon, I couldn't concentrate. Aiden bounced his leg up and down, his foot noisily tapping out an anxious rhythm on the scuffed floor. The sound echoed off the classroom walls covered in outdated posters of celebrities holding books and encouraging me to *READ*; it set my teeth on edge the longer I had to listen to it. I glared at him from under my eyelashes, watching as he rubbed a hand agitatedly across his forehead and squinted at his book, his mouth turned down into a frown. He seemed distracted, like maybe he was reading the same sentence over and over again too.

I was about to tell him to quit with the foot-tapping when the bell rang and a herd of students filtered in, filling up the classroom with their noisy chatter. Our English teacher, Mr. Kline, stood behind his desk in his favorite lumpy cardigan with the leather elbow patches, looking worn out even though class hadn't officially begun yet. His eyes darted to Aiden in his seat, then over to where I sat. I had a pretty good guess why he was already looking fatigued.

I guess rivalries aren't just exhausting for the two people engaged in them.

But Mr. Kline took a deep breath and cracked open his lesson plan, carrying on bravely like he wasn't dreading opening up the classroom for discussion and the arguments that were most certainly going to follow.

"Let's talk about your reading from yesterday."

My hand was up in the air before he'd even posed a question.

"Yes, Josephine," he said, trying to smile at me, "please share your thoughts with the class."

I sat up straighter in my seat and recapped everything I'd read this week in *The Grapes of Wrath* (which I'd already read multiple times). But the longer I spoke, the more confused I felt. Aiden didn't try to cut in once, and he didn't raise his hand either. Instead, he just sat there, rubbing his forehead and looking like he was about to slump forward onto his desk and take a nap right in the middle of class.

Mr. Kline asked another series of questions, this time calling on a few other kids who weren't raising their hands and looked terrified to be put on the spot. But still, no word from Aiden. Not even when I successfully commandeered the discussion and steered it away from our reading to a lengthy diatribe against Truman Capote and everything he'd ever written.

Not a word.

Halfway through class, Aiden stiffened in his seat, his back a collection of rigid lines visible through his t-shirt. He stared at a spot in the corner of the classroom with wide eyes, his mouth stretched into a tight line. He sat so still, I wasn't sure if he was even breathing.

I was so distracted by Aiden's sudden shift in mood that I forgot to raise my hand to answer Mr. Kline's question, and he took that moment to start a gleeful monologue about the wonders of hidden symbolism in 20th-century literature. I craned my neck to peer at the same corner Aiden was so fixated on, but saw nothing out of the ordinary, just another faded poster, this one featuring the alarmingly piercing stare of Nicolas Cage for America's Libraries.

Not exactly something I'd like to be caught staring at, but Aiden didn't seem to share my same concern. He stayed like that, tense and unyielding, ignoring me and everybody else until the bell rang and our classmates began to trickle out.

He slowly packed up his untouched notebooks while his eyes flickered over to that same corner.

"What are you staring at?" I blurted out before I could stop myself.

His hands froze on his backpack as his eyebrows shot up in surprise. "Nic Cage, of course. He's impossible to ignore." He tried to smile, but only one corner of his mouth lifted. I rolled my eyes and went to step around his desk to look more closely at the wall he'd been so obsessed with. But before I could Aiden caught the strap of my backpack and gave it a tug, nearly sending me colliding into his chest.

"Better get to class, Jo," he said as he fiddled with the fraying strap. "Your perfect attendance is on the line."

"Something you know nothing about," I muttered as he dragged me out the door with him until I yanked my backpack free from his grasp. I spun around, ready to tell him to get his hands off me, but he was gone. He'd already taken off down the hall, his blond head of hair bobbing in and out of the swarm of students until it disappeared entirely in the crowd.

He didn't show up for chemistry. Or calculus.

And when I saw him at lunch, he had his pill bottle back in his hand.

□ □ □

"I thought we'd discussed that you aren't allowed access to the gavel anymore," Aiden hissed in the nearly empty library. "You almost cracked the table that one time."

"Because I was imagining it was your big head," I whispered back before turning to pass out the Pearson High School Student Council agendas I'd just printed out, the paper still warm in my hands. Aiden chuckled dryly as I rounded the table, and he snatched the only remaining agenda. I didn't try to take it back; I already had it memorized.

"Besides, I'm the only one who can be trusted with the gavel," I said pointedly. "I wasn't sure if you'd even show up today."

"And leave you to overthrow my cabinet?" he asked with a frown. "Never." He tried to slide the gavel out of my hands, but I only clutched it tighter.

"*Our* cabinet, you mean. We are *co*-presidents if you recall."

"How could I forget with you reminding me every single day since the election?"

The rest of our student council filed into the room and took their seats, their mumbled chitchat filling the silent spaces of the tiny Pearson High library.

"Why weren't you in chem today?" I asked over the low hum of conversation, trying to steer the topic back to my original point. "And you skipped calculus." My words came out like an accusation, a suspicion.

"Well, well, well. Looks like you missed me," he said with a smirk.

"Hardly," I scoffed.

Mr. Gunderson, the current teacher assigned to supervise our meetings, cleared his throat as he pulled out a chair and sat down. He kneaded his temple with his knuckles like he was warding off a headache. "Let's get this over with," he sighed, picking up his agenda. Then, as if realizing he'd said that thought out loud, he turned crimson and busied himself with reading the printout.

"I call this meeting to order." I banged the gavel on the table and everyone but Aiden jumped and quieted instantly.

Aiden scanned the agenda and rolled his eyes before saying loudly, "Half of this is obsolete; we discussed most of these items in our last meeting."

"You mean your 'coup,'" I hissed back.

"Call it what you want, President Crew, but there's no point in wasting everyone's valuable time." Aiden smiled at Mr. Gunderson, who beamed back and nodded gratefully. "So, for the blood drive tomorrow—"

Blood drive. Somehow hearing the words out loud was worse than typing them onto the agenda. My stomach dropped to the floor as the room started to spin. I gripped the gavel tightly in my hands and tried not to sway on my feet.

"Josephine, are you all right?" Our treasurer, Liz, leaned forward in her seat to get a better look at me. "You look pale. And clammy."

"I'm fine," I answered back, my voice low and rough. I couldn't stop thinking about all the needles, and the needles coming into contact with my skin, and—

I closed my eyes and tried to concentrate on not puking all over Aiden's jeans.

"Well, let's assign checkpoints, crowd control, and staff liaisons…"

I barely registered him droning on and on, and I didn't have the mental or physical energy to resent that he'd completely taken over the meeting. What I really wanted to do was sink down into a chair and let my face rest against the cool surface of the table, but Aiden had refused to sit, so I refused too. I stood next to him, hardly hearing a word anyone said until he gently slid the gavel from my hands and slammed it onto the table.

"Until next time! Great work everyone, thanks." Aiden's cheery voice rang in my ears, startling me so thoroughly, I nearly fell over as the rest of our student council packed up their backpacks. Liz lightly touched me on the arm and told me she hoped I'd feel better soon. Mr. Gunderson actually whistled on his way out the door.

"Welcome back, Jo," Aiden said loudly. "Did you hear your assignment for the homecoming dance?"

"My—wait, what?" I was so disoriented, I forgot to correct him about my name.

"You're on trash duty."

I must've looked like I was going to wrestle the gavel out of his hands and do some serious damage with it because he laughed once and said, "I'm kidding. Relax. Caleb volunteered for trash duty, which is super weird now that I'm thinking about it." He paused expectantly as if waiting for me to laugh, then rushed on when all I offered was a woozy grimace. "Anyway, all that's left to do is count the homecoming ballots…" he said, trailing off as he tapped a bright orange box decorated with tiger stripes that was resting on the table. "Hey, are you okay?"

Now that all the talk of needles was over and done with, I could breathe normally again. The whole meeting flashed before my eyes like an awful, slow-motion train wreck; me just standing there, mute and ineffectual, next to Aiden and his dazzling leadership skills. After the coup, this was a problem.

After I'd barely scraped a win in the election, this was unacceptable.

When I first found out Aiden was also running for school president, I couldn't say I was surprised. I welcomed it, even; relishing in yet another opportunity to defeat him. He may have had the football team, the dance squad, the German club, the astronomy club, and half the debate team, but I had the marching band, the theater kids, the French club, the art club, the other half of the debate team, *and* most of the school paper.

My bedroom became my war room as Cat, Rose, Ethan, and I hunched over whiteboards covered in strategy and flyers covered with my face. I may sometimes struggle in the social department, but my sister and best friend do not. They had connections, and I wasn't too proud to use them. Not to mention, I had a truly fantastic platform, and I was sure my classmates that I'd known since birth really wanted to support me.

Or maybe it was Cat's suggestion that I promise pizza every Friday in the cafeteria. We'll never know.

Our presidential campaign was a slow descent into smear politics and ruin. Battle lines were drawn, friends turned into foes, and a small fight broke out in the quad after lunch one day. Okay, maybe it wasn't that dramatic, but the fight *did* actually happen on top of some of our campaign posters, so it totally counts. And our classroom bickering became so extreme that all our teachers nearly quit calling on Aiden and me entirely.

On the day of the election, we were summoned to the principal's office. Mrs. Cartwright looked at us over her wide desk and folded her hands primly, gravely even. Her solemn expression was in sharp contrast with her hot pink pantsuit.

"I'm afraid we have a tie."

"*What?*" Aiden and I both said at the same time.

"Yessiree, an actual tie. The school is split."

"I'm sure some kids are absent; can't we call them and—"

"Ms. Crew, we are not extending this election for another hour, let alone another day. I'm pretty certain you and Mr. Mitchell have given me at least three new gray hairs from all this unpleasantness." She patted her stiff updo with a sheepish grin, but when neither Aiden nor I laughed, she frowned and got down to business. "You two will be co-presidents. And no," she said when she saw the horror on our faces, "the matter is not up for discussion."

I couldn't look at her or Aiden as I fumed, so instead I focused on the giant Texas flag hanging behind her desk, the single white star swimming in my vision as my head spun.

"Now y'all run along to class. It's going to be a great school year, I just know it." She sounded like she was trying to convince herself, not us.

"Heaven help us," I heard her murmur as she slammed the door in our wake.

"Josephine."

The feeling of Aiden's hands on my shoulders, warming through the sleeves of my shirt, snapped me back to the present. "Josephine," he said again, "do you need to go to the nurse's office?"

I stared at him blankly. "You called me Josephine."

The corner of his mouth twitched, revealing the shadow of his dimple. "Yeah, well that's your name, isn't it?"

I batted his hands away and he held them up in a gesture of surrender (I should've taken a picture) before shoving them into his pockets.

"I'm fine," I said, stuffing my binder into my already bursting backpack. "Let's just count the ballots so we can get out of here." I slid into a chair and grabbed the lid off the box, then started rifling through the scraps of paper for the final homecoming court nominees.

Aiden, Aiden, Aiden—his name was everywhere. What a shocker. I glanced over to where he was keeping a tally in his notebook, bracing for him to gloat, but he merely continued counting names as I read them out loud, his face surprisingly neutral.

My stomach gave a jolt when I opened up the next folded ballot and read the name written on it. My own. I quickly slid my hand down to the pocket in my dress and crumpled up the small slip of paper before Aiden could notice. But my sabotage was in vain; my name was still in there a handful of times. Whenever I saw it scrawled across a ballot, I felt sick again. So I quietly demolished each vote for me as Aiden finished tallying. If he thought it was odd that my name wasn't mentioned once, he didn't show it.

"That's it," I mumbled, as my fist closed around the wadded up paper in my pocket. "Looks like the prince will finally get his crown."

He dismissed my comment with a flippant wave of his hand and frowned. "Are you sure you're okay, Josephine?"

My stomach somersaulted again. I shut the bright orange ballot box and slid it across the table to him. "I told you, I'm fine."

"Whatever. You just don't look so good."

"Yeah, well your eyes all over my legs would beg to differ. Have a nice night, Aiden."

I spun on the heel of my boot and walked out the door. His shocked silence was all I needed; I was already feeling better.

Point to me.

But as I walked to the parking lot, all I could hear was the sound of him saying my name, over and over again, marching in time with my steps on the pavement.

Josephine.

Josephine.

Josephine.

I F I DIDN'T have a perfect attendance record and a masochistic desire to keep it that way, I would've skipped school on the day of the blood drive.

I stood in front of the doors to the gymnasium for a full ten minutes before working up the nerve to go in. A few nurses passed by and gave me knowing looks before the doors swung shut behind them. I tried to plaster a smile on my face, but I think I just came off as sweaty and manic.

I really, really hate needles.

After one final deep breath, I pushed through the doors and stared straight ahead at the cluster of volunteers sitting in the bleachers on the side of the basketball court. I didn't let my eyes wander to the tables heaped with medical equipment and all the you-know-whats.

Aiden was already standing there on the gym floor in front of everyone, his hands on his hips as he surveyed the group of student council members and the handful of kids that volunteered to help out (or maybe they just wanted a free pass out of class for the afternoon).

Save lives, skip Spanish.

The cheap lights flickered overhead as I quickened my pace to the meeting point, not wanting Aiden to rally the troops without me. I wondered if this was even a sanitary place to host a blood drive. How very like him to overlook such meaningless details like cleanliness or proper hygiene. He probably felt right at home here amongst the smell of old sweat and the layers of discarded gum wrappers.

Aiden glanced over his shoulder to see me barreling through the crowd to get to him, so he quickly turned and started without me. Of course.

"All right, so the nurses will be opening the doors to the donors in about five minutes—"

"And by nurses, he means his mother," I added, coming to a stop by his side.

"Yes, my mom will be here," Aiden continued, not skipping a beat. "Stay on task, Josephine."

Josephine.

Grabbing a clipboard from the table next to us, I gripped it tightly in my hands, barely resisting the urge to throw it at him and run out of the gym screaming. I was so anxious that morning when I got ready for school that I had accidentally pulled my hair back in the tightest ponytail imaginable. I was starting to worry that it was actually cutting off the circulation to my brain.

Aiden leaned over to pick up a stack of papers covered in charts that coordinated the volunteers and their station rotations. "Katlyn, could you pass these out?" he asked, handing them to our secretary.

"Sure thing, Aiden," she said, her lip-glossed smile glistening under the poor lighting. She fluffed her hair a few times before sauntering up the stands to hand out the flyers. Aiden's eyes darted to mine as he opened his mouth to say something.

"Anyway," I cut in, trying to maintain some semblance of control over the volunteers, "you all have your handouts with your positions, so go make yourselves useful."

"And if you feel woozy," Aiden said, with another sharp glance at me, "make sure you get help. We don't want anyone passing out on the floor, okay?"

Katlyn laughed far too loudly, like he'd just made the most hilarious joke. She was always favoring Aiden, sending out his emails and reminder texts, then conveniently forgetting to send mine. She smiled at him adoringly and he smiled back. I'm surprised she didn't address him as "Mr. President."

I stepped in front of Aiden, blocking his game of eyeball "you hang up first" and waved my slip of paper in front of his face. "You assigned me to pass out cookies."

"Yeah, so?"

"So that means I'll be in the room with... with all the... you know," I stammered, unable to say the word "needles" out loud.

"It's on the way out, away from... everything. Is there a problem?"

He *had* positioned me as far away from the action as possible, but still; it wasn't far enough. Obviously he suspected something, but he was waiting for me to ask to be removed or to just come out and admit my weakness.

Fat chance.

"Nope, no problem," I said tightly before I slipped into my mom's patented Pageant Voice—all honey, sickly and sweet. "I hope this goes swimmingly for you, Mr. President. I hope it's the crown jewel of your administration and the reason you get into the college of your choosing. You did lobby for it quite persistently, after all." I batted my eyelashes at him and he frowned.

"*Our* administration, you mean, Madame President."

I snorted and walked away, leaving him to wrangle the rest of the volunteers.

The cookie station ended up being not so terrible. For one thing, I got to eat a bunch of cookies. The nurse I was stationed with kept handing me more as she told me about her boyfriend and the fight they'd had the night before over her dog peeing on his rug. The more I nodded along, the more cookies I got. She was sweet and funny, and, most importantly, distracting. If I didn't think too closely about what was happening behind me, I could manage to keep the feeling of nausea at bay.

All I had to do was hold out a cookie to anyone who walked by the table. I didn't make eye contact or look at their bandaged arms. It was just, "here's your cookie, now leave."

"We've got a fainter!" came a yell from across the gym. My curiosity got the better of me, so I took the risk and swiveled around in my folding chair to see who'd succumbed. My mouth full of chocolate chip cookies fell open when I saw Aiden sprawled on the filthy gym floor, his eyes closed and his forehead covered in a sheen of sweat.

"Sweet mother of pearl," I whispered under my breath, accidentally spitting cookie crumbs all over my pants. "He fainted. He actually fainted." My new nurse friend Cathy looked sideways at me, probably concerned that I'd said that sentence with so much joy.

"You'd better go help the poor boy, he looks terrible!" she crooned, clutching at her chest. She took the cookie out of my hand and shoved me out of my seat. "Go on now."

Cathy didn't look like she'd be handing me any more cookies until I obeyed her orders. I wanted to argue back that we were in a roomful of medical professionals, so what exactly was I going to contribute? But after one look at her suddenly stern face, I nodded and closed my mouth. Picking my way through the maze of tables, I kept my gaze trained stubbornly on the ground until I reached the spot where Aiden was lying on the floor and swatting at all the hovering hands reaching down to help him.

As I leaned in to get a better look, my foot bumped into something on the floor. When I glanced down to see what it was, my eyes caught on something small, shiny, and cylindrical—a metallic pill canister. I crouched down to pick it up, shoving it quickly into the pocket of my jeans.

"Josephine!" a voice called from the surrounding huddle the moment I stood back up. "Can you walk Aiden over to the nurse's office? Grab him a cookie on the way out, he's a bit peaky."

The voice came from none other than Betty Mitchell, Aiden's very own mother. She was crouched down on the floor, dressed in navy scrubs like the other nurses, and propping her son's head up with her hand. She smiled at him ruefully and he grimaced before closing his eyes again. "I tried to warn him this might happen—he gets a little lightheaded at the sight of blood, but would he listen to me?"

"Mom, stop talking," Aiden murmured, his words slurring together. "Just stop."

She laughed and pulled him up by the arm until he was seated on the dirty gym floor rather than lying on it. "Let this be a lesson to you; mother knows best."

Christmas had come early.

Ten points to me for not being the one on the gym floor with my mother stroking my hair off my forehead in front of the entire blood drive full of students and medical staff. This victory tasted even sweeter than the half dozen cookies I'd just thrown down.

"Up you go," Betty said to Aiden as she gently helped him to his feet before dragging him over to me. "Josephine? All the other kids are occupied, can you take him? He needs to get out of this room. I'm sure Cathy can hold down the fort for a moment while you're gone." She tucked a stray blonde curl behind her ear and smiled at Aiden, but as he leaned into her, a shadow crossed her face like a wispy cloud passing over the sun. A moment so brief, you could almost miss it. By the time she turned back to me, the shadow was gone. She was all sunshine and daisies.

I blinked and tried to think of what to say, but before I could summon an excuse, she was handing her son off to me. I hesitated, not sure what to do with my hands. Aiden was walking like he'd never taken a step in his life, all clumsy and tripping over his feet, so I grabbed his arm and slung it across my shoulders. He staggered into me, and I nearly tipped over. Despite our nearly identical heights, he was way heavier than he looked.

I tried not to notice that I could feel the hard muscles of his chest under his shirt as we tumbled past Cathy, who cooed sympathetically and tossed me another cookie on our way out of the gym.

I shoved the cookie in Aiden's mouth. "Remember; mother knows best."

He closed his eyes and chewed, his face solemn and still.

I choked on a laugh and dragged his heavy self out the doors. I had to wrap my arm around his waist as we slowly walked down the hall past all the faded lockers and the hand-painted posters screaming about the homecoming dance as we trudged across campus to the nurse's small corner office at the front of the school. Aiden mumbled something through his mouthful of cookie, his face pale under the stark fluorescents.

"What was that? I can't understand you with all that food in your mouth. Where are your manners? What would mother say?"

He swallowed his bite and peeked his eyes open wearily. "I hate you."

I grinned back. "The feeling is mutual."

He sank his face into my shoulder and let me lead him the rest of the way to the nurse's office with his eyes closed. I could've done something truly terrible or embarrassing to him right then and there; he was so vulnerable and entirely in my power.

I could've, but I didn't, and I think that shows great self-restraint. True maturity.

But right before we went into the main office, I paused to snap a selfie with Aiden tucked into my arm, looking like he was weeping onto my shoulder. I sent it to Rose and Cat. They immediately responded with a lot of question marks and exclamation points.

"Did you just take a picture of us?"

"Shh, shh. You're hallucinating. Don't worry your pretty little head about a thing."

"You think I'm pretty?" he asked, his breath warm against my neck.

I pulled open the door to the front office and his nose bumped into me, pressing against my collarbone. Goosebumps rose up along my arms as I stepped around the school secretary's desk (her eyes went wide as she stopped mid-sentence during her phone call to watch us) and shoved him through the last door.

"The prettiest, Aiden. Absolutely stunning."

"You smell nice. Like cake."

He fell into the chair at the nurse's station and blinked sleepily at me. Then he reeled back in surprise as if he'd only just realized what he'd said out loud. "I've got it from here, thanks," he murmured, trying to sit up straight and regain whatever scraps of dignity he had left. But a moment later, he groaned and tipped his head back against the wall, clearly still too nauseous to be dignified.

"You dropped these," I said, fishing the pill bottle out of my pocket. It glinted under the lights as I tossed it to him.

Even though he was woozy, he still caught it with one hand, his face pale and his eyes round. He didn't thank me. He didn't say a word.

"What's with the pills?" I asked, my curiosity getting the better of me and stealing any limited tact I possessed.

Aiden slid the canister into his own pocket, the pills rattling with a tinny noise. He sighed and leaned his head back against the wall once again. "I get headaches," he said simply.

"Let me guess—from being around me."

He laughed once and swiped a hand across his forehead still shining with sweat, his blond hair sticking to him in clumps. "I'm sure you're a contributing factor." He closed his eyes and turned his face away from mine in dismissal.

I had more questions, but just then our ancient school nurse, Mrs. Layton, bustled over and started fussing over him. She patted him roughly on the cheek and said, "Don't feel bad, sonny, there's always a fainter."

I swallowed the laugh that was threatening to burst out at any second. "Mr. President," I coughed, saluting him as I backed out the door.

His mouth twitched, but he kept his eyes shut tight and hissed, "Go away."

I hummed to myself as I walked back past the school secretary who was now whispering into the phone about how Aiden had to be carried to the nurse's office like it was the latest hot gossip.

I floated down the hall; I was practically skipping. I waved at kids I normally ignored, I smiled at passersby like we were the best of friends.

And to think I almost stayed home today.

Eight

I WAS SMUG when I walked into debate practice that afternoon, still riding my high from half-carrying Aiden to be nursed back to health by the ninety-year-old Mrs. Layton, who still made us lie down with a hot water bottle on our heads (no matter what was ailing us) while she hand-fed us animal crackers and told us stories about when she was a student at Pearson High and how she was "quite the looker" back in those days.

Every time I thought about it, I sighed with contentment.

So when I walked into the auditorium and saw Aiden already standing on the stage and leaning against the podium—the perfect picture of health—I nearly swallowed my tongue. He was chatting up Ms. Torrence, who had the nerve to blush and swat him on the shoulder before taking her seat in the front row with her stopwatch in hand. The rest of the team was scattered throughout the room where they broke into smaller groups that got to enjoy the luxury of practicing unsupervised. A flicker of irritation went through me when I looked at Ms. Torrence perched in the front row. Apparently she still felt like she had to babysit Aiden and me as we adjusted to our new partnership.

After I climbed the short stairs to the stage, I tossed my backpack at his feet and crossed my arms, smiling sweetly. "And how are you feeling, Aiden? Still swooning?" I reached over to brush the animal cracker crumbs that lingered on the front of his gray t-shirt, but he grabbed my wrist to stop me.

"Mrs. Layton sends her love," was all he said in reply, his hazel eyes dark and narrowed. He let go of me to pull his stopwatch out of his backpack. The skin on my wrist tingled where he had touched me. I half expected to see scorch marks left behind from his demon hands.

"Negative today?"

"Obviously," I snapped, still rubbing my wrist behind my back. I dug through my gigantic backpack to pull out my laptop and waited for Aiden to do the same, but today he didn't even do that. He just stood at the podium, in that wide, overly confident mansplaining way of his, and waited for me to join him.

"What, no notes today? Still too dizzy to read?"

"I don't need them," he said, his voice low and dismissive. He glanced down at the laptop in my hands. "But apparently you do."

I did not deign to respond, but when I stood at the podium, I bumped him with my hip to move him out of the way. "I'm opening. Let's begin." He had no chance to argue, so he clicked his stopwatch and began his completely annoying and unnecessary scrutiny of me as I delivered the first negative construction.

I started with the overview, carefully unraveling the affirmative argument Aiden and I had presented on Tuesday at our last practice. After only one or two glances at my notes, I poked holes in the resolution while pressing deliberately on the few weak points in our case that our opponents were bound to notice at the tournament this Saturday (if they were any good, that is). Our stopwatches ticked quietly in the background as I leaned forward and relaxed my grip on the podium, letting myself get caught up in the rhythm of my words.

I didn't let Aiden's obnoxious staring interfere; I crushed it.

At the exact eight minute mark I finished speaking and gestured for Ms. Torrence to begin the cross- examination. She sat up straight in her seat like she was bracing herself, her face solemn like a soldier bravely gearing up for battle. But once again, her questions were light and easy to work around. I idly tapped the surface of the podium as I answered; Aiden shifted on his feet impatiently.

"Please, hold your applause," I said under my breath while Ms. Torrence scribbled notes on her clipboard and shouted out encouragement like, "Wow, Josephine! Incredible! Well done! You've already convinced me!"

I didn't need her approval, but that didn't mean I didn't like it or soak it up like she was throwing buckets of sunshine at me.

Aiden was quiet for a moment while I closed my laptop and shuffled through some of my handwritten notes. "That was reasonably well done," he finally consented with a nod.

"'Reasonably well done.' Such high praise coming from you. I'm going to write about that in my journal tonight. 'Dear Diary, you would not believe what *the* Aiden Christopher Mitchell III said to me today…'"

He scrunched up his nose. "Why do you always call me that?"

"Are you kidding me?" My eyebrows shot up in surprise. "That's how you introduced yourself to the whole class when you moved to town."

"Yeah, and I was also twelve. Are you still the same person you were when you were twelve?"

I squirmed under his glare, because if I was being honest, I was pretty much exactly the same when it came to Aiden. We might as well still be in Mrs. Crabtree's class, both of us on the edge of our seats, our hands waving wildly in the air.

I ignored his question. "You're like a '90s child actor, like Jonathan Taylor Thomas." He scoffed and knocked my notebook off the podium with his own. I caught it before it fell and started ticking off names with my fingers. "Or Chad Michael Murray, Vanessa Anne Hudgens—"

"Wow, you watch a lot of TV. No wonder your grades are suffering."

Rose watches a lot of TV, I wanted to argue, *and our house is too small.* But I just let my lips curve into a knowing smile and shrugged one shoulder. "Tell me, did your parents used to take you to audition for commercials?"

He looked at me for a long moment before he sighed and ran a hand through his hair. I'm sure somewhere out there a girl is shedding tears of joy over the rippling waves of his golden hair. It was like a field of wheat swaying in the breeze of a sunlit afternoon.

I shook my head and took a step back. "Your turn."

Aiden elbowed me aside as he stepped up to the podium and clicked his stopwatch once again. He picked up where I'd left off and continued to break down the affirmative case. He was annoyingly charming when he spoke, animated and articulate as he wove my argument in with his until it was seamless. He even made Ms. Torrence laugh twice. I cleared my throat noisily and waved my stopwatch around to remind him of the time. Now I was the one tapping my foot impatiently.

Ms. Torrence attempted to pepper him with questions, posing as the affirmative side in favor of mandatory voting, but she still seemed to have no idea what she was doing, so I volunteered to take over. "May I, Ms. Torrence?" I tried to be the picture of politeness, just like my mother had drilled into me.

More honey, less vinegar, Josie.

It worked. Ms. Torrence sagged in her seat and resumed taking notes. "By all means, Josephine. Take it away!"

I smirked at Aiden and began my rapid-fire cross-examination of him, throwing questions and verbal assaults like fistfuls of darts. He deflected each one and turned them back on me so quickly it seemed effortless. It was like a dance—sidestep here, twirl there, our arguments pressing together before we pushed off and spun in opposite directions.

We were both out of breath as the stopwatches ticked through the final remaining seconds. Then Aiden dipped his head and smiled at me, that gleaming Golden Boy smile of his, and for the briefest moment, my mind emptied and I completely forgot what I was going to say next.

He leaned into the podium and whispered, "Time's up, Jo." Then he turned to Ms. Torrence. "Who won?"

Her eyes darted back and forth between us as she chewed on her lip and fiddled with her pen. "You're both winners! That was excellent!"

Aiden and I both sighed at the same time; there's nothing more stupid than the "everyone's a winner" mentality. Obviously, there can only be one winner. Only one of us could be the best.

"I think I won," I offered in a casual tone, turning to lean against the podium like Aiden. "While your performance was 'reasonably well-done,'" I said, mimicking his voice, "all of your arguments were a little contrived. Some would even say unoriginal."

"Some, as in *you*," he muttered, rolling his eyes. "And of course it's a little contrived, we have to prepare these statements ahead of time."

"Young Aiden, so narrow-minded, so stuck in his ways." He snorted and crossed his arms. "You need to add a little pizzazz to it, liven things up. Maybe go off script every once in a while."

"Pizzazz?" He laughed. "That's rich coming from you. You're unbelievably predictable. Same clothes, same comebacks, same answers; same Josephine day in and day out."

My face flushed and my breathing stuttered. "You don't know anything about me," I whispered fiercely, wishing my cheeks would stop burning in such an obvious way.

"But I do. You watch me, and I watch you. That's our thing, right?"

I gaped at him as the horror of what he had said rose up in my chest. "You… we… I don't know what you're talking about." I forgot about Ms. Torrence sitting in the front row, and the rest of our team milling about the auditorium in various stages of practice. The world had been reduced to Aiden and me, standing an inch apart, both of us glaring so hard I was surprised laser beams didn't shoot out of our eyes. He glanced at the podium, and I thought he might kick it or pick it up to smash it over my head. But when his eyes flicked back to me, they landed on my mouth.

The moment stretched between us, taut and tense until it broke with Aiden's heavy exhale.

"Oh, get a room already!" someone called out from the darkness of the audience. I stiffened and jerked back, feeling a new wave of heat wash over my face. I squinted past the spotlights to see who'd dared to hurl such an insult at me and froze when I saw Tim Boren heaving himself up out of his squeaking auditorium seat with a grin. His letterman jacket stretched tight over his shoulders as he slow clapped and looked around, hoping everyone else would join in.

But it was silent. Our team knew better than to clap along. Tim was co-captain of the varsity football team with Aiden and definitely not interested in speech and debate. The only thing he liked to debate was which party he was going to on a Friday night.

"Did you get lost, Tim?" I called down from the stage. "The football field is that way." I pointed out the doors and shooed him with a flippant hand. He rolled his eyes at me and yelled over to Aiden, "Grab your stuff and let's go! Coach wants us in the locker room in five minutes."

Aiden turned his face to look at Tim, but his body was still angled toward mine. "For what? Practice doesn't start for another thirty minutes."

"Special pre-game meeting. Let's get outta here—unless you have some unfinished business to attend to?" He waggled his eyebrows suggestively at me and I mimed vomiting behind the podium. Tim guffawed loudly. "Cute, Josephine. Very cute."

Aiden sighed as he bent down to pick up his backpack. "Meet at my house tonight," he said quietly.

"Excuse me?"

"To finish our practice. The tournament's on Saturday."

"I know when the tournament is—"

"Then you know we need to practice again. I have the game tomorrow, so I won't have time then. Just meet me at my house. 7 o'clock."

I was stunned. I hadn't been to Aiden's house since his birthday party in the seventh grade when his mom made him invite everyone (the small handful of us, that is).

"Fine," I heard myself agreeing.

He brushed past me and jogged down the stairs over to Tim who was yawning widely.

Did I just agree to willingly go over to Aiden's house tonight? I wanted to shake myself by the shoulders and shout, "What are you thinking?!"

His territory, his house, his rules.

My blood was still boiling and my face was still hot. I swear Tim's booming voice was echoing through the room, bouncing off the high ceiling of the auditorium and slamming back into me with the force of a punch.

Oh, get a room already.

I hated when people did that, when they assumed that an argument was a secret smoke signal for desire or a billboard that screamed, "Take me, I'm yours!" Sometimes a fight was just a fight.

I should know. That's all Aiden and I do.

Ms. Torrence peered at me over her glasses. "Do you want to continue, Josephine?" Her voice was soft, her tone compassionate, pitying even. Like she knew something I didn't. I grabbed my backpack and stuffed everything back inside before turning to her. "No, I think we're done here."

I marched stiffly down the stairs with my head held high even though I was shamefully walking out on my own debate practice (again). Halfway down the aisle I saw Brandon Lopez headed in my direction, straight from his own debate round. He didn't see me standing right in front of him; he was flipping through his notes, his forehead all scrunched up in concentration.

"I need to talk to you," I said when he nearly ran into me.

"Oh, okay," he said, stumbling back a step and only halfway paying attention. He started pulling another notebook out of his backpack. "Did you want to practice or something?"

"Just follow me." I didn't mean for it to come out like a command, but my voice was rough and, well, commanding. Brandon's dark eyebrows shot up in surprise, but he didn't argue when I tugged him by the sleeve to the auditorium doors. I could hear Ms. Torrence trying to reestablish some semblance of order after all the disruptions to our practice, but I ignored everything else and just kept walking with Brandon trailing along in my wake, the sleeve of his t-shirt still pinched between my fingers.

My palms were sweating by the time we'd made it to the empty hallway. The doors swung shut behind us as I turned to face him. His eyes were still glued to his notebook. "Did you see that *New York Times* article about voter turnout in rural areas—"

"Brandon, do you want to make out with me?" I blurted out, cutting him off. I figured bluntness was the only way to go. Just get it out and over with.

Somehow his eyebrows went even higher—they were nearly grazing his hairline at this point. He blinked his brown eyes at me and dropped his backpack on the floor. "Um, what?"

"I asked if you—"

"I heard you. I guess I'm just... surprised?"

My eyes narrowed but my face felt like it was on fire. "Like a bad surprise?"

He considered me for a moment, then swallowed. When he finally spoke, his voice came out higher than usual. "No?"

I wished it hadn't sounded like a question when he'd answered me.

We stared silently at each other for a few more seconds while the fluorescents flickered overhead. He was clearly waiting for me to explain myself and my sudden desire to kiss him, but I had nothing reasonable to offer him and I was afraid of what I'd say if I tried to explain.

I could see why Rose and Cat had put him on the list. Brandon was cute, clean-cut, polite, and a decent debater—he'd made it nearly as far as me in the state tournament last year. Plus, he was taller than me, which I liked.

He was your classic nice guy.

I cleared my throat and pointed at the doors that led out to the parking lot. "So, should we—"

"Yeah, sure. Okay, yeah." He slowly picked up his backpack and nodded a few times. I hoped that wasn't more evidence of him trying to convince himself that this wasn't a terrible idea.

I wasn't so sure myself.

I let him lead me out the school doors and over to his truck in the school parking lot, my heart hammering the whole way. He asked me a few stilted questions about the tournament, but I couldn't think of anything to further the conversation, and my mouth was suddenly bone dry. My nerves were getting the best of me; I'd only been kissed once, and it was during a game of spin the bottle freshman year. A five-second kiss with Nolan Price that was more braces clashing than actual lips touching—I hardly think that counts.

As we weaved between the few remaining cars, I saw Tim and Aiden heading to the field house. Even though he was fifty yards away and had his back to me, somehow Aiden stopped and spun around, just in time to see me sliding into the front seat of Brandon's black Silverado.

I could feel his gaze on my back, like a knife, slicing me clean through.

I slammed the door shut and faced Brandon, who bit his lip shyly. He fiddled with the radio, switching from station to station before shutting it off with a sigh. My stomach dropped when his eyes caught on my mouth. I was starting to second guess this very stupid, very impulsive decision. My hand snaked across the seat toward the door handle, but before I could make a hasty escape, Brandon leaned forward and pressed his hand to my cheek, pulling my face slowly toward his.

I closed my eyes as his lips landed on mine, warm and light. We fumbled for a moment, our noses bumping as we both awkwardly readjusted in our seats. But after a few minutes, we got the hang of it. He put a hand into my hair and leaned into me, this time kissing me in earnest. His mouth was soft and tasted like cinnamon from that gum he was always chewing. Brandon really seemed to know what he was doing, which made up for my lack of expertise. As far as I could tell, he was an excellent kisser.

It was nice; he was nice. After a while, I pulled back and asked if he could drive me home. He shook his head as if trying to clear it before nodding. His mouth looked swollen and his eyes were hazy. I felt a strange twinge of satisfaction knowing that I'd made him feel that way.

It was easier to talk to Brandon on the drive to my house now that the kissing was done. I asked him about his practice rounds, and he asked me about mine, but every time he brought up Aiden my stomach twisted itself into a knot. I could ignore that if I concentrated on Brandon's voice and his latest findings on voting patterns in the Midwest.

Although I wasn't looking forward to seeing the smug looks on their faces, I had to admit that Cat and Rose were right. I *did* feel a little better.

I could almost pretend that I didn't hear the words still ringing in my head.

Oh, get a room already.

You smell nice. Like cake.

I could almost pretend I was thinking about the feel of Brandon's lips on mine, and not the feeling of Aiden's eyes on my back, right in between my shoulder blades, like a pressure point demanding to be acknowledged.

Almost. But not quite.

Nine

BRANDON DIDN'T TRY to kiss me goodbye once we got to my house. He put his truck in park and darted a glance at me. "Listen, Josephine, I'm not really looking for anything serious—"

"Ugh, Brandon. Stop," I groaned. "Relax. I'm not trying to date you or anything. You're off the hook." He sank into his seat and released a giant breath, running a hand through his short dark hair. I rolled my eyes. "Try not to look so relieved."

He laughed softly and ducked his head. "I mean, don't get me wrong, *that* was great," he said, gesturing between us with a blush. It was like he couldn't even bring himself to say out loud that we'd just kissed.

"You don't need to tell me how great I am, I already know," I said with a snort. I tried to summon some of my usual bravado, but truthfully I just wanted to get out of there.

Brandon laughed again and leaned across me to push open the truck door. "Well, thanks."

"You're welcome, I guess?" Such sweet parting words. "See you at school," I said as I climbed out.

I couldn't stop picturing his relieved expression when I said I wasn't interested in pursuing him. It's like I could almost hear him saying, "Whew, dodged that bullet!"

He's probably still scared of me. Or intimidated, if we're being generous. But that just sounded like dressing up fear in a different outfit and pretending it was something else. I'd made out with the guy, no strings attached, and he still didn't look back as he pulled out of my driveway and sped away, his tires spinning in the loose gravel.

There is no justice in this world.

When I got inside, there was no one there to greet me or to ask me how my day was. Dad was still at work and Mom was nowhere to be found. Maybe she was preening around town, or maybe she was locked in her room, crying over her old high school yearbooks or something else equally depressing.

I looked around my house and sighed. There were no family pictures on the walls, no crayon drawings or painted handprints preserved and cherished. But my mother's old pageant trophies and silver-framed glamour shots were displayed on a small shelf above the TV, with her beloved Miss Carl County crown nestled on its plush velvet cushion beside them.

If you squinted, it almost looked like Rose and I didn't live here. My parents must walk around with their eyes permanently scrunched up.

"Rose?" No answer. I texted my sister.

I have breaking news. Where are you?

She didn't respond for a while. I sat at the kitchen counter, piled my textbooks around me like a fort, and got to work until my phone pinged with a message from Rose.

What's the news?!!? I'm thrifting for a new dress for the dance this weekend!!!!!!! Want to meet me and Cat?

My sister was an enthusiastic texter; all the emojis and all the exclamations, all the time. I shuddered as I read through her text.

No thanks, I would rather bathe in acid. I'll tell you later tonight.

I'd make her wait. It served her right for trying to make me go shopping.

I tried to lose myself in my homework, but it was hard to focus; all I could think about was how I was about to go to Aiden's house to practice for our debate. How did he get me to agree to such a ridiculous proposition?

Time seemed to speed up the closer it got to 7 o'clock. The time displayed on the microwave was glaring like an overly bright neon sign; a constant reminder of the stupid agreement I'd made. At 6:45 I finally gave up, put my textbooks away, and gathered my debate materials.

I resisted the urge to go into the bathroom and fix my hair or change my clothes, or anything else that was a waste of my time. Instead, I grabbed the keys to the beater and made myself get in the car and drive the four minutes to his house. I drove in silence with my heart in my throat and my hands gripping the wheel tightly until I pulled into his flowerbed-lined driveway. Aiden's house was small but well taken care of. Something I couldn't say about my own, except for the small part.

I stood on his front porch for a ridiculous amount of time with my hand poised over the door ready to knock, feeling like I was walking straight into the lion's den. Willingly. Stupidly. A moth that had been fluttering near the porch light suddenly dove straight into the bulb and was zapped. It fell at my feet, twitching pathetically on the ground. I'm not a big believer in signs, but that did not seem like a good one.

Gritting my teeth, I tightened my ponytail, then forced my knuckles to rap sharply on the door three times. Seconds later, a tiny thing that looked like Aiden answered the door. She swung her head around, her pigtails swaying back and forth, and asked, "Who are you?"

"I'm Josephine." She blinked expectantly as if she wouldn't let me pass until I gave her more information. "I'm here to see Aiden." I shivered after the words came out.

Another tiny human shoved his way through the doorframe, his mouth smeared with some kind of red sauce. "Are you Aiden's girlfriend?" he asked with a slight lisp.

I tried to hide the horror on my face, but I must have failed miserably because both the miniature Aiden's laughed and grabbed me by the hands to pull me inside. "Aiden!" his sister screamed down the hall with her hands on her hips, "your *girlfriend* is here!"

"No, no, I'm not—He's not—we're..." But Aiden's younger brother and sister didn't listen to a word I stuttered out. They ran off, apparently bored with humiliating me. Soon their screeching and the sound of the television filled the next room.

"Don't mind Beau and Lacy," another voice sang out from the kitchen, "they live to tease. Ignore them or you'll just fuel the fire." Betty Mitchell, still in her scrubs from work, ambled into the entryway with a dishrag slung over her shoulder and the smell of lasagna wafting behind her. "It's nice to see you again, Josephine," she said warmly. "Aiden should've invited you over earlier, you could've eaten dinner with us!"

I smiled stiffly, trying to imagine what it would be like to sit at the Mitchells' dinner table and share a meal together, but the thought was so absurdly strange I couldn't even fathom it. By the time I'd opened my mouth to refuse the dinner invitation that hadn't actually happened, Mrs. Mitchell had already moved on. "He told me you were coming over to practice for your big debut this Saturday."

I nodded mutely and she took that as permission to start asking me questions about different debate techniques and which ones I preferred and why. She seemed sincere and genuinely curious, but I could barely find the words to answer her. I wasn't used to anyone caring or trying to understand me on this level. My throat tightened painfully, and my shoulders hunched in on themselves, curling around me protectively like I could shield myself from the onslaught of human interest.

Don't be rude, Josie, answer the nice woman's questions. And quit slouching.

My mother's voice rang in my ears so loudly, I could hardly hear Mrs. Mitchell and her earnest kindness. The walls felt like they were closing in. Walls covered in family photos and framed crayon drawings, even a collection of terribly painted handprints, forever memorializing her children and her love for them.

My eyes focused on a giant family portrait hanging over the small fireplace. I picked out Aiden immediately; it must've been taken shortly before they moved to Pearson because it looked like twelve-year-old Aiden Christopher Mitchell III in all his glory. His younger brother and sister were even tinier, huddled around him and grinning widely. But behind Mr. and Mrs. Mitchell (both younger, blonder, and thinner) was a tall boy, also blond, and smiling like he had a secret.

"I didn't know Aiden had an older brother," I blurted out in the middle of Mrs. Mitchell's question about the guidelines of a Lincoln-Douglas debate. Betty's brown eyes widened at my question, and she turned to look at the portrait I'd been openly staring at.

"That's my Wes," she said softly. "He passed away some time ago."

My chest heaved in a painful lurch, and I wasn't sure why. I didn't know this boy, and I barely knew this woman. But a loss is still a loss, and the unfairness of it all sent a shuddering ache through me just the same.

"Aiden doesn't like talking about him—" his mother started to say, just as Aiden himself walked down the hallway, finally gracing us with his presence. He was wearing a clean t-shirt and looked freshly showered, his blond curls dark and damp against his head. I looked away at the sight of his bare feet. It was strangely intimate to see him like that, all scrubbed clean and shoeless.

"You're here," he said quietly with a weird look on his face.

Did he think I wasn't going to show? Then he would've won.

"Let's get started," he added quickly. No greeting, no "welcome to my humble home" hospitality or awkward shuffling from the lack of it.

Betty Mitchell smiled at her son and waved me toward him. "You two have fun! If you get hungry, let me know and I'll heat something up for you in a jiffy." She grabbed Aiden by the arm and planted a kiss on his cheek. I expected him to brush her off or scowl in annoyance, but he just stood there and let her do it. He met my gaze boldly, as if daring me to make fun of him and his family, but what he couldn't know and what he would never understand was that my throat had closed up and had made it nearly impossible for me to speak, let alone sling insults.

I couldn't remember the last time my mom had touched me like that, with such casual affection and easy tenderness.

I hated that I envied Aiden. And I hated that he probably knew that I did. It must've been written all over my sorry, emotionally-deprived face.

Aiden turned down the dark hallway and I followed, feeling like I was stepping off a cliff. But I was so numb, I doubted I would even feel the crash landing.

Oh, get a room already.

Tim's heckling followed me into Aiden's bedroom as he leaned across me to pull his door shut behind us. He was standing so unreasonably close, I could smell the soap he used in the shower—clean and a little spicy.

He stepped to the side to let me survey his room. I scanned the simple space, hoping to find something embarrassing to hold over his head. But there was nothing except a queen-sized bed (unmade), a desk in the corner (just as cluttered as mine, if not more), and the rest of the narrow room was buried under bookcase after bookcase. I wanted to circle the shelves and take my time reading every spine.

I glanced at his nightstand, wondering if I'd see the mysterious pill bottle for the supposed headaches, but the small table was disappointingly empty besides a lamp and a small, framed picture of his family, in which Wes was noticeably absent.

"Are you done snooping? Or should I leave you alone in here for a few minutes?"

I glared at him and gripped the straps of my backpack. "What, no alter for blood sacrifices?"

"I put that away when I have guests over. It tends to unnerve them."

"Same with your voodoo doll with my face on it?"

Aiden pretended to kick something under his bed. "Oops, forgot to hide that."

I bit my cheek to keep from laughing. "By the way, your football gear reeks," I said, nodding toward his gym bag tossed in the corner and spilling out onto the floor.

He snorted and threw his backpack on his bed. "Then you'll feel right at home."

"I thought you said I smelled nice? Like cake."

What was wrong with me? We obviously had an unspoken agreement to never bring that up again, and now I'd broken it.

Aiden blushed furiously, and it was fascinating to watch. The color started high on his cheekbones, then bloomed to cover the rest of his face in a bright revealing pink. "Obviously, I was delirious," he said after clearing his throat.

"I think that might've been the sanest you've ever been," I retorted.

It was like I couldn't stop the word vomit from spewing out all over him. Aiden watched me, his expression suspicious as I busied myself with pulling out my laptop and powering it on.

After setting up our workstations—Aiden on his bed, me at his desk—he finally broke the silence by blurting out, "I saw you get into Brandon's truck after practice today."

"I saw you seeing me get into Brandon's truck after practice today."

He waited for me to elaborate. I waited for him to drop it.

"So, did he give you a ride home?"

"Yep, he drove me home."

Again, Aiden waited for me to say more. Again, I ignored his opening.

"You know he placed thirteenth at the state tournament; he totally lost it during the cross-examination."

"What's your point?" I huffed.

"I just thought you had higher standards, that's all."

He knew what had happened in Brandon's truck. I could tell by the way he was looking at me with his condescending mouth pulled into a frown.

"I do. Brandon's a nice guy." *And a good kisser*, I almost added, as the taste of cinnamon filled my mouth. But instead, I bit my lip and turned back to my notes. "And he's tall."

"He's not *that* tall." Aiden leaned forward, his bed creaking beneath him. He lowered his voice like he was about to reveal a secret, something truly shocking. "Also, did you know he competed in the poetry round last year? Poetry." He dragged the word out, enunciating every syllable. "And he didn't even place."

A hysterical laugh almost burst free from my chest, but I didn't want to give Aiden the satisfaction. It's a known fact that debaters hold a lot of (probably unfair) disdain for the speech side of the tournaments.

"Interesting," I replied.

"What's interesting?"

"That you're so intrigued by the subject of Brandon driving me home." But we both knew I was referring to something else.

Aiden scratched his head and grabbed the nearest notebook he could find, flipping it open with a flurry of pages. It was his chemistry notes, not his debate prep. He didn't seem to notice as he hunched over and pretended to read. "It's not interesting, I'm just trying to have a civilized conversation with you, that's all," he mumbled.

"Civilized... you and me? Please." I laughed and leaned across his bed to flick his notebook shut, then tapped the cover. "Wrong notebook, Mr. President. Why so distracted? It couldn't possibly be the thought of Brandon kissing me in his truck that has you all flustered, could it?"

I didn't know what possessed me to say such a thing. Especially since I was still mid-lean, halfway stretched across his bed, and hovering right over him. I immediately regretted saying it when I saw the look on his face. His eyes were piercing as he glared at me, the rest of his features dipped in shadows from where his desk lamp refused to shine. He looked down at my mouth once before glancing away.

"You can do whatever you want, Jo. I don't care." He leaned back against his headboard, looking wrung out. I sat back down in his desk chair, smoothing my ponytail for something to do with my hands. "Let's begin," he said, not pausing to see if I was ready.

Ten

W E DIDN'T TALK for the rest of our practice unless it was specif-
ically about the debate.

We both stayed on our opposite sides of the small room, avoiding
all scenarios that involved eye contact as we pieced together our game
plan for Saturday. We were politely indifferent with each other as we
offered articles we'd read and evidence we'd collected. Even our level
of bickering was at an all-time low. Aiden seemed too tired, and I felt
too awkward to summon any spite when he would interrupt me or
insist that his opening statement was better (it most definitely was
not).

After practicing for a few hours, I had to admit we were *good*. Our
separate arguments meshed together to form a platform so unstop-
pable that anyone challenging us would most likely end up in tears.
For the first time since my team had betrayed me and hijacked control over the tournament, I felt hesitantly optimistic.

At the end of our session, Aiden shut his laptop and ran his hand
across his forehead, ruffling his blond hair as he looked me in the eyes
for the first time since The Brandon Incident. We stood in unison, the
air tense and tight in the crowded space of his room. I bent down to
pick up my backpack, tossing in each item mechanically while Aiden
stood there hovering over me.

When I straightened, he rubbed his jaw and frowned, looking like
he wanted to say something. Between the bookshelves and the desk
and his bed, there was hardly any room to stand, leaving me basically
zero personal space in my enemy's inner sanctum.

It was not ideal.

My heart started racing as he took yet another step closer, the toe of his bare foot nudging against my shoe. Aiden blinked a few times, his eyelashes fluttering softly like the moth I'd seen outside his front door earlier. Another bad omen. He finally opened his mouth, only to snap it shut once again.

Then his expression hardened. "You need to leave. Right now," he said looking over my shoulder rather than at me. The planes of his face were rigid, his mouth pulled into a thin line. There wasn't a dimple in sight.

"Wow, okay." I tried to hide the surprise I felt at the sudden dismissal, but I'm sure it was as obvious as the sickening bloom of a black and blue bruise. "Got it." I shot him one last glare, but he didn't even bother looking up to receive it. I didn't say goodnight as I darted out of his room, and he didn't offer to walk me to my car either. His bedroom door closed behind me with a soft thud.

I turned around to stare at the shut door, the solid dark wood now the humiliating symbol of Aiden rudely kicking me to the curb. I tightened my ponytail and adjusted the straps of my backpack, waiting for my heart to calm down. But it didn't, which only made me feel more stupid.

Everything had gone according to plan: I came, we practiced, and now I was going home.

Everything was fine, right?

I was about to aim a swift kick of my own at Aiden's offensive bedroom door when I heard a strange sound coming from inside his room. It was hard to describe—kind of like a slow ripping sound, or the long, drawn-out sigh of a zipper. Whatever it was, it made all the hairs on the back of my neck stand on end.

His door rattled once, and then everything was quiet. My heart went into overdrive.

It's fine. I'm fine. Everything is fine.

I repeated that to myself as I slowly backed away and quietly snuck down the hallway until I was met with the sound of urgent whispering filtering in from the kitchen. "You need to talk to him," Betty said softly, her voice low and anxious.

"I know, I know. I'm just trying to think of the best way to approach him. You know how he gets whenever I bring it up," a tired voice answered. I was pretty positive it was Mr. Mitchell—Aiden's father.

I froze at the end of the hallway, eyeing the front door warily. Maybe if I ran really fast no one would see me. But then there was the issue of the door opening and closing noisily. I clenched the straps of my backpack and prepared to bolt, not wanting to interrupt whatever discussion was happening in the kitchen between Aiden's parents.

"Maybe I should talk to him after the game," Mr. Mitchell said. "I don't want him distracted. He needs to focus."

"You know, there's more to life than—Oh, Josephine!" Mrs. Mitchell came out of the kitchen and rounded the corner, nearly slamming into me. Her eyes were red, and her mouth was small and puckered. No more sunshine and daisies. "Did you need something? Is everything all right?"

"It's fine, I'm fine. I'm just heading home," I muttered, trying to slide past her to the door.

Mr. Mitchell leaned against the kitchen entryway and folded his arms across his chest. "That's for the best. Aiden needs to get his sleep," he said. His tie was loose like he'd yanked it free the moment he stepped off his used car sales lot, Mitchell's Motors. He had the same blond waves his son did, and when he smiled softly at me, I saw he had the same dimple too.

The Mitchells were both smiling at me, but neither of them looked very happy. Everything about them seemed stiff and forced. "Drive safe now," Mr. Mitchell said as he opened the front door and gestured for me to leave. He closed the door in my face before I could utter another word.

My hands were shaking as I fumbled with my keys and zipped out of the Mitchells' driveway, nearly knocking their garbage cans over. I didn't stop shaking the whole way home, but I couldn't really put my finger on why. I drove faster than I normally did, feeling like if I slowed down, I'd have to stop and look more closely at all the thoughts racing through my mind, rapid-fire and wild.

Rose was watching TV with Dad when I walked into the house. Somehow, she'd convinced him to turn on a rerun episode of *Project Runway*. He was frowning at the TV and checking his watch, literally counting the minutes until it was over. A pile of Chinese takeout boxes was heaped on the scarred surface of the coffee table. I was pretty sure our family single-handedly kept the three restaurants in Pearson open for business—we're not exactly what you'd call "domestic."

Rose stood when she saw me come in through the door, her expression eager. "You're free, Dad," she said, tossing him the remote, which he caught and twirled like a baton.

He passed her the last fortune cookie in exchange for total TV control. "Sleep well, little ladies!" he said, nestling deeper into his chair as the opening notes to Sports Center rang through the house, mixing with his content sigh. I didn't ask where Mom was—I doubted he knew anyway.

I grabbed a container of spicy orange chicken and followed Rose down the hall to her room, where she pulled me onto the bed and all but screamed, "Dish! What happened?"

At first, I thought she was referring to the strangeness I'd just experienced at Aiden's house, but then I remembered our text exchange earlier this evening; I'd all but forgotten about Brandon.

I pretended to drumroll with the chopsticks clutched in my hands. "I made out with Brandon after practice today."

"What?" Rose screeched and fell back squealing onto her pillows. "Tell me everything. No holding back."

So I did. She was the perfect audience, gasping in all the right places and grinning like a fool by the time I was finished. I may or may not have skipped all the parts where I was awkward and sweaty.

"So, what's going to happen next? Do you *like* Brandon?" She wiggled her eyebrows up and down.

I absently picked a sliver of orange peel off a piece of the now-cold chicken and shrugged. "Um, I doubt anything will come from it."

"You don't like him," she said simply.

"And he doesn't like me," I added.

Rose waved her hand dismissively as if that was beside the point. "You need more, I think."

"What, more propositioning guys to make out in their trucks?" I winced and nearly started sweating again.

She laughed. "Well, I definitely think you could use more of that. But no, what I meant was, I think you need someone who challenges you a little more." She didn't offer any suggestions for who she thought that would be, and neither did I. Instead, I shoved my mouth full of Chinese food and stared at the worn floral comforter on her bed.

"Remember," she said, glancing down at something in her hand. *"Follow your heart and you will find the true happiness you seek."*

I set the empty takeout container on her nightstand and pinched my lips together. "Quit feeding me your fortune cookie wisdom."

She laughed and handed me the other half of the cookie. "But really, how do you feel now? A little more relaxed?"

"I'm completely zen," I said flopping down next to her. "I will be super chill from now on."

She laughed and tried to push me off the bed. "Then why did you look so serious when you got home?"

I swallowed. "I looked serious?"

"Spooked, even."

For some reason, I didn't feel like explaining what had happened at Aiden's house; I didn't even want to tell her I'd been over there. "I'm just nervous about the tournament on Saturday." The words felt clunky in my mouth. I don't think I'd ever admitted to having nerves before, but I was surprised by how true the admission felt.

Rose sat up and tugged on my arm until I was seated beside her. She pulled the elastic out of my hair and smoothed it down, then started working the strands into a braid crown. Her fingers were light and soft, soothing and familiar. "You and Aiden will absolutely kill it. No question. If you can avoid killing each other first, that is."

"I make no promises," I said drowsily, feeling like a sleepy cat.

She snorted and continued braiding my hair in the easy silence that followed.

You and Aiden.

I was nearly asleep by the time she'd finished and patted me softly on the head. "There. A crown for the queen."

I stood up and kissed her on the cheek before crossing the hall to my own room. "Don't stay up too late texting sweet nothings to Jordan," I whispered before shutting the door.

She rolled her eyes and whispered back, "I make no promises."

I felt like I was floating outside my body as I sat down to work on my homework. I outlined my next English term paper, finished a chemistry assignment, did my history reading, and looked over my debate notes one last time. Then, I opened my laptop and looked at all of my college applications: Stanford, Columbia, Princeton, Yale. The deadline was approaching, and I was nearly ready, but every time I thought about submitting them, I felt like I was going to throw up.

For as long as I could remember, I've wanted to be somewhere other than Pearson, Texas. I've worked and studied and volunteered, giving everything I had to produce a resume so unfailingly perfect that no college would dare to reject me.

But they still could.

And then where would I be?

I scrolled through the applications, looking at all my gold stars and grand accomplishments, feeling the surge of pride I felt every time I saw them lined up like that, all neat and tidy and unabashedly mine. But when I got to the essay questions, the screen turned blank, the blinking curser reminding me that I had nothing to say with every one of its winks.

Share your story, they asked me. *Tell us about you.*

How was I supposed to tell them that my story hadn't started yet? That I was still in the prologue, waiting to turn the page, to skip to the good part?

I slammed my computer shut and rubbed my face. My eyes felt heavy and strained. I avoided looking at the clock, not wanting to know how late I'd stayed up; because this is what I was good at, this is what made sense to me. The longer I worked, the harder I pushed myself, the more at home I felt in my skin. I felt grounded, like I'd just finished meditating or repeating positive affirmations to myself.

What does that say about me? That I only feel like I can breathe when I'm buried?

I don't really want to know.

I collapsed on my bed, still fully dressed with my shoes on and everything, and fell asleep within seconds. But I tossed and turned all night. I couldn't stop hearing that strange sound or seeing the even stranger look on Aiden's face when he unceremoniously forced me out of his room.

But mostly I kept hearing my sister's voice repeating:

You and Aiden.
You and Aiden.
You and Aiden.
I rolled over onto my stomach and shoved my head under a pillow.
Me and Aiden.

Eleven

I WOKE UP to the sound of shouting.

I sat up in confusion and stared at my still-booted feet hanging off my bed, blinking blearily a few times before another rush of angry yelling filtered in under my door.

When I glanced at the clock on my bedside table, I yelped. I was running seriously behind. I grabbed the closest clean clothes I could find and blessed Rose for braiding my hair last night, thus saving me a step in my morning routine.

When I skidded into the kitchen, I found the source of the shouting match. Rose stood facing off across from our mother over the rickety kitchen table, still covered in the grocery bags from last night's takeout.

"Missy told me she overheard you and Cat yammering on and on about your big date to the dance this weekend." Mom's face was lovely even when livid, which was an extremely irritating thing to have to deal with first thing in the morning. "Did you really think we wouldn't find out?"

Rose glared at her with tears shining in her eyes, but she didn't deny it. She'd probably already tried that route and failed.

Dad was hiding halfway in the fridge, the gallon of milk hanging from his loose grip as he watched the conversation with the same interest he usually only reserved for sporting events. I grabbed the gallon from him and set it gently on the counter, not feeling like cleaning up spilled milk if he decided to join in on the screaming match.

The only time our absentee parents ever paid attention to my sister and me was when a boy entered the scene. Well, pretty much only Rose's scene—my lack of experience wasn't anything to write home about.

If either of our parents ever heard a rumor concerning one of their daughters and a boy, they'd both perk up and remember that they're the ones in charge here. Then they'd shake the proverbial dust off and fire up the old, "if you live under my roof, then you follow my rules" speech they kept on standby for these special times. There was nothing that scared my parents more than the thought of teenage pregnancy. Living with them was like living with a giant billboard written in bold print, *"Don't make the same mistakes we did!"*

A big mistake, according to them. And a mistake not worth repeating.

Rose closed her eyes and took a deep breath as if trying to regain her composure. "You're completely overreacting. It's just a *dance*! What's the big deal?"

"The big deal is that you're not allowed to go out with anyone, anywhere, until you're out of high school and out of this house," Mom said primly, smoothing down her blouse.

"Your mother's right. Don't argue with her, Rose," Dad quipped, apparently deciding to join the fray after all. "That's final." The fridge door slammed shut behind him, punctuating the seriousness of his statement.

"You two are utterly ridiculous. Maybe I'll move in with Jordan since you think that's the next step after a first date!" Rose wailed as she abandoned her cool, collected tactic and went straight for total meltdown.

I needed to intervene and fast. I stood in front of Rose and turned to face our parents. "Look, she won't go, okay? I'll make sure of it."

Mom and Dad both paused and eyed me skeptically, but I held their gazes steadily. I could see them wrestling with their desire to shove the responsibility of parenting off on me, but also wanting to maintain some sort of control over the situation.

But I knew them well; *not* parenting always won.

"You see to it, Josephine," Mom added pointlessly. She gave Rose one more warning look before exiting the kitchen in a huff and banging the bathroom door shut behind her, the sound of her hairspray can hissing noisily in the sudden silence.

Rose played the part of the properly abashed daughter well. She hung her head solemnly (a little too solemnly, I might add), and left to get her backpack from her room without looking at me. Mournful music spilled out from under her door as Adele warbled on depressingly about lost love. Rose was really laying it on thick.

"Well, I'm glad that's settled," Dad said cheerfully as he abandoned his cereal in favor of a granola bar (much more conducive to a clean escape). "Tell your mama goodbye for me!" he called over his shoulder on his way out the door and away from the possibility of any more drama.

I made some toast for Rose and me in the now quiet kitchen, then packed our lunches to take to school before heading back to my room to grab my backpack. I carefully organized my books and binders, gently sliding in each item while counting my pens and gathering my highlighter collection. I finished the soothing ritual by slowly pulling the zipper shut.

Swinging my backpack over my shoulder, I went into the kitchen to finish my toast. Mom finally emerged from the bathroom, filling our tiny house with an unholy amount of fumes from her assorted hair products. I coughed, nearly choking on my jam. "You're killing the environment with all that stuff," I wheezed as she blew through the kitchen in her hurry to leave before Rose or I could need anything else and ruin her morning further.

She click-clacked across the floor in heels much too high for a real estate agent and blew a kiss to no one in particular. "A little hairspray never hurt anybody," she said as she shimmied out the door, "and you could use a little on those flyaways, Josie. I left the can on the—" The door slammed shut, cutting off her totally unnecessary instructions. As if I didn't know where her collection of hairspray was. As if I was going to use any.

I chewed on my last bite of toast and clenched my hands into fists to keep myself from checking for the supposed unruly hairs my mother had mentioned. "The coast is clear," I yelled down the hall as I stuffed my lunch into my backpack. Rose's music abruptly switched off. She poked her head out her door and grinned.

"You are an angel," she crooned as she pranced down the hall. "I don't deserve you!"

"No, you don't," I said, sliding her lunch into her backpack. "Now don't do anything I wouldn't do this weekend, young lady."

She groaned. "Ugh, don't say that. That leaves me with no options!" She snorted as she took a giant bite of her toast.

I laughed, but it sounded hollow in my ears. "Grab the keys, we're going to be late."

She skipped outside, twirling around in her bright purple dress and singing a Taylor Swift song about true love and parking down by a lake as I climbed in the car after her with a lump in my throat. Rose didn't notice that I was quiet the whole drive; she chatted endlessly about the perfect dress she'd found last night with Cat while I mentally high fived myself for resisting the urge to bury my face in my backpack and cry.

No options—is that really what my own sister thought of me?

□ □ □

Every Friday, the entire population of Pearson, Texas engaged in what I could only call total mayhem. Because every year as autumn descended on our fair town, Friday meant football, and football was life.

For everyone, it seemed. Except for me.

Today was game day, in case you missed it.

Our school hadn't made it to the state playoffs since my dear old dad led them to victory back in his senior year, so I don't know why everyone got so excited about such mediocrity, but here we are. Even Cat and Rose—fairweather football fans at best—succumbed. Cat showed up to school with Ethan's jersey number painted on both her cheeks in our school's heinous colors of purple and orange.

"*Et tu*, Cat?" I groaned at the sight of her painted face beaming at me from the other side of my locker door. "Ethan's a benchwarmer," I reminded her.

She smirked. "A very cute one, at that." Then she gave my outfit of jeans and a black t-shirt a once-over. "It's game day," she said, stating the obvious. "Aren't you supposed to be in your marching band uniform?"

"Yeah, where's your school spirit?" Rose raised her eyebrows as she shook out the many ruffles of her insanely purple dress (she wouldn't be caught dead in something as boring as a school t-shirt).

I grinned. "One of the many perks of being both student council president—"

"—co-president," coughed Rose.

"—and a captain in the marching band is that I disbanded the archaic tradition forcing us to wear those hideous uniforms to school. I consider it one of my greatest accomplishments." I took a bow.

"Quite the achievement," Cat said in a muffled voice from where she was rooting around in her locker.

Rose laughed and offered me a round of applause before running off to go see a group of juniors down the hall. Cat finally emerged from the abyss with a small container in hand. She shook it a few times, then peered into her mirror and began sprinkling glitter in her short, messy waves.

"Glitter, Cat? You've got too far. I can't save you now." I leaned back against my locker and closed my eyes. I'd meant it as a joke, but it came out too matter of fact.

"It's our senior year, Josephine! It's okay to have fun; you should try it sometime." Her voice was grave; I could tell she didn't mean it as a joke. She sighed before adding, "You're my best friend, and I'll love you until the day I die, but sometimes I wish you'd let everyone else in every once in a while."

I stood up straight and scowled at her. "What does parading myself around with glitter in my hair have to do with 'letting people in' anyway?"

Cat shook her head sadly, almost as if she was disappointed in me. My stomach swooped when she said, "It's because you're fun, Josephine, and funny too. But you never let anyone besides me and Rose see that side of you. Maybe every now and then you could let your hair down." She frowned up at me with her hands on her hips, a sharp contrast to the cheery paint and glitter sprinkled all over her. "Not just metaphorically, but literally. You've been wearing that same uptight ponytail since kindergarten."

I gestured wildly to the top of my head. "Come on, look at my fancy braid crown today!"

"I know Rose's handy work when I see it. I want *you* to choose something different, to try something new."

Anger flared through me at the end of her lecture. "I'm so sick of people saying things like that to me." Unbidden, Aiden's snide voice whispered through my mind: *you're unbelievably predictable. Same clothes, same comebacks, same answers; same Josephine, day in and day out.* "Why does everyone assume I'm not happy the way things are?"

Cat stuck her chin up, quietly refusing to back down. She blinked at me and asked, "Well, are you happy?"

I opened my mouth to say an emphatic "*Yes,*" but just then the bell rang. Cat gave me one of her knowing smiles again, like she was waiting for me to catch up, and squeezed my arm. "I'll see you in chem," she said before running off to her first period.

I sat down in my English class in a huff. I was furious; I was fuming. And when Aiden walked in after me, I hit him with one of my best and nastiest glares. He tried to glare back but ended up flushed and fumbling as he slid into his seat, as if my anger had actually left him off-kilter.

I muttered to myself for a few minutes, blaming Cat and Rose, Aiden and my parents, and anyone else who had the nerve to bother me in such a blatant way, before Mr. Kline started class. He adjusted his round glasses and said, as he always did, "Let's talk about your reading from yesterday. Any thoughts?" My hand shot straight into the air, beating Aiden's by a few seconds.

"Yes, Josephine, go ahead," Mr. Kline said without looking up from his copy of *The Grapes of Wrath.*

As I flew through my answer, breathless and quick, I settled into myself, feeling every inch of me realign as I let the rest of my anger float off me in waves. I could raise my hand and spout off answers. I could both annoy and impress my teachers; I could both inspire and intimidate my peers.

I could do that.

But when I finished giving my answer I sank into my seat, feeling small and deflated. It had felt good at first, to prove what I knew, to answer succinctly and show the breadth of my skill, but it was only temporary. And after the initial rush... I felt empty.

Because I was only just starting to see (much to my annoyance) that maybe Cat was a tiny bit right. Maybe I was the one who was actually scared but dressing it up in a different outfit, calling myself a perfectionist to make myself feel better.

I didn't raise my hand for the next question.

Aiden angled himself in his seat to study my face after he'd answered Mr. Kline unopposed. He raised his eyebrow like it was a question mark. Just the sight of him waiting for me to cut in was like a slap to the face, a bucket of ice-cold water. It shook me out of my existential crisis and sent my hand flying into the air before Mr. Kline had even finished asking his next question.

Aiden's mouth curved into a private little smile as he turned back in his seat, drumming his fingers on his desk and not even bothering to crack open his book. We spent the rest of the class period in a heated debate over the root of selfishness and whether or not greed was properly represented in the novel.

Mr. Kline eventually sat down on his desk and started taking notes, nodding along with some of our points (he would probably quote us the next time he covered this material, but he definitely wouldn't credit us). The rest of the class just looked bored as they doodled or daydreamed, waiting for Aiden or me to grow tired and give up.

But my arguing felt like crawling through mud—sloppy and slow. My heart wasn't in it no matter how much I wanted it to be.

The bell rang out shrilly, effectively cutting off Aiden's final and long-winded remarks about themes and whether or not authors intend for their work to be analyzed at this level. Everyone scurried out the door until Aiden and I were the last students in the room. Once Mr. Kline noticed that he was alone with us, he tugged on his ratty old cardigan, mumbled something about needing his morning cup of coffee, and booked it out of there with an already full mug in his hands.

Aiden didn't get up to leave and neither did I. We just sat there in the quiet as the noise from the hall pounded against my ears. I glanced down at my backpack and sighed. Suddenly, I didn't think I could carry the weight of it anymore. That creeping feeling of despair was rising up in me again now that the clock had run out and the questions were all answered.

"You're awfully quiet today, Crew."

"You're awfully annoying always, Mitchell," I said back with another sigh. But even my insult didn't have the same bite it usually did. Aiden's brow furrowed as he opened his mouth to say something else.

"Don't," I said quietly. Then I picked up my too-heavy bag and left without another word.

□ □ □

"Pass me the hot glue gun," I said from where I was half-hidden under a dozen layers of tinsel and papier-mâché. Greg snuck his hand under the trailer and handed me the hot glue gun, nearly dripping the lava-like goo all over my jeans.

"Watch it," I mumbled, jerking my hand back just in time.

"Sorry!" Greg yelled to me under the float, accidentally sending a tumbling handful of confetti down into my face. "Sorry again!"

I watched his feet slowly shuffle away to a different section of the student council homecoming float, off to assault some other poor soul trapped under the trailer like me.

I loathe group projects; nobody pulls their weight, and if they do, I usually end up redoing their part anyway because they didn't do it right. Working on a homecoming float is the ultimate group project on steroids, only add glitter and dangerous power tools.

It's any wonder we make it out alive.

We'd been working on our float for weeks, and by "we," I mean I'd been coming in early or staying late to fix everyone's haphazard work.

"Pass me the stapler," I called out to no one in particular.

A hand reached under the float where I was positioned in the back, putting the finishing touches on the giant signs that screamed, *"Go Tigers!"* hanging off the end of the trailer.

"Thanks—" I started to say, until I saw Aiden's head pop under the bumper.

"Are you sure you've got it secured?" he asked, eyeing my collection of staples, hot glue sticks, and duct tape. "Do you need a hammer and nails, or maybe I should just start mixing some concrete?"

"You're hilarious," I said without looking at him. "You know Caleb is driving the float, right? Caleb. If he manages to avoid driving us off a cliff, I will consider this a smashing success."

Aiden grimaced before standing back up. "You have a very low bar for measuring success," he said. "And there are no cliffs in Pearson."

I stuck my head out from under the trailer. "It's Caleb. He would find one." We both turned our heads to see the junior class vice president, Caleb Rand, spraying cans of silly string reserved for the parade up his nose, all the sophomore boys surrounding him guffawing loudly. Aiden and I shared what I could only call a conspiratorial grin, until I got a grip on myself and said, "Get back to work, Mitchell. I'm sick of picking up your slack."

Before he could think up what I'm sure was going to be a lackluster comeback, our ever-faithful leader, Principal Cartwright, wandered over to interrupt. "Well, how are my favorite co-presidents doing today? My, my, the float sure is beautiful!" She eyed the explosion of orange and purple with a satisfied smile. "Go Tigers!" she cheered.

"Go Tigers," Aiden and I both said a little less enthusiastically in response.

"All right, I'll leave y'all to get back to your work," she said before shuffling away in her baby pink kitten heels.

"She checked that box off real quick." Aiden laughed. "I don't think she's your biggest fan," he said giving me side-eyes.

"Me? You're the one who nearly started a food fight during the election, I was just—"

"Aiden! Could you come help me with this sign?" Katlyn simpered from the other side of the float where she was holding up a poster board to staple. She could have easily stapled it if she stood on her tiptoes, but I'm sure the damsel in distress tactic worked very well for her.

"Sure, Kate," Aiden said, slipping on his golden grin. "Madame President," he said to me with a bow before walking away.

For the next twenty minutes, I listened to the two of them flirting while I finished gluing the rest of the streamers, burning my fingers with the glue gun repeatedly. All I could see was the backside of the trailer, but it's not like I needed a better view to know exactly what was unfolding only a few feet away from me. Every time Katlyn giggled, every time Aiden showed off, my mind painted a picture with blinding clarity. I could see him in his homecoming crown, twirling her across the dance floor, the two of them glowing, floating on air, with the unfailing belief that the world was theirs.

But then that image would flicker and fade until all I could see was my parents, packed full of promise and potential with nowhere to go but down.

Caleb blew an airhorn, nearly making me jump out of my skin. I was hot and exhausted, but the parade was about to start and I still had to go check on the marching band and the drama club (which I'd combined with the French club so I didn't have to keep helping with more elaborate floats).

I crawled out unseen from under the trailer and formed my mental checklist. There were too many things to do and too many places for me to be, but I *had* to sign up and show up. What if I missed the one thing that gave me the competitive edge I needed on my applications? I wasn't very superstitious, but I shuddered over open spaces in my schedule like other people flinched when they saw black cats or walked under ladders. Too much free time was like opening an umbrella indoors—I just didn't do it.

I stuck my stapler in the back pocket of my jeans and worked my way to the other side of the parking lot, dodging my overly hyper classmates and smiling stiffly at anyone who waved at me; everyone was buzzing with excitement over the game. My shoulders felt tight as I walked. I was still trying to shrug off that strange suffocating feeling I'd felt this morning. I was still trying to work out how I felt every time I heard Cat's question repeating like a broken record: *well, are you happy?*

Of course, I'm happy, I mumbled back, arguing with her even though she wasn't here. *I'm surrounded by all the things I love.*

I could see her shaking her head and sighing. Like it was annoying that I still wasn't getting it. I took a deep breath in through my nose, just like Cat's mother suggested I do when I'm feeling tense. But it didn't help.

Because you can be surrounded and still feel alone.

Twelve

I F THERE'S ONE thing I hate, possibly even more than Aiden, it's the stupid marching band hat I'm forced to wear on a weekly basis. In front of everyone. While playing the flute. If captain in the marching band didn't look so good on my resume, I would've tossed my feathered hat in the dumpster a long time ago.

I pulled on the too-tight chin strap and watched the purple plumes sway in the mirror. "You can glare at it all you want, it's not going to burst into flames," Amelia said from the bathroom sink next to mine. "And it's not going to make it any more attractive either."

We both grimaced. Her hat was too big on her head; it kept sliding down over one eye. Both our faces were beet red and shining with sweat. Seriously, who decided that marching band uniforms needed to be so stiff and suffocating? I could do without all the pomp and circumstance—I just wanted some air flow.

We'd just finished marching in the homecoming parade, and my ears were still ringing from the enthusiastic playing of my bandmates. I was pretty sure the Pearson High fight song was going to be stuck in my head until the day I died. I'd hopped around from the marching band to all the other floats I was supposed to be riding on, ending with the student council one at the front. Aiden was already in his horrendously neon orange football uniform, waving at all his adoring fans like the prince he thought he was. Almost the entire town was out for the parade, sitting in rusty lawn chairs and cheering their little hearts out while a handful of floats did a few loops around the school.

It was kind of tragic when I thought about it too closely.

Aiden openly smirked at me when he saw me hoist myself up onto the slowly moving float in my horribly unflattering uniform. "Nice hat," he said before turning to throw a fistful of candy to some kids running after us. I recognized his little brother and sister at the front of the pack of feral children.

"Nice pants," I said back with a sniff. "Traffic cone orange is really your color."

We spent the rest of the parade standing on opposite sides of the float and ignoring each other.

I turned off the water in the bathroom sink and grabbed a paper towel, wiping my hands then dabbing it across my face in vain. "Touché," I said to Amelia with a sigh. "Break's over. Let's go face the music."

We grabbed our flutes and lined up with the rest of the band as we prepared to fill our designated spots on the stands. A few of the clarinetists were already playing the opening bars to "We Are the Champions," which I thought was a bit optimistic considering how bad our team was, but all anyone could talk about was how *this* year was going to be different. Because *this* year, Aiden was going to take us all the way to state.

I'd seen him play. It's kind of hard to miss the action when you're trapped in the bleachers surrounded by screaming fans. He *was* good. Of course he was. He's the Golden Boy after all, and being the star running back is part of the gilded package deal. I knew it from the first time I saw him pass the ball to his newfound friends back in the sixth grade, and I knew it now after watching every single one of his games.

He was good. And it was annoying.

The sun was setting as we piled into our stadium seats; the bleachers were still unbearably hot from the afternoon's heat. "Wouldn't it be nice if our uniforms included shorts?" Eric, one of our trumpeters, complained from behind me.

"But then our legs would stick to the bleachers, and that would be worse," Amelia answered. "We'd probably pull up the layers of gum too," she added with a frown.

"Gross, that's all I'm going to think about now," I mumbled as sweat dripped down the back of my uniform.

Our conductor, Mr. Stevens (who insisted we call him Larry) was waving his baton, signaling for us to get ready to play. We started a rousing rendition of "Sweet Caroline," and by rousing, I mean that we hit every other note, and the people sitting next to us were scooting over to get away from the racket by the time we'd finished.

I never said we were an exemplary band of players. I blame the hats.

Across the aisle, Cat and Rose were taking their seats. They waved at me before joining the throng of other orange and purple-clad kids in the riotous student section. I clutched my flute tightly in my hands; all the noise and all the people were already starting to get to me, and the game was only just beginning.

Our band played off and on through the first quarter (we were winning, all thanks to Aiden), and the crowd was absolutely losing their minds. They stomped their feet on the metal bleachers and roared the fight song every time we scored. My bandmates weren't any better. When they weren't playing, they were screaming along with everybody else. "Fake left, go right!" Eric wailed in my ears, waving his trumpet around madly through the air.

I was suffering from acute secondhand embarrassment just from watching the entire town's certifiable behavior.

Halfway through the second quarter, Aiden ran to the sideline and took his helmet off, bending his head to tell the coach something. His hair was matted and dark, his eyes squinting like he was in pain. I didn't remember seeing him take a hard hit. "What's wrong with Aiden?" I heard myself asking Eric.

"What are you talking about, he's playing like a *god*," he exclaimed in my face. I reeled back and tried not to roll my eyes. By the time I looked back to the field, Aiden's helmet was on again and he was out in the huddle with his teammates.

Right before halftime, Larry started flirting with the choir director, Ms. Oh, and let us have a break before our big performance on the field. "I'll be back," I mumbled to Amelia, before nestling my flute in its case and jogging down the rickety bleachers. I felt better the moment I was free from the band section. Turns out breathing fresh air that hasn't been recycled by thirty other players blowing into their instruments at top volume is instantly reviving for the soul.

I found Cat and Rose seated at the back of the student section. Cat was still doused in glitter, now with the addition of Ethan's jersey to complete the look. Rose had her version of school spirit on with her violently orange '70s jumpsuit—the color clashing horribly with her auburn hair—but because the universe is incredibly unfair, she was still glowing under the stadium lights. I felt completely ridiculous standing there in my feathered hat and starchy purple pants.

When I slid onto the end seat next to Rose, she jumped in surprise and shoved her hands behind her back, clearly trying to stash something away. "Josephine! What are you... why..." She fumbled through something to say, trying to hide her discomfort along with whatever she'd flung behind her back.

Cat's eyes wouldn't meet mine. "I'm going to get some popcorn," she mumbled, looking relieved she had an excuse to leave this suddenly awkward moment. Her hand landed softly on my shoulder where she squeezed me once before heading down the stairs.

When it was just my sister and me, I darted my hand out and grabbed the paper she was hiding. "What incriminating thing do you have here?" I asked with a laugh until I read the top of the pamphlet and my mouth fell open.

"You've got to be kidding me," I whispered. I waved the pamphlet in her face with shaking hands. "A *pageant*, Rose? Really?"

She grabbed it back from me and folded it into her purse. "This is why I didn't want to tell you," she huffed. "I knew you'd react like this."

"Of course I would. This is insane."

She closed her eyes and exhaled heavily. "No, it's not. Not all of us are as smart as you or want to be in every single club like you. I want to get out of Pearson too, and maybe this could help me earn some money or—"

"This is exactly the kind of thing that's going to get you stuck here!" I didn't mean to yell, but I kind of had to with how loud it was up on the stands. We were the only ones left sitting as the entire student section rose to their feet with a swell of screaming.

She crossed her arms, giving me a glare that rivaled mine. "Just because that's what happened to Mom, doesn't mean it will happen to me. You sound just like them, you know," she spat. "Worried over nothing. I'm *not* Mom. Besides, it wasn't the pageants that got Mom stuck here, it was—"

She snapped her mouth shut, a brief flash of guilt crossing over her face.

"You mean *me*," I finished for her. "She got stuck here because of me."

Her words stung. I tried to ignore the leftover prickling feeling from them as I carried on, desperate to convince her to change her mind. Part of me knew I was being irrational, that I was making this a way bigger deal than it was, but I couldn't seem to stop myself once I got going. I couldn't stop seeing Rose bent over a vanity mirror next to our mom, sharing a can of hairspray the way we used to share disdain for everything our mother stood for.

I wasn't blind. I saw the way Mom looked at her—like Rose was her last great hope. She's the daughter that doesn't always storm off or spit spiteful things that actually reveal how much she cares. She laughs at our parents' immaturity and shrugs off their neglect.

Easy, breezy, beautiful Rose.

And then there's me—a stiff wind that plows right into our mother's face, blowing her perfect hair into her perfectly glossed lips.

Tell me, which daughter would you prefer?

Which daughter could you see in a crown?

I'd never felt so alone as I did in that moment. It felt like Rose was on one side of the bleachers and I was on the other, with more than a below-average marching band sitting between us. It had always been just the two of us, maybe not against the world, exactly, but against our parents and their refusal to move on from the past.

"I don't think you should do it," I said harshly, grabbing onto her arm like a lifeline.

"I don't really care," she said back. "You think you know everything, but that couldn't be further from the truth, Josephine. Sometimes you're completely clueless."

Her eyes flickered after she'd said it like maybe she knew she'd taken it too far. The purple feather on my hat dipped forward in the breeze, tickling my nose and making my eyes water. "Fine. It's your life. You can be as stupid with it as you want to be." I barely got the words out; my throat was so tight.

Her mouth puckered into a small frown like it did when she was trying not to cry. I stood up and crashed down the noisy metal bleachers, nearly tripping over every step along the way. I didn't go back to my bandmates (who were in the middle of butchering Lady GaGa's "Just Dance"). I ran down the remaining steps while the commentator's voice drawled over the speakers that, *"It's halftime, folks,"* and nearly ran straight into my parents at the bottom.

They were lined up with the other alumni, all poised and polished, ready to be put on display as part of the celebration of homecoming courts of yesteryear. They stood, sparkling and laughing with the other high school sweethearts who'd gotten married and never left town, still straddling the line between growing up and staying young, with one foot in the hallowed halls of Pearson High and the other on their mortgages and kitchen counter bills.

My stomach twisted at the sight of my parents holding hands and lighting up for their friends. I wondered if everyone knew that my dad usually slept on the couch.

I ran past them to the other side of the bleachers, skulking miserably in the shadows. From my hideout, I watched my bandmates clomp down the stairs and line up to march onto the field. A brief commotion broke out as Amelia, Eric, and everyone else looked around for me. But after only a minute of half-hearted searching and shrugging, they all shifted forward to fill in my space and carried on.

Like I was that easy to replace.

They started playing the school's fight song as they broke into their formation on the field with the color guard following behind. I tore off my hat and tossed it on the ground, then sniffed loudly into my sleeve while my classmates cheered and stomped their feet, their thunderous applause ushering their beloved team back into the locker room for halftime.

I leaned against the bleachers, feeling wretchedly sorry for myself. And the worst part was that I couldn't shake the urge to go back and apologize—to Rose, to my bandmates, probably to anyone who was seated near me that had to endure all my yelling or flute playing. I just wanted to be angry right now, not angry and apologetic. My breathing was shallow as I held onto the burning feeling in my chest. If I focused on that, then maybe I wouldn't feel the sinking in my stomach or the stinging in my eyes.

The door to the locker rooms opened with a bang. Aiden strode out and slumped against the brick wall of the field house, his chest heaving and his helmet hanging loosely in his grip. I froze, still half-hidden in the shadows, unsure where to go or what to do.

"What's wrong, son?"

Mr. Mitchell walked up to Aiden with his hands in the pockets of his khakis, his golden hair gleaming under the lights.

"I'm fine," Aiden said through gritted teeth.

"You're not fine. I saw you rubbing your head during the last quarter." He crossed his arms and looked Aiden up and down. "Your mother thinks you haven't been taking your meds—"

"Maybe I haven't been." Aiden's voice was quiet, but the confession carried all the way to my ears despite all the noise coming from the bleachers above us.

"Aiden, you know you can't be skipping doses." Mr. Mitchell's voice oozed with firm fatherly concern. He tried to take Aiden by the shoulders, but his son pushed him away.

"They make me feel weird, I hate it. It makes everything fuzzier, duller. It's harder for me to remember things."

Mr. Mitchell glanced around hurriedly as if to make sure they were still alone. "I thought that was the point, toning things down. Pain management."

"Yeah, well, how do you expect me to compete in Saturday's tournament if I'm not at my best? I can't stumble my way through this, I need every advantage—"

"But look at you! I bet you have the start of a migraine right now, don't you?"

Aiden slumped down even further but didn't answer.

I felt like the world's biggest creep for eavesdropping on this obviously private conversation, but it was too late for me to go anywhere else. If I tried to escape, Aiden would see me and know I'd been listening. Even though I'd been curious about the pills, this wasn't the way I wanted to find out. I do have boundaries, you know.

So I sank further into the darkness and tried to focus on the marching band's halftime performance (did we always sound that bad?), but it wasn't enough. The Mitchells and their argument still rang out into the night.

"We need to contain—"

"—and control. I *know*."

After a strained pause, Mr. Mitchell said, "This isn't like you, son. It's your senior season, all eyes are on you. These games could determine everything. You know the recruiters are here to see you play. Now is not the time to be acting out—"

"It's never the time." Aiden's voice was sharp. It sliced clean through the conversation, effectively severing anything else his father had to say.

Mr. Michell rubbed his forehead in a gesture identical to his son's and sighed. "Finish the game. We'll talk at home." He walked away without looking back.

At that precise moment, my phone trilled noisily in my pocket. I tried to silence it, but of course, since the universe hates me, I accidentally turned the volume up louder instead. Aiden's head whipped over to find me half-crouched in the darkness, purple pants and all, with my feathered hat lying in the dirt.

His eyebrows shot up in surprise. We stared at each other for a long moment, neither of us saying anything. Just then his team ran out of the locker room, all of them slapping their helmets and yelling loudly, riling up the crowd to a new level of frenzy. Aiden's helmet was still in his hands, but he didn't make a move to follow his teammates.

His gaze flicked back to mine. Suddenly, his eyes went wide and he gestured me forward frantically. "Josephine, come here!"

Even though I knew he knew where I was hiding, I slunk further back. I was not in the mood to deal with him and whatever drama he was going through. I had enough of my own.

Aiden made an exasperated noise and jogged over. He stood so close to me, I could see every shade of green and brown in his wide eyes; all the little flecks of gold. "Don't move." He sounded angry, but he looked terrified. He reached out a hand and put it on my waist, slowly tugging me closer to him.

"What do you think you're doing?" I said, shoving him hard in the chest. "Get your hands off me."

But he didn't release me. Instead, he placed his other hand on my lower back and said, "*Josephine,* listen to me. Don't—"

He didn't get another word out. He groaned and ducked his head, his eyes screwed up as if he was in pain. His hands gripped me tightly as a strange sound filled the air between us, like someone slowly ripping a piece of paper in half, but amplified by a thousand. A loud humming filled my head and my chest, beating along with the rhythm of my pulse.

"I'm sorry," he whispered, his hair brushing against my cheek.

And everything went dark.

Thirteen

I WOKE UP to the sound of shouting.

I sat up in confusion and stared at my still-booted feet hanging off my bed, blinking blearily a few times before another rush of angry yelling filtered in under my door.

When I glanced at the clock on my bedside table, I yelped. I was running seriously behind—

And all of this was eerily familiar. I looked at my jean-clad legs and plucked at the cotton of my shirt—when did I change into this? I very distinctly remembered wearing a very distinct marching band uniform last night at the game. Until halftime. I remembered fighting with my sister (all too vividly), and I remembered hiding out under the bleachers (like a coward) and overhearing Aiden and his father arguing.

And that's when things got fuzzy. Aiden's eyes, wide with fear. His hands clutched at my waist. That odd hissing, tearing sound and then—

Shouting from the kitchen.

I tried to concentrate, to dredge up my memories of the second half of the football game or how I got home last night. But nothing—I couldn't remember a thing.

Another shriek from Rose rattled the walls of my bedroom. I sighed and heaved myself out of bed, thinking about how I was going to strangle her for waking me up this early on a Saturday. A storm to rival the one in the kitchen was brewing outside my window. The clouds were billowing and dark; lighting forked in the distance.

I stumbled into the kitchen just in time to hear my mother say,

"Missy told me she overheard you and Cat yammering on and on about your big date to the dance this weekend. Did you really think we wouldn't find out?"

Rose's eyes filled with tears as she jutted her chin out and didn't deny a thing.

Again.

"What's going on?" I asked, still feeling slow and sleepy like I was swimming through syrup. "I thought we already went over all of this yesterday?"

Dad poked his head out from the fridge with the gallon of milk gripped tightly in his hands, his bowl of cereal forgotten on the counter. "Yesterday? You knew about this, and you didn't say anything?" he asked, having the nerve to look annoyed with me. As if our family had any communication skills at all.

"You and Mom just talked to Rose about this yesterday! I already told you I'd make sure she stayed home."

Rose was mouthing, "Thank you!" over Mom's shoulder, her hands folded together as if in prayer. I raised my eyebrows back at her in surprise. I thought she'd still be mad at me after our fight last night, but she was smiling like all was forgiven. Like it had never happened at all.

"Is this some kind of joke?" I asked, confusion coloring my voice.

No one laughed. Mom puckered her bright red lips into a pout. "Honestly, Josephine. You have the strangest sense of humor. Why would this be funny?" She was still seething, her face blotchy under her flawless makeup.

She was wearing the exact same thing she wore the last time they'd had this argument: the tight short skirt she claimed was "business casual" because she wore it with a blazer. Her hair was tucked behind her ears and rippling in bronze waves down her shoulders. Just like last time.

But my dad's polo shirt was a different color: blue, not green. Rose had on a pair of paint-splattered overalls that I'd never seen before, with dangling earrings that caught the light of the morning sun. I looked down at my wrinkled t-shirt and jeans again.

It was all the same. But it wasn't.

"This is a weird prank to play at 7 a.m. on a Saturday," I finally said with a scoff.

"It's Friday," Rose said, her voice rising at the end like it was a question. "Game day. Remember?"

They all blinked at me, their argument temporarily forgotten.

Game day.

I ran back to my room and slammed the door. With shaking hands, I picked up my phone from the nightstand where it was still charging. The date on the screen said Friday.

Friday.

Again?

A loud tapping noise startled me out of my reverie. I dropped my phone on my bed and spun around to see Aiden Christopher Mitchell III standing in our dead flowerbeds with both hands pressed against my window, his face wild and panicked.

"Josephine," he said, his voice muffled by the glass. "I need to talk to you."

Just when I thought this morning couldn't get any weirder. I slid the window open, and Aiden sighed with relief. "I wasn't sure if *you'd* actually be here. Last night..." He groaned and ran a hand through his hair, his forehead shining with sweat.

"You look like you ran all the way over here."

"I drove. But I was hurrying. I needed to see you."

Oh, get a room already.

I stiffened and stepped back.

"Hey, are you—" Rose gasped as she threw open my bedroom door and saw Aiden's sweating face at my window. "What are *you* doing here?" Her eyes narrowed in accusation as she swung her gaze between Aiden and me.

He blurted out, "I'm giving Josephine a ride—" at the same time I said, "He was trying to toilet paper our house!" in a loud voice.

Rose's mouth tipped into a tight, thin line. "Mmhm," she said as she slowly backed out of my room and mouthed furious things at me from behind her hand that implied I had a lot of explaining to do. "I'll see you at school!" she added brightly. It sounded like a threat.

"Really? TP-ing your house? And at 7 a.m.?" Aiden rested his forehead against the partially open window, his blond hair splaying out in every direction. That's when I noticed he was still in his pajama pants (bright blue and too short, like he'd just outgrown them). "I only did that once in eighth grade. Give me a little credit."

"Twice. You're forgetting freshman year with Tim Boren."

Aiden scrunched up his face like he was searching through all the terrible things he'd ever done to me, and then gave a weak laugh. "I forgot about that."

I waited expectantly, tapping my foot.

"Sorry," he mumbled grudgingly.

"Now, are you going to explain what's going on? Why you're perched at my window like the world's most irritating bird?"

He chewed on his lip for a moment before saying, "Your morning—it's the same as it was yesterday, isn't it?"

My heart thudded dully in my chest. "How did you—"

"The conversations, the way everyone's acting... It's basically identical, right?"

"Yes." It was suddenly difficult to swallow. "Except the weather," I said softly, pointing behind him to the dark gray clouds promising rain. "And Rose's clothes, my dad's shirt. Little things are different."

He watched my face carefully like he was expecting me to start hyperventilating or something. My hands were shaking from that encounter in the kitchen, the same old argument, the torrent of bitter words. My chest tightened with a rush of panic when I finally realized that my family wasn't in on this, that it wasn't a joke or some elaborate yet slightly lame trick.

My back straightened as I peered down at Aiden. "That doesn't explain why you know any of this."

He sighed and leaned heavily into the window. "I can see the cracks in everything."

I blinked. "Are you being philosophical right now, Aiden? Because I really can't deal with—"

"*No.* I mean literally. I can see the cracks. And last night at the game, we fell in one."

More blinking from me. "Are you on drugs?" His shiny silver pill canister flashed in my mind. "You're doing drugs and you drugged me! At the game!" I thought back to how strange I'd felt, the buzzing in my head, my shallow breathing, Aiden standing too close to me.

The way the humming intensified until it was all I could hear and then—

I woke up at home in my bed. To the same shouting I'd woken up to the day before. Word for word.

"What am I on?" I looked around my room, half expecting to see psychedelic swirls or hear Bob Dylan wailing in the background (obviously my frame of reference for drug usage is not that creative).

"Josephine! Listen to me!" Aiden climbed through my window without my permission and landed in a heap on my bedroom floor. I was too stunned to say anything as he rose and brushed himself off. He grabbed me by the shoulders and said, "Tell me everything you did yesterday morning before school."

"What are you talking about?" I tried to brush him off but he wouldn't budge.

"Just tell me," he said in a strangled voice. "Please," he added as an afterthought.

I didn't want to tell him about my parents fighting with Rose in the kitchen. That felt too personal, too intimate. I couldn't hand him that kind of humiliating information; he would most certainly use it against me.

"I got ready, ate some toast, and made lunches for Rose and me to take to school. That's basically it."

"That's basically it, or that's actually everything you did—"

It took a significant effort not to roll my eyes. "Well, I came in my room after and got my stuff together, and then yes—that's it. Rose drove me to school. Why are you asking me this?"

His hands were heavy on my shoulders as he glanced around the room in a haphazard way. But he wasn't snooping around my bedroom like I had when I'd been in his. This was different. He was serious. Shaking, sweaty, and stone-cold serious.

He bent his head to look me dead in the eyes. "Do it all again," he said quietly. "I want to show you something."

"But why—"

"Josephine," he said slowly, his voice rising the way it always did when our fights would escalate.

I could still hear my mom's hairspray hissing in the bathroom. "Okay, okay. Fine," I whispered. I pushed his hands off me and looked at him through narrowed eyes. "But you stay here. Do not come out of my room."

"Fine," he said, flopping down on my bed.

I cringed, unable to decide which was worse; Aiden lounging on my bed like he owned the place or Aiden following me around my dingy house like a shadow where my mother could catch us together.

"Get going," Aiden said as he reached for the book on my nightstand and started thumbing through the pages. He appeared to be the picture of casualness, like it was totally normal for him to be stretched out across my comforter, but his face was tight and agitated as he watched me.

My jaw clenched tightly as I swung my door open and quickly closed it behind me, praying that no one in my family developed a sudden interest in me or the state of my room. The hallway was mercifully empty. Rose was still barricaded in her room with Adele, whose mournful cry was shaking the walls of the house. I crept past the bathroom door where my mother had set up camp and hurried into the kitchen, ready to get Aiden's weird instructions over with. Dad had already left for work, but forgot to put the milk away (again). I stared at the sweating jug resting on the yellowing counter and sighed.

I'd been desperate to escape Aiden and his riddles in my room, but now that I was here alone in the kitchen (and still convinced I was tripping on drugs) I wasn't sure what to do. But I was starving, so I grabbed the loaf of bread from the pantry and popped two slices into the toaster.

I opened the fridge and put the milk back in its proper place, then pulled out a bag of baby carrots and two apples and started assembling the same lunches I packed for my sister and me every day of the week. My shoulders loosened as I dug through the cupboard for the peanut butter; it felt good to fall into a familiar pattern after such a strange and jarring start to my morning.

But it's the same morning as yesterday! My mind yelled at me on an endless loop, running through all the bizarre similarities just in case I'd forgotten. I ignored my internal fretting and buttered the toast before slathering it with raspberry jam.

The kitchen lights flickered. I paused and peered up with a frown.

Suddenly, the air felt weird; it felt dense, like there wasn't enough space for me to be standing there in the kitchen. Like the air itself was trying to squeeze me out. I dropped the butterknife I was holding. It clattered loudly, splattering bright red jam in a violent slash across the counter.

My mom slammed the hairspray bottle down in the bathroom. She was nearly finished primping and would be coming down the hall any second now. I grabbed a rag and wiped the counter before quickly rolling down the tops of our brown paper sack lunches. The lights flickered again.

My heart hammered as I ran down the hall and back toward my room. As I ran, I heard that same slow hissing sound I'd heard last night at the game, that same sound I'd heard coming from Aiden's bedroom the other night too. I lunged for my door and raced inside.

Aiden was no longer lounging on my bed. He was pacing back and forth across my room, his bare feet leaving tracks on the old carpet. He froze when I swiftly shut the door behind me.

"Aiden," I panted. "What is—"

"Pack up your backpack and get ready for school. The same way you always do."

I slowed my breathing, trying in vain to calm myself down. But even though I was most definitely freaking out, I could still take the time to be annoyed that Aiden was ordering me around without offering any explanations. I crossed my arms over my chest and opened my mouth to argue.

His face slightly softened. "Just do this last thing, Josephine, okay? You'll see."

"Fine," I muttered, pushing past him. I tried not to let my expression reveal how much he was starting to scare me. He hovered behind me and watched as I gathered up my books and tucked them into my backpack. I zipped up my pens and pencils and all my spares in the same order I always did, systematic and precise, sliding in my laptop last.

My lamp flickered and the air tightened around us until it was hard to breathe. Aiden's eyes were fixed on the wall behind me. When I followed his gaze, I didn't see anything unusual, but all the hairs on my arms were standing on end as the soft hum of voices filled the room, like a radio turned down low.

"More cracks." Aiden sighed like he'd known this would happen.

"What the—"

"I swear I'll explain everything. But we should go." He reached out and grabbed my hand as he tried to pull me out my bedroom door. The humming noise slowed and then stopped, my lamp flickering one last time before burning brightly again.

"Stop!" I whispered fiercely, flinging his hand from mine. I could still hear my mom's towering heels clicking on the linoleum. If I burst out of my bedroom with Aiden Christopher Mitchell III in tow, all sweaty and pajama-clad, I'm pretty sure she would murder me. Or him. Or possibly both of us, with her red painted lips twisted into a grimace.

"Now what did I tell you, Josie? Boys will always get you into a world of trouble…"

I blocked the door with my body, my arms stretched wide and my face framed in panic. Aiden nearly slammed into me in his rush to get out. "What are you doing?" he said too loudly. "We need to—"

"Go. Yes, I know. But we can't go out that way. My mom will see you."

"So?"

"Are you really that dense?" His frown deepened as he considered me, glancing between us and the door. "Oh. I see," he said, as he finally processed the implication. His face flushed as if he'd only just realized that he was all but on top of me, pressing me back against the door. He stepped back and tried to shove his hands in his pockets, but they slid down his thighs ineffectively—he was pocketless in his PJs.

Aiden must've rushed over here the moment he woke up. His urgency and his pale face made my heart thrum with anxiety. "I'll go with you," I consented. "But you better explain yourself. And you need to change; I'm not walking around in public with you dressed like that."

He nodded, not even bothering to argue. For once. I should've memorialized the moment with a photograph or a decorative plaque or something.

He gestured to the open window. "After you," he said with a slight bow.

"You first, I insist."

Our mock politeness was all sugar-coated sharpness. Truthfully, I didn't trust him at my back, but I also didn't want him to watch me heave myself out the window to potentially fall face-first onto my sun-scorched lawn.

"Fine." He easily jumped out the window and started walking toward his truck. Even though I was a little more than freaked out and still 80% convinced that I was drugged, I did have some of my wits about me. I grabbed my backpack before I slid out the window, landing lightly on my feet. I was still in the clothes I'd fallen asleep in, but I didn't have enough time to care.

Aiden was already in his white Tacoma. He mimed honking the horn and mouthed for me to hurry up. I scowled as I ran to the passenger side and flung the door open, climbing in before anyone could see me or murder me or, worst of all, wonder what in Sam's Hill I was doing getting into Aiden's truck willingly.

With my hands untied and everything.

"Start talking," I snarled as I slammed the door shut behind me.

Fourteen

B UT AIDEN DIDN'T immediately launch into an explanation, and he didn't start baring his soul or sharing his secrets.

Instead, after about a minute of driving in silence, he pulled over on the side of the road next to a vacant field. "Is this where you're going to bury my body?" I asked, rolling my window down. "It's a little too obvious. You could do better."

He rolled his eyes and gestured down at his pajama pants. "I need to change, remember? I have extra clothes in my gym bag." That was all he offered by way of explanation as he swung himself out of the truck and pulled a bag out of the backseat. He made his way around over to my side and stuck his head through the open window.

"No spying," he said. And I realized then that he was changing his clothes with the truck blocking him from the rest of the road.

"As if I would want to see any more of you than I already have to," I said primly, turning my head in the opposite direction, my cheeks flaming.

He laughed and dropped his gym bag in the dirt with a dull thud. I heard the rustling of fabric as he lifted his shirt over his head, and my cheeks burned even hotter.

"I know you're tempted to turn around, but please try to resist," he said in a muffled voice.

"If this is your attempt to distract me from the crisis at hand, it's extremely pathetic. Even for you."

Aiden grumbled something under his breath, then threw his bag in the truck. "Okay, I'm decent," he said, climbing back into his seat. "Better? Can you be seen with me in public now?"

I surveyed his faded jeans and gray Pearson High football t-shirt. "The purple and orange really make your eyes pop," I said with a snort.

He grinned and I was suddenly aware that we were trapped together in a tiny, enclosed space with nowhere else for me to go when I couldn't stand to look at him a moment longer. It didn't matter that he had explaining to do, or that I was desperate to understand what was going on, every inch of me felt too tight and overly exposed as he sat there staring at me, his grin fading away.

He cleared his throat and glanced out the window. "Looks like it's going to rain."

"Are you seriously trying to talk about the weather right now?"

He took a deep breath and shook his head, his golden hair flopping over his forehead. "Remember how I told you that I get headaches?" he asked softly. "Really bad ones—"

"—and it's all my fault, I know. You've made that very clear."

He chuckled and started the truck once again, pulling back onto the main road. "That was obviously a joke, Josephine. Now can you be quiet for one second? No more interruptions." His eyes flashed nervously in the rearview mirror. "I just need to get this over with," he said, sitting up straighter in his seat. "When I was a kid, the headaches would come and go, but as I got older and started to go through puberty—"

"Wow, this is taking a turn," I cut in.

"—the migraines got worse," Aiden finished with an exasperated sigh, his hands gripping the wheel tightly. "That's also around the time I started remembering things… *more clearly.*" The last two words were said with an emphasis I didn't understand.

"Don't be coy with me now, Aiden. What's that supposed to mean?"

He chanced a glance at me before his eyes drifted back to the road. "I have a photographic memory. Like, next level photographic."

I thought about how he never needed to look at his notes or the way he caught the tiniest mistake only moments after I'd given an answer. I thought about how it always felt like he'd been one step ahead of me since the moment I'd met him.

"I *knew* it!"

Aiden's mouth twitched like he wanted to smile. "Let me guess; you knew I couldn't be *that* smart on my own?"

"Exactly," I said, feeling smug. I felt like I'd caught him cheating.

"Well, I hate to break it to you, but I am," he said, his dimple flashing briefly. "Don't look now, Crew, your jealousy is showing again."

I sniffed. "I'm not jealous."

"Your bright red face and beady eyes are saying otherwise."

My eyes narrowed even further. "So, you had headaches, developed a perfect and convenient photographic memory, and what? Now we're... repeating the same day again?"

I said the last part casually, trying to play it cool, leaving it open for him to reveal the very late punchline of his very stupid joke. Relaxing into my seat with an ease that was entirely forced, I tried to come across as totally fine with Aiden's weirdness and the too-small space of the truck (our elbows kept brushing), but, if I'm being honest, I was definitely starting to panic.

"Kind of." He swallowed. "This is where it gets weird."

"Oh, *this* is where it gets weird. I'm sorry, I thought things were already weird."

Aiden chose to ignore me. "The headaches got worse, and I started—" He paused and exhaled heavily. "I started hearing things, seeing things."

I remembered what he'd said in my room, *I can see the cracks in everything.*

"You started seeing cracks—the cracks in what?"

He gave me a sidelong glance, his mouth tightening. "I guess the only way to describe it is... time."

"You see the cracks in time," I deadpanned. "All right, I'm done. Pull over."

"Why? I'm not—"

"Just pull over, Aiden!"

He'd been driving aimlessly in circles around the town square. After I'd screeched at him, he frantically veered off the side of the road next to an old gas station with only two pumps. Carl, the old manager who used to personally hand pump everyone's gas, waved at us from his little booth and saluted us with his coffee cup.

I unbuckled my seatbelt and threw the passenger door open.

"Josephine! Wait—"

Aiden's voice was cut off as I slammed the door behind me. I was done with him and this joke or whatever trick he was trying to pull on me. I was in yesterday's jeans and t-shirt with my hair still woven into an elaborate braid crown that didn't feel like me. All I wanted was the shower I never got to have and a moment of quiet to collect myself, but no. Instead, I got Aiden and his drug-addled tale of cracks in time.

I hefted my heavy backpack over my shoulders and turned to head home. But before I took more than two steps, I remembered my mom and dad dressed for work this morning and Rose heading out the door, ready for school. She usually slept in until noon on Saturdays. I frowned. Obviously, things weren't adding up the way they were supposed to.

But I didn't want to believe Aiden, and how could I? He sounded like a raving lunatic.

I clenched my jaw tightly, just giving my dental hygienist more reasons to worry about me and the state of my teeth, and tapped my foot as I thought over my options. Aiden's truck was still idling beside me on the side of the road as he waited to see what I was going to do.

I needed to prove him wrong.

So, I spun on my heel and changed directions, heading toward the school. Aiden slowly drove alongside me, but I kept my gaze trained on the road and refused to acknowledge him. A minivan honked behind him before swerving to pass our ambling and angry parade—Aiden had to be driving less than five miles per hour.

"Would you just get back in the truck?" he called out through the open window.

"No."

"Why are you going to school?"

I ignored him and picked up my pace. My boots crunched noisily in the loose gravel on the side of the road as I pictured how ridiculous his face was going to look when I marched into the empty school parking lot and proved once and for all that it was indeed Saturday morning, and he was indeed an absolute idiot.

My heart hammered in my chest as I jogged the last fifty yards to the school, which is no easy task in ankle boots.

It's Saturday. Today is Saturday. Today you will compete in the debate tour-nament, and you will win, and then you will binge-watch the PBS Masterpiece series of your choosing rather than going to the homecoming dance, and it will be marvelous. Today is Saturday.

I repeated the words in my head like a mantra. I repeated them when I saw the parking lot packed full of cars; I repeated them when I saw the cheerleaders bouncing around in their uniforms and squeal-ing about the upcoming game, and I still repeated them even when I heard Cat yelling from the open front doors of the school, "Come on, Josephine! The bell already rang!" her glittery hair shining in the barely-there sun.

I stared at the faded brick building of Pearson High School with my mouth hanging open in shock. "No," I whispered when I saw the "IT'S GAME DAY!" banner slung over the entrance, painted in bright purple and orange. "No, no, no, no, no," I choked out when I heard Katlyn's chipper voice announcing, *"Remember, this is your last day to buy homecoming tickets at the discounted price!"* over the school's PA system.

It was Friday.

Somehow, impossibly, it was Friday all over again. And the only ones who seemed to know were Aiden Christopher Mitchell III and me.

I slowly turned around to face him. He'd parked his truck and was standing a few feet behind me, watching as the realization finally sunk in. Thunder rumbled overhead as we looked at each other. A few guys from the football team called out to him as they ran past us on their way into the school, but he ignored them. The last stragglers made it through the doors just as the final bell rang, leaving the parking lot empty except for the two of us.

"I was ten the first time it happened—the first time I saw some-thing from another timeline." Aiden swallowed and waited for me to interrupt him, but I didn't.

I couldn't think of a single thing to say.

"One day my mom came home from the store, and I asked her if I could have some of the chocolate ice cream she'd bought." His eyes went all fuzzy as he remembered. "She got the weirdest look on her face; she was so confused. And then she told me she didn't get any ice cream." Aiden dipped his head and gave a humorless laugh. "I dug around in the freezer afterward, convinced she was lying because I *saw* her buy it." He shook his head and rubbed his jaw roughly. "That night I overheard her tell my dad that she'd been holding the chocolate ice cream in her hands in the frozen aisle of the grocery store, and then had decided not to get it. She'd put it back."

Aiden closed his eyes as raindrops started spilling from the sky and sprinkling over us. "It started happening more regularly, and so did the headaches. I would see flashes of things that didn't really happen, hear things that weren't actually said. But all of it was blurry and a little off, like living in this strange feeling of perpetual déjà vu. It was confusing and disorienting, and it was hard to know what was real anymore."

He shoved his hands into his pockets and finally opened his eyes to look at me, squinting through the rain. "Every time I brought it up—the voices I heard, the things I saw—my parents freaked out. Understandably so, I guess. My mom put me in therapy. She thought I was acting out because I needed help processing my pre-pubescent feelings or something. But my dad was more concerned about the headaches. They took me to see some specialists he knew from med school—"

I found my voice again. "Wait, what?"

"My dad used to practice medicine," he added when he saw my confused face. "He was a general practitioner."

My mouth popped open in surprise. I tried to reconcile Mr. Mitchell of Mitchell's Motors with the doctor Aiden was describing. It just didn't add up.

"Then what happened?" I asked in a whisper.

"We spent a week in Dallas where the specialists ran tests, and they did more MRIs than I could count, but they couldn't figure it out. All they could offer us was that my brain scans showed 'an unusually high amount of activity' in my hippocampus, which obviously didn't solve anything."

He sighed. "And I didn't want them to run any more tests. I was starting to feel like a glorified lab rat at that point, so we went home. But my headaches had become pretty unmanageable, so my dad started giving me different medications to try." Aiden grimaced and rubbed his head, like just talking about those migraines was giving him another one.

I pictured his dad flipping through a prescription pad, frantically trying to find something, anything that could help his son. I wondered how far he went. I wondered if that's the reason he was selling used cars now.

"We finally found a combo of drugs that worked," he said with a shrug, "and things were better for a while. The headaches came less frequently... and so did the other stuff." He kicked at the ground with his shoe, scuffing the toe on the black asphalt. "But when I was twelve, I got sick of it, and I quit taking them for a few days. The drugs make me feel weird. They make me feel... less-than. Like I'm not operating at full capacity."

The fight I overheard at the game between Aiden and his dad came rushing back to me.

I thought that was the point, toning things down. Pain management," Mr. Mitchell had said.

Contain and control.

"So after a few days of not being on the meds, my memory was sharper than ever, but the headaches had come back too. That's when I actually saw a crack for the first time." He shuddered and looked down. "There was one on my bedroom wall, just barely visible. Like the hazy outline of something familiar, but I couldn't quite place it. I heard a strange humming, like static filling the air." He paused and ran a hand through his rain-dampened hair. "I don't know how else to describe it, but when I reached out and touched it, I ended up here."

"At Pearson High?" I asked, scrunching my nose.

"No," he laughed, then gestured around us. "*Here,* in the alternate. This is an alternate timeline. Different in some ways, but exactly the same in others."

An alternate timeline.

My brain was screaming for him to slow down as it struggled to digest every outlandish thing he said. I looked around me, expecting to see something that proved what he was saying was true, but all I saw were the familiar front doors to Pearson High and the school secretary peering at us suspiciously through one of the front windows. Everything looked the same. Except for the weather.

The rain started falling harder, plinking noisily on the cars in the parking lot.

"But how—I mean, it's just so—" I was having a hard time forming a coherent sentence. My heart was in my throat and my eyes were shining with unshed tears. I was teetering on the verge of a very embarrassing breakdown; all it would take was just one more thing to push me over the edge and send me falling. Because I knew now that he wasn't tricking me or making this up.

Aiden's not that imaginative.

"Come on," he said softly, tugging me by the elbow. "You don't look so good. Let's get out of the rain and then we can figure out what to do next."

I jerked out of his grip and hissed, "This is insane—*you* are insane. How can you be so casual about this?"

He stopped and rubbed his face tiredly with his hands, and when he looked back at me his expression was hard, his mouth drawn into a tight line. "Because it is my life, and I've had to deal with this for a long time. Trust me, I'm anything but casual. But it's raining, and you look like an angry wet cat."

I bristled and opened my mouth to argue, but my retort died on my lips when he pointed to the window and said, "Plus Ms. Candor won't stop spying on us through the blinds. Let's not deny her the opportunity to hand you a tardy slip." His face softened as he looked at me from under his eyelashes. "It's going to make her whole year."

He turned toward the school, and when he opened the front door and held it for me, it was more of a challenge than an invitation.

I stood there for a moment, indecisive and soggy, as I considered him. I didn't know where else to go or what else to do. The dingy halls of Pearson High beckoned to me, safe and known and familiar. I gripped my backpack straps as I brushed past him into the front office, leaving a trail of wet footprints in my wake. There was nothing left for me to do except follow him. I was not about to stay out there in the rain in some alternate timeline by myself.

Even if that meant a tardy slip.

Fifteen

"It's not like this is really going to affect your perfect attendance record, you know," Aiden said with a smirk, waving his own tardy slip back and forth. I scowled at him and crumbled the note in my fist as we walked down the empty hall toward our English classroom.

My carefully constructed reality was crashing down at my feet, completely blown up by Aiden and his weird mutant abilities, and he thought this was a good time to make stupid jokes about attendance records. I stopped in my tracks, my boots squelching wetly on the slick floor.

"This is all your fault," I said, shoving him in the chest. His eyes widened as I pressed his back into the lockers lining the walls. "Why did you bring me here with you? I didn't want this."

"I didn't try to bring you! I was trying to move you out of the way, but you wouldn't hold still, and we just sort of... fell in." His gaze was a pointed accusation.

Don't move.

Josephine, listen to me—

His warnings flooded my memory along with the feel of his hands gripping my waist and his hazel eyes only an inch away from mine.

"Remember when you came over the other night for debate practice?" he asked, moving a step closer.

My heart started to race but I tried to keep my face blank when I nodded.

"That night in my room, there was a crack. Right behind you."

You need to leave. Right now.

I looked at his abrupt dismissal with new eyes. The way he'd glanced over my shoulder, the way he was so adamant that I leave right then. I could still hear his door clicking shut softly behind me, followed by that slow tearing sound that left me shivering and confused.

Aiden was watching me carefully. "And then at the game, there was another one. A huge crack, the biggest I'd seen since that first time I crossed over."

My eyebrows pinched together. It felt like I was trying to solve a puzzle with half the pieces missing. "But... why?"

He folded his arms over his chest and sighed. "Look, I wish I had more answers for you. But, honestly, this has only happened to me a handful of times."

"Oh, so you actually have no idea what you're doing, is what you're trying to tell me."

"Actually, Jo, I—"

"Josephine."

His smile sliced across his face, all shining teeth, and one dimpled cheek. "Maybe you could be Jo here."

"I'm not a 'Jo' in any time or place or reality or whatever," I snapped. "Josephine, always."

"Okay, Josephine," he said, his smile only growing wider. "What I was trying to say is I know enough about this place. There are a few rules—"

"Of course, because made-up timelines must have rules."

He pushed off the lockers where I still had him pinned. He got right in my face and said, "I'm serious. We have to do things slightly different here. Whatever your first impulse is, ignore it. That's the normal timeline trying to take over."

"But I *want* to be in the normal timeline," I said fiercely, "that's just fine with me if it takes over."

"We do not want that happening." He glanced around nervously as if he was worried we'd be overheard. "I know you felt it this morning. In your room. That energy in the air?" His voice was barely a whisper, his lips too close to my ear.

Oh, get a room already.

I gulped and shook my head, stumbling back a step. "Felt what?"

"The timeline. I could see the cracks forming in your room when I had you go through your normal routine. I was trying to show you."

All the hairs on the back of my neck stood up as I remembered. That strange sound, the air rippling. I didn't trust myself to speak without squeaking, so I nodded.

"I was trying to show you that this is real, that I wasn't making it up. And if you do things the same way you did yesterday, those weak spots, those spaces in between timelines start to show. If we try to make it identical to our timeline, it could converge, and I don't think that's a good idea. It could change things, alter our histories. The domino effect alone could be catastrophic."

I must've not looked very convinced, because he sighed and leaned back against the lockers. "The year we moved to Pearson, I only crossed over to this timeline once. And I wasn't careful; I didn't do things differently. The timelines started to merge, and I could see things in my home starting to vanish. A picture here, a throw pillow there. Little things." He rubbed his jaw, resting his chin in his hand and looking much more tired than any seventeen-year-old boy had the right to look. "Do you really want to mess around and risk losing something bigger? Something more important than a pillow?"

I repressed the shiver snaking its way up my spine. "Okay, okay, I get it. Don't do things exactly the same as I did yesterday. That doesn't sound that hard."

"You'd be surprised," Aiden mumbled. His eyes traced curiously over my face like he was searching for something. "So let's go."

"To class? We are."

"No, let's get out of here." He waved down the hall with a flippant gesture. "We don't need to go to English to discuss Steinbeck again. In fact, we definitely shouldn't. Let's just go."

I stared at his expectant face and suppressed a hysterical laugh. I was not about to go run off with Aiden on some crackpot adventure. No thank you.

"You can do whatever you want," I heard myself say dismissively, even though I was secretly terrified to be left on my own in the middle of the crackpot adventure we were already on. I tried to sound braver than I felt. "*I'm* going to class."

It was the only thing I knew how to do.

I stomped down the hallway with my tardy slip still crumbled in my sweating hand, straining my ears to hear if Aiden was following behind me or if he really was going to ditch school and leave me on my own. Mr. Kline's head swiveled to mine when I yanked the classroom door open. He eyed my pink tardy slip and pursed his lips, clearly annoyed at me for interrupting what I can only assume was his own *Dead Poets Society* moment in the lecture, only lacking all the inspiration and gravitas of Robin Williams.

"Nice of you to join us, Josephine. Take your seat. We were just discussing—"

"—modern themes in *The Grapes of Wrath*, I know," I muttered, annoyed with him for being annoyed with me. I snapped my mouth shut when his eyebrows shot up in surprise.

I was already very bad at this. There is nothing more dangerous to a know-it-all than *more knowing*, and as someone who'd already gone to this class and completed this day, I was like a greedy cheater with all the answers written on the back of my hand.

"That's right," he said with a sniff. "Who can—" his voice broke off when Aiden barreled through the door behind me. "Oh. You're both here."

I don't know if I imagined it, but it looked like the whole class deflated along with Mr. Kline. Like they were all disappointed we'd showed up.

My hands clenched my desk as I slid into my seat. Aiden took his spot across from me and tossed his backpack on the floor. *"Josephine,"* he whispered. He kept trying to meet my gaze, but I was feeling too overwhelmed by everything he'd told me to look at him. My eyes wandered the classroom, glossing over all the familiar posters of celebrities holding books as my head swam with a weird feeling of déjà vu.

So much was the same, but if you looked a little closer, the differences were there. Mr. Kline wasn't wearing his droopy old cardigan, he was wearing a trim leather jacket. With fringe on the arms and everything. Like he'd actually driven a motorcycle to school. If I didn't believe we were in an alternate timeline before, I would now. The Mr. Kline I knew was too timid to do anything but walk to school with his sweater wrapped carefully around his shoulders.

"Josephine," Aiden whispered again. "Quit ignoring me."

I angled my body away from him and shot my hand in the air when Mr. Kline said, "Who can describe Ma's role in the family?" He looked around the room hopefully, as if waiting for anyone else to volunteer, but mine was the sole hand flapping around in the air. "All right, Josephine, take a swing at it."

How about a grand slam or a home run or whatever other sports reference he was implying when he said I should, "Give it a try."

I launched into the same answer I'd given last time, pausing for emphasis halfway through when I saw Mr. Kline picking at his nails rather than paying attention to me. I powered through my explanation, making sure to cover everything I remembered from the reading. But my words slowed and stuttered when the lights started to flicker, the air filling with an electric charge and that same low tearing sound I'd heard before. My mouth snapped shut as I gripped the edge of my desk with shaking hands, like that gesture alone could save me.

"I think the whole thing is a sham," Aiden said loudly without raising his hand. "I think Steinbeck was an overly sentimental writer who took so much pleasure in his overstuffed descriptions that he forgot what he was actually trying to say."

I finally chanced a glance at Aiden and was surprised to see that he was still staring at me even while verbally assaulting John Steinbeck. He widened his eyes and shook his head slightly in warning.

I slumped in my seat, feeling completely exhausted. When I'd raised my hand, I hadn't deviated from the answer that I'd given the day before; it was pretty much word for word. But Aiden's response was entirely different than yesterday's. As he veered off into his Steinbeck rant, the air settled and the lights returned to their normal unattractive glaring selves. A few kids looked up and frowned, but flickering lights weren't that unusual at Pearson High, so they thought nothing of it.

"I hate this book," Aiden finished solemnly, tying up his diatribe with a nice little bow and the slightest wink at me.

Mr. Kline blinked at him, looking like an owl in his round glasses and fringed jacket. I was suddenly possessed with the untimely urge to burst out laughing. I had to bite my cheek to keep my mounting hysteria from bubbling up and spewing out all over the rest of the class and poor Mr. Kline, who was still twitching behind his desk.

"Strong words today, Mr. Mitchell. Your opinions on the subject have been noted." Mr. Kline swallowed. "Anyone else?"

Aiden leaned back in his seat, looking pleased with himself. I, on the other hand, was fully starting to panic. Neither of us made a peep for the rest of the hour. I sat squirming at my desk, sitting on my hands in case the urge to answer came over me again, until the bell rang shrilly and it nearly made me jump out of my skin.

"Come on," Aiden said, already standing with his backpack on his shoulder. "Now do you want to leave? Now do you believe me?"

I nodded mutely, hating him for being right and hating myself for insisting on coming to class anyway.

We were the only ones left in the room. Even Mr. Kline had left, probably to go complain about us in the teacher's lounge. They liked us well enough on our own, but when Aiden and I were together and taking over the class with our one-upping and bickering? Not so much (I was convinced they had a dartboard with our pictures on it).

Aiden reached down and pulled me up out of my seat, his hands sliding from my shoulders down the length of my arms, sending a shiver through me.

"I don't need your help," I said, trying to sound assertive and authoritative, but my voice came out all wrong and breathless. He slowly lifted his hands away, but his eyes were still roaming all over me, and everywhere his gaze landed was as heavy as a touch.

"Why are you looking at me like that?" I blurted without pausing to think.

He ignored my question as we left the classroom and entered the bustling hallway that was overcrowded with students and posters screaming about homecoming.

"There's something else I need to tell you." He said the words all slurred together like they were tripping over themselves in their rush to get out.

"Please tell me it's how to get out of here?" I said too loudly over the roar of raucous kids too amped up on football and the promise of tonight's glory.

Aiden shushed me and glared before looking around to make sure no one had overheard us. He leaned in and whispered, "Could you maybe try harder not to yell about our little situation?" Then he added, "Tomorrow morning we should be back at home on Saturday. But no, that's not it."

"Wait, you already know when this will be over?"

"Yeah, I always just repeat the day and that's it." He shrugged as if to say, "duh." Like I was dumb for not understanding his time-hopping ways.

"That's oddly specific," I said skeptically as we wove in between classmates slamming their lockers shut and filing into classrooms.

He frowned and shifted his backpack on his shoulders. "I like to think about it like the other side of yesterday."

My hands roamed to the top of my head where I tried to tighten my nonexistent ponytail. Curse Rose and this braid crown I will never be free of. "Sure, because that makes perfect sense."

Aiden watched me fussing around with my hair, his eyes following the stray strands that had escaped from the braid. He swallowed, suddenly looking nervous, the tips of his ears turning red.

The hallway was starting to empty and neither of us was running to make it to our next class yet. At the end of the hall, I could see Cat waiting for me, leaning against my locker and tapping on her phone. I wanted to call out, to elbow everyone else out of the way and ask her to come save me from Aiden and the rest of this insanity. But before I could, he lunged for the nearest door and yanked it open, pulling me in roughly behind him.

When he flipped on the light switch, a single lightbulb flared to life, swinging on the end of a decrepit-looking chain and offering us next to no light. I surveyed the narrow room completely stuffed with cleaning products. It was so cramped in here, that no matter where I turned I bumped into some part of Aiden invading my personal space.

"Is *this* where you're going to bury my body?" I asked, looking at the mop in its bucket. "Again, you need to work on your creativity."

"No, I did not bring you into the janitor's supply closet to murder you," he said in a strained voice. "I told you I need to tell you something."

"You're just full of surprises this morning. Do you come with an off button?"

"I just need to get his over with," he said, his jaw clenching. The lightbulb swayed back and forth between us, lighting up his face one second, then casting it in shadows the next. "I feel weird not telling you."

"Oh, you've been meaning to tell me something other than the fact that your life is the premise for the new and upcoming Marvel movie? You already have the child actor name…"

His mouth twitched like he wanted to smile but wouldn't allow himself to. In the end, his exasperation won. "Look, I know you overheard that argument I had with my dad at the game."

His sudden switch in topics left me scrambling for something to hold on to. "What?" I said, shaking my head and trying to keep up as my back pressed against the wall of shelves behind me. "I mean I wasn't *trying* to eavesdrop—"

"Whatever, I don't care. I know you heard what he said about my meds. The ones that help prevent all… this," he said, shrugging one shoulder. "The truth is, I'd been skipping doses all week."

"Why?" I asked, my brow puckering.

He chewed on his lower lip, looking down. "For the tournament," he mumbled so quietly I wasn't sure I'd heard him correctly.

My head tipped to the side. "Excuse me, did you just say that you quit taking your time-travel meds so you could best me in the speech and debate tournament this Saturday?"

"They're not 'time-travel meds,' whatever that means."

"But you quit taking them," I said, a slow grin sliding across my face, "because you know I'm the superior debater, and you needed your weird little mind tricks to beat me!" I jabbed my finger into his chest triumphantly.

He flicked my finger away and rolled his eyes so hard I thought they were going to get stuck in the back of his head. "We're on the same team, Josephine, I wasn't trying to beat you. I was trying to compete *with* you so we would win. But, like I was saying," he said, obviously annoyed at me for hijacking his secrets, "I skipped some doses to see how it would feel. It was fine at first, but then I started seeing a few cracks—small ones. I saw one in English on Wednesday." He coughed and rubbed the back of his head. "You may have noticed."

I thought back to his staring, his stiff posture and agitated watchfulness. "The Nicolas Cage wall," I whispered.

He laughed softly. "The very one. And then after the blood drive, I quit taking them entirely. I'd missed enough doses that once the meds got out of my system, I felt so clear. I hadn't felt like that in a long time."

I thought back to his flawless debate performances, the way he hadn't had to look at his notes once. The debate performances I'd had to grudgingly admit (if only in my head) were perfect.

His voice got quiet. "So, I kept skipping. The headaches didn't come back right away, and I thought I had it under control, but then Thursday night there was another crack—way bigger this time—and after you left my house, I ended up here again. And, well, Josephine... I—we—you..."

He groaned and ran both his hands through his hair until all of his honey-colored blondness was staggered in wild, rippling waves. "I kissed you, okay? Yesterday. At debate practice."

"You—we—I—" Now it was my turn to be speechless. "I think I would remember if you even attempted to kiss me."

"It was here. In this timeline," Aiden said, gesturing around us and accidentally knocking a jug of bleach to the floor in the process. "I told you, I have to be careful when I'm here. I can't repeat the same choices I do in my real life. I have to keep it *alternative*." He said the word slowly, enunciating every syllable, stretching out the word until it sounded twice as long. "It has to be different. *I* have to be different."

"So different for you means kissing me? In the middle of debate practice?" My voice was getting shriller by the second.

He shuffled his feet, kicking at the drain in the middle of the floor. "There was a moment during our practice." His cheeks were tinted a bashful shade of pink. "You know what I'm talking about."

I knew exactly what he was referring to, but I wasn't about to let him know that. "And what moment would that be?"

"That moment!" He leaned in until our eyes were nearly level, his face hovering just an inch away from mine. My breath stuttered, then snagged in my throat. "That moment when I could've kissed you but didn't."

We were suspended in time, right then and there. Half of me was back on that creaky old stage, one hand on the podium, clenched tightly into a fist. The other half of me was trapped in a janitor's closet, caught in the space between what could've been and what could happen now.

If I wanted it. If I moved another inch.

Both halves of me had Aiden standing in front of me. Both versions of him wore that same fierce expression—the one I'd thought meant he was possibly on the verge of kicking over the podium and storming out, but with added hindsight, I knew meant something else entirely.

The same wild hazel eyes, the same sharp inhale.

He wanted something, but it wasn't a violent fit of rage like I'd assumed.

It was *me*.

Aiden stepped back and tucked his hands into his pockets, a gesture I was starting to familiarize myself with as a nervous tic.

"You liked it."

His eyes widened. "I liked what?"

"You liked kissing me, didn't you?"

"What are you talking about?" He scoffed but it came out a little strangled. "I *had* to. I didn't feel like ripping open another gaping hole in the universe, so I took one for the team."

"Oh, please. Just admit it. You liked it."

The strangest part of all this was how much it annoyed me that he knew what it was like to kiss me before I knew what it was like to kiss him. Yet another thing for him to hold over my head; yet another way in which he'd beaten me.

Point to Mitchell.

He opened his mouth, ready to retort, but then he paused and squinted at me. He looked like he was mulling something over, like he was weighing his options. He looked the way he did before he called me out in class when he knew I'd gotten the answer wrong.

His freaking Cheshire Cat face.

"So what if I did."

He stepped in closer, reached his hand out, and gently ran his thumb across my cheek, letting it slide across my face until it landed on my bottom lip. "So what if I can't stop thinking about it. So what if maybe I want to kiss you again."

I was frozen. We stared at each other for a long beat, both of us breathing hard. My face was flushed and my stomach was swooping, but still, I just stood there. Letting him touch me like that.

"So what," he said again, that time in a whisper. He dropped his hand and stepped back, a soft smile on his face. A smile that looked like a secret.

I tried to glare at him, to summon any kind of resentment or anger I could, but all I felt was a different kind of burning that I wasn't sure what to do with. He'd struck a match, then flicked it carelessly at me, watching to see if the flames would devour me.

And he *liked* it.

This was a whole different kind of game, a new kind of psychological warfare. One I wasn't sure I knew how to play, or if I wanted to play at all.

But I swallowed all of that down. I took the match and I stepped on it, crunching it under my boot.

"Well, I hope you enjoyed yourself because that is never, ever going to happen again," I said harshly as I yanked the door open and walked straight into the loving arms of Principal Cartwright.

Sixteen

"**J**OSEPHINE! WHAT IN the name of all that is holy are you—*Mr. Mitchell?*" Mrs. Cartwright gasped theatrically as Aiden tumbled out the door after me. "My, my, what a surprise." Except the way she said it made it sound like she wasn't surprised at all. "Now, y'all know you can't be canoodling here in the janitor's closet, especially when you're supposed to be in class!" Her narrow eyes landed on me. "What would your mama say?"

It was mortifying.

Mrs. Cartwright didn't wait for me to find my voice (which is a good thing because it was long gone). She put her hands on her hips and said, "Actually, I'm sure your mama was caught doing this very same thing in this very same closet when she was a student at Pearson High. With your Daddy, of course." Then she winked at us.

I wanted the timeline to rip open under my feet and swallow me whole. Blink my existence right out.

"Mrs. Cartwright, you've got it all wrong—"

"She just can't keep her hands off me," Aiden said, with a small, private smile that completely blew things out of proportion.

My face flamed as Mrs. Cartwright shook a finger at us and said, "I'm sorry, but I'm going to have to write you up for this, no matter how adorable it is. Lunch detention should teach you a lesson." Another wink.

I was ready to light the school on fire. She pulled a notepad out of her suit jacket (fuchsia—what was with this woman and the color pink?) and scribbled a note that I read upside down in horror.

Caught these two necking in a supply closet—have them help make copies in the teacher's lounge or something.

"Here, give this to Mrs. Goldwyn; she should get you sorted out. All right, no more of that! Save some of that fire for after school, hmm? Bye now!" She waved her manicured hand at us and went back to traipsing down the hallway.

"I. Cannot. Believe. You," I choked out.

Aiden's grin twisted into a tight straight line. "Oh, relax. None of this means anything."

So what if I can't stop thinking about it.

"I know it doesn't, but that doesn't mean I'm enjoying it! This whole day is a nightmare." Tears prickled in my eyes, furthering my humiliation. Because, no matter what timeline I'm in, the universe despises me.

"Hey," Aiden said softly, nudging my chin up with his knuckle. "I'm sorry. It was just a joke. I didn't mean to upset you."

So what if maybe I want to kiss you again.

"Since when do you care whether or not you upset me?" My voice was laced with bitterness—barbed and cutting.

He stepped back and slid his hands into his pockets. "I do care."

"Oh, please." I started walking toward our chemistry classroom even though I would probably answer everything the same as I did yesterday and tear another hole in the timeline. Whatever that meant. But Cat was there. And even if she wasn't exactly *my* version of Cat, it's still some version of her, and that would be comforting enough.

"Josephine, why would you choose to go repeat a class when you could do absolutely anything you wanted to today? Anything at all."

His words stopped me short.

You're so predictable.

He walked over to where I was standing frozen in place and turned me to face him. I could feel the heat of his hands as they pressed into my arms, squeezing gently. He had that same edge about him that he'd had all morning—all wild eyes and impatience. Maybe a little bit of recklessness, too.

"We can be anyone we want to be today."

"What if I just want to be myself?" I asked in a small voice.

"I happen to like who you are every other day of the week," he said with a nod. I nearly choked in surprise. "But I think there's more of you in there. I'd like to meet her."

Cat's question crashed into me. *Are you happy?*

Most of the time I thought I was. I had my books, I had the friends I needed, and I had my future. All the possibilities far away from Pearson that I'd been dreaming about every single day of my life for as long as I could remember.

I was happy. But most of the time I felt like I was still waiting for my life to start.

Like I was still waiting to meet that girl inside me too.

"It's like what I said when I called this place 'the other side of yesterday,'" Aiden rambled on. "It's kind of like we're in a fan fiction of our lives." He paused, the hint of a blush darkening his cheeks. "You know how some writers take characters and stories they love and they make it a little different, they make it their own—"

"I know what fan fiction is," I said, holding a hand up. "But Aiden, now I need to know. Do you read fan fiction?" He swatted my hand away and looked down.

"There's some decent stuff out there," he mumbled. I fell into a fit of giggles as the thought of Aiden scrolling through Twilight fan fiction pushed my hysteria over the edge.

Aiden ignored my laughter. He was watching me with that piercing stare he usually reserved for particularly difficult math problems. Then his face relaxed a little as if he was one step closer to solving it.

"Truth or dare," he said.

"Excuse me?" I asked, still gasping for breath. "I know you have the emotional range of a twelve-year-old, but are you seriously asking me to play truth or dare?"

"Challenging you, you mean."

My jaw clenched as that familiar heat of loathing crept up my neck, paired with the crawling pressure of needing to win absolutely. Entirely. I exhaled heavily, already sliding on my game face. "Truth," I said, picking the lesser of two evils, not trusting him for one second with a dare. Not when he had his game face on too.

Plus, I could always lie.

"What's the lowest score you've ever gotten on a test?"

My stomach dropped. Like I would ever admit such a weakness to my nemesis. Aiden tapped his foot and hummed the *Jeopardy* theme song as I squirmed under his steady gaze, wrestling with what to do.

"85%, trig test last year."

"You little liar."

"How would you know if I'm lying or not?"

"You're chewing on your bottom lip and your eyes are all twitchy. You do that when you're lying."

I scowled. "Fine. 80%."

He surveyed me for a moment in silence as if waiting for me to show more revealing tells, or perhaps burst into tears. "80%, how embarrassing. Tell me, how do you sleep at night?" He couldn't keep a straight face. "Your turn," he said.

"Truth or dare." I crossed my arms tightly over my chest, still seething.

"Truth."

"What's *your* lowest score?"

"So unoriginal, Josephine. I'm disappointed." He sighed. "81%," he said with a grin. "That extra 1% I have on you must kill you. Tell me, how do you sleep at night?" he asked again.

"I sleep just fine."

He wasn't lying. I already knew his lowest score because I'd memorized his ID number and compared his scores against mine every time they were posted. Which wasn't stalker-ish at all; it's knowing your enemy.

The bell rang again.

"Let's get out of here," I heard myself say.

Aiden's eyes widened. "That's the second time you've ever surprised me," he said, looking smug.

"When was the first?" I asked, my heart thudding out a warning.

"When you kissed me back."

He laughed as my jaw hit the floor, brushing past me as the hall filled once again with the noisy buzzing of kids heading to their next classes.

"Are you coming or not, Crew?"

I marched determinedly past him without another word. I wasn't going to let him win this.

Point to me.

We waded through the mass of bodies, trying to make our way out undetected, but the excitement over the game was so palpable, it was almost impossible to walk through. "Why of all the days you could make me repeat, does it have to be Homecoming? I can think of about 361 other days I'd like to do over," I said, not looking at him, still fuming from the kiss comment.

"361? That's specific."

"I'm also excluding winter formal, Sadie Hawkins, and prom."

"It sounds like someone has a phobia of dancing."

"I'm an excellent dancer, actually." The words came out of my mouth before I realized what I was saying.

Aiden's eyes gleamed. "I'll have to see some evidence of said dancing abilities and make my own judgment."

Truthfully, I didn't know if I was a good dancer. I'd refused to participate in any of the dance classes my mom had signed me up for when I was a kid in the hopes that I would succumb to the siren call of the spotlights. I hid my ballet slippers, tap shoes, and (no, I'm not kidding) jazz dance shoes, and locked myself in my room, refusing any form of bribery in the process.

I'd only ever danced with Rose and Cat, which mostly comprised of jumping on Cat's bed whenever we listened to boy bands from the '90s. It wasn't the actual dancing that deserved my scorn and ridicule. It was the whole ritual of it all. The elaborate ways people asked each other to the dances, the over-the-top dresses and tuxedos, the hotel rooms and the "this is the best night of our lives" speeches from all the starry-eyed girls.

If that was going to be the best night of my life—the peak of my existence—then that was the most depressing thought of all.

If that was going to be the best night of my life, then that would make me my mother.

"Get used to disappointment, Golden Boy."

"You think I'm golden?" he asked, his lips quirking into a smirk.

"No, *you* think you're golden. You and everyone else in this ridiculous town."

We'd nearly made it to the front doors of the school when I planted my feet and stuck my arm out to stop Aiden from bursting into the front office. He collided with me and groaned, "What now? We're almost home free."

"We can't just walk out the front doors. We'll be seen!"

I peered through the skinny window in the door leading into the main hub of the front offices. I could see Mrs. Cartwright stalking back and forth, a pink blur in front of Ms. Candor's desk, which was blocking our exit, the two of them talking animatedly.

My face burned as I imagined their conversation. *"You'll never guess who I just caught tumbling out of the janitor's closet!"* I could almost hear our principal simpering. Ms. Candor would be on the edge of her seat, her tight curls bouncing as she bobbed up and down with the clunky school phone clutched in her hand, her fingers twitching like she couldn't wait to start dialing. That woman could mobilize a gossipy phone tree faster than anyone else in town. I couldn't decide if her specific skillset was horrifying or impressive.

"I dare you to—"

I glared and smacked him on the chest before he could even finish getting the words out. "Don't even think about it. I am not running out that front door."

Aiden snorted and mumbled something that sounded suspiciously like "wimp," tapping his chin thoughtfully. "Well, then we only have one other option." He turned and pointed back down the nearly deserted hallway to the emergency exit.

Alarm will sound if door is opened.

My eyes widened at the warning written in screaming red letters. "But the alarm—"

He grinned. "Exactly."

This was not the Aiden I knew. He wasn't politely thinking about how the teachers would have to stop their lessons, or how everyone might have to evacuate the building; this version of Aiden seemed to delight in the possibility of a little extra chaos, egging me on as he toed the line we normally didn't cross.

"You know what? I'll let you dare me since you copied my truth on your first round. I'll let that be your freebee. It was incredibly lame, and you need to redeem yourself."

I wanted to argue, but I also didn't want to push against his sudden burst of goodwill and make him change his mind. So instead, I lifted one eyebrow and said, "I dare you to run out the emergency exit."

"Only if you follow."

"Deal."

We started sprinting down the hall, dodging the last few dawdling kids. And because I have terrible luck, Rose happened to be one of them. She was flirting with Jordan next to his locker, squeezing his arm as she flipped her hair over her shoulder and giggled, but her mouth hung wide open when she saw me hurtling down the hall with Aiden running wildly by my side.

I ducked my head and pretended like I didn't see her, rounding the last corner and nearly crashing into the Pearson High trophy case, chock-full of legends who'd never left Pearson and never moved on. Golden trophies and gleaming medals flashed from behind the smudge-free glass case as we ran past. I tried to avoid looking at the framed photographs of the teenage version of my dad, who was holding the state championship trophy and looking happier than I'd ever seen him look in my entire seventeen years of life.

Right before I turned away, one name stamped boldly on a plaque caught my eye.

Wes Mitchell.

"Wait," I said, sliding to a stop.

But Aiden had already slammed his hands on the emergency exit, the door flinging open with a loud, rusty-hinged *creak*, followed by the blaring of an even louder alarm. I gave an involuntary yelp as I flung myself out the door behind him, the shrieking siren a twin pulse to my pounding heart.

Seventeen

I WAS PRETTY convinced Aiden's brother was still alive in this time-line. After all, I'd just seen his name featured in the shining trophy case of a school he most definitely had not attended.

But that was impossible.

You still think some things are impossible? My brain snickered at me like I was slow and stupid. *Look around you.*

I was reeling from the shock of it when we got to Aiden's truck and climbed inside, just barely missing the rain that had started falling again. Aiden was too busy laughing over our dramatic exit to notice my silence at first. He peeled out of the parking lot before we could see if everyone was following protocol and evacuating the school.

"See, now you're getting the hang of truth or dare," he said as he sped down the road, his windshield wipers sliding noisily across the rain-spattered window. "What does that say about you and me if running out an emergency exit door is that intense for us?" He slumped in his seat and shook his head, bemused, his gaze flicking over to mine when I didn't answer. "You okay? Did the game already break you? You look like you've seen a ghost."

I have, I wanted to say. But I didn't. I couldn't. I was so caught off guard, I didn't know how to bring up the subject without sounding totally tactless. I mean, what if I brought it up and it was just another Wes Mitchell that happened to live in Pearson?

Aiden never mentioned his brother; obviously, it was an off-limits subject. A sharp pain needled its way through me as I thought about Rose and the possibility of me losing her—

Nope. I couldn't even finish that thought.

So I kept my mouth shut. Especially since Aiden was smiling at me with that wide easy grin of his as if he was happy to be ditching school with me. I was both surprised and irritated by how much I liked the thought of that. And for the briefest moment, we weren't fighting. Like maybe our being here in this strange place had caused us to lay down our weapons and draw up a temporary ceasefire.

"Where are we going?" I asked, changing the subject.

"I have a few ideas," he said, refusing to explain further.

Forget what I said about liking this temporary truce—he was starting to annoy me. But no matter how much I bugged him about where we were going, no matter how many questions I threw at him, he dodged them all. "You need to live a little," was all he said.

"What, like you're some wild child out on a bender for life? You're nearly as uptight as me."

"Maybe at home. But not here. I don't need to be."

"Why?"

"It's not your turn to ask me a question."

"Fine, then go ahead and ask me. Truth or dare."

"Nope, I'm saving mine for when we arrive at our destination."

Five minutes later, we pulled into the parking lot of Applebee's; Pearson's finest dining establishment.

"Seriously? Applebee's?" I asked, totally unimpressed with his big surprise.

"Save your disdain and follow me." He hopped out of the truck and waited for me to join him, scattered raindrops landing on his t-shirt.

I *was* hungry. In the commotion of waking up in an alternate time-line, I'd forgotten to eat my breakfast and it was nearly noon.

When Aiden held the door open for me, I was greeted with the dulcet tones of someone wailing a Mariah Carey song completely off-key. There was a chorus of cheers and the sound of clinking glasses. And next to the hostess table, a big sign written in neon pink letters that read, "Mom's Happy Hour! Bottomless Drinks and Karaoke!"

"Oh no. No, no, no. Nope. I'd rather face lunch detention with every single one of our teachers thinking I made out with you in a broom closet. Take me back to school."

"Not a chance. You can't be trusted back there. You fall too easily into old patterns and habits; you'll get us sucked into the void for sure."

I grimaced and glanced over my shoulder at the crowd of middle-aged women swaying with their frosted glasses in the air, now singing along to Whitney Houston.

This was going to be terrible. I better get a lot of appetizers out of this.

"Fine. But you're buying me lunch."

"Of course," he said.

"But it's not a date."

"Of course. We're just two friends—"

"—we're not friends—"

"—who have casually kissed, no big deal—"

I must've looked murderous because Aiden cut himself off and bit his lip like he had to physically restrain himself from continuing his little tirade.

"Get your wallet out. I'm starving." I marched over to the smiling hostess and asked for a table for two as far away from the moms and the karaoke as possible.

But it wasn't far enough.

I ordered six appetizers as punishment.

"How'd you know about Sad Mom Karaoke Hour anyway?" I asked between mouthfuls of buffalo wings.

"My mom used to come."

I nearly spewed ranch all over him. "Betty Mitchell is into karaoke?"

"She loves it."

I thought of Mrs. Mitchell, the mother, the nurse, the woman mourning the loss of her son, and tried to picture her swaying on a small stage while singing, "Man! I Feel Like a Woman!"

I leaned back into the booth seat and giggled into my soda.

"You don't have to put everyone into boxes, you know," Aiden said as he scooped up some spinach dip with his chip.

"What's that supposed to mean?"

"You like boxes. You like order and consistency. You make snap judgments about people and then you never let them evolve from what you originally thought about them."

"That's not true!"

He scoffed. "That's what you did to me."

Okay, maybe that was true.

"Well, most people choose to stay in their boxes," I answered back, picking up a mozzarella stick and dunking it in the little pot of marinara sauce. "I don't keep them there."

Aiden was thoughtful as he stole the last wing from off my plate. "Truth or dare," he finally asked, raising one eyebrow at me.

"Truth," I said, as the karaoke blared loudly in the background, now playing "(I've Had) The Time of My Life."

He sighed and shook his head. "Are you really never going to pick dare? I didn't know you were such a little chicken."

I swallowed. Those are fighting words.

He fought back a grin as if he could see the internal battle raging inside me over which humiliation would be worse—completing his dare or letting him win.

"Fine. *Dare*," I choked out as my palms started to sweat.

"Oh, I think you know what the dare is."

I stood robotically and walked over to the crowd of dancing moms, feeling like I was floating outside of my body. But reality crashed into me as I tapped one of them on the shoulder and said, "Would you mind if I sang a special song for that special guy over there?" I tried to look like a lovesick schoolgirl; I batted my eyelashes and sighed dramatically like Rose does whenever she thinks she's in love again.

"Oh honey, of course you can!" she crooned, grabbing the microphone from the stumbling mom who'd just finished her performance. "Anything for young love!" She was dressed in expensive-looking athleisure wear with a full face of makeup on, like she couldn't decide if she was going to the gym or a gala. "Aren't you Jenny's little girl?" she asked, peering tipsily at my face as she led me over to the tiny stage in the corner of the restaurant.

I resisted the impulse to deny it. "I'm Josephine Crew," I said stiffly in grudging acknowledgment.

"I knew it! You look just like your mama. I bet you can sing like her too!" She raised her glass and all her friends cheered and followed suit.

Everything in me was screaming to get out of there. The only thing that could've made the situation any worse was if my mother walked through the doors of Applebee's right then and there and saw me standing on a stage with a bedazzled microphone in hand. I didn't think I would survive the smug look on her face or the false hope that would surely fill up her eyes.

But I couldn't leave. I refused to give Aiden the satisfaction of watching me walk out on a dare.

I woodenly approached the ancient karaoke machine and started scrolling through the menu, impatiently clicking through the song selection until I found exactly what I needed. I squared my shoulders and closed my eyes for a moment, finding peace in the fact that if I was going to embarrass myself in front of everyone, then at least I was going to take Aiden down with me.

He'd walked over and pulled up a chair right in the middle of all the moms. I was disturbed by how many of them he knew by their first names. They fawned over him and tousled his buttery blond hair, asking him how long we'd been together.

"It's new," he said, trying not to laugh. "Very new. We're still in the honeymoon stage."

"Oh, sweetheart, that's the best part!" They all continued to twitter around him like a flock of rhinestone, denim-clad birds until the opening notes to "You're So Vain" started blasting through the restaurant.

At first, I kept my eyes trained on the lyrics scrolling over the tiny screen, not wanting to see the looks on everyone's faces as I hesitantly worked my way through the first verse, singing about yachts and apricot scarves. But then as the chorus picked up, I found myself peeking, and what I saw nearly made me fall over.

All the moms had their lipsticked mouths popped open in shock as they watched me serenade my apparently brand-new boyfriend with the words to Carly Simon's revenge song.

You're so vain, I'll bet you'll think this song is about you—
Don't you?
Don't you?
Don't you?
Aiden's eyes were watering with the effort of not laughing. When

our gazes met, it was almost too much. But I carried on valiantly, singing directly to his face, enunciating every time the lyrics reminded him just how vain he was.

It was glorious.

Halfway through the song, I started loosening up; the stiffness left my shoulders as my foot tapped along to the rhythm of the music. Before I knew what was happening, I was dancing around the stage, and by the time I'd hit the last stanza, I'd hopped off the small platform, shimmying toward Aiden in his seat. His eyes widened in surprise when I sashayed over to him and sat on his lap while belting out the last few lines of the song.

Purely for performance purposes, of course.

Aiden wasn't laughing anymore. His eyes burned into mine as the last notes faded away and the machine shut off, filling the room with a silence much more deafening than the music had been. His hand tightened around my waist as he pulled me into his chest. "What a show. I could tell you meant every word." His tone was all mock-sincerity, but his breath was warm against my ear, his nose skimming along the back of my neck.

I pushed off him and took a bow. The moms started clapping hesitantly, clearly confused by what they'd just witnessed. One of them sauntered over and took the mic out of my hands, all but dismissing me from their group.

"Who's up?" she whooped into the microphone. "How about some Destiny's Child!"

My chest was thrumming with the thrill of victory, but that wasn't the only thing. I'd never admit this to Aiden, but it was actually *fun*. I'd had fun singing in front of a group of tipsy moms at Applebee's in the middle of the afternoon.

"Josephine?" a familiar voice exclaimed, and my stomach bottomed out.

It was Cat. And Ethan. Standing at Applebee's in the middle of the afternoon.

"Cat!" I called out, stretching out her name so that it sounded like two syllables. Anything to buy me more time. "What are you doing here?"

"It's Friday," she said simply, still staring at me. "Ethan and I always go out to lunch on Fridays."

Not in my timeline.

Aiden shot a quick glance at me and shook his head as if reminding me not to say anything stupid. "Hey, Ethan," he said to Cat's boyfriend who was eyeing the moms squealing over their rendition of "Survivor" with amusement.

Ethan turned to me, "I didn't know you could sing, Josephine," he said with a grin. "That was impressive." He elbowed Cat, but she ignored him.

"What are *you* doing here?" she asked, folding her arms over her Pearson High t-shirt. I stared into the cartoon tiger's giant eyes rather than hers. "We were, um, we just—I—"

"Debate practice," Aiden offered. "I made Josephine come here to practice because I was starving, and then, well, the music took ahold of her." He gestured back to the karaoke platform and smirked. "When the muse calls, you better listen."

I wanted to throw the purple karaoke machine at his big head. "We should go—" I said at the same time Aiden said, "Come sit with us! We have tons of food."

I glared at him, trying to communicate silently that the last thing I wanted to do was sit with my best friend and her boyfriend, to whom I'd repeatedly complained to about Aiden. Like on a daily basis. Hourly, even. We all had classes together; it's not like they hadn't seen the two of us together before. They had, thousands of times. But this felt different. This was away from school and under the rosy glow of a chain restaurant that was currently hosting a very pitchy happy hour.

This was Aiden and me spending time together intentionally.

And Cat was suspicious. She kicked me under the table and said, "I need to go to the bathroom, do you, Josephine?"

"Nope. I just went," I lied.

She kicked me under the table again and narrowed her eyes at me. "I don't want to go alone, come with me."

Ethan snorted into his chips and dip as Cat pulled me by the neck of my t-shirt and dragged me away from the table. "Why do they travel in packs?" I heard him asking Aiden as Cat shoved me into the bathroom at the end of the dimly lit hallway.

"Josephine Crew," she cried out the moment the door shut behind us. "What is going on with you?" Cat is significantly shorter than me, but when she's mad, she fills up the room with her quiet indignation. Well, usually it's quiet. This version of Cat seemed to be more of a yeller.

"Nothing! Nothing's going on. Aiden dragged me here—"

"—and forced you to sit on his lap and *serenade him*?" she screeched.

"That was a joke, Cat. Relax."

"It didn't look like a joke. It looked like you were about to grab his face and start making out with the guy." She paused for emphasis. "With *Aiden*," she reminded me unhelpfully. "Who you supposedly hate, remember?"

"I do hate him."

"Mmhm."

We stared at each other in silence for a moment while the strains of "Wannabe" pulsed through the cheaply painted walls surrounding us. Cat softened a bit, then laughed. "Remember that dance we made up to this song in third grade?"

"How could I forget. It was one of our best." Apparently, my mom was a big Spice Girls fan back in her day, and when we were ten, Cat and I stole her beloved concert t-shirts out of her dresser and really went for it, practicing our choreography all afternoon in front of my closet mirror, with Rose calling out the steps from my bed with the stern attitude of a strict ballet instructor.

When my mom got home from work and saw us in her prized memorabilia, the shirts spilling off our shoulders in that oversized way, I thought she was going to be mad at me like she always was. But instead, she smiled and took a video of us performing. I think that was one of the only times I've ever made her proud—prancing around like a background dancer in a low-budget music video.

I never wore that t-shirt again.

Cat smirked as she danced a square step around me, swinging her arms exaggeratedly, but her eyes looked a little sad.

"Ugh, don't remind me," I groaned into my hands. "We were horrible."

"We were," she said gently. "We've known each other a long time, Josie." I cringed at the old nickname I'd outgrown like an itchy sweater that never fit quite right in the first place. "Long enough for me to know how much you hate that nickname." She sighed and took my hands in hers, her eyes round and watery. "I thought we told each other everything."

"What—we do, Cat. I swear! There's nothing going on. It's not like that. We—" I started and stopped multiple sentences, trying to find the right words to describe what was happening between me and Aiden.

We're two time travelers out enjoying a change of scenery!

We're a couple of overachievers that need to blow off some steam before we explode!

Aiden's ringing voice broke through my mental stammering.

We're friends that have casually kissed, no big deal.

"I don't know what's going on," I finally said in a soft voice that sounded nothing like my own.

"And that's the first honest thing you've said to me today," Cat replied with a small smile, squeezing my hand.

She didn't make me explain, and she didn't press for more answers. That's the thing about best friends—they know when to push back and they know when to retreat. But mostly they know you better than you know yourself, and the way Cat was looking at me made me think she knew something I didn't.

There's nothing worse to a know-it-all than not knowing.

Eighteen

"**W**ELL, THAT WAS weird and awful," I said to Aiden as I waved goodbye to Cat and Ethan from the shotgun seat of the Tacoma. Cat shot me meaningful looks from where she sat in Ethan's car, which heavily implied that while she might be temporarily letting me off the hook, her generosity was not going to last forever; I would eventually have to explain myself and this thing with Aiden. I tried not to gulp when she winked at me as they drove away.

"What was weird and awful?" Aiden asked.

"Lunch, obviously. That was—"

"—perfectly pleasant. I don't know what lunch you were at, but I had fun."

It had been so strange to see Cat and Aiden joking around, talking like old friends. Which I guess they were. I guess all those times she didn't join in on my Aiden bashing, she wasn't just letting me take the proverbial first swing, she actually didn't have anything to add.

They were friends.

It left me feeling tilted, like the earth wasn't spinning at precisely the same angle I'd thought it was.

Aiden smiled. "I've always liked Cat," he said, hammering the final nail into the coffin full of things I'd thought to be true. "I can see why she's your best friend."

He reversed out of the parking spot and said, "Where to?"

I fiddled with my hands in my lap, trying to think of something off-beat or forbidden, something I'd never allow myself to do in my real life. But my mind was disappointingly empty.

Was I really this boring?

"I don't know," I huffed. "You think of something. You're the X-Man here."

"That's not the first Marvel reference you've made today. I didn't know you were such a fan."

"I'm not," I said honestly. "Rose and Cat always make me go see the movies when they come out because they think I need lessons on being a teenager. They want me to have some speaking points to reference when I'm conversing with The Youths."

Aiden laughed loudly but didn't disagree. What I didn't tell him was how long I spent falling down the Wikipedia rabbit hole after I saw each movie, trying to follow the interconnecting characters and plot lines. I could keep that little tidbit to myself.

"Besides, I hardly think you can make fun of me for referencing movies basically the entire world has seen. Let's not forget which one of us reads fan fiction," I added.

He scratched the side of his head idly—too idly—and didn't comment.

"Wait—you don't just read it, you *write* it, don't you?"

Aiden gripped the steering wheel and whipped his head over to me. "You should know that I happen to have a very engaged readership—"

I was squirming in my seat, bouncing around in excitement. "This is amazing. What's your username? I'm looking it up right now," I said, pulling out my phone.

"Sorry, the fan fiction website doesn't exist in this reality."

"You're such a liar. I *dare* you to show me." I sounded just as juvenile as he did when he'd dared me to do karaoke (maybe even more so).

Aiden groaned and drooped in his seat, letting his forehead smack the steering wheel. We hadn't even made it out of the Applebee's parking lot yet. "TheTrueBoyWhoLived." He spat the words out like they were burning his tongue.

A long, strained silence stretched between us. He broke first and started laughing so hard he was in tears. "I know, it's ridiculous. But I made the account when I was *thirteen*. Thirteen-year-old Aiden thought he was particularly clever."

I rolled my eyes. "I've met thirteen-year-old Aiden. Believe me,

I know." I typed his username into the website and immediately his profile popped up; it was teeming with years' worth of stories. I grinned as I scrolled down the list of titles, all Harry Potter-related, of course. They had to be, with a username like that.

"This is literal torture," Aiden complained as he watched me click on the most recent story (written only a month ago, I should add). "Don't sit there and read it in front of me!"

"Why not? I want to join your avid readership."

Aiden grabbed my phone and clicked the screen off before tossing it back in my lap. "You can read that later. I know where we need to go."

"Where?"

He just smirked and said nothing, clearly reveling in lording our destination over me. Well, after the fan fiction reveal, I couldn't really blame him—he needed a win.

He pulled onto the main road in town and drove for two minutes before stopping at one of the only small shopping centers we had, all the buildings a dingy pale yellow in desperate need of a new paint job. "Grocery shopping, Aiden? Color me unimpressed."

"No, over there." He took me by the chin and turned my face in the opposite direction, to the rundown shop in the corner of the complex.

My pulse quickened at the feel of his fingers on me. I smacked his hand out of the way and squinted at the sign, trying to read it, which was nearly impossible since half of the neon letters were burned out. "A comic book store?"

"The hidden gem of Pearson," Aiden said proudly. "Come on, you'll love it." He pulled into a parking spot and hopped out of the car, practically bouncing on the balls of his feet. I followed a few steps behind him, bracing myself for the dimly lit shop full of limited editions in crisp plastic sleeves, and a manager named Steve who knew the history of every single issue of *The Amazing Spider-Man* in chronological order.

"Jeff!" Aiden called over the door chime as we walked into the store (Steve, Jeff—I was pretty close), which had much better lighting than I'd assumed it would.

"Is that Aiden I hear?" The voice came from behind a register on a counter completely overloaded with stacks of comics. "Well, I'll be. I haven't seen you in ages." A thin, wrinkled face popped out from behind a teetering column of *Justice League* that looked dangerously close to falling over. "What brings you in?"

"Just browsing," Aiden answered, nudging me forward. "I brought a new recruit."

Jeff grinned and leaned on the counter, tipping his square glasses down his nose. "Are you ready to begin the initiation process?" he asked in a low voice as he blinked at me from under his bushy gray eyebrows. He had on a starchy, white collared shirt that was buttoned all the way to the top, and when he stepped around the counter to reveal his jean shorts and cowboy boots, I was so distracted I all but forgot what he'd asked me. Jeff's juxtaposition made my eyes hurt—but somehow it worked on him.

"I—um, what?" I took a step back and bumped straight into Aiden's chest.

He laughed and I could feel the sound of it rumbling against my back. "It's a joke, Josephine. This isn't a cult, it's a bookstore." He put a hand on the small of my back and led me over to the nearest shelf. "Take a look."

My skin was tingling where Aiden had touched me. To avoid looking at his face, I crouched down to scan the titles on the lower shelves, but Aiden had already wandered away to look at a bookcase across the aisle that seemed to be on the verge of tipping over, it was so overstuffed.

I had to admit, the store was actually very cool. It had a lost-in-time kind of feel to it, with cushy reading chairs stuck into random corners and endless towers of comics to choose from. It was the kind of place you could easily lose track of an entire afternoon.

With Aiden's back to me, I started looking through the comics in earnest. While the movies tended to be a little on the over-dramatic side for my taste, I couldn't deny my interest in the storytelling. I picked up a worn-out issue of *Wonder Woman* and started to read.

"Did you know Wonder Woman was first introduced way back in 1941?"

I turned around to see Jeff standing behind me. He was shorter than I'd realized, barely coming up to my shoulders. "Lots of Nazis in these comics, just so you know," he said in a gentle warning voice.

I stifled a laugh. "Yeah, I've noticed that."

He blinked owlishly and gave me a shy smile. "You're Josephine Crew, right?"

First Applebee's, now this; it was impossible to remain anonymous in Pearson. I couldn't seem to outrun my last name no matter how hard I tried. "Yes?" My answer came out like a question.

"I thought so. Your dad talks about you all the time. I hear you're quite the brain, very talented. A bit like Diana here, hmm?" he said, tapping the cover of the issue I was reading.

My mouth opened and closed uselessly. I couldn't decide which part was more shocking: my dad reading comics, my dad being friends with Jeff, or my dad talking about me while reading comics with said friend Jeff.

Jeff looked at me curiously, as if he was waiting for me to be as impressive as my father said I was, but all I could do was stand there completely flabbergasted. "Um, okay," was the only thing I could think to say.

He shrugged and ambled away, his boots clicking on the floor while he whistled along to the Joni Mitchell song playing on his ancient radio. My hands fell to my sides, the comic book dangling in my limp grip. The sad thing was I didn't know if this was something my dad did in the alternate reality, or if he came here in our timeline too.

I didn't really know him all that well. But, apparently, he knew me. Much more than I thought he did, at least. That realization left my eyes stinging and my throat feeling too tight. I jumped when Aiden tapped me on the shoulder and hurried to wipe my nose on my sleeve. I wondered if he'd heard what Jeff had said to me.

"I knew you'd like it here." Aiden smiled and gestured to the issue of *Wonder Woman* still held in my hand.

"It's all right," I said as I gingerly set the comic back down, not wanting to reveal exactly how much I loved this weird cozy store with its chairs and crackling radio and Jeff and his boots.

Aiden's gaze turned scrutinizing when I sniffed once again. "Are you okay?"

"I'm fine. It's just really dusty in here."

He glanced over his shoulder. "Did Jeff say something?" he asked in a low voice. "I love the guy, but he doesn't have the sharpest people skills. He spends too much time alone—"

"And not enough time dusting. I told you, I'm fine." I tried to brush past him, but he crossed his arms and blocked the aisle. His shoulders filled the narrow space and left me no choice but to stay where I was even though I was more than ready to move on from his inquiry and the strange ache in my chest. "Is this how you usually wow the ladies? Fine dining at Applebee's followed by impressing them with your nerdy knowledge?"

As soon as the words left my mouth, I realized I was grouping myself in with all his flirtations and conquests. I stared at the shelves behind him, pretending to scan the titles and resisting the humiliating urge to cover my burning face with my hands.

"I've never brought anyone here," he said simply, waiting until I looked him in his hazel eyes. "Come on, I want to show you something." He pulled me by the arm to the back of the store where the shelves were even dustier and the music was nothing but the faint hint of a song.

"Pretty cool, right?" He pointed to the oldest editions that were held in glass cases, their illustrations faded from time and all the fingers that had gripped them too tightly. I was a sucker for old books, no matter what kind they were. And apparently Aiden was too. It was odd seeing him like this, all lit up like a kid at Christmas. He was animated as he pointed to the different issues he'd read, telling me which ones he wished he could afford to take home with him.

"So which Marvel movies are your favorite?" he asked. "Since you're such an expert."

I rolled my eyes. "I'm not an expert—"

"Wait, pause. Say that again, but nice and slowly this time. I want to savor it."

"Oh, shut up." I tried to punch him on the arm, but he easily blocked me. His long fingers wrapped around mine, squeezing gently before dropping my hand.

I looked away first and cleared my throat noisily. "*Doctor Strange*, I guess. Until he joins up with the Avengers, that is." I shuddered at the thought. Those movies were my nightmare (far too much teamwork). One corner of Aiden's mouth turned up. "Interesting."

"And why is that interesting?"

"You chose a story with a brilliant, highly driven but egotistical main character. Hmm, I can't see why you'd identify with that." His voice was buried under so many layers of sarcasm I lost count.

In less than a second, my entire body was flooded with all-consuming indignation. It burned through me as my eyes narrowed into slits and my mouth popped open to retort.

"I'm kidding!" Aiden said, shaking me by the shoulders. He laughed and the other side of his mouth curved up into a full grin. "You should see your face right now. It's kind of terrifying." He leaned in closer and smiled even wider. "Absolutely terrifying," he said again but in a much softer voice.

I huffed and looked away, feeling stupid for my overreaction. "Of course it was a joke. Except for the part about me being brilliant and driven."

Aiden rubbed the back of his neck, looking like he was about to start laughing again. "Anyway, I think you'd like the actual comics. Obviously, their storytelling is superior to any movie—"

"Obviously. Rose has banned me from talking during most movies because she says I start every sentence with, 'well, the book was better...'"

And with that, we fell into a lively debate over movie interpretations and artistic license. We stood across from each other, both of us leaning against the display case as we took turns abusing the movies that had ruined our favorite books. I complained about *The Giver*; Aiden could hardly find words to express his disappointment in the *Percy Jackson* franchise; and we both agreed that turning *The Hobbit* into three separate movies was unforgivable.

I don't know how long we stayed like that in the musty backroom of Jeff's store. It felt like ages; it seemed like a blink. But our conversation never turned into a fight, and for once neither of us were trying to prove a point. We were just talking. Almost like we were friends. Or something similar.

My face flushed when I realized I'd been studying the way he moved his hands when he spoke. How he nodded along when I said something he liked, his lips quirked like he was a second away from laughing. Or the way that dimple on his cheek would appear in a flash, then disappear just as quickly. I was so distracted that I actually forgot to scowl or make a rude remark when he interrupted me. Instead I just waited, genuinely curious about what he would say next. Surprisingly curious.

"You know, my brother loved comics," Aiden said quietly. "My brother Wes." He tapped his fingers against the glass and stared down at the faded editions below us.

I stiffened and held my breath, waiting for him to say more. This was the first time I'd ever heard Aiden say a word about his older brother. I knew next to nothing about the situation, only that he didn't like to talk about it. I waited for him to go on, to give me something. But he didn't. He just scuffed his foot on the old, checkered linoleum, his face drawn and sad.

"I bet you miss him," I said slowly, dragging out the words while I tried to think of something else to say. I circled around the display case to stand next to him.

"Every single day."

"I'm sorry," I said. And I meant it. We stood shoulder to shoulder in the silence, both of us lost in thought. I wanted to be patient, to let Aiden steer the conversation, but too many questions were climbing up my throat and nearly spilling out of my mouth. I couldn't stop thinking about the trophy case at Pearson High. "Aiden," I said, hesitantly, unsure how to ask what could potentially be an awkward question, "is your brother—"

But I swallowed my words when I saw how he was looking at me. He had that same wild look in his eyes that he'd had that day at debate practice—the day when he'd wanted to kiss me but didn't.

Aiden raised his hand, hesitating a moment before letting it land softly on my face. He cupped my cheek in his warm palm, letting his fingers drag along the ridge of my cheekbone. I froze as all the air left my lungs. My stomach dipped all the way down to my toes as heat rushed into my face, pooling at the very spot he was touching me.

"Truth or dare," he whispered.

I couldn't answer. I knew what he wanted me to choose.

He was waiting for my permission; he was waiting for my surrender.

I tried to find my voice, but it had left the building. All I could think about was Aiden's hand on my cheek and the fact that he was hovering only a few inches away from me, asking me questions with his eyes that I didn't know the answers to.

This wasn't the kind of thing I'd ever prepared for. No amount of studying could've helped me in this moment.

If Aiden Christopher Mitchell III is leaning in like he's about to kiss you, do you:

a. Let him
b. Slap him in the face, or
c. Run far, far away

Option C was looking pretty good right now. I didn't like how out of control I felt, with how hard my heart was pounding, how sweaty my hands were, or how I was leaning in too.

I didn't like that I wanted to choose option A.

So I pulled back, turned on my heel, and ran right past the dusty aisles, past Jeff and his eyebrows dancing to Bon Jovi, and out the front door.

I waited for the sounds of footsteps in my wake, or a hand to grab me by the shoulder and ask me to stay. But all I heard was my own feet hitting the cracked pavement, and I didn't feel any hands reaching out to stop me.

Aiden didn't follow, so I just kept running.

Point to Mitchell.

I was pretty sure I was in the negatives by now.

Nineteen

I WENT FROM one place of books to another.

I didn't know where else to go. I didn't want to go back to school, and I didn't want to go to my house, so I went to the one place I truly felt at home. After walking through the town square for all of five minutes in the too-hot-for-October weather, I was actually glad Pearson was so small and I could get wherever I wanted to on foot relatively quickly. It wasn't raining anymore, but the air was muggy and warm as I crossed the lawn to the public library. The small but tidy gray stone building was nearly as old as Pearson itself, its tall, arching windows winking merrily at me in the barely-there sun.

When I walked through the library's heavy oak doors, my body instantly relaxed. The smell alone revived me like nothing else could. I pulled in deep lungfuls of musty air, the scent of old paper and generic cleaning products more potent than even the strongest smelling salts.

If there was going to be one place I missed when I left Pearson, this would be it.

I was five years old when my mom brought me and Rose to the library for the first time. We were temporarily involved with a play-group until she realized that "playgroup" wasn't a secret code for "drop your kids off and go get your hair done." We only went to one meet-up before Mom called it quits. I don't remember everything about that day, but I do remember her wrinkling her nose at the smell and vowing that she would never set foot in the library again.

Even at the young age of five, I could tell that my mom and I were different. She didn't like the things I liked, and I didn't like the things she liked. But I still tried to please her, to impress her, to get her to notice me. I watched the other mothers at the playgroup doting on their darling daughters—reading them books with their arms wrapped around their tiny shoulders—and wondered what I was doing wrong.

I asked her to read to me. Her lips puckered into a pout as she glanced at the old clock ticking on the wall and took the book with a sigh. I sat next to her on the vinyl-covered couch as she thumbed through the story, skipping words and entire pages at a time. I remember tugging on her sleeve, ready to tell her that she wasn't reading it right when she said, "Josie, you know Mama hates to read. It's just not my cup of tea." She tossed the book in my lap and slumped in her seat.

Her eyes were wary as she watched the other moms at the library, women from our town who were a little older, a little wiser, a little more experienced than she was. She reapplied her lipstick and straightened her back, holding her chin up high. "Now, go stop your sister from throwing all those books everywhere." She pointed over to where Rose was hyperactively yanking everything off the shelves with the other toddlers wreaking havoc. Mom's eyes flicked over to the clock again.

I knew right then and there that she wouldn't be bringing me back to the library anytime soon, and that thought made me sad. I loved the orderly aisles of books with their colorful spines all lined up in careful rows. I loved that it was so quiet you could even hear the crisp turn of a page.

And I think some part of me loved it because my mom didn't.

So I marched over to the librarian's desk and got myself a bright yellow library card. I held that little plastic rectangle lightly in my grip, feeling like I was holding the world in my hands.

I didn't need anyone to read to me. I could read to myself.

The library hadn't changed much in the years since then. It was small and understocked, but I still loved it; it was one of the few places where being alone didn't feel lonely.

I roamed the narrow aisles, trying unsuccessfully to keep my low-key panic at bay. Normally, I reveled in the quiet of the library, its always-reliable peacefulness, but today it was too much. I needed something to distract me from my racing thoughts, not a deafening silence that made my whispered worries sound like someone had handed them a megaphone.

I tried to browse for something new to read, but I felt hot and restless, picking up books at random and setting them back down without bothering to crack any open. After agitatedly working my way through the entire library three times, I finally gave up perusing and pulled out my phone. I almost called Rose or Cat, but my finger hovered over the call button uselessly. I wanted them to come down here and remind me how much I hated Aiden, to listen to me bring up all our past grievances as I ranted about how much he annoyed me and got under my skin.

But then I thought about him smiling as I sang karaoke and the way he scanned the shelves of comics while joking with Jeff, his face open and curious.

That Aiden got under my skin in an entirely different way.

I knew it wouldn't work if I called my sister and Cat to come rescue me. I could already picture them exchanging glances like they'd known this would happen all along. So instead of calling anyone, I tapped on my phone's web browser and found myself scrolling through Aiden's fan fiction. I curled up in one of the moth-eaten armchairs and started to read.

Of course it was good. I always knew Aiden was a good writer (much to my dismay). He had a deeply relatable voice that made the dialogue snap into place like the crack of a whip. He plucked at plot holes I'd never previously questioned, unraveling them until they became something new. As I read through his stories, I saw how he took the characters I knew and loved and turned them into something else. Not in a bad way, but in a way that made me miss my ten-year-old self with an overwhelmingly sharp pang of nostalgia.

And he'd made Hermione the hero.

Of course he actually did have an engaged readership. They peppered him with questions and asked when new chapters were going to be posted. And he took the time to respond to every single one of them, no matter how ridiculous some of the comments were.

Suddenly, this wasn't funny anymore. My chest felt tight as I shut my phone off and closed my eyes. I groaned as I smacked my head onto the non-fiction shelf behind me.

"What's the matter? The history of the Transcontinental Railroad got you down?" My back stiffened at the sound of Mrs. Grady—Pearson's omnipresent and wizened librarian—coming from the aisle behind me. I immediately jumped to my feet. There was something about her that made it impossible to sit in her presence.

There were rumors that she lived at the library—no one ever saw her anywhere else. Her shoulders were permanently hunched like she was always protectively bent over her books. And even though I'd never returned a single book late or damaged, she still didn't like me.

But she didn't like anyone.

"Sorry, Mrs. Grady—"

"Aren't you supposed to be in school, young lady?" she wheezed while stacking books back on the shelf from the rickety cart she pushed around. With a pointed frown at me, she straightened the ones I'd accidentally knocked over when I'd smacked my head on the shelf.

"Free period," I lied, chewing on my lip.

She looked at me skeptically through the space between book spines, but she must've seen the mix of shame and humiliation on my face, so she left me in peace with only the sound of her squeaking cart as a response.

I deflated against the bookshelf and sighed.

What was I doing? Everything was spinning out of control. I wanted to gather up all the pieces of my life and hold them tightly to my chest, to rearrange them back into their familiar pattern and let them be.

I wanted to put everyone back inside their tidy little boxes. Including me.

And especially Aiden.

Insufferable, infuriating Aiden.

I made sure Mrs. Grady was nowhere in sight before I started rearranging the books by color. Sometimes I did that when I was stressed or needed to clear my head (maybe I really should take up yoga). The books felt cold and heavy in my hands as I worked my way through the rainbow. Maybe it wasn't the colors themselves that I enjoyed;

maybe it was the cleanup afterward. The Dewey Decimal System is a cure-all for overthinking.

"Fancy meeting you here."

The sound of Aiden's whisper sent a shiver up my spine. I slowly turned to face him. He was leaning against the shelf opposite of mine with his arms folded over his chest, watching me sort through the piles of books.

"How'd you know I was here?" I asked in a hushed voice.

"I thought to myself, 'what would Josephine Crew do if she could do anything in the whole wide world with zero consequences? Hmm, I know—maybe rearrange books at the library and torment poor Mrs. Grady.'" His mouth tipped into a smirk.

I hated that I couldn't stop looking at his mouth.

I narrowed my eyes and waited for him to tell me how he actually found me.

"I texted Cat, and she texted your sister," he said sheepishly. "Rose used Find My iPhone and tracked you here."

I pulled my silenced phone out of my pocket and, sure enough, the screen was blinking from Rose's tracking and about a hundred messages from both her and Cat that all contained too many emojis and exclamation points.

The little traitors.

"Okay, you found me. So what."

So what if maybe I want to kiss you again.

I screamed internally and Aiden blushed as if he was remembering his words at the exact same moment I was. I felt off-balanced and out of focus. Like I couldn't remember how to play the game.

Or what the point of the game was in the first place.

"Look, Josephine, we don't have to—"

"Truth or dare," I blurted, cutting him off.

I thought he'd argue and say it wasn't my turn to ask, but he sighed and ran a hand through his hair, making the back of it stick up. I wanted to reach out and smooth it down. I wanted to—

I shook my head, trying to clear it. We needed to get out of this dimly lit library with all its quiet solitude and private corners and delicious-smelling books before I did something that was incredibly stupid, and that I would most certainly regret.

"Dare," he finally said, his voice a challenge.

"I dare you to tell Mrs. Grady you've had a crush on her for years, and that you've only just worked up the nerve to tell her."

My cheeks flamed at the words *crush* and *years*, *nerve* and *tell her.*

Something was seriously wrong with me.

Aiden didn't even blink. He marched off down the aisle with me following in his wake, listening for the sound of Mrs. Grady's squeaking cart until he found her in the romance section (of course).

"Mrs. Grady!" She shushed him and went back to her shelving. Aiden swiveled the cart around until he was facing her. "Mrs. Grady, I have a confession."

"Young man, you owe this library $13.89 in late fees. Have you come to settle your balance?"

I croaked out a loud laugh and nearly sank to the floor. Aiden stammered out an apology and took out his wallet, fishing through it until he found enough change to cover his fines.

"Thank you. You and Ms. Crew are excused from the premises until you can both show a bit more restraint and decorum." She turned away without another word, her tight gray bun vanishing behind the next aisle over.

I took out my phone and snapped a picture of his stunned face. "I call this one 'Boy, Interrupted,'" I said, cackling into my hands.

Aiden smiled his best and biggest smile, just like the first day I saw him in the sixth grade. It's the kind of smile that made me sit up a little taller, the kind that made me wonder what I needed to do to keep him smiling at me like that.

"Are we good?" he asked softly.

"Are we ever?"

He paused for a moment. "Fair point. You want to get out of here?"

The sound of Mrs. Grady's cart was coming down the aisle again.

"Definitely," I said as we sprinted out the door.

The clouds hadn't let up all day; they still hung heavy and low in the sky, drooping with the potential for another downpour. The air was hot and humid, making my clothes stick to my skin as I climbed into Aiden's truck.

School was just getting out. It was strange to think that I'd been there only this morning, listening to Aiden convince me that reality was flexible, and that time had cracks in it.

I was starting to forget that this wasn't real. At least for us, anyway.

Aiden started to drive even though we hadn't decided where to go next. If I thought getting out of the library was my safest bet, I was seriously an idiot. Being in the small, enclosed space of Aiden's truck was much, much worse. We kept stealing glances at each other while our arms brushed across the center console, but neither of us moved. We just stayed like that, barely touching and barely speaking.

This was worse than fighting. Much, much worse.

"Truth or dare," Aiden said at last, breaking the silence.

"Truth."

"What are you most afraid of?"

I let my head tip back against the seat as I stared out the window. The obvious answer would be needles. Or I could just as easily say that I was afraid of the dark or clowns or big hairy spiders, but the truth tumbled out before I could stop it. "I'm afraid that I'm just a big fish in a really tiny pond."

I could feel Aiden's eyes boring into the back of my head, but I didn't turn around. I kept staring out the window, watching the familiar landmarks of Pearson roll on by. The churches on every corner, the rusty water tower, the 7-11 where Dad used to take Rose and me to get Slurpees when we were young. The yawning patches of land were flat and open, tired and lonely looking.

What if this was the only view I'd ever know?

"That's not possible," he said back quietly.

I let his words sink in, settling deep inside me as I closed my eyes and asked, "Truth or dare?"

"Truth."

We drove in circles around the town, asking each other questions we'd never taken the time to ask before. I learned that Aiden has a deep hatred of mustard, that he'd broken his left arm three separate times, and that he rereads *The Lord of The Rings* every Christmas. He found out that I'm allergic to strawberries, that I've never broken a bone or had stitches, and that I watch *Little Women* when I feel sad.

The longer we talked, the more things I wanted to tell him. I could feel my mouth moving in an endless stream; I could hear myself revealing things I'd never planned on telling anyone, especially not Aiden. But still, I didn't stop. There was just something about this day. I felt cracked open and tipped over; now everything was spilling out. So we kept on driving and filled the truck with our secrets, the tiny things that added up to make us who we are.

He asked me which university was my dream school. "Columbia," I said with a wince, hoping that I hadn't just jinxed myself. "What about you?"

He paused and rubbed the hard angle of his jaw before setting his arm back down next to mine on the center console. "University of Texas," he said after a minute. "It's my dad's alma mater."

I tried not to scrunch my nose, but I must've because Aiden rolled his eyes. "Not everyone wants to leave Texas, you know."

"But don't you want to go somewhere new? Try something different?"

Aiden's phone rang before he could answer, breaking the stiff silence that was slowly starting to strangle us. He glanced down at his phone and sighed. "Hey Mom," he said once he answered. He listened to her talk for a minute, driving with one hand on the wheel. "Okay, okay," he mumbled, darting a glance at me. "I'll go get them. It's fine. Yeah, I'll still have time to do the parade."

The parade. How could I have forgotten? I felt an intense urge to go to the school parking lot to make sure Caleb didn't destroy the float I'd been working so hard on. My hands were itching to hold the hot glue gun, to make sure all the details were properly in place.

Aiden hung up his phone and flipped a U-turn in the middle of the road. "I gotta go pick up Beau and Lacy from school. My mom is stuck at the hospital and my dad's still at work."

I watched him out of the corner of my eye as he drove, trying to ignore the nagging question that kept popping up every time Aiden shared another truth with me. We'd kept up a steady conversation over his likes, his dislikes, and everything in between. He'd easily woven in stories about his family, bringing up his parents and his little brother and sister multiple times—but only mentioning Wes's name once. I chewed on the inside of my cheek, debating for a moment whether or not I should ask. But my curiosity won out in the end.

"What about Wes?"

Aiden's face froze and he stared out the windshield; his one hand on the steering wheel was gripped so tightly, his knuckles were white. "My brother Wes isn't here," he said in a small voice.

I immediately regretted asking the question. Just hearing him say the words out loud made my chest expand in a strange way. It filled me up until I couldn't stop myself from reaching out and resting my hand on Aiden's. He hesitated for a split second before flipping his hand over so it was palm up and tangled my fingers with his, squeezing me lightly. We drove like that for a while, neither of us mentioning the fact that we were holding hands. A comfortable silence stretched between us until all thoughts of his siblings and the homecoming parade had floated away.

My mind was empty except for the parts of my brain that handled nerve signals and synapses. That part was lit up like the sky on the Fourth of July as Aiden slowly moved his thumb in a circle across my skin. Every other part of me ceased to exist in that moment. I was now fully contained to my left hand, folded into Aiden's, our fingers laced together and pulsing in time with the rhythm of our heartbeats.

□ □ **C H A P T E R**
Twenty

I LOOKED UP in surprise to see that we'd already arrived at Pearson Elementary school. I chanced a glance at Aiden and saw that he looked a little dazed too, like he didn't remember driving here. We both looked down at our hands still entwined on the center console. Aiden inhaled sharply and turned to face me at the precise moment the back doors of his truck were thrown open and the two miniature Aidens hopped into the backseat.

Aiden frowned as I pulled my hand out of his grasp, but before he could say anything, his sister Lacy squealed, "Are you taking us to get ice cream?"

Beau and Lacy immediately popped their heads over our seats and started begging, their tongues lolling out like rabid little puppies. It was disturbingly effective. Aiden groaned, but it turned into a laugh. "All right, all right. Fine. Just quit making those faces at me before I agree to anything else."

The two blondes in the backseat cheered and wiped the drool off their faces before sliding into their seats. As Aiden pulled out of the school parking lot, they jabbered on and on about their days, only pausing to ask questions about tonight's parade and game. Aiden must've seen me rolling my eyes every time they said the word "homecoming," but he didn't comment on it.

"Are you Aiden's girlfriend?" Lacy asked, her pigtails swinging as she held her hands up to her chest. "He talks about you *all* the time," she crooned.

"Only to complain," Aiden said to me, but he added a wink.

I could still feel the shape of his hand around mine. I sat on it so I didn't do anything else stupid.

"No, I'm not his girlfriend. I'm just here for the ice cream."

That sent them back into their cheering madness. Aiden grinned at me, and my heart somersaulted in my chest. We pulled up to Dairy Queen where we ordered four Oreo Blizzards. He then drove over to a small park nearby, and Lacy and Beau ran with their ice creams straight to the playground. Aiden and I walked over to the swings and sat down, watching the wild things do the monkey bars.

"Truth or dare," he said in between mouthfuls of Blizzard.

I still didn't trust him with a dare. Or me. "Truth."

"Why do you really hate homecoming?"

His question surprised me. It caught me off guard in such a way that the truth came bubbling up before I could stop the words from coming out. "Because my mom loves her homecoming crown more than she loves me."

I clamped my mouth shut as Aiden and I looked at each other, our swings slightly swaying in the warm, rain-scented breeze. His face softened, which was exactly what I didn't want to happen. I didn't want anyone feeling sorry for me.

Especially him.

He let the moment pass without comment. He just tucked away my answer like he was saving it for later. Probably to use against me in a future argument.

"Truth or dare," I asked after a long moment.

"Truth."

Beau shrieked as Lacy pushed him down the tallest slide; Aiden smiled. I stirred my soupy blizzard around a few times as I watched him watching them. "What happened to Wes?"

He slumped on his swing and set his spoon down, letting his ice cream rest on his thigh. "He died in a car accident. He swerved and hit a tree."

A horrible, pointless accident.

He didn't look away from the playground when he said it. His eyes stayed trained on his little brother and sister as he gently kicked off the ground and sent his swing rocking in a graceful motion. My Blizzard soured in my stomach, making me feel sick. "Aiden," is all I could think to say. I didn't say anything else because what is there left to say when the unimaginable happens?

"I like it when you say my name," he whispered. He finally looked up at me, his hazel eyes the only spot of brightness in the storm threatening to spill open overhead.

"Aiden Christopher Mitchell III," I said back, just as softly.

"No. Just Aiden."

Our swings fell into a similar rhythm as we swayed back and forth. I broke the silence first. "Can I ask you something?"

"That depends on the question."

"Why didn't your older brother get the name? Why wasn't he Aiden Christopher Mitchell III?" I'd been wondering that ever since I'd found out that Aiden wasn't actually the firstborn.

Thunder crashed loudly in the distance and Lacy screamed. Aiden and I both jumped and almost dropped our forgotten half-eaten Blizzards.

"Because my mom liked the name Wes." His lips twitched but I couldn't tell if it was a smile or a frown. "She always wanted to name her son Wes."

"Tell me more about him."

Aiden eyed me carefully like he wasn't quite sure why I was interested in hearing more about his brother.

"Please," I added with a small smile, trying to look reassuring.

Aiden toyed with the scattered wood chips beneath his feet as we continued to swing back and forth. He was a little stilted at first, as if he hadn't spoken out loud about Wes in a long time. But the longer he spoke, the more relaxed he became until eventually all his self-conscious sadness was wiped from his face and replaced with an easy affection that reminded me of his mom. "Wes knew how to throw a football before he knew how to walk," he said with a chuckle.

He told me stories about them growing up together in East Texas, with a sprawling backyard so big they could almost get lost in it (and sometimes did). His eyes drifted out of focus as he remembered forts built and fought over, all the movies they watched on repeat, and the summers spent at his grandma's house near the Piney Woods. He told me that with Wes being four years older than him, he'd always looked up to his big brother, that it was impossible not to.

"When I started getting the headaches along with the enhanced memory, he didn't treat me differently like our parents did. He thought it was awesome." Aiden looked up wistfully at the sky. "He used to show me a page out of a book for less than five seconds, and then have me repeat it to him, word for word. It was a game we'd play—he loved it. That's when he got me into comic books; he thought maybe I could relate to some of the freakish characters," he said with the ghost of a smile. "He was the kind of guy people always liked. He was confident and funny, charismatic and easy to be around, you know? He made people feel good."

"Hmm, it sounds like Golden Boys run in the family," I said before I could stop myself.

But Aiden only snorted and shrugged. "It was easier for Wes than it is for me."

My lips pursed into a frown. "What are you talking about, you're exactly the same. You sound just like him—well, except for the 'easy to be around' part. Personally, I find you very grating," I said with my chin held high and a very unconvincing sniff.

He laughed and swung his swing closer to mine so he could nudge me with his elbow. "Whatever you say, Josephine." But then his smile slowly melted off his face. "It was easier for Wes," he said again softly.

I watched him carefully swaying on his swing as I tried to unpack what all of it meant. What all of *Aiden* meant, every single syllable of him.

I thought about what it must be like for him, to be weighed down by a name so heavy with expectations. And how it must've been hard to follow in the footsteps of a brother who was given a name simply because their mother loved it. Loved him. A different sort of family bond without all the complicated shades of duty and obligation.

Our eyes met and I gave him a tiny nod, hoping it conveyed what I didn't know how to say. I knew what it was like to carry around a last name you weren't sure what to do with yet.

Thunder rumbled loudly overhead again. The tiny Aidens ran over to us, sticky and sweaty and ready to go home. As his brother and sister raced each other back to the truck, Aiden reached out and took my hand in his. "Thanks," he whispered.

"For what?" I asked with a tilt of my head.

"For asking. For listening." He threaded his fingers through mine, and my heart started pounding. "Honestly, I didn't know you were capable of being quiet for that long."

"You are ridiculous," I snapped. His eyes lit up with suppressed laughter as I yanked my hand out of his grip (and told my embarrassingly overactive heart to calm down). Leave it to Aiden to ruin what could've been a nice moment.

The two of us were quiet on the short drive to his house, but Lacy and Beau filled up the car with their noisy teasing and their unending chatter. Every time I would sneak a peek at Aiden, he was already looking at me. The air between us felt charged, all stirred up and agitated. I sat on my hands for the entire drive.

As we pulled into the driveway, he said over his shoulder, "All right, you two. Get out of here."

Beau made kissing sounds before he slammed the truck door and ran toward the house, both he and his sister howling with laughter. "*Josephine and Aiden, sitting in a tree...*" they sang out from the safety of the front porch.

"I said, get out of here!" Aiden yelled back in exasperation, before flopping back in his seat. I turned to look out the window before he could see my pink cheeks.

Just then, another car pulled up into the driveway and Aiden Christopher Mitchell II climbed out and walked over.

Aiden's father.

And he was wearing scrubs.

"Hey, thanks for picking them up, I wasn't going to make it to the school on time," he said once Aiden had rolled his window down. His dad smiled and ran a hand through his honey-colored hair in a gesture very much like his son's.

"No problem. But I did hop them up on sugar, so good luck with that."

Mr. Mitchell rubbed his forehead and sighed. "Your mother's going to strangle you. Then I'm next." He turned to me. "Josephine, right? What are you two up to? Homecoming prep?"

I nodded at the same time Aiden said, "Yeah, we gotta get to the parade, Dad."

"Sure thing. But stay off your feet, son," Mr. Mitchell said in a warning voice. "You've got a big game tonight—"

"I'm aware," Aiden replied woodenly, a forced smile on his face.

"Now, tonight when you get the ball, you need to…" Mr. Mitchell rambled on and on about passing and running and yardage and touchdowns, and a bunch of other things I didn't know about and didn't care to either. Aiden nodded along, letting his dad do most of the talking and offering little in the way of responses. I was starting to zone out from pure boredom when the air rippled around his truck and the sound of muted whispers filled the air along with that faint tearing sound.

His dad didn't seem to notice the changes as he reminded Aiden that the recruiter from UT was going to be at Pearson High tonight. "Just play the game you always play, and they'll be begging to have you," he finished as he slapped the hood of the truck and grinned at Aiden. "Well, you two go have fun, but stay off those feet!" he reminded one last time before throwing us a double thumbs up and jogging over to the house where Lacy and Beau jumped into his arms as soon as he opened the front door.

The air tightened around us, relentlessly squeezing in a slow pulling motion that left me clutching the side of my door and panting for breath. All of Aiden's warnings about falling into familiar patterns and old habits rose to the surface as he put his truck in reverse and sped out of the driveway, moving away from whatever was happening in front of his house. He didn't say anything while we drove. Raindrops pelted the windows as the clouds finally burst, no longer able to hold themselves together.

"So, your dad," I said once the air had stilled and settled around us, and once my heart had returned to its normal place in my chest. "He's still a doctor in this timeline." I wiped my sweaty hands on my jeans and sank into my seat.

"Yep."

Aiden didn't elaborate, he just chewed on the side of his cheek and stared out the wet windshield. He must've had the exact same conversation with his dad before the homecoming parade yesterday. And today, Aiden slipped up and repeated it, word for word. Nod for nod.

Once he'd pulled into the Pearson High parking lot, he finally glanced at me and loosed a deep breath. "Here's a truth for you: I don't really like football all that much." After his confession, his face was dipped in such guilt and embarrassment, I wondered if he'd ever said that out loud before.

I slapped a hand over his mouth and his eyebrows shot up in surprise. "Don't say that! Every time you speak such blasphemy in the great state of Texas, an angel loses its wings."

He huffed out a laugh and pried my hand off his face. He held it for a moment before letting me go. "You're funny, you know. Even when you're annoying me, you're always making me laugh. But that makes you even more annoying because sometimes I just want to be mad at you."

I grinned because I knew exactly what he meant.

"I swear I won't reveal your sordid little football secret. So why do you play if you don't like it?" I asked.

"Because it makes them happy." Them—his parents, our classmates, the great state of Texas.

"But it doesn't make you happy."

He shrugged. "Since when does that matter? We play the game because we're good at it," he said softly. Sadly. He wasn't talking about football anymore. "You know that better than anyone."

Twenty-One

WE DIDN'T MARCH in the parade; what was the point? Instead, Aiden and I raced to the football stadium and ran up the bleachers, dodging everyone we knew and ignoring our responsibilities to the school on this most sacred occasion of homecoming. We leaned over the railing at the top of the bleachers, watching the slow and clunky (not to mention comically disorganized) crawl of the trucks and trailers heading out of the school parking lot.

I felt a secret thrill watching everything unfold without me. It was like this one strange day had turned my entire life into confetti, and when I woke up here with Aiden, I'd thrown all the pieces into the air. Now I was watching each individual particle float gently back to earth, some scattering in the wind because they didn't matter nearly as much as I thought they did.

Our teachers taught, the floats floated, and tonight the marching band would march—all without me there, desperately clutching everything between my hands. It felt like a giant exhale to be standing there, shoulder to shoulder with Aiden. It was as if this heavy, pressing weight had shifted off my chest, and for once I could stand up straight, sit still, and watch the sunset.

I couldn't remember the last time I'd looked up at the sky just because it deserved to be noticed.

The rain had stopped, but the clouds still looked torn open in swirling shades of angry gray, with soft oranges and pinks spilling from their centers like a popsicle that had melted all over the sidewalk, dripping and sweet.

"Tell me more about the timeline," I said, turning to face Aiden.

We both held our breath when the student council float veered too close to the side of the road with Caleb grinning wildly behind the wheel.

"You've seen it," he said, gesturing around us. "What else do you want to know?"

"Do you usually go to school, or do you like to run off and Ferris Bueller it all day?"

Does today matter to you as much as it matters to me?

I gripped the railing tightly in my hands while Aiden considered. "It depends. Most of the time, I find something else to do. It's kind of risky to be so close to what I spend my normal day doing. But there are some things I want to repeat."

"Or do-over," I added.

"Exactly."

Like the moment at debate practice.

Neither of us mentioned it, but we didn't need to. It sat between us like an obnoxiously loud unanswered question. We both looked at each other out of the sides of our eyes as we leaned over the railing of the stadium seats. The lights on the field were already on, buzzing and too bright. The game was going to start soon, but Aiden hadn't said anything about it.

"We should practice for tomorrow," I said. "We don't want to wake up with everything back to normal and then completely bomb the tournament, right? We need to stay sharp. Keep our eyes on the prize. Finish strong." I was rambling and saying embarrassingly generic things that were better left to coaches and their pre-game locker room speeches.

Aiden tipped his head back and laughed. "Go, team, go."

My face flushed as I scowled and said, "You know what I mean. Do you want to practice or not?"

He tapped his chin and smirked. "I don't think I need to. But if *you* need to, by all means…"

He wasn't rising to the bait. I wanted to drag us back to our safest places—the debate stage, the classroom, the student council table with our gavel in hand. I wanted him to annoy me or fight with me so I didn't have to keep feeling this way. I didn't want to keep noticing the way the setting sun lit up his hair with a warm rosy glow or the way his eyes softened a little in the corners when I made him laugh.

And that freaking dimple. I really had to stop thinking about that or I was going to reach out my hand and touch it lightly with my finger.

So I started reciting our opening argument like a crazy person, launching fact after fact at him like they were hand grenades in my last-ditch effort at self-defense. The words flew out of me in a rush, as if the faster I said them, the further away from these feelings I would be. If I built a strong enough case, bulletproof and impenetrable, then I could crawl inside it and never look back.

Aiden watched me with a strange look on his face. He didn't time me or clock my words-per-minute pace. He just leaned back against the creaking chain-link fence and listened, his easy posture the complete opposite of mine.

By the time I'd finished, my chest was heaving and I was utterly exhausted. I wanted to sink inside myself like I always did when my heart felt too exposed, too ragged and raw. Because my grand plan didn't work (surprise surprise) and the more Aiden stared at me, the more I didn't want him to look away.

"If you give the argument like that tomorrow, then we'll win for sure. How could anyone refuse you?" he said.

I waited to see if he'd follow it up with an eye roll or sarcastic dig at me and my lack of research skills, but he must've meant it because all he did was smile softly. "You're a force, Josephine."

"Do I scare you?" I blurted out.

He raised one eyebrow. "Scare me?" he scoffed. "Never." But he slid his hands into his pockets like he was shoving the rest of his answer away from me.

"Never? I don't intimidate you?" I leaned in a little closer and his breathing hitched.

"Okay, fine," he said after a long pause. "Maybe you intimidate me. Just a tiny bit. Like a sliver. Only on my bad days, like if I'm sick or I didn't get enough sleep or—"

My shoulders slumped as I sagged against the railing next to him, bumping my elbow into his.

"What's wrong?" he asked, his brow furrowing.

I sighed. "Sometimes I get tired of trying so hard." I'd meant to say something about how all the boys at school were scared of me and there was nothing I could do about it, but what came out was that sad little truth instead.

"Me too," Aiden said, his sigh an echo to mine.

He didn't add anything else—he didn't need to. A simple sensation started in my chest, then rippled through me, warm and steady like the sunset shining in our faces.

This must be what it feels like to be perfectly understood.

His hand found mine on the railing. He trailed a finger over the ridges of my knuckles as if he was memorizing the shape of them, like he wasn't in any rush to go anywhere else or *be* anyone else. It was a slow and aching feeling to know that we were here alone and that maybe, for once, we could stop acting like we had something to prove.

Aiden's eyes burned into mine and mine burned right back. "You have your game face on," he whispered.

"It's my only face," I muttered.

"No, you have a lot of different ones. Like that face you make when you're trying not to laugh even though you know I'm hilarious. Or your face when you're looking at your sister—soft, but a little bit fierce too. Or your classic Annoyed Face, which is the one you make any time Ms. Torrence tries to coach you on debate techniques."

I rolled my eyes and he laughed.

"But this one," his finger traced along the edge of my jaw, "is my personal favorite."

I shivered and took a step closer. "Ask me," I breathed.

His hand moved from my face to my hip, his fingers wrapping around me gently one by one. "Truth or dare." His eyes stayed trained on my mouth.

"Truth."

Aiden's grip on me loosened like he was going to let go. He deflated with disappointment; half his face lost in the shadows—like the last dregs of his hope had rushed out of him leaving him empty.

I grabbed his face and kissed him. For the first few seconds, we both had our eyes open, like we were still assessing the situation, unsure of the other's intentions. But then his eyes closed and his hands circled my waist as he responded to my kiss, and I forgot to think. I didn't wonder what it meant. I didn't ask myself what I was doing.

My brain almost shut off entirely.

Aiden kissed me the same way he argued—fervent and feverish. His mouth slid against mine as he tipped the kiss even deeper, demanding more and more of me. And I was finally willing to give it. We broke off the kiss at the same time and looked at each other with wide eyes before both of us burst into relieved laughter.

I used to think I was so smart, but obviously I'm nothing of the sort because if I really was, I would've done that a lot sooner. Aiden pressed his forehead to mine, our breath mixing in the barely-there space between us. I was pretty sure he was having the exact same epiphany as I was.

We were mirror images of wanting as we both leaned in again, finally in perfect agreement about something.

My hands tangled in his hair, tugging through his messy golden waves as he tightened his hold on me so I could feel the warmth of his fingers searing through my t-shirt. He pulled me closer until our thighs were brushing, our legs knocking noisily into the metal bleachers. It was our same old dance, only now it felt entirely new; a different kind of push and pull, of give and take.

I liked this version way better.

Aiden pulled back and looked at me with a hazy, half-crazed expression. "Never mind. This is my new favorite Josephine face. You look like you've just been hit over the head with a gavel." He laughed near my ear, sending a new wave of chills down my spine.

I tried to glare at him. "I'm sure you've imagined doing that a million times."

"Hitting you over the head with a gavel? No. Kissing you? Definitely."

"You liar. You have not."

Aiden kissed my cheek, then both my eyelids, my nose, and the side of my jaw, his lips leaving a trail of heat behind them. "Why do you think I've been working so hard to get your attention?"

His revelation stopped me short. My mind was racing, trying desperately to sort through years' worth of grudges and grievances. I examined all of our battles and shouting matches with a brand-new lens that I'd never once considered.

Aiden working hard to get my attention. Aiden trying to impress me. Aiden wanting to kiss me.

I scoffed, but it just brought our lips closer together and my breath stuttered. "You did a terrible job of trying to get me to like you."

"I never said I was good at it." He grinned before pressing another kiss to my jaw.

"So Golden Boy isn't good at everything," I said in an extremely self-satisfied way, even though my heart was in my throat. "Someone alert the media."

"I think I like you better when you're not talking."

"Nope, it's too late. You've already admitted that you're completely obsessed with me and—"

He interrupted me with a long kiss, and I raised zero objections as I threw my arms around his neck and kissed him back.

His lips tasted like spearmint and sweet relief.

"So, am I a better kisser than Brandon?" Aiden asked a while later.

"Hmm, your performance was reasonably well-done," I answered, imitating his not-so-high praise of me during debate practice.

Aiden snorted and put a step between us. "Well?"

"Why is it always a competition with you?" I smacked him on the chest, and he grabbed my hand and held it against his shirt. I could feel his heart racing. It would've made me feel smug if mine wasn't racing just as frantically.

"Says the girl who counts her blue ribbons every night before she goes to sleep," he quipped.

"Fine! Yes, Aiden, you're a better kisser than Brandon Lopez. You win."

"Say it again," he said with his best and widest grin.

"Oh, shut up—"

We both silenced the other with a kiss.

But Aiden was right (I still hate saying that). Because this kiss mattered when the other one didn't. Brandon kissed me like he knew how to kiss, but Aiden kissed me like he knew *me*.

And he wasn't going to run off screaming in terror, even if he was the tiniest bit afraid of me—just like I was of him.

Can you even call it falling if there isn't a little fear?

Twenty-Two

O H, GET A *room already.*

If only Tim Boren could see us now.

As if on cue, reality started creeping in with the sound of people milling under the bleachers, chatting loudly back and forth. Then I heard the one thing that could get me to stop making out with Aiden. Well, make that two things—my parents.

"Get down," I whispered shrilly as I yanked Aiden away from the railing. We crouched down on the top row of seats and peered through the gaps in the fence.

Why, when we had the entire town of Pearson available to us, did we choose our high school bleachers on the night of the homecoming game as the place to finally give in and admit that maybe we didn't actually hate each other? The same place where my parents were standing below us, huddled together with the rest of the alumni waiting to storm the field?

I went to tighten my ponytail but instead came back with handfuls of hair, wildly raked through by Aiden's fingers. My braid crown was toast. "My parents cannot see us. They're going to take one look at me, and they'll *know*. My mom has a sixth sense about this kind of thing."

"Know what?" he asked, only half-listening as he tugged on the hem of my t-shirt, pulling me closer.

"Aiden!" I snapped, wrenching out the last of the pins holding my braid in place. I ran my hands through my hair as it tumbled down in dark waves over my shoulders. Aiden's eyes went wide; I honestly didn't know if he'd ever seen my hair down before. "Focus! We need to get out of here."

The bleachers rumbled with the sudden sound of a flood of spectators climbing up the stairs. I grabbed him by the hand and pulled him in the opposite direction, down the less-crowded stairs on the other side of the stands—where we ran straight into my sister at the bottom.

There was no escaping my family.

I winced as Rose did a double-take, her mouth falling open exaggeratedly like a cartoon character. I tried to drop Aiden's hand but that only made him clutch mine more tightly in his. He didn't seem doubtful at all. He was completely confident and collected, like it was perfectly normal to kiss his nemesis on the bleachers. I, on the other hand, was slowly dying in a shame spiral. Rose chewed on her lip like she was trying not to laugh as she watched me squirm.

"This isn't what it looks like," I said, stalling.

Aiden snorted. "Actually, it's exactly what it looks like."

I could've strangled him.

Rose slowly looked me up and down once before her eyes settled squarely on my face. I was frozen under her sharp gaze, bracing myself for the onslaught of highly personal questions I definitely did not want to answer. "You look happy," she said simply, her mouth tilting into an easy smile.

Like that was all that mattered.

Was I happy?

I was still fumbling for something to say when Jordan Hernandez walked up and slung his arm around my sister's shoulders before handing her a giant soda in a Styrofoam cup. She beamed at him like he'd given her the world. "Hi," he said to us with a crooked smile.

Cat chose that moment to run over to us, her painted cheeks and glitter-covered hair sparkling under the stadium lights. She paused to smirk at my hand still entwined with Aiden's, her grin growing wide and toothy when she saw my beet red face, but then she got down to business. "Aiden!" she panted. "Ethan said Coach Callahan is freaking out—you're supposed to be in the locker room."

He blanched and loosened his grip on my hand. "I gotta go," he whispered.

"What? You're actually going to play?" I frowned as he shuffled his feet in the gravel.

"Of course he's going to play!" Cat said, fully caught up in the mania that is Texas football. "Get going!" she yelled at Aiden, clapping her hands loudly like she belonged on the sidelines with all the polo-clad coaches.

Rose danced around in her orange jumpsuit (apparently that heinous thing stayed the same no matter which timeline we were in). "Let's go find seats," she said, pulling on Jordan's arm. "Aren't you supposed to be in your very attractive marching band uniform?" she called back to me. "I miss the feather. Come find us before halftime!"

The three of them bounded up the bleachers, leaving Aiden and me alone but completely surrounded by people.

Of course he's going to play!

Supposed to, supposed to, supposed to.

I turned to face him. "What was all that talk about 'be who you want to be, Josephine!' We're in an alternate timeline, and you're *still* going to do something you don't want to do, because..."

I trailed off, waiting for him to explain himself. But he wasn't listening; he wasn't even looking at me. His eyes had gone all wide as he stared at something over my shoulder, his mouth pinched together in a tight line. Now he was the one who looked like he'd seen a ghost.

"Aiden!" a deep voice called out.

When I turned to see who it was, I was greeted by the sight of a tall blond boy. He looked like Aiden with a few more years added to him. And even though I'd only seen a picture of him once, I recognized him immediately.

Wes Mitchell, in the flesh.

I stumbled back and bumped into Aiden. He grabbed me by the elbow to steady me without looking away from his brother. "I didn't know you were coming tonight," he said to Wes. Aiden looked at him like a starving man at a buffet, his eyes bugging out of his face as he tried to take it all in.

"I wouldn't miss the big homecoming game," Wes said, slapping him on the back. He turned his bright blue eyes to me, assessing. "Josephine Crew." He said my name like he knew me. "Has my baby brother finally won you over?" he asked, raising his eyebrows at Aiden's hand still resting on my arm.

I opened and closed my mouth uselessly a few times; I was at a complete loss for words. Wes Mitchell was alive and well in this timeline, elbowing Aiden and smiling at me. I'd had my far-fetched suspicions all day, but seeing him standing there right in front of me was another thing entirely. And from the way he was grinning and all but winking at the two of us, it seemed like he knew a lot more about me than I knew about him. Like Aiden had actually confided in him that he *wanted* to win me over.

That little detail was almost as shocking as the whole Wes-is-here-in-this-timeline thing.

"Dad's going to lose it if he sees you're not in uniform yet," Wes said, giving his brother a light shove toward the field house. "Your girl isn't going anywhere; go change. I've gotta go meet up with the other honorary alumni. Good luck!" Wes ambled off like he did this kind of thing all the time—living, breathing, going to football games. The works. I watched the rest of the alumni greet Wes with cheers and more back-slapping. The prodigal son returned.

Aiden swallowed and finally spared me a glance.

I carefully placed a hand on his forearm. "I thought you said your brother had an accident."

"He did," Aiden said quietly, looking down. "Just not… here. He goes to school at UT in this timeline. I didn't think he'd come home for the game; I didn't think we'd see him today."

My hand slipped off his arm and fell back at my side, my brow furrowing as I thought back to Aiden's carefully chosen words before we'd picked up his younger brother and sister.

My brother Wes isn't here.

"But why didn't you just tell me?" I asked, thinking about Wes's name written in scrolling letters on the plaque in the trophy case.

"Because I've never told anyone." He hung his head, his face flushed and guilt-ridden. I knew he must've been thinking about all the moments he could've told me the truth today but didn't. "Look, I—I should've said…" He sighed and took me by the shoulders. "I should've said a lot of things. I just didn't know how."

There was once a time when hearing Aiden admit that he didn't know how to do something would've utterly delighted me. It would've made me feel powerful and victorious as I smugly added another tally mark to my scorecard. But now when I heard his admission, his small and tired confession, it didn't have the same effect on me like it once would've. It didn't make me feel like I was winning.

It just made my chest ache.

I took his hand in mine and gave it a squeeze. There were I lot of things I wanted to say, too. But I guess I didn't know how to either.

Aiden's face was lost in shadows as he turned away from me. "I've gotta go. Meet me here after the game." He started walking toward the locker room.

"Are you crazy?" I had to yell over the din of our classmates and the entire town of Pearson clambering across the metal bleachers, plus the off-beat rendition of "Crazy Train" the marching band had started playing above us (they weren't any better in this reality, unfortunately). "What about 'converging timelines' or whatever? If you go play, you'll play exactly the same game you did last time. Won't you."

It wasn't a question.

I could see the truth all over Aiden's face. He wouldn't be any less than his best in front of his parents, our school, our town—

In front of the brother who should've lived to see him play in the first place.

"I'll do things a little differently this time, it'll be fine," Aiden said, trying to sound self-assured. But he just sounded scared. He didn't know how to walk away; he didn't know how to disappoint the people he loved.

There was nothing I could do but watch him leave. I stood there for a minute, unsure where to go or what to do as Aiden marched with a stiff back toward the locker room and the team that depended on him. A sudden weariness fell over me, heavy and deep. I hated that Aiden wouldn't say no to everyone else even though he obviously wanted to. And mostly I hated that I understood why.

We play the game because we're good at it.

I pressed a hand to my mouth where Aiden had kissed me only a few minutes ago, surprised to realize that I missed him already—his voice, the low sound of his laugh, the heat of his body next to mine. My face flushed. The intensity of my awareness of him was humiliating. I barreled through the crowd, not really caring where I was going, but needing to move, to do something instead of standing there and feeling like someone who'd been left behind.

It's just a game, I told myself. *He's just playing the game.*

And then when it was all over we would... what? Go back to truth or dare? Go back to being people we're not?

I could still feel his hands on my waist and the smile on his lips as they pressed against mine.

My mom's lilting voice drifted over to me from across the bleachers. "How does my hair look, Bradley?" she asked, patting one manicured hand over her perfect curls.

"Fine, darling. It looks just fine." My dad hadn't even glanced back at her. He was too busy eyeing the field, waiting for the players to come out.

I dove behind the dumpster I'd been pacing near and hid like a coward, still certain that my mom would know I'd been kissed if she caught one glimpse of me. I peered around to see her pressing her hands down her too-short skirt, smoothing it into place. She turned to my dad, who was dressed in his best sports jacket, cowboy boots, and jeans. "Have you seen our girls yet?"

My heart sped up. *Our girls.* Me and Rose. She never referred to us like that, with ownership and a hint of pride.

My dad glanced around as if expecting to see Rose and me pop up next to them. "Nope, I haven't. Not yet." He straightened as someone called out to him in greeting, grabbing his hand in a hearty handshake. Dad seemed to grow a few inches when he was back under the stadium lights. He looked younger too. Lighter. Like he remembered who he was when he was back at the place where he'd been at his happiest. This version of him whistled along to the marching band (now playing "Eye of the Tiger") as students and faculty filed in to take their seats.

But as I watched my mom fluster and fidget over herself and my dad, I felt like I'd caught them in a strangely intimate moment. It was like seeing her without her makeup on (which rarely happened). She threw back her shoulders and I imagined her on this very field all those years ago, adjusting her crown and her satin sash, fixing her best gleaming pageant smile on her face.

Back when she thought the world was hers and she could do any-thing and be anything she wanted to be. But instead, she became a mother when she was barely older than me. Does it even count as growing up if the growing happens that quickly? Growth is slow and steady, something that happens over time like the sprouting of a ten-der plant. But for my parents? Their version of growing up was more akin to being shoved off a cliff, a swooping plunge into adulthood.

I don't know if they ever landed on their feet.

For the first time, I imagined what that had felt like—to fall in love before you were ready to, ushering in a lifetime of other things you weren't prepared for either. My heart thrummed as I glanced back and forth between them, their faces blurring into mine and Aiden's. I wondered if I knew what I was doing. If I was ready for feelings this big.

I wondered if any of that would matter by the end of this game; or if we'd even make it to the end of this game.

"Good evening folks, it's Tiger time here at Pearson High, and boy oh boy, is it going to be a good game tonight! Here comes our team onto the field, let's get on our feet and give them a proper welcome!" The drawling voice of the announcer was drowned out by the sound of stomping feet and adoring screams.

The stands exploded into thunderous applause as the players ran onto the field in a rush of purple and orange, a dizzying combo that should've made us all sick. I walked over to thé side of the low chain-link fence surrounding the permitter of the track that circled the bright green football field.

The best patch of grass in the otherwise dry town of Pearson, Texas.

I could see Aiden's family perched in their seats in the front row at the fifty-yard line. They cheered and yelled along with everyone else, none the wiser—Wes Mitchell the loudest of them all. And seated next to them was the recruiter from the University of Texas, shaking hands with Mr. Mitchell as they prepackaged Aiden's arranged future with a nice tidy bow.

Aiden shoved his helmet on and huddled with his teammates.

The ref blew the whistle, and everyone collectively held their breath.

I held my breath for the entirely different reason of waiting for the universe to crack in half and suck us into the endless void.

Aiden looked over his shoulder and found me. He nodded once.

And then he began to play.

Twenty-Three

I'D NEVER BEEN so invested in the outcome of a high school football game in my entire life.

I was about ready to paint my own face orange and purple and scream at the refs for every bad call if it meant that Aiden and I could walk away from this unscathed. I pressed against the fence, gripping it tightly in my hands. Turns out football is far more interesting when the stakes are higher—like possible timelines converging higher. My whole body felt tense and wound too tight as I stood on my toes and craned my neck, not wanting to miss a single second as the clock lit up and started counting down every painfully long minute of the first quarter.

"Our Tigers are ready to prove that they're the true kings of the jungle tonight. Come on, let's make some noise for our boys!" the commentator yelled into the crackling PA system as everyone cheered in response. Even though I still rolled my eyes, for once I wasn't trying to tune him out; I was focused on his every over-enthusiastic word.

It wasn't so bad at first.

Every time Aiden touched the ball it was like time stood still. He darted in and out between the players, engaged in a dance that I couldn't even begin to understand as he ran alternate routes, avoiding the same plays he'd executed the last time he'd played this game. His teammates ran in circles around him, their confusion obvious as he deviated from the previously called plays.

Well, at least that's what I thought he was doing; I wasn't watching all that closely last time.

"There's the handoff to Aiden Mitchell... that kid is moving so fast, no one can touch him... and he takes it all the way home, just like we knew he would! Touchdown Pearson!"

The stands erupted with euphoric cheers. I found myself joining in, clapping so hard my hands were stinging as Aiden ran back to the sidelines with his teammates, all of them chest-bumping and hollering just as loudly as their fans.

But poor Coach Callahan was agitated and fuming as he stood there in his tight orange polo, clutching his clipboard. He called Aiden over and smacked him on the side of his helmet, waving his arms wildly and pointing to the quarterback as he screamed things I couldn't hear.

Aiden took off his helmet and nodded a few times, then shook his head once. I could see his mouth moving along to the words, "Yes sir," "No sir," while the coach continued to lecture him for ignoring the playbook. Then he shoved Aiden down on the bench and offered him some water with a grudging back slap.

They *did* just score a touchdown after all.

But as soon as Aiden returned to the field, he went right back to ignoring the coach and running rogue, slipping in and out of the plays with a slightly chaotic yet masterful touch. The crowd was eating it up, chanting his name as the marching band butchered "We Will Rock You" in the background.

Coach Callahan ripped his hat off his head and threw it on the ground in frustration. But he couldn't stay mad for long because whatever Aiden was doing, it was *working*. Somehow, we were still winning, and he was successfully keeping this reality alternate.

Win-win.

I was surprised to feel my lips turned up into a smile. Even I couldn't summon my usual disdain for the game. I tried to tell myself I was just caught up in the drama of our situation, but truthfully, I think I just liked watching him play.

Once we'd made it through the first quarter, I started to relax and let my hands loosen their death grip on the fence post. I was even considering going to sit by Rose and Cat for the rest of the game, but by the time the second quarter began, something changed.

Aiden was getting sloppy.

The quarterback threw him a perfect pass, a breathtaking spiral that made grown men weep into their hands from the sheer beauty of it. Aiden caught it effortlessly, the ball thudding dully against his chest, and he started to run, nimbly dodging anyone that came near him. But a few seconds into the play, he hesitated. He gripped the ball tightly in his hands, his back tense as he swerved around yet another player attempting to tackle him. There were too many of them, and they were coming too fast.

I remembered this moment from the homecoming game in our timeline. It was impossible to forget since Eric had been yelling his frantic commentary so loudly in my ears that I almost turned around and smacked him with my flute. "Fake left, go right!" he'd screamed, waving his trumpet wildly in the air.

"And Mitchell's got the ball—he needs to run for his life or that boy will be flattened like a pancake!" the announcer drawled just like last time.

Aiden paused; I could almost hear him thinking over his options and the consequences of each choice. His gaze flicked to the stands where his family was standing in the front row, screaming louder than anybody else.

He faked left and went right. Just like last time.

The air rippled around him like a pebble tossed into still water, the stadium lights flickering as he ran. My heart pounded in my chest as Aiden stumbled, nearly dropping the ball before he quickly changed directions and ran straight into the massive arms of the other team. The crunch from the impact reverberated in my ears as Aiden went down, fumbling the ball in the process. The opposing team grabbed the ball and off they went, running straight down the field completely unopposed to score a touchdown. The air squeezed around me with its vise-like grip until it was hard to catch my breath.

There was a collective wave of purple and orange outrage. Coach Callahan was livid. I was surprised actual steam wasn't rising from his bald head as he waved Aiden over and the rest of the team followed, crowding around the two of them. I leaned forward, trying to get a better look at what was happening, but all I could see was a mass of teenage boys and grown men acting like teenage boys as they yelled over a game that shouldn't have mattered as much as it did.

Aiden's shoulders slumped as if he could feel the weight of everyone's disappointment. His head dipped low as he rubbed the space between his eyes and frowned at the ground. He looked like he did when he couldn't figure out the answer in calculus—annoyed and ready to stab someone's eye out with a pencil (usually mine). I watched him staring at the scoreboard, his foot jangling anxiously on the ground while he waited to get back on the field.

Even if he didn't like football, I think he disliked losing even more.

By the time the coaches had finished their yelling and the team was running back out on the field, the game had descended into pure chaos. Everyone was screaming and stomping loudly on the bleachers, adding to the pandemonium. The enthusiastic drumline crashed their symbols together over and over again, the sound ricocheting off me and shattering whatever nerves I had left. I wanted to march up to the nearest percussionist, grab his giant cymbals out of his hands, and throw them into the dumpster.

I could see Amelia and the other kids from the marching band pointing down at me with confused looks on their faces since I wasn't up there with them. I'd never skipped a game (perfect attendance record all around) and to see me standing there without my uniform or flute in hand must've been a shock to the system. I waved them off; I was pretty sure they could manage without me.

Every time I thought the game was veering into safe territory, it bounced back to how it had been the last time Aiden had played, like a rubber band snapping into place. It didn't matter how differently he played, everyone else just course-corrected and sent him back to the original play. And Aiden slipped back into it, too. No matter how hard he tried or how much he wanted things to be different, he couldn't outrun his competitive side. He couldn't outsmart the Golden Boy trying to edge his way back in.

It felt like we were balancing on the edge of a knife, waiting to see which side we'd tumble over. The air was tight and constricting as it shivered around me. It felt like it was trying to squeeze everything—me, Aiden, the entire football field and the stands full of people—through a space that was suffocatingly too small. Like we were about to hurtle down a dark, narrow tunnel through time and space and probably never emerge again.

As the clock ticked down the final seconds of the second quarter, Aiden stopped in the middle of the field and bent over, clutching his head as he took in deep lungfuls of air. My stomach dropped at the sight of him curling in on himself like that. I wanted to run onto the field, grab him by the hand and get him out of there. But before I could swing my legs over the short fence, the whistle blew and the teams started jogging over to the locker rooms for halftime.

Aiden staggered for a moment before following them on shaking legs.

I glanced behind me to see Mr. Mitchell get up from his perch in the stands with a stark frown across his face. On one side of him sat the UT recruiter in the orange hat who was tapping away on his phone, looking bored and unimpressed. And on the other side was Wes, his eyebrows drawn together as he whispered something in his mom's ear before rising to his feet. I pushed off the fence and started running through the crowd, past the marching band filing down the bleachers to line up on the field, and past the concession stand that permanently smelled like burned popcorn. I heard someone calling out my name, but I ignored them and kept running, shoving bodies aside in my rush to get to Aiden before his dad or Wes beat me to it.

I found him outside the locker room, leaning against the faded brick wall, his helmet hanging loosely in his hands. Just like before. The air was shifting around him, strange and shuddering. It made his face look out of focus and far away.

"Aiden!" I called out over the tumult of noise as I ran across the cracked and scarred pavement, dodging all the kids and parents acting like children. He didn't look up; I wasn't sure if he could hear me over the tinny sound of footsteps clanging on the bleachers or the music blasting through the old PA system.

I finally made it to where he was standing with his eyes closed, the air still crackling with static around him.

"It's my turn... to take you somewhere," I wheezed between gasping breaths. I reached out and pulled the helmet from his hands.

His eyes flew open. "But the game, we're tied—"

"You can't be serious. None of this matters—it isn't even real."

Aiden slid his back against the wall of the field house and slumped down further. An awkward silence fell between us as the realization of what I'd said fully sank in.

"I mean, *some* of this is real—at least I think it is—I don't really know, I just—" I stammered, my cheeks blushing a bright pink as I shook my head, wishing he would understand. "You can't keep playing, Aiden. Don't you feel it?" I waved my hands around us, hardly able to get the words out, the air felt so strange and tight in my lungs.

His mouth tucked into an even deeper frown. "But I can't just quit."

"Why not?"

"They—"

"I'm not asking about anyone else. I'm asking about *you*."

He opened his eyes and shook out his sweat-dampened curls. Somewhere out there a girl was imagining running her fingers through those golden locks.

Maybe that girl had always been me.

"Come on," I said. "You don't have to stay. You don't have to prove anything." He looked at me hesitantly, chewing on his lip as he thought it over. Then he inhaled sharply, holding his breath for a moment before releasing it with a sigh. Finally, he nodded. So I took him by the hand, and we ran.

"Aiden!" his dad called out from behind us. Aiden's hand tightened around mine as we ignored him and kept on running.

"Aiden!" Wes yelled after us, his worried voice mixing with their father's shouts. I thought Aiden might break my fingers, he was gripping them so tightly, his mouth drawn into a thin line. I knew how badly he wanted to turn around, to put his helmet back on, to finish the game. But instead, he gritted his teeth and kept running, our feet slapping loudly across the asphalt of the parking lot.

He only let go of my hand once we got to his truck. In one fluid motion, he had his jersey off, followed swiftly by his shoulder pads. I could see his chest heaving from underneath his sweat-drenched undershirt as he dropped them into the truck bed with a dull thud. Aiden motioned to his helmet still clutched in my hands. "Just toss it in," he said flatly.

I nodded and threw the helmet into the back of the truck with the rest of his discarded gear. He didn't look at me as we flung open our doors and climbed inside, but once we were seated, he took me by the hand and threaded our fingers back together.

"Where to?" he asked halfheartedly, his face half-lit from the blinding beams of the stadium lights.

"Just drive north."

Neither of us tried to fill the quiet while he drove. The clouds still hung low in the sky, blocking most of the stars from view as they blurred out my window. Aiden gently squeezed my hand, his back ramrod straight as the lights and the sounds of the Pearson High homecoming game faded behind us. He seemed to visibly relax the further away we got from the field. His breathing was slow and easy by the time I told him to turn left at the next fork in the road. He raised an eyebrow as he signaled but didn't question me.

We pulled into the deserted parking lot of the Carl County Regional Airport. Aiden's brow was knotted with worry as he glanced at the time illuminated on the radio; the third quarter of the game had surely started. He was obviously still obsessing over it no matter how much he pretended to be at ease. He roughly ran a hand through his hair, then turned the truck off with a sigh.

"Welcome to my favorite place," I said throwing my arms out wide and knocking my hand into the side of his face.

Twenty-Four

"**I**S THIS WHERE you're going to bury my body?" Aiden asked, lowering my arms with a frown. "It's perfect—no one will ever find me here." He squinted as he took inventory of all the concrete and chain-link fences. "But, seriously, this is your favorite place? That's depressing, Josephine. Even for you."

I rolled my eyes and opened my door. "Come on."

Aiden plucked at his undershirt (which, I must say, did not smell so great) and looked down at his mud-splattered football pants. "I guess I should probably change," he said.

"I mean, I wasn't going to say anything—"

"Oh please. Yes you were." He chortled and climbed out the driver's side before sliding his shirt off with a wince and tossing it into the truck bed. Aiden looked every inch the Golden Boy, standing there shirtless with his hands on his hips, surveying me and the rundown, sorry excuse for an airport. He already seemed lighter without his football pads on, beyond the literal weight removed from his shoulders.

I tried not to stare, but I was most definitely staring.

Aiden smirked as he pulled another one of his Pearson High football t-shirts over his head (did he have an unlimited supply of those things?), then said, "Or I could just stay shirtless if you'd like. You seem to be enjoying the view." His cleats clattered noisily as he added them to the pile in the back of the truck.

"I don't know what you're referring to," I sniffed primly.

But he must've seen my flaming cheeks in the orangey glow of the street lights because he snorted as he dug through his duffle bag.

"Well, it looks like I'm stuck in these pants," he said with a groan, shaking out his now-empty bag.

I bit my lip and tried to swallow my laugh. "That's okay. Like I said, traffic cone orange is really your color."

Aiden grinned and finished lacing up his sneakers. Then he stood and opened his arms wide in invitation. I was going to complain that he was disgusting and sweaty, but as he wrapped his arms around me, and my cheek pressed into the soft fabric of his shirt, I couldn't bring myself to say a word.

He just smelled like Aiden.

He pressed a kiss into my hair and said, "So why is this junkyard your favorite place? Is it even operational?"

"You'll see."

I pulled him by the arm to the far side of the parking lot where the fence blocked the path to the dangerously pothole-ridden single runway the airport could boast.

"I dare you to hop the fence," I said, wagging my eyebrows.

"Done."

Aiden lithely climbed up the side of the fence until he nearly fell at the top. He barely landed on his feet in time as he tucked into an awkward half-roll like an action hero that hadn't read the script all the way through before attempting a stunt.

"That was graceful," I said, snorting as I pushed open the unlocked side gate right next to where Aiden had clambered over the fence.

He glared at me, still in his fumbling crouch. "The gate was unlocked? I hate you."

"Yes, you've made that very clear," I said with a laugh. "And I didn't think you were actually going to try to Spider-Man your way over the fence. Don't take that as a compliment; the keyword being 'try.' You looked nothing like Spider-Man."

Aiden brushed his hands off on his hideously orange football pants and tried to look more dignified than I'm sure he felt. "You dared me, so..."

"So, obviously you had to." I stood in front of him, suddenly feeling shy and very aware that we were extremely alone in the dark at a nearly-abandoned airport.

He shivered as if he'd noticed that fact at the exact same time as me.

"How did you know that gate would be open?" he asked, his eyes still narrowed.

"Because it always is. It has been for years."

"You've got some explaining to do, Crew," he said as he pointed to the tiny tower across from us that was airport control.

I shrugged. "This is the way out."

He tipped his head to the side. "Of Pearson?"

"Pearson. Texas. All of it."

He nodded and looked around with renewed interest. "I take it you mean 'the way out' symbolically because, seriously, does anyone actually fly out of this airport?"

"Private planes, yes. Small ones. And not many of them." I took him by the hand and my heart jumped when he laced his fingers through mine.

Would I ever get used to us touching so casually? I doubted it.

I stopped on the runway and tugged him down to the still-warm asphalt. We laid on the ground, shoulder to shoulder with our hands clutched together between us. "Sometimes I come here at night when I can't sleep," I murmured to Aiden and the few stars that were peeking through the clouds.

"You, Josephine Crew, upstanding citizen and president of Pearson High—"

"—you mean co-president, Mr. President—"

"—not only sneak out of the house but illegally trespass on private property?"

I blinked at him as the realization of what he'd said sank in. "That would be correct."

He burst out laughing and rolled into my side. "I would've never guessed. That's the third time you've ever surprised me."

Making Aiden laugh like that felt like I'd caught a whispered secret in between my hands—soft and rare. I held that feeling in my chest before letting it go, imagining it scattering in the wind.

"I know, I know. Boring, predictable, and always consistent... it's Josephine Crew." I applauded into the quiet. "And the crowd goes wild."

He shrank into himself a little, looking properly abashed. "You know I only said that to annoy you since you'd said my debate argument was contrived."

"Which it was," I mumbled into his shoulder. "But you were right. I *am* predictable. Predictability feels safe, it feels comfortable—"

"But you're not boring," he cut in. "You're easily the most interesting person I know."

I tried to hide my smile, but the more I tried to fight it the wider it became.

We laid there in silence for a few minutes, staring up at the sky as our mutual understanding stretched between us in the form of a new, blaring, unanswered question: would tomorrow find us here, lying side by side, both of us vulnerably exposed in this temporary truce?

Did it have to be temporary?

"The night my brother died, I'd been fighting with my dad," Aiden said suddenly, his voice cracking through the easy quiet. "We'd been fighting a lot lately because I didn't want to take the meds anymore. I didn't like the headaches, of course—they suck. I can hardly see when they get that bad." He rubbed his forehead and grimaced. "Everything's fuzzy and every noise is too loud." He shuddered and took a deep breath. "It's the worst.

"But I liked everything else that came with it. Sometimes the pain was worth it." He smiled wistfully. "On one of my good days, when I'm feeling clear and the headache hasn't come yet, it feels like I'm floating along, like I'm just swimming through words. I have perfect recall—everything I've ever read, every movie I've seen or song I've heard—it's all just sitting there waiting for me. It makes me feel expansive, untouchable, even. My mind feels like this incredible carnival, all lit up and in motion, just teeming with the possibility of everything."

I could see a younger Aiden, skinny and blond, pouring over piles of books on his bed, remembering all the information in picture-perfect detail. A small part of me seethed with jealousy. I'd always felt like I had to work so hard in every subject; nothing has ever felt truly effortless to me.

"But my parents were completely stressed out." He swallowed. "I mean, I get it. Their kid was suddenly hearing voices and remembering things in a weird, slightly-off way. And half the time I could barely function because of the headaches. I told you about all the tests those specialists ran, all the labs and MRIs," he said as he glanced over at me. "None of that helped. So my dad started messing around with this other doctor that was running clinical trials on a few different migraine medications. Some of the side effects were... less than pleasant," he said with a frown. "So I would skip doses sometimes. I felt like I was walking around in a fog, like the carnival had been shut down and packed up, you know? I hated losing my perfect recall. I hated that I had to slog through homework that should've taken me seconds to finish. I hated how the meds slowed me down when I could've been running laps around everyone."

His eyes flashed under the half-hidden moon. "It drove me crazy. I don't know if you know this about me, but I hate to lose." He winked.

I barked out a laugh. "I would've never guessed," I said, reaching out to softly touch his face, letting my finger rest in the shadow of his dimple just like I'd always wanted to.

He leaned into my touch and gave me a small smile. "Anyway, one night my dad and I really got into it. I'd heard my parents arguing that morning over what to do about me, and I'd stewed over it all day. I hated feeling like their problem instead of their child. So, we fought.

"I remember my mom trying to calm us down, but we both let our tempers get out of hand and said some things we didn't mean. My dad even told me that he was probably going to lose his medical license because he'd been prescribing so many things for me. That he'd let the drug trials go on without reporting any of his findings to keep me safe, and a few other doctors had noticed. People were starting to ask questions. He said I was being ungrateful."

Aiden closed his eyes and took a deep breath, his sigh ruffling my hair as he wrapped his arm more tightly around me, his hand resting lightly on my waist.

"Wes had gone out that night—" His voice got so quiet, I had to strain to hear him, "—but I called him and begged him to come home. I'd locked myself in my room and wouldn't talk to anyone but him. And the headache I'd been trying to manage for a few days was getting, well, extremely unmanageable. It was agonizing."

I could feel the beat of his heart through the fabric of his shirt.

It started pounding faster and faster, and I braced myself for what I knew was going to come next.

"I kept expecting Wes to burst through the door, to come to my rescue like he always did. I wanted him to tell our dad that he was being unreasonable and that I was fine. That I'd be okay, and all of this was just some big misunderstanding. But none of that happened."

My heart started racing just as quickly as Aiden's.

"I was lying on my bed in the dark with a stack of pillows over my head, trying to drown out the whispers I was hearing, the strange flashes I saw. Then the phone rang. And my mom screamed. She screamed so loud I thought my head would split in half." His breathing staggered as he paused.

"My dad came into my room and told me that Wes had been in an accident. His voice was mechanical, completely void of every feeling like he was the one who had died. I yelled at him and told him to get out. I called him a liar, I told him he was crazy. Wes was fine; he was on his way home right now."

Aiden exhaled heavily. I wondered how long he'd been holding that breath; I wondered if he'd ever told this story out loud before. "The moment my dad shut my door, I saw the crack. It was thin and spindly like the wall had suddenly quit holding itself up. It looked like everything was caving in, which I guess maybe it was." His eyes were still closed as he repeated, "Everything was caving in.

"My head nearly exploded, and the only thing that made it feel better was when I got closer to that crack in the wall. So I reached out a hand to touch it, and then I woke up back in my bed, headache-free, to the sound of my brother singing in the shower."

Aiden choked out a laugh. "He was a terrible singer. Truly horrible. But I threw myself out of bed and ran into the bathroom. And when I saw him standing there all covered in soap and yelling at me to get out, I just burst into tears. Full-on sobbing. It really freaked him out," he said with a watery smile. "My parents too. I kept telling everyone what had happened, but no one knew what I was talking about. My dad didn't remember anything about the meds, and my mom didn't remember anything about the fight, and Wes, well, Wes was *there*. Alive. So, I started piecing things together. Things were the same, but slightly different. My headache was gone, and I didn't have to take a cocktail of pills. For the first time in a long time, I felt free.

"I convinced my family to go to the lake that day. We went and picnicked and had this insanely perfect afternoon, real Norman Rockwell stuff. The weather was beautiful, warm and partly cloudy so it never got too hot. My parents weren't fighting for once. Instead, they laughed and joked while they chased Beau and Lacy around on the beach, spreading out blankets for us to eat hot dogs on and holding hands when they walked along the water's edge. Wes and I swam until we'd totally exhausted ourselves, then laid on our towels near the shoreline while the sun went down. Everyone was sunburned and happy when we walked back to the car that evening; it was the best day I could ever remember having. And that night when Wes went out to his friend's house, I didn't call him and make him come home. I waited up until I heard him come in through the door at his curfew. I just laid there in my bed, crying into my pillow, feeling like I'd won. Like I'd made things right."

I squeezed his hand and he squeezed mine back. "But when I woke up," he said, "Wes was dead, my headache was back, and my mom wouldn't come out of her room." He sniffed loudly. "I took my meds that day because I couldn't see straight and I needed to help with Lacy and Beau. The cracks went away. So did the whispers. So did Wes.

"For a while, I thought maybe it was a dream, some kind of wish-fulfillment thing I'd conjured up the night my brother died. But a few months later, it happened again. We'd moved to Pearson by then." He glanced at me and smiled softly.

I looked back at his first day in Mrs. Crabtree's class with new eyes. This tucked-in boy, in desperate need of a haircut, trying to stake a claim in a place that was new to him, in a life that felt stretched too thin by loss and pain.

And I'd been there trying to snatch it back from him, greedy and spiteful just because I thought my claim mattered more than his. "I'm sorry," I whispered, feeling a hot wave of shame melt over me from the top of my head clear down to my toes.

"Don't be, Josephine." He turned his face into my neck, sliding his nose down the length of my jaw. "I wanted to pick a fight just as badly as you did," he said, tangling his fingers in the knotted mess of my hair and tugging gently. "Fighting with you felt purposeful. Stupid, but purposeful." He pressed a kiss against my skin, so gently I barely felt it at all.

Aiden rolled back and stared up at the sky. "So, every once in a while, I'd forget to take my meds," he continued. "Or I'd skip them just to see what happened. And every time I did, I saw the cracks again. I saw possibilities."

"And you wanted them," I said back softly.

"Who wouldn't?"

"How often do you come here?"

"Not as often as I want to," he said shrugging his shoulder and jostling my head. "But when I miss Wes more than I can handle, I have to. I like coming here and seeing things how they *should* be. My brother's alive and well, living his life as he was meant to. My dad kept his job, my parents don't fight as much. Everyone's just happier."

Something in my chest gave a sharp twinge when he said that. "What about you?"

"Sometimes I am too."

"Only sometimes?"

"On days like today, I'm definitely happier." He smiled at me like I had something to do with it. "I get a second chance. To fix things that need to be fixed. To try again. To kiss the girl."

He leaned in and pressed his lips to mine. His kiss was warm and soft, nothing like our frantic kissing on the bleachers when it had felt like the whole world had caught fire and we were watching it burn. But I think I liked this one even better. It felt like Aiden was giving me a piece of himself he'd hidden away from everyone else. This kiss didn't feel like the white flag of surrender; it didn't feel like a fight at all.

His hand tugged at my waist, pulling me closer to him as we lay there under the barely-there stars and the flickering street lights of the Carl County Regional Airport. My favorite place in the world.

On the best day of my life so far. But the day was nearly over.

"Aiden," I murmured.

"Hmm," he said, his face still nuzzled into my neck.

"You know, it's not your job to fix everything."

Aiden pulled away from me and sat up in a rush of movement. "You don't know what it's like," he said after a beat too long.

I sat up and turned his face to look at mine, my fingers splayed on the smooth angle of his jaw. "What's that supposed to mean?"

I could feel him clenching his teeth together before he got the words out. "You're trying to defy everyone's expectations. Especially your parents. I've known you for a long time, Josephine; I've seen the way you act around them." He searched my face as if he was looking for something. "You want to be different than who they expect you to be. You like the fight."

"So?" I tried not to squirm under his assessment—it was hitting a little too close to home.

"So, you don't know what it's like trying to achieve every expectation, spoken and unspoken. It's a totally different feeling."

I unfolded my mental scorecard and examined its contents, mentally filling in the gaps with what I now knew. I saw Aiden over the years, signing up for every club, every AP class and test. Aiden, dedicating his time and energy to a game he didn't even like to play. Aiden, who didn't know how to say no, who didn't like to let people down.

Aiden Christopher Mitchell III, the boy so extra they had to name him thrice.

"But you're trying to be two sons in one, Aiden."

He stiffened at my words, his face wooden under my touch. "So what if I am?"

"Listen to yourself. That's ridiculous and impossible. It's not fair to you or to them. It's not honest, and it's not real. None of this is real."

"How do we know *this* isn't more real than our other life?"

I shrugged. "Because it's not ours. Not really."

"You don't know what it's like," he said again, this time in a whisper. "To watch my parents missing Wes. To have to see that gaping hole every single day. To watch my dad go to a job that he hates because he thinks he failed both of his sons when really this is all my fault."

I opened my mouth to object, but he ignored me and pushed on, jerking his face out of my grip. He stood up to pace around me and tried to shove his hands into his pockets but came away frustrated when he realized he was still in his uniform. "To see Beau and Lacy look at pictures of Wes like he's just someone they used to know, like a random acquaintance or a relative twice removed, not their brother. And to see my mom overworked and exhausted at the hospital because we can't afford these meds I have to be on to keep me rooted in reality. I hate it. All of it."

He threw his hands up to the sky and made an angry noise so that even the stars could hear his exasperation. "They should be watching *Wes* play football, not me. He loved it, he lived for it. They should've had recruiters come to his games, to give him scholarships... but I'm all they have left." All the fight seeped out of him in a sudden rush. "And that's never going to be enough. It shouldn't be enough."

What he really meant but didn't say was, *"I'm not enough."*

I could see it in the set of his shoulders and the way he sank into himself in defeat, like he couldn't hold his head up for one more second. "I didn't take my meds. I fought with my dad. And then I called Wes and made him come home. I set things in motion that never should've happened. It's my fault, I know that."

"Aiden," I said, standing up to face him. "Look at me."

He stubbornly ignored me and held his gaze to the ground, chewing on the inside of his cheek.

"Fine. Don't look up, I don't care." I crouched down so he had to meet my gaze. I stared into his hazel eyes and said, "None of this is your fault. You were a kid—you're *still* a kid. And you're dealing with something that no one should ever have to deal with. It's loss, it's grief, and I'm sure it's heavier than anyone could imagine. But the one thing you can let go of is that stupid lie you've been telling yourself since the night Wes had the accident: this is not your fault. You don't have to make up for anything. And I don't think your brother would want you to. Or your parents."

Aiden blinked a few times, his eyes wide as he stared at me.

"You don't have to hold all of this on your shoulders," I said, waving around us. "You can let it go. No amount of do-overs is going to make it okay. But you'll be okay, eventually. You will."

He sighed and opened his mouth, his eyebrows all pinched together. He was making the face he always makes when he's about to pitch his opening argument.

"No," I said, holding a finger up to his lips before he could get a word out. "I'm not going to let you fight me on this. I'm right and you know it."

Aiden exhaled and all of the struggle seeped out of him. He wrapped his arms around my waist, pressing his face against my neck as he folded me into him. "Thank you," he said against my skin. "Thank you for saying that."

He didn't cry—I think he knew that would've embarrassed us both tremendously. But he didn't let go of me. We held each other like that for a long time, both of us breathing softly, easily.

Sometimes it's nice to be held. Sometimes it's nice to have someone to hold.

When he finally pulled back, his eyes weren't quite as shadowed. "Are you ready to go home?"

I knew he didn't mean my house. He looked a little shy when he'd asked, like he wasn't sure what my answer would be.

This entire day had felt like a hall pass. But what do you do when you hand your hall pass in?

You go back to class.

Twenty-Five

WE LEFT THE airport and started driving without a destination in mind.

I fidgeted in my seat, unsure what to say. Aiden fiddled with the radio, looking distracted and far away like he was still caught in the snare of his memories and hadn't decided if he wanted to climb out yet. After all the things we'd said to each other, I didn't know how to act around him. But for once, not knowing didn't feel quite so terrible. It felt a little bit like a cross between freedom and uncertainty—and I was surprised to find that I liked it.

We'd been slowly chipping away at each other's defenses all day long, but our time at the airport had sent the rest of our walls tumbling down. So what do you do after all the barriers are gone, after you've cleared away the rubble and let the dust begin to settle?

You see each other clearly. Maybe for the first time.

"Did you want to go see your brother?" I asked hesitantly. "I understand if you do."

Aiden tucked a loose strand of my hair behind my ear, his fingers sliding down my neck as he smiled. "I'll see him later when I get home. Besides, he's probably off with friends or something anyway. Just living his life like normal." His eyes flicked back and forth between me and the road. "And he thinks it's weird when I follow him around," he said with a shrug.

"I'm sure that doesn't stop you from following him anyway," I said, raising one eyebrow.

He laughed softly, his hand brushing against my collarbone before putting it back on the wheel. "No, it doesn't. But like I said, I'll see him later." He bit his lip. "I—I want to stay with you."

His face was careful, but his chin was lifted, strong and square, his jaw a sharp angle in the low light of the truck. A challenge. A different kind of dare.

"I want to stay with you too," I said back so quietly I wasn't sure if he'd heard me. But he must've because he lost the careful edge to his face. Instead, he just looked happy. Happy, and more than a little relieved.

We weren't ready to say goodbye yet. We both knew things would be different when we woke up tomorrow, and I don't think either of us was ready for that. Things had changed again. It wasn't just a mutual loathing or a mutual attraction simmering between us any-more, now it felt like something more.

"I have a dare for you," I said over the music blasting in his Tacoma (apparently, Aiden is a big Carrie Underwood fan—who knew). "Turn down your angry girl music and listen to me."

He scoffed and mumbled something about my lack of refined taste. "But it's not your turn. You dared me to jump the airport fence, and I nearly broke my neck. That means it's my turn to make you do something very stupid instead."

He left one hand on the wheel and moved his other to rest on my leg, squeezing it once. My heart started racing as I squirmed in my seat. He smiled smugly to himself.

"Eyes on the road, Mr. President," I said, but my voice came out embarrassingly breathy. I coughed, trying to clear my throat. "But this is a really good dare. Are you… scared?" I clucked like a chicken, and he rolled his eyes, his lips twitching into a half-smile.

Aiden tapped his fingers on my leg as he considered. "Fine. But you're skipping a turn after this."

I paused dramatically before saying, "I dare you to toilet paper Tim Boren's house."

"Are you kidding me, Josephine? That's your big dare?"

"Why are you acting like you're so mature and above it all? You're the one who started this game in the first place—a game usually reserved for preteens and slumber parties. Do you accept my dare or not?"

"Oh, I accept. But only if you TP Mrs. Cartwright's house."

"I'm not going to TP our principal's house! She'll have all the toilet paper analyzed for fingerprints, and then she'll put me in lunch detention until I graduate. Probably after too."

"But tomorrow, none of that will matter. Are you… scared?" He started clucking as he squeezed my thigh again.

"Fine! Fine. I'll do it." I scowled at him, but I was secretly thrilled. I'd always wanted to TP someone's house. I'd only ever been on the receiving end of toilet-papering (thanks to Aiden), and this end looked like way more fun than the early morning cleanup.

Aiden grinned as he flew down the road to the dollar store. We ran inside and loaded up on toilet paper and cheap snacks because we were starving. The girl ringing us up snapped her gum loudly and raised her eyebrows, looking unimpressed; it was extremely obvious what we were about to go do.

"You two have fun," she said in a monotone voice as she handed us our overflowing bags.

We tore through town with the windows down, sharing a giant bag of Doritos as the hint of autumn air filtered into the truck. Aiden held my hand while he drove, like he didn't want to let go of me even for a second. We kept glancing at each other out of the corners of our eyes when we thought the other wasn't looking. I smiled into my shoulder as Carrie Underwood sang about another husband who'd done her wrong, and Aiden sang along loudly in the background.

I could do this tomorrow too, I thought to myself. *I could do this every day.*

I think this could become my new normal.

Aiden grinned at me like he was thinking the same thing.

"You're up first," he said. "Mrs. Cartwright's is on the way to Tim's."

"Why do you know where she lives? That's gross and weird."

"Yes, Josephine. I'm secretly in love with Mrs. Cartwright. I sit outside her window every night, whispering sonnets at the stars while her husband snores through his sleep apnea mask."

"Ew, how do you know her husband wears a sleep apnea mask?" I asked with a laugh.

"Josephine, Josephine. You don't listen to anyone. That's why I'll always be the more effective and more beloved leader of our hallowed school."

I glared at him and punched him on the shoulder, hating that he was probably right about that. He laughed and turned his face, kissing me quickly before looking back at the road. "Mrs. Cartwright spends at least half the morning talking about her husband's snoring. I hear it every day when I'm prepping announcements. Haven't you noticed?"

I blushed in my seat and was grateful he couldn't see me in the dark. I usually spent the whole time we did the morning announcements watching Aiden and his golden hair, obsessing over everything he did or didn't do so I could add it to my list of complaints about him.

Or maybe it was a list of something else entirely.

He slowed the truck down in front of a small brick one-story house, with a tidy porch boasting two matching rocking chairs. It even had a white picket fence. "Madame President," he said, handing me the first roll. "I wish you luck."

I blanched and held the roll of toilet paper tightly to my chest. "Wait, you're not coming with me?"

"This isn't my dare." He laughed and more or less shoved me out of the truck, clicking the locks down once the door shut behind me.

I stood there fidgeting on Mrs. Cartwright's lawn with a roll of toilet paper clutched in my sweaty hands, fighting the impulse to turn around and beg Aiden to let me back in the truck. I shook off the urge to flee as I squared my shoulders. This was it; these were my last few moments to be stupid and not overthink things.

To act young and dumb for a minute. To maybe like it a little.

I threw the roll into her large persimmon tree that was heavy with fruit. It sailed out of my grip and tangled into the branches before falling out the other side and landing in the damp grass. I laughed even though no one else was there to hear me. Then a pair of hands wrapped around my hips, and I nearly yelped.

Aiden chuckled into my ear and spun me around. He pulled another roll of toilet paper out of the bag he'd set on the ground. "I couldn't just watch you do it. I *have* to help. My inner twelve-year-old is screaming."

I grinned and grabbed another roll. We tossed them back and forth, shaking with silent laughter as we absolutely covered Mrs. Cartwright's perfectly maintained front lawn and shrubs. Part of me was freaking out that she would catch us and that we'd get in trouble, but the rest of me was having too much fun to care.

I couldn't remember the last time I'd acted without thinking it over from every possible angle. I couldn't remember the last time I'd done something stupid just to say I did.

Maybe I never had.

A porch light flicked on, and we froze. I'd been wrapping Aiden up like a mummy (because why not?) and when the soft golden glow spilled over us, I dropped the roll I was holding and put my hands up in the air.

Aiden snorted into his toilet paper-covered shoulder. "We're not under arrest, Josephine," he hissed.

I slowly backed away as Mrs. Cartwright's magenta bathrobe and scandalized face came into view. "Is that Aiden Mitchell and Josephine Crew?" She gasped into the night air. "Well, I'll be—"

We didn't wait to hear what she'd be. Aiden grabbed me by the hand, and we booked it back to the truck, with toilet paper trailing behind us as we ran.

"Sorry, Mrs. Cartwright!" I blurted over my shoulder. I couldn't help myself—once a teacher's pet, always a teacher's pet.

Aiden's tires squealed as he peeled out of the driveway and raced down the quiet street, leaving Mrs. Cartwright's shocked face and pink bathrobe behind.

"We are the worst," I said into my hands. "She definitely hates us."

"I'm pretty sure she already did." We looked at each other as another wave of childish giggles hit us. "I'm surprised you didn't stay and offer to help her clean up the mess," he said, nudging me with his elbow.

I wanted to argue, but he was totally right. Just thinking about Mrs. Cartwright scowling as she scooped up piles of damp toilet paper from her manicured yard with her manicured hands was enough to make me slowly die of shame. I curled up in the front seat and groaned. "I'm a terrible delinquent."

"You just need more practice," Aiden said with a wink.

"Would you TP Mrs. Cartwright's house in real life? In our time-line?"

"Never. I'm not that brave," he swallowed, looking stricken.

I sniggered. "Looks like you need more practice too."

Moments later, we pulled up in front of Tim's house. The narrow street was completely lined with cars; it looked like the entire school was there. Aiden's eyes widened. "I forgot. It's Friday."

"So..."

"So, Tim has a party at his house almost every Friday night after the game."

I grimaced. A Tim Boren party was one of the last places on earth I wanted to be. Aiden ran a hand through his hair and made a face similar to mine. I could feel the bass pumping from inside the house, rattling my bones from where I sat in the truck. I peered out the window just in time to see someone jumping from the roof down into the glowing pool below.

"This looks like the start of a CW show," I said, shaking my head.

"Which CW show?"

"All of them."

Aiden laughed but didn't disagree. "Do you usually go to his par-ties?" I asked, curiously. I realized that for how much I knew about Aiden, I had no idea what he did every weekend.

"Sometimes," he shrugged with a sigh. "If there's nothing else to do. Or when my dad wants to analyze game film before I've even taken my uniform off." He scoffed, trying to look annoyed, but his face fell and his eyes darkened until I could barely see them in the dim glow of the streetlights. Obviously, football was not a safe sub-ject. Or his dad.

But thinking about Aiden at one of those parties was even worse. I imagined him inside Tim's house, flirting with other girls, dancing with them, his body pressed up close against theirs. My eyes nar-rowed as I glared at the house in front of me.

"You look like you're going to light something on fire," Aiden whispered. "You usually reserve that face for me." His eyes drifted to my mouth.

I blushed all the way to my hairline. I wasn't about to admit that

I was suddenly seething with jealousy at the thought of Aiden with anyone other than me.

"So what are we going to do?" I asked, waving out the window as I tried to change the subject. "Let's just leave." Clearly, I'd never been to one of Tim Boren's raves, and I had zero desire to change that.

Aiden shook his head. "A dare has been dared," he said, his eyes flashing as he grabbed another roll of toilet paper and spun it in his hands. "I'm not letting you out-TP me."

He jumped out of the truck and ran through the poorly lit front yard, throwing the toilet paper back and forth through the darkness. He made a remarkable mess in a matter of minutes. Even I was impressed. A few people coming in and out of the party gave Aiden strange looks when they saw him demolishing the Boren's yard, but he didn't care; he just waved or called out a greeting before returning to his vandalism.

When he finally ran out of toilet paper, he jogged back over to the truck where I was crouched down in my seat hiding. "Okay, dare complete," I hissed. "Let's go."

He opened my door and leaned over to unbuckle me. "But I have another dare for you," he said with a smile that made my stomach drop. "And it requires you to go inside."

"*Inside*? Tim Boren's party? Hard pass." I tried to re-buckle myself, but he put his hand over mine.

"Yes, inside. I dare you to walk in there and kiss me in front of everyone."

"You cannot be serious."

He smiled and nodded before pulling me out of the truck. "Extremely serious. Are you scared, Josephine? Am I to remain your dirty little secret?"

He was making a joke, but he wasn't laughing. He had that same look on his face that he got right before we started debating. His eyes flashed and his mouth quirked up as if he was waiting for me to back down. But underneath it all was a kind of hopeful nervousness that made my heart swell. His blazing gaze was filled with the same silent question we'd been asking each other all day.

Is this real?

He bit his lip and looked down at our entwined hands and that's when I knew; he wanted me to want to kiss him in front of everyone. I think we were both looking for some kind of reassurance—something to prove that maybe this wasn't a fluke, that today didn't have to be some small, strange blip in our lives.

"After you, Mr. President," I said, trying to keep my voice steady as I gestured at the house. His surprised face snapped up to meet mine, the unspoken question still there, but a little quieter now.

I'd finally found my answer.

My face was flaming when he pushed open the already ajar front door. Music pulsed through the house as we passed bodies swaying into each other in the dim light, everyone talking loudly over each other and dancing in an off-beat, slightly manic way.

As we crossed the bright orange shag carpet of the spacious family room (Tim's parents probably loved that it was Pearson High Tiger Orange), a low voice called out over the noise, "Mitchell! Where'd you go at halftime? Coach was losing it!" Aiden stiffened next to me as Tim rounded the corner and came between us, throwing an arm around each of our shoulders. "But dude, we won! Go Tigers!" he howled, flicking his sweat-soaked hair out of his eyes. I was pretty sure he hadn't showered after the game.

"Go Tigers," I said back weakly, my legs buckling under his leaning weight. Tim Boren was a walking cliche no matter which timeline we were in. He slapped us both roughly on the back before ambling off to a group of girls who were waiting for him by the pool table.

Aiden was staring after him blankly as the news of Pearson High's homecoming victory hit him. "We won," he said. "They didn't need me." He sounded confused, like the thought of him not needing to carry the team or anyone else was completely foreign to him, some abstract concept he'd never considered before.

"I told you," I said, leaning in so he could hear me over the pulsing music. "You don't have to hold all of this on your shoulders."

He shook his head in disbelief, but a wide smile stretched slowly across his face. Leisurely, even. Like he'd only just realized that maybe he could loosen his grip on his life a little. But then that smile slid into a dangerous-looking smirk that made my stomach flip as he pulled me over to the large brick fireplace at the front of the room. He stood there expectantly, waiting for me to make the first move.

I took a deep breath and leaned forward, catching his lips in a kiss before I had another second to reconsider. He immediately put his arms around me and pulled me to his chest as our classmates bumped into us, dancing wildly to the rhythm of the music.

I kissed him and forgot that we were in a room full of people I didn't like all that much. I even forgot to worry about everyone else's opinion or the gossip that would surely fly across the school halls come Monday morning.

But what I didn't want to forget was this: Aiden's fingers tipping my face up to meet his and my hands pressed against the nape of his neck. The horrible Eminem song playing in the background. How my feet were sinking into the worn carpet, my shoes squishing in some mysterious spilled substance.

I didn't want to forget the way Aiden looked at me when he pulled back with a smile on his face. Another one of those secret smiles that said he knew something I didn't. But I knew something he didn't know too. I felt it pass through my mind like a whisper, the barest hint of an idea.

You like him. More than you ever hated him.

When we stepped back, nothing happened. We weren't greeted with thunderous applause or screams of shock. Tim didn't yell, "Oh, get a room already!"

No one said a word. The clumsy dancing continued, idiot kids kept jumping from the roof into the pool, and the crowd gathered around the pool table cheered as someone scored. No one cared that Aiden Christopher Mitchell III and Josephine Crew had just kissed in front of everyone because to them we were just another pair of people making out at a stupid party. There were probably dozens of couples locked in similar embraces around the room.

The truth was, we didn't matter nearly as much as we thought we did. I couldn't decide if that was disappointing or a gigantic relief.

Aiden tucked my hand into his. "Now stand on the table and make a speech about what a superior president I am. Maybe throw in that I'm a better kisser than Brandon too."

I plucked at the front of his t-shirt, pulling him in until my mouth was hovering over his. "Not going to happen," I said, our lips brushing before I shoved him lightly in the chest, his breath caught in his throat until he burst out laughing. "Besides," I added, "I swore to faithfully uphold the truth when I was sworn into office, and I cannot tell such blatant lies."

"We weren't sworn in; Mr. Gunderson just handed us the gavel and almost started crying."

"Still."

Aiden was laughing, but his eyes burned into mine. "Well, only the first part would be a lie. You already admitted I'm a better kisser than Brandon."

I scoffed as I pulled him by the hand past the swarm of partying kids and out the front door. "Yes, but can you recite me poetry like he could?" I asked him over my shoulder.

Aiden snorted and mumbled something along the lines of, "He only got seventh place," but once we were at his truck and clear of all the noise and the chaos of Tim Boren's house, he reached around me to open my door and whispered in my ear, *"Sometimes with one I love I fill myself with rage for fear I effuse unreturn'd love, but now I think there is no unreturn'd love, the pay is certain one way or another. I loved a certain person ardently and my love was not return'd, Yet out of that I have written these songs."*

Heat filled my cheeks as I stood there gaping. He swung the door open and gently nudged me into my seat. "Walt Whitman," he said, before slamming the door shut.

I bit my lip, trying to keep my smile from searing across my face, catching like wildfire until every inch of me was consumed. Aiden grinned in an entirely self-satisfied way as he flipped the radio on. Carrie Underwood was wailing about another man who'd broken her heart.

"So tomorrow," Aiden said, staring out the window as he backed away from Tim's house.

"So tomorrow," I said back. Carrie filled the silence with her talk of keying cars and smashing headlights while Aiden hummed along.

I took his hand and held it between mine.

We'd crossed another line by coming here, and we both knew it.

Now all that was left was to cross the line of tomorrow.

Twenty-Six

FOR TWO NON-DELINQUENTS, we were getting pretty good at sneaking.

"Slow down," I hissed as Aiden pulled his truck onto my gravel driveway. "Now turn the headlights off."

Aiden made a noise of amusement but flicked the lights off all the same. I squinted through the windows to see if my parents had left any lights on in the house, or if I could see any angry silhouettes waiting up for me.

We'd never really discussed a curfew before. There hadn't been a need to.

I could feel Aiden watching me. "Wow, your parents must be intense."

"Only when it comes to boys," I grumbled back.

He joined me in peering through the window. "So I take it you're not going to run in there and tell them how we spent our day, hmm?"

"Yeah, not so much."

He laughed dryly. "I'll give you a free pass tonight, but you're going to have to tell them eventually."

"Says who?"

"Well, I plan on occupying a lot of your time in the future." My stomach swooped at the meaningful look he gave me. "They'll probably want to know where their daughter is."

"You'd be surprised," I said, looking back at the dark windows of my house.

"Then they'll at least be wondering why you're suddenly in such a fantastic mood all the time. I want to get the credit I deserve."

"You are impossible," I said, smacking him on the arm, "and incredibly annoying, not to mention big-headed, and—" He caught my hand and pulled me to him, silencing me with a kiss. I didn't object.

"Okay, I have one last truth or dare for you. There's something I want to know," I said, brushing the hair off his forehead.

"Ask away."

"What happened after you kissed me? That first time. At debate practice in this timeline."

Aiden's smile had started out soft and sweet, but by the time I'd finished asking my question it had stretched into a wide and wicked grin. "I bet this has been bugging you all day, hasn't it?"

"I decline to comment."

"That's what I thought," he snickered. "Well, if you must know, the whole team started clapping. And Ms. Torrence threw her clipboard in the air and yelled, 'Finally!'"

I blinked at him. "Seriously?"

He blinked at me. "No." His smile turned sheepish. "I ran out the door before anyone could do or say anything."

"*What?*" I screeched, grabbing his face in between my hands. "You're telling me that you kissed me in front of everybody, and then you *ran*?"

"Yep."

My hands fell back in my lap as I doubled over with laughter, cackling at the thought of a panicked Aiden booking it out the emergency exit door after making a move on me.

"You're never going to let me live this down, are you?" he asked, rubbing the back of his neck.

"Never ever."

He sighed and ducked his head. "I suppose that's only fair."

Another wave of laughter washed over me as I watched him squirming in his seat. Once my hysteria had finally calmed down, I tipped my head back against the headrest and tried to catch my breath. "I guess I should go," I whispered. Aiden's hand found mine on the center console. "I'll see you at school in the morning. Don't be late."

He snorted. "I'll be earlier than you," he said, squeezing my hand lightly before letting me go. "Tomorrow."

We couldn't stop saying that word.

I leaned in for one last kiss. He tugged me closer like he wanted to ask me to stay but wouldn't.

"See you then." I slid out of the car. He started to back out of the driveway but stopped when I motioned for him to roll the window down. "Make sure you shower," I said as I poked my head through the window, raising my eyebrows with emphasis.

"Yeah, you looked like you could hardly stand to be near me, I must smell terrible," Aiden replied, rolling his eyes. I smirked and leaned against the truck door. He didn't move to drive away, and I didn't start walking up to my porch. We just continued grinning moronically at each other.

You hang up first.

No, you hang up first.

"All right, get out of here," I said, tapping the hood of his truck, my cheeks pink with embarrassment; we were nauseating. He shot me one last smile as he backed away. I stood there on my dead front lawn, watching his truck fly down the road until it vanished from view. And for a brief moment, I considered pulling my phone out, my fingers ready and willing to dial Aiden's number and ask him to come back. I wanted to climb inside his truck and stay with him.

To pretend the sun would never rise. To freeze time. To stop it right then and there.

But I left my phone in the back pocket of my jeans, already knowing that staying with Aiden wouldn't make this frantic feeling go away. Because deep down I knew that if I stopped time, if I kept things exactly the way they were, then I would miss out on everything that happened next. All the possibilities lying before me just waiting to be chosen.

My breath emptied from my chest in one great exhale. I could do it. I could face the sunrise and still believe that the feelings stirring in my chest would stay with me through the morning.

Tipping my head back, I looked up at the stars as I walked to my front door and wondered if they were the same ones I looked at every night before I fell asleep. I slowly opened the door, making sure not to let the rusty hinges announce my arrival, then shut it softly behind me as I tiptoed down the hallway, avoiding all the squeaky spots on the floor.

But my efforts were in vain—my mother was sitting at the kitchen table under our ugly chandelier that needed nearly all its lightbulbs replaced, waiting for me. "Josephine Crew," she said, with a glare. "Do you have any idea what time it is?"

I glanced at my phone and saw it was nearly midnight. I also saw the string of missed calls glowing across my screen. "Sorry," I mumbled, as guilt and annoyance fought for center stage. "It won't happen again," I lied, because according to Aiden, this was going to be a regular thing.

"Where were you?" she asked, peering at me through narrowed eyes. She was wrapped in her silk robe, her makeup stripped from her face. She looked tired and older than she usually did, but prettier somehow.

It made me feel small when I saw her glowering at me like that.

"I was at the game and then I... hung out with Aiden," I answered truthfully. I might as well do a trial run in this timeline to see if my mom would freak out as spectacularly as she would in mine.

Her eyes widened. "Aiden Mitchell?" she laughed and slapped the table, making me jump. "You sure know how to pick them, Josie."

I grimaced at the nickname but didn't correct her. She shook her head and stared at me for a long moment, her expression unreadable. "Just be careful."

My hands gripped the kitchen chair in front of me when I nearly tipped over in surprise. Just this morning—or yesterday morning, or whatever—my mother's face had been beet red as she'd told her daughters that under no uncertain terms were they allowed to go out with anyone until they'd graduated and moved out of her house, or some other variation of "it's my way or the highway."

"What—I—we—" I couldn't think of a single coherent response.

She patted the seat next to her, and in my state of shock, I sat down. "I saw you at the game," she said softly, tucking her red hair behind her ears and smoothing it back.

I hadn't known she'd seen me. I thought I'd been the one seeing her.

"I hardly recognized you when you ran past me, you looked so grown up." Her voice sounded strange and far away.

I grit my teeth and swallowed all the words rising up in my throat. Who did she think she was, getting to suddenly be sentimental? Since when did she care?

"Seeing you like that made me feel—"

"Let me guess. Old," I said in a monotone voice.

She winced. "I was going to say it made me remember what it was like to be your age. When the world is your oyster and all that." She waved her hands dismissively before folding them primly in her lap and sighing wistfully. "What a feeling, Josephine. And it'll be gone before you know it."

I braced myself for what was surely going to be her next sentence—her "back when I was Miss Carl County" speech I'd heard a million times before. I braced myself for her to steer the conversation back to her, just like she'd always done in that subtle (and sometimes not-so-subtle) way of hers. The way she made it painfully clear that there wasn't any room for me at her table.

You can't sit here, she seemed to say with every uninterested glance. *This seat's taken.*

I froze in my chair like an actual deer caught in the headlights. A stupid, naive deer who prances out onto the road, time and time again, expecting things to go differently than they do. But the car always comes speeding down the road, and either the deer runs off, skittish and scared, or *bam*—the deer is finished.

What's the definition of insanity again? My mother and me.

Her wistful sigh turned sour as she frowned. "I'm sorry that sometimes I try to take that feeling away from you."

This was definitely an alternate reality because I've never once heard my mother use the words "I'm sorry" before. Not after all the times she was hours late picking me up from school, or the six separate years she'd forgotten my birthday, or when she'd spelled my name wrong when she'd embroidered it on my backpack (in purple—my least favorite color).

She always huffed and told me I was ungrateful or too impatient. Always the burden she'd been forced to carry in her delicate hands.

Honestly, Josephine. Must you be such a thorn in my side.

"I'm a jealous woman," she said simply. "Always have been. Always will be." She shrugged and wrapped her blush pink robe more tightly around herself. "My mama used to say that my pride would be the death of me. Maybe she was right after all."

It wasn't an explanation, but it was more than she'd ever given me before.

"We all swear we aren't going to turn out like our parents," she said, pressing her hands flat against the table, her simple golden wedding band glinting in the low light. "We all swear it," she mused quietly, "but I think you just might be one of the few who keep that promise." Her voice sounded tired and bruised. But I could've sworn there was a hint of pride there too.

She shook her head and her eyes fell on me, piercing and sharp.

Eyes like mine.

"Mom," I blurted out. "Do you want to come to my tournament tomorrow?" The words slipped out of me before I'd really thought them through. But there was something about the sad set of her mouth and the way she was looking at me—like she didn't know me but wished that she did.

Or maybe this day had left me feeling a little more tender, a little more torn open than I usually was. I kept thinking about Aiden's voice rumbling in my ear as we lay on the airport runway when he told me about the brokenness in his family he so desperately wanted to mend. How they actually missed each other when someone wasn't around.

I wanted that. Still. I wanted to miss her, and I wanted her to miss me.

My mother's eyes widened in surprise. "All right, Josephine. I'd like that very much." We both stood and stared at each other awkwardly before she turned and padded down the hall to her bedroom. "But don't wear all that black, honey. It washes you out," she said over her shoulder.

I awarded myself a bonus point for not telling her exactly where she could stick that comment.

Mom paused with her hand on the doorknob. "Did you sing at Applebee's today?" she asked turning back to face me, her expression unreadable.

Curse the Sad Moms and their big mouths.

I sighed. "Yep. Carly Simon."

She straightened her shoulders like she was straightening her crown. "That's my girl," she said softly.

My mouth tugged up into a smile as she shut her door.

After a much overdue shower (was it just me or was the water pressure better in this reality?), I threw on pajamas and crawled into bed, feeling like I could sleep for the next two days straight. But instead of falling asleep, I flopped around on my bed, fluffing and rearranging my pillows and trying to get comfortable as the nerves from the past day finally caught up with me.

Was I ready to go home? To fall back into old habits and familiar patterns because they were known and easy, or would I want something else? Something more? Something slightly uncomfortable, but maybe a little bit better. Different and sometimes surprising.

But still me.

I sat up against my pillows and reached over to my desk to grab my laptop. The glow of the screen illuminated my face as I pulled up my always-open tabs with my college applications.

Share your story, they asked me. *Tell us about you.*

A flash of recklessness pulsed through me as I imagined my essays like a game of truth or dare. These schools wanted to learn about *me,* not some version of me I thought would impress them the most or look good on paper. Like a pinned-up golden star or a bright blue ribbon.

I stared at the blinking cursor. Could I dare to share my truth?

I started typing. My fingers flew across the keyboard as images from the past day filled my mind—moments where I could feel all the pieces of me aligning in a way I'd never thought possible. I wrote about the things that made me happy—like debate and books and my sister and Cat—without stopping to wonder if those angles were flattering or if I needed to tack on anything else at the end like hastily finished extra credit work.

I may or may not have even mentioned Aiden a time or two.

His words from this morning came back to me in a rush as I wrapped up my essay with a confession that I was surprised to find I was more than okay with admitting.

I think there's more of you in there, he'd said. *I'd like to meet her.*

The honest truth was that I didn't know my whole story yet, but that was okay. I was only just beginning to see that maybe not knowing was the whole point.

I wrote until I couldn't keep my eyes open any longer, then shut my computer with a sigh that felt like a breath I'd been holding onto for years. It didn't matter that what I'd written down wouldn't save or crossover with me when I went back home. It was inside me, waiting to come out, and it would still be there for me tomorrow, too. A small smile flitted across my face as I finally drifted off to sleep, holding every version of me loosely in my hands and wondering who I'd be when I woke up again.

Twenty-Seven

I BOLTED UP in bed the next morning, grabbed my phone off my nightstand, and checked the date before falling back onto my pillows in relief.

Saturday.

We were back.

The sun was streaming in through my window, revealing a clear, unquestionably bright blue sky. I hopped out of bed with a literal spring in my step and tapped out Aiden's name into my phone. A brief scroll through our past messages revealed that we'd only ever texted threatening things about homework assignments or snipes over student council business. Sometimes we threw in an occasional rude meme to mix things up.

I took a deep breath and typed out the words, *home sweet home.*

I wanted to break the ice, to show him that I could bring parts of that Josephine—the alternate, slightly less-uptight version of me—back with us. That I wouldn't just go straight back to sending hostile messages about group projects or club minutes.

I wanted to show him that I still wanted him.

My phone stayed silent as I threw on my pencil skirt and fitted blazer (all in black—what does my mother expect me to do, wear a yellow suit?) and the only pair of high heels I owned that I pretended I hated but secretly loved because they made feel like I was about to take someone down in court. I grabbed a hair tie off the bathroom counter and started running my hands through my hair, pulling the strands into my signature ponytail, uptight and unyielding.

Blinking at myself in the mirror, I dropped my hands back down to my sides and let my hair settle in waves around my shoulders before flicking the hair tie back on the counter. I didn't need it today.

My fist hammered on Rose's door as I yelled, "I'll see you at the school! Try not to cheer too loudly for me when I win!" She groaned back a muffled incoherent response, probably still face down in her pillows. Down the hall my parents' bedroom door was still shut, too. I paused with my hand poised ready to knock, unsure what to do since the moment I'd shared last night with my mom didn't carry over into this reality.

Could those versions of mother and daughter, tentative as they are, exist here too?

I grabbed a sticky note off my desk and wrote down the information for the final debate round, then quietly stuck it to their door.

After gathering my laptop and notes into a tidy pile, I tucked them into my backpack and plucked a banana out of the fruit bowl before bounding out the door.

Well, as much as a girl can bound across her lawn in heels.

I still hadn't heard from Aiden, but that was fine; I was going to see him in just a few minutes anyway. I hummed along to the radio as I pulled into the nearly empty parking lot, grinning when I saw I'd beaten him there. Soon this lot would be full of buses and cars carrying kids from all over the Carl County school district. This tournament determined who would go to regionals.

Aiden and me, obviously.

The auditorium doors swung shut behind me, echoing loudly in the quiet dark space. I flipped the lights on and made my way to the stage, running my hand along the rows of seats as I walked, my shoes click-clacking noisily in the cavernous room. The stage had two podiums angled toward each other and facing the audience, with a long table next to each podium. We wouldn't be in the auditorium until the final round at the end of the tournament, but I liked seeing the stage set up like this. I liked the quiet, the still in the air before the words were flying and the stopwatches were ticking.

"I made sure to get the largest tables available," a voice rang out from behind me. Ms. Torrence flicked another row of switches on the wall behind her so the spotlights shone brightly on the stage. "You'll have plenty of space—which both you and Aiden have repeatedly reminded me you need," she mumbled loud enough for me to hear.

I shifted on my feet and chewed on the inside of my cheek while trying not to laugh. That version of me—that girl who needed space and walls and extra elbow room on the debate stage—seemed like a distant memory. She's a little faded around the edges, like an old photograph I'd been holding onto for years, nearly torn to shreds from gripping it so tightly.

"I think this will do nicely," I said to Ms. Torrence since I couldn't explain everything else I was thinking or feeling. "It looks great."

She sagged into a seat on the front row. "Well, that's certainly a relief."

I smiled at her widely and she glanced over her shoulder in a twitchy way like she was resisting the urge to check if someone else was standing behind her. I guess I didn't smile at Ms. Torrence very often. The moment stretched on for too long and my cheeks felt weird from ginning at her, so we both cleared our throats and busied our hands with our bags.

"Good luck today," Ms. Torrence said after a minute of silence. "I'm sure you and Aiden will do a wonderful job. I have to admit, when he first came to me with the idea of pairing you two together, I thought—" She stopped talking abruptly, her cheeks reddening.

"Wait, it was *Aiden's* idea to have us debate together?" I asked incredulously, my voice rising an octave.

Ms. Torrence stared longingly at the auditorium doors as if hoping someone else would rush in and save her. "Well, yes, it was his idea," she said, smoothing down her short hair nervously. "And he made me swear not to tell you. I thought it would be a disaster, but he was insistent." She wrung her hands and shrugged before glancing back at the doors again. "So, we took it to the team, and they voted. It was unanimous."

I was stunned. I couldn't decide if I was annoyed or impressed with Aiden's subterfuge. But the longer I thought about him seeking out Ms. Torrence and convincing her and the rest of our team to pair us together, the more it made sense to me.

Why do you think I've been working so hard to get your attention?

A sudden warmth filled my chest. It slowly expanded, spreading its way through me until it felt as if every inch of me was glowing. A few days ago, this news would've made me livid. I would've been angry and suspicious, wondering what Aiden was up to and how he was trying to sabotage me.

But today it just made me happy.

Ms. Torrence was still rigid in her seat as if bracing herself for my inevitable blowup.

"Okay. I guess I'll go get set up," I said after another awkward minute of silence. "Which classroom are we in first?"

She loosed a breath and whipped out her clipboard, thumbing through the papers in a flurry. "Mrs. Parker's Freshman English. Room 102," she answered as more of my teammates finally filtered into the auditorium, all clad in their own black suits. Ms. Torrence's smile widened now that she had other pupils to fuss over who actually needed her cheerleader antics and semi-tough love.

I gathered my stuff and was just about to sneak out the door to go stake out my territory in room 102, when Ms. Torrence called out, "Time for our huddle!"

I swallowed my groan as I turned back to my team, who was indeed huddled together in a circle with an empty spot saved for me, their ever-faithful captain. I tucked myself into the circle, scanning the familiar faces for Aiden's, but he wasn't there.

"Has anyone seen Aiden?" I hissed to the person standing next to me, stiffening once I realized it was Brandon Lopez that I was currently elbowing in the ribs.

He peered down at me with a hesitant smile. "Maybe he's already in the room?"

"Yeah maybe," I said quickly, trying unsuccessfully not to be awkward or to remember the taste of cinnamon from when he kissed me. He shrugged and looked away, already moving on.

Ms. Torrence started making a speech that sounded vaguely like some of Hillary Swank's lines from *Freedom Writers*. I fidgeted the whole time, anxious to get to the classroom and to find Aiden.

"Anything to add, Josephine?" she asked with surprising deference to me.

"Um, what? Yeah, go, team, go," I said pumping my fist in the air. Everyone laughed while Ms. Torrence gave me an exasperated look, and our huddle scattered before she could make us stick our hands in the middle and start chanting. I glanced at my phone again to see if I had a message from Aiden, but all I saw was a slew of texts from Cat and Rose wishing me good luck and that they'd see me for the final debate.

Maybe it was a little presumptive of me to invite people to the final round before I'd even made it, but oh well. I'm presumptive, and I was also going to win.

The English classroom was small and cramped with its rows of desks and colorful posters reminding all the freshmen that they could be anyone they wanted to be if they just believed! But still, no Aiden. I set my laptop up at the small table right in front of the poster of a tiny cat dangling from a rope and yelling for me to *"Hang in there!"* I scowled at it the same way I used to when I was a freshman in this very classroom (Mrs. Parker really needed to redecorate).

The clock ticked loudly as I strummed my fingers restlessly on the table. A few moments later, my opponents walked in, immediately blanching when they saw me standing at the tiny podium to the left of my table.

"Cassie," I said, to the first girl. "Amanda," I added, nodding to the second. They both mumbled quick and unenthusiastic greetings before hunching their heads together over their table and whispering back and forth with worried glances at me.

I tried and failed not to smile. I'd pummeled them individually last year, and I was sure it would be no different this time around. Cassie was a mumbler and Amanda said, "um," after every other word. It was almost too easy.

Next, our judge came in, a squat, middle-aged man I'd never met before who looked less than thrilled to be judging a high school debate tournament on a Saturday morning. His name tag boasted, "Hello, my name is Doug," across his broad chest. "Some game last night!" he said when he saw me standing on the Pearson High side of the room. He didn't wait for a response from me before he launched into a play-by-play of his favorite football moments.

I stared at judge Doug blankly, hearing him but not registering a word he'd said until Aiden finally burst in through the door behind him, sending my heart into overdrive. Doug noted Aiden's face and verified his name on the clipboard with his mouth set in a hard line, already forming opinions about Aiden and our debate with his preconceived notions about last night's game. "Nice of you to show up, Mitchell," he sniffed.

I sighed. We were going to have to dazzle him.

"Where have you been?" I hissed to Aiden as he dropped his pile of stuff on the table. "And why are you all sweaty again?"

"I'm here, okay?" Aiden ran a hand over his forehead, flicking his hair back from his face.

I frowned as I gave him a once-over; his tie was hanging loosely from around his neck, his white collared shirt only halfway tucked in. "You could've put in a little effort, you know."

He hastily tucked in his shirt and slid his fingers along his tie, straightening it before smoothing down his jacket. Even disheveled, Aiden Christopher Mitchell III could pull off a suit. It was annoyingly distracting when I would've preferred to be mad at him for showing up late *and* looking like he'd just rolled out of bed.

"I'm sorry," he whispered back, barely making eye contact. "I need to—"

"All right, my little debaters," the already bored Doug said in a condescending voice. "Let's get this show on the road."

Our opponents sat primly waiting at their table while Aiden and I struggled to get our act together. My cheeks flushed as I stumbled into my seat, the two of us knocking into each other like we'd never walked in the same room together, let alone practiced debating on the same team. Not exactly the intimidating persona I wanted to open with.

"Let's begin," said Doug with a glance at his watch. "Archer High, you have the affirmative. Take it away."

Cassie stood and gave us one last wary glance before launching into her opening statement. "Abraham Lincoln once said that 'the ballot is stronger than the bullet,'" she said in her monotone mumble, basically butchering the quote in her rush to get it out. "We believe that voting should be compulsory in a democracy for the following reasons," she continued, after pausing to noisily clear her throat. I jotted down notes while she spoke, smiling to myself as she cited all the sources on voter turnout that I knew she would, and prepared for the cross-examination.

Aiden hadn't moved. He just sat there next to me, staring at nothing and sweating through his suit. I kicked him under the table, and he barely reacted. "What's your problem?" I whispered through gritted teeth.

He shook his head and started scribbling notes on his blank notepad. Before I knew it, the first affirmative constructive speech was over and it was time for our first cross. I clutched my notes and went to stand, but Aiden beat me to it and hurried over to the podium.

He leaned into it like it was the only thing in the world holding him up, and asked "Does anyone know what the point of this is?" He gestured to the opposing team, to me sitting stiffly in my seat, and to our bemused judge, who was slouching sleepily in his chair and probably wondering if it would be frowned upon if he got his phone out.

I was too stunned to flip through my notes, to move from my chair, to even blink.

"What's the point?" Aiden continued. "For weeks we plan out our arguments and we prepare for every counter. We recite them over and over again, and for what? To prove *what*, exactly? That one team is better at googling than the other? Or better at memorizing quippy comebacks and prepackaged answers? That isn't how real life works, you can't just know everything you're going to say in advance like that. How about we do some *real* debating? Let's pick a new topic and 'take it away!'" he said, mimicking our judge's bored, nasally tone. "How about it? Let's have a real debate." He slapped the podium with his hand and everyone in the room jumped except for Doug.

Cassie and Amanda both stared at him, then stared at each other before finally shifting their gazes to stare at me.

"Aiden," I muttered as the shock wore off and I jolted out of my seat. "Why don't I take the cross—" I tried to pull him back by his suit jacket, but he swatted my hand away with a manic expression that made my insides twist into a horrible, knotted mess.

Hang in there! the cat on the poster reminded me with a wink as Aiden and I stood there, face to face behind the beat-up old podium, in the tiny too-hot classroom.

"We need to use some of our prep time!" I yelled to the now very interested Doug, who'd sat up straight in his seat once Aiden had started his strange soliloquy. "Stop the clock."

"Just when things were getting interesting," he mumbled, rifling through his binder full of guidelines and regulations. "Whatever, I don't care. Do you?" he asked our opponents who sat frozen at their table. They chanced a glance at Aiden, who was gripping the podium like he was about to start making another speech. They wisely shook their heads.

"Take five," Doug yawned.

"Better make it a full ten," I huffed as I dragged Aiden out of the classroom and across the hall, then straight through a familiar narrow door. I thought he would fight me or try to run off and take over the podium again, but Aiden offered no resistance as I shoved him into the janitor's closet. I slammed the door shut behind us before remembering to turn on the light.

"What do you think you're doing?" I wailed into the darkness. "We practiced for this, we were completely prepared! And I thought after everything that happened yesterday, we'd come back and try this out. That maybe we could make it work; make *us* work." The tone of my voice swung back and forth between enraged and hurt as I tried to sort through everything I was feeling. "But I should've known you'd do something stupid to sabotage me…"

Rage won as I ranted into the shadows, too afraid to turn on the light. It was easier to cling to my self-righteous anger like the life preserver it was when I couldn't see his face.

But I stopped talking when I heard Aiden slump against the door and sigh, the sound muffled like he'd dropped his face into his hands. "We didn't go back, Josephine."

Twenty-Eight

"WHAT DID YOU say?" My hip bumped into a teetering stack of brooms, sending one sailing across the floor with a loud *whack*. "That's not funny," I whispered shrilly as my hands scrambled blindly against the wall in search of the light switch. Now I was desperate to turn the light on, to see his laughing face as he shook his head and told me he was just kidding.

Aiden beat me to it. He flipped the switch and the single lightbulb lit up, illuminating the wild look in his eyes and his blond hair all askew. "I'm telling you, we didn't go back. We're still in the alternate." His voice was serious and firm without the slightest hint of a joke.

My heart stuttered as I stumbled back, nearly knocking over the supply shelf on the wall behind me. "But you said that you always wake up where you—"

"I know what I said! But that didn't happen."

"How do you know?" I asked, slicing into him with a skeptical look. "How do I know you're not just screwing around?"

"Because when I woke up this morning, my brother Wes met me at the table and wished me luck over his bowl of cereal." Aiden closed his eyes and smacked his head against the door with a thud. He sighed and massaged his temple, his mouth puckered into a deep frown.

It was Saturday—I knew that. But it wasn't *our* Saturday. We'd crossed over into tomorrow, but we'd stayed exactly the same. We were stuck in the wrong timeline.

"What do we do?" I asked quietly, trying to shove my panic back down, but it was rapidly rising in me, blisteringly hot.

"I don't know." He kept rubbing his forehead and squinting like he was in pain.

"Are you okay?" I reached out and took his hand in mine, lacing our fingers together.

He smiled weakly. "It's just a headache. I'm fine."

"But I thought you didn't get those headaches when you're in this timeline?"

Aiden's hand tightened around mine as he grimaced. "I usually don't."

We stared at each other under the glow of the swaying lightbulb. I pulled my stopwatch out of my blazer pocket. "We've nearly used all of our prep time. What should we do? We need to get back in there—"

"I think we have to throw the tournament." He winced and dropped my hand, looking down to avoid my gaze.

"*What*?" My voice came out like a screech. I coughed and tried to clear my throat. "What did you just say?"

"We can't do things like we normally would. I don't know what will happen if we do."

"We'll lose, that's what will happen! Is that why you were acting all crazy during the cross-examination? 'Let's have a real debate!'"

Aiden pinched the bridge of his nose and nodded. "We can't win, we have to keep things different. Think about the other timeline," he said, folding his arms over his chest. "Don't you remember what I told you about the last time I wasn't careful here? I saw things disappearing."

"But I thought you just saw a pillow vanish. Or a picture frame or something."

"It's more than that, Josephine." He swallowed. "It's moments forgotten and lost. I saw things changing. And maybe it wouldn't seem like a big deal at first. Maybe it would just be something small like you notice a few things in your room are gone or misplaced. But what if it affects more?"

He tried to pace around the closet, but there was hardly enough room for two people to stand in there, so he just walked in a tight circle and ended up exactly where he'd started. "Say Ms. Isaacs forgets to give us our history exam on Monday. Or maybe Cat suddenly doesn't like to draw anymore. Or maybe she dumps Ethan and Rose runs away. Or my mom shaves her head and my dad wins the lottery, or maybe he just disappears altogether—"

"Okay, I get it. We don't know what will happen. But we can't just *lose.*"

He looked at me with one corner of his mouth pulling up into a sad smile. "Would that really be the end of the world?" he asked softly.

"Yes, actually, it would."

I could handle skipping class and pretending my responsibilities didn't exist for a day. I could throw out the gavel and not show up for the homecoming parade, but this? I'd never intentionally done badly at something in my entire life.

Just thinking the thought left a terrible, bitter taste in my mouth.

"But Aiden, why are we still here?"

His gaze shifted to his feet. "Maybe we could just stay," he said quietly. "Would that really be the end of the world?" he asked again. When he met my eyes, he looked nervous. Like he'd just revealed something tender and small that he'd never told anyone before, and he was waiting to see what I'd do with it. Would I throw it on the floor and smash it, or crumple it up like some scrap paper that didn't matter? Or could I handle his admission gently, with careful hands?

My shoulders loosened as I reached out and touched his cheek. "We can't stay here, Aiden, because it's not ours. This life, these versions of everyone—they don't belong to us."

Aiden bit his lip and leaned his face into my hand. "But we could make it ours. We wouldn't even know the difference after a while." The air shimmered around him as soon as the words left his mouth, tightening and squeezing until the tiny closet felt like it was going to close in on us. Aiden's face screwed up as if he was in pain.

I gripped his arms and inhaled sharply through my nose, trying to get more air into my lungs. "But shouldn't we know the difference?"

I didn't know what else to say. I tried to imagine if this was the only place I could be with my sister, if this was the only way I could see Rose living the life she was meant to live. Would I be able to just walk away? To pretend like it wasn't more real to me than anything else out there?

I couldn't look him in the eyes and tell him that I wouldn't do the same thing.

I leaned forward and pressed my mouth softly to his. His arms circled around me as he kissed me back, warm and sweet, then buried his face in my neck and sighed. My mind was whirling, ticking along with the frantic clicking of my stopwatch as I tried to find some sort of solution, something that made sense.

How were we going to get home?

I leaned back to look at his face. "Can you see the cracks right now?"

Aiden nodded slowly with his eyes still closed. "They're everywhere."

I peered around the room, wishing I could see what he saw, but the only thing my eyes landed on were discounted cleaning products covered in cobwebs and neglect.

"Maybe you should touch one?"

"But I can't," he said, his voice rising in alarm, "we don't know what will happen—"

"I don't think we have any other options."

I ran my fingers through his hair as I mentally laid out all the pieces of the puzzle, shifting them this way and that, trying to see the complete picture but feeling like I'd been stuck with an instruction manual for the wrong game. I thought about everything that had happened yesterday, all the things I'd ignored because I was too caught up in our games. Too caught up in Aiden.

"Think about it. Nothing about this timeline makes sense. Why would your family have moved to Pearson without Wes's accident or your dad losing his job? Why do some things stay the same here, but other details don't?" Aiden stiffened but didn't answer. "All of those choices would've had consequences like they did in your real life, wouldn't they? Your life here wouldn't play out in the same way."

Still, he stayed silent. Of course he already knew all of this. He was the smartest person I knew.

It could change things, alter our histories, he'd said to me. *The domino effect alone—*

Now *I* was starting to get a headache. "Maybe we don't need to throw the debate. Let's go out there and take first place, and maybe that's what will bring us back home," I said, half kidding, half hoping he'd go for my nonsensical plan and let us win.

"Wow," he chuckled dryly. "You really don't like losing."

My lips pinched together in a tight line. "Says the boy who wouldn't walk away from a stupid football game last night even though he was tearing the fabric of time... or something equally dramatic."

"Fair point."

Point to me, indeed.

"Come on, Aiden, let's just try."

"But what if—"

"—what if everything changes?" I guessed, tugging on his jacket to pull him in closer. "Maybe Ms. Isaacs will forget to give us our history exam on Monday. Or maybe Cat suddenly won't like to draw anymore. Maybe she will dump Ethan and Rose will run away and your mom will shave her head while your dad wins the lottery. We don't know. We'll never know. And we're not supposed to."

Aiden looked at me skeptically but didn't argue. His mouth creased into a frown as he rummaged through his pockets. "We're out of time, aren't we?" he asked after a quick glance at his phone. He slid it back into his suit and squared his shoulders, straightening his tie before leaning in to kiss me quickly. "You ready?" His expression was grim but determined.

I could work with that.

I smoothed my hands down my skirt and nodded. Everything else might be up in the air, but at least I had the always reliable structure of policy debate to hold onto. "But *please* don't go back out there and continue to desecrate the sacred rules of debate; it's sacrilege," I pleaded.

Aiden smiled but his eyes looked far away. "I thought it was very *Great Debaters* of me."

"Not so much. You're no Denzel Washington."

He rubbed his hand along his forehead again as he reached across me to open the door.

"Are you sure you're okay? Your head—"

"It's fine," he interrupted. "I'm fine. Let's go wipe the floor with them. If we're going down in flames, at least we'll go down as champions, right?"

We play the game because we're good at it.

We both laughed weakly even though nothing about this was funny.

Judge Doug looked eager when we walked back into the room. He even rubbed his palms together, like he couldn't wait for Aiden to start ranting again.

I marched over to the podium with my head held high and said, "Let's begin," without another glance at gleeful Doug or the reluctant opposition still seated at their table.

Cassie scrambled to her feet as I fired off my first question. "You argue that mandatory voting does not infringe upon a citizen's individual liberty, but you cannot deny that forcing someone to comply with a policy they may not wish to participate in is the very definition of infringing upon an individual's right to choose, isn't that right?" I spoke with such vigor, I think I scared Doug, who shrank back down in his seat as he looked mournfully at his stopwatch.

"What I meant by that was..." Cassie mumbled into her notecards as she shuffled through them haphazardly, "what we meant to say is that civil liberties—I mean, wait." She fumbled and dropped half her notecards, and Amanda darted out of her seat to grab them off the floor. "Doesn't an individual forfeit their full rights to participate..." Cassie fanned herself with her remaining notecards as she continued to stumble her way through her answer.

Of course, a part of me (okay, a really tiny part of me) felt bad watching her fold under the pressure, but when I was in the middle of a debate round, my competitive side was fully in charge. I just couldn't help myself.

The three minutes flew by as I carefully wove through my line of questioning and dismantled our opponents' plan line by line. I felt invigorated by the time I'd finished; I had to repeatedly remind myself not to grin gloatingly. But the same couldn't be said for Aiden—he had on his Cheshire Cat face as I slid into my seat.

"That was reasonably well-done," he whispered on his way to deliver his first negative construction.

I rolled my eyes and bit back my smile.

Poor Amanda did not fare much better with Aiden once it was her turn for the cross-examination; he completely eviscerated her. I sat on the edge of my seat, watching him casually lean against the podium as he turned every question she threw at him back in her face. It made me want to forget the rest of the tournament and drag him back to the dark janitor's closet.

Something was very wrong with me.

He grinned at Amanda as he presented his final question, and she stuttered under the full gleam of his Golden Boy smile. Forget his super-powered super memory, Aiden probably only won his debate rounds by flirting with his opponents or charming the judges. Tapping my pencil impatiently on the table, I cleared my throat loudly as the urge to kiss him vanished and annoyance took its place. I elbowed him sharply as we traded places at the podium and Aiden nearly snorted.

As the round dragged on, Doug looked painfully bored, and he wasn't even trying to hide it. He sighed loudly multiple times, fiddling with his stopwatch noisily on the desk until my slitted gaze forced him to stop. I'd nearly forgotten the crisis at hand—that we were currently stuck in a timeline we didn't belong in—I was so caught up in the tournament and the rush of adrenaline that flooded my body every time I stood to speak. But as we neared the end of the debate, Aiden started gritting his teeth and rubbing the side of his head more frequently. I nudged him with my knee under the table, trying to see if he was okay, but he just gave me a half smile-half grimace and shook his head.

Once both sides were finished, Doug scanned over his sloppy notes (all three sentences of them) and sighed. "Sorry, ladies. Even with their rocky start, Pearson High smoked you. I was rooting for you too," he said sadly to Cassie and Amanda, who just looked relieved this weird round was over for them. "Better luck next time," he added, giving them an aggressive thumbs-up.

I would've glared at him for his obvious favoritism, but it wasn't worth it because we'd won.

On to the next round.

Aiden laid his head down on the table as I packed up our supplies. "Okay, you're obviously not fine." I scanned the now abandoned classroom and saw nothing amiss. No ripples, no branching cracks, no gaping holes into the void.

"My head is killing me," he muttered distractedly.

I rubbed my hand in small circles on the back of his neck. "Do you want to stop? We don't need to—"

"No. Let's go." He clenched his jaw and stumbled his way out of the classroom. I glanced at the cat poster one last time and prayed to it for strength before shutting the door behind me.

Twenty-Nine

DESPITE AIDEN'S HEADACHE and our ever-fraying nerves, we sailed through our next six rounds with perfect ease. When Aiden was on, he was *on*. His easy charm and razor-sharp focus were impressive on any day, but today it was spectacular. I'd also like to humbly (okay, not so humbly) admit that I was also totally on fire. Every argument I made was a steel trap, enclosing the opposing team in cages made of their own words, forged by debate skills inferior to ours.

After every debate, we sank into our seats and waited for something to happen. With each round we won, I wondered if that's what would finally push us over the edge; if that victory would be the thing to merge the timelines and bring us home. So we waited, still and tense as the air grew tight around us, leaving Aiden clutching his head in pain.

But nothing changed. We were winning, but it wasn't enough.

By the time we broke for a late lunch, both of us were exhausted and teetering on the brink of a breakdown. I felt the thrill of victory, but it was overshadowed by the looming relentless question of how to get back home. Aiden slumped in the seat across from mine at our designated team table in the cafeteria. I watched him anxiously as the rest of our teammates filtered in, talking animatedly about their own triumphs and losses. Brandon shyly told me he hadn't lost a poetry round yet. At that, Aiden managed to lift his head up to shoot Brandon a dirty look before letting his face fall back on the table with a loud smack.

"Is Aiden all right?" Ms. Torrence asked me, her brow knit with worry as she peered at him over her glasses.

"Yeah, he just has a headache," I muttered, even as my stomach tied itself into yet another knot. I wasn't sure how much longer we could hold this all together with our bare hands, sheer will, and dumb luck. I couldn't see any cracks or tears like Aiden could, but I felt the strange charge in the air and the tightness in my lungs like there wasn't enough oxygen in the room.

I sank into the chair next to Aiden's just as the officials announced the final debate round. It was the two of us versus the team from Southwick High—Jared and Kyle. No surprise there; they were the only contenders. I tapped Aiden on the shoulder and pointed to the large sign posted with our scores. "Champions," I said, splaying my jazz hands.

He smiled weakly before groaning and tucking his head back into his arms crossed on the table. Through the small window in the cafeteria doors, I could see people filing into the auditorium across the hall, the friends and family who'd come to watch the final rounds of the day. The back of Mr. Mitchell's head floated by with Mrs. Mitchell in tow as they joined the other people ambling in. But one face stopped to peer into the window—Wes's.

"Aiden," I whispered, poking him on the shoulder again. "Your brother's here."

He stiffened and sat up with a jolt. "I'll be right back," he muttered as he stood, tugging at his tie to loosen it. I watched him walk unsteadily to the double doors and push them open, his brother greeting him with a grin and a slap on the back.

Wes's expression slid from casual to serious as their conversation began. I stared at the small window, studying Aiden's body language as they spoke. He slightly swayed back and forth like he was shifting on his feet; he ran a hand through his hair and shrugged the way he did when he was trying to look nonchalant; and when his hands fell to his sides, I would've bet almost anything that he'd shoved them into his pockets.

I knew Aiden well. I'd spent all of my teenage years watching him, obsessing over all the things he said and did. And right now it was as clear as day to me: he was struggling; he was holding on for dear life.

I was in the middle of debating with myself over whether or not I should go to him when I felt the shift in the air and heard that strange sound again. The soft hissing. Like the slow ripping of a sheet of paper.

I scrambled to my feet and ran to the doors, nearly knocking Aiden over in my hurry to open them. Wes's face flickered like the light of a candle about to go out. He looked slightly hazy and a little off-balance as he offered me a smile in greeting and went on talking to Aiden. The air was even tighter over here; the electric current running through everything made all the hairs on the back of my neck stand on end.

I tugged on Aiden's hand, but he ignored me, his eyes wide and trained on his brother's face. I could see him drinking in every detail, every minute mannerism, soaking it up like it would never be enough.

"Anyway, don't worry about the game," Wes said, bumping Aiden on the arm with his fist. "But you should tell Dad the truth, you know."

"Tell him—tell him what?" Aiden stammered.

"That you don't want to play anymore."

"But—why would you—I never said—"

Wes laughed and gave me a look that said, "Can you believe this guy?" Like I was in on the joke. "It's pretty obvious that your heart's not in it. You want to win, but just because you like to win. Not because you actually enjoy it." He paused and lifted an eyebrow. "Am I right?"

Aiden pressed his lips together and looked down.

Wes sighed. "You should tell Dad," he said again. "You've got a lot of other things going for you." He gestured at all the kids loafing around in their best suits, then nudged me in the side with his elbow as if he was including me on the list of things Aiden had going for him. "You've got your own life to live."

Aiden swayed into me as he gaped at Wes.

"You'll be fine. I just know it." Wes's eyes were full of something I couldn't quite name as he stood there smiling at his little brother. It looked like a mix of pride with a dash of admiration, but mostly it was just a heaping helping of love. My throat felt too tight as I watched

Aiden wrestling with his emotions. He sniffed and looked down at the scuffed linoleum floor of the hallway.

"And good luck in there!" Wes called over his shoulder as he opened the door to the auditorium where Beau and Lacy were waiting to drag him to their saved seats. Beau made kissing sounds when he saw me standing there with Aiden, and Lacy howled with laughter.

Aiden didn't even react. He looked like he was closing in on himself, like he'd slammed his doors shut and pulled the blinds down, all hollowed out and vacant.

"Are you okay?" I asked because I didn't know what else to say.

"Not really, no." He turned to walk away but instead came face to face with the towering trophy case where his brother was immortalized on the golden plaques and shining trophies. The lights flickered overhead and the air shivered around us as Aiden winced into his hands again.

I thought of his brother's face fading in and out of view. I thought of Aiden's onset of headaches and how the air tightened around us like it wanted to squeeze us out. I thought of the way he tried so hard to do things differently here, but everything always seemed to end up the same. It was like no matter what we'd done yesterday, our reality kept trying to pull us back in. Real life kept calling and Aiden couldn't go on ignoring it anymore.

"Those cracks, those rips in the timeline—" I shuddered as the air seemed to tug on me in acknowledgment, "—they're trying to take us back, aren't they? It's supposed to merge, isn't it? Only now we've stayed too long, and that's why your head is hurting again, right?"

Aiden didn't answer my questions. He stared at his brother's name carved into the gilded awards. Pearson High's pride and joy, star running back, Wes Mitchell. "Remember how I told you about that day when the timelines almost merged?"

"I remember," I said, gently taking his hand in mine. "You said it was the year you moved to Pearson."

His gaze shifted down, the golden flecks in his eyes flashing in the overhead light. "I told you I was at my house, right? There we were, sitting around the family room like we had been the day before, everyone doing their own thing. My dad had the TV on; my mom was reading; I was playing cards with Beau and Lacy. But Wes was there, too. He wasn't out with his friends, he was just sitting on the couch, talking with us. It felt so normal, so right, to have him there at home. But that was only the second time I'd crossed over to this timeline. I didn't realize that I needed to pay attention to the details. I didn't want to get up and leave or do anything different. All I wanted was to sit at home with my family, whole and complete, just for a minute. But one by one, little things started to disappear. Evidence of Wes. He started to slip away—his voice, his laugh, all of him.

"It scared me." Aiden's grip on my hand tightened. "I didn't want to lose him again. I thought about what I'd done the last time I'd been there, how I'd taken the day of the accident and made it different. So I got up and left. Just walked out in the middle of the conversation. I let the moment unfold the way it could've, the way it *should've* if Wes was still with us. I changed the day. And everything was okay."

All the pieces clicked into place. Aiden's insistence that we had to keep things separate, his determination to make things right for his family. He couldn't stop clinging to the second chance he'd never actually received.

"He's what anchors you here, isn't he? Your brother."

Aiden bit his lip and slowly nodded.

"It's not just about the timelines merging," I said, leaning back to look at him. "I think you just wanted to make a space where things could be different, where *you* could be different. A space where you didn't have to miss your brother or feel like you'd let anyone down. A do-over," I said softly. "The other side of the day you wish had never happened."

Aiden shrugged one shoulder in a noncommittal way, then slumped against the trophy case, looking tired and defeated. It was enough to break anyone's heart.

It most certainly broke mine.

"Aiden," I said carefully, "I think it's time to go home."

He sniffed again and kept his eyes trained on the floor. "And how are we supposed to do that?"

"I think you know."

"I'm not in the mood for riddles, Josephine," he said as he kneaded his knuckles against the side of his head and grimaced.

I was standing so close to him, his back was pressed against the trophy case. I pinned him there with my hands and my gaze until he had no choice but to look at me. "You don't need an alternative reality to be someone else. You don't need to apologize for anything or try again. And Wes doesn't need you to build him a different world so you can keep saying goodbye."

The air shifted again like it was trying desperately to slide us back to what was right, to where we belonged, but Aiden still had one foot on either side of the door.

"We can't go back because you're not letting go. You need to let *him* go, Aiden."

I'd known it was true the moment I'd seen them standing together in the hallway—Wes's gleam fading away while Aiden did his very best to hold on, willing him into existence. I'd only just figured it out, but Aiden must've always known; since the first time he'd crossed over and turned that nightmare of a day into a blissful afternoon at the lake.

But how do you let someone go? Is it one single decision? Or is it a million tiny choices that slowly relax your grip until all you have left are half-remembered memories and a partially healed-over hole in your chest?

I'd never wished harder to have the right answers than I did at that moment.

Just then, my family came shuffling down the hall. My mom was in her best dress, her hair and makeup predictably flawless, with my dad in his nicest polo. They looked fidgety and nervous like they weren't sure where to go or what to do. Once they saw me standing there the three of us waved uncomfortably like we were acquaintances who'd only met a few times.

It was weird. But it was something.

Rose was right behind them, rolling her eyes at their awkward hesitancy as she herded them into the auditorium. She gave us a bright smile and a thumbs up. "I hope you crush them!" she said gleefully before the doors swung shut behind them

Aiden watched all of this unfold without a word. After a minute, he finally spoke. "I'm turning eighteen next week. Then I'll officially be older than Wes." His face crumpled.

All I could do was put my arms around him as we watched the rest of the people filing into the auditorium. All the people who were trying their best to love us. We stayed like that for a long time until the hallway was empty and we were alone.

"I think that's why I've been seeing so many cracks lately," he said quietly. "As soon as I skipped one dose of meds, there they were." I could feel his pulse jumping where my cheek was resting against his neck. "It's hard for me to stay in control when I'm feeling so much."

He paused, then laughed softly, his breath warm against my ear. "That's probably why you fell in here with me. You definitely leave me feeling more than a little out of control, Josephine."

"Control is overrated," I whispered back. "You can't run away to a place where nothing bad ever happens. You can't control every aspect of your life." As soon as I said the words, I knew they weren't just for him.

Just then, the cafeteria doors burst open behind us, and the rest of our team filed out. "There you two are!" Ms. Torrence panted. She had both of our backpacks clutched in her hands (no wonder she was sweating). "You're supposed to be on stage already! Go!" She dropped our cumbersome backpacks at our feet and ushered our teammates into the auditorium or off to their own final rounds.

Aiden took a deep breath and handed me my bag, looking resolved. "Come on," he said as he shouldered his own backpack and pulled me through the auditorium doors. "We've got a debate to win."

We passed by Rose who was in the middle of persuading our parents to quit hovering in the back of the room and to go take seats near the front instead. Cat was there too, following along in their wake. She was glitter-free today, but she had "Go Josephine!" scrawled on one cheek and "Go Aiden" on the other. I scowled in embarrassment, but my eyes started stinging when I saw her smiling at me from the crowd. Aiden's family was sitting in the front row like they were used to coming to cheer for him.

"Are you ready?" Aiden asked, his hand resting on the small of my back.

Ready for what? I wanted to say. *Who can ever be ready?*

But instead, I nodded, and we turned and marched solemnly up the stairs to the stage.

The spotlights were bright and glaring; I could feel the heat pouring off them as I slid into my chair at the Pearson High table. Jared and Kyle assented to nod in our direction as they took their seats across from us on the opposing side. I pulled out my laptop and shuffled through my papers, but Aiden just sat there, staring out at the audience.

The district official in charge of the tournament stood at the front of the stage with a microphone in hand, welcoming everyone to the final debate of the day. She turned and beamed at both sides, making a considerable effort to look neutral as she nodded at the four of us. "Pearson High, y'all are affirmative."

I went to high-five Aiden under the table (we were solid for both sides of the debate, but affirmative was where we did our best and most brutal work), but he didn't notice. He was already halfway out of his chair when he said, "I'm going to take the opening." He paused and dipped his head, giving me a small smile. "If that's all right with you, I mean."

"Sure," I said hesitantly, hopefully.

I wiped my sweaty palms on the smooth fabric of my skirt as Aiden stood and walked to the podium. He placed his hands gently on the dark wood and scanned the crowd just like he did on his first day of school in Mrs. Crabtree's sixth-grade class. He was surveying the audience, slowly and meticulously searching through the sea of faces as if he was looking for something. And when his eyes flicked back to land on mine, he smiled softly like he'd found it.

I sat up taller in my seat, hoping I'd measure up under a gaze like that. Aiden's mouth twitched and he shook his head as if he'd read my mind. *Stand down, soldier,* I could almost hear him saying.

Maybe we didn't need to measure anything after all.

He inhaled sharply, then exhaled the words, "Let's begin," and started delivering his opening statement. Jared and Kyle hunched in their seats and quickly scribbled notes while Aiden took them through every point of our case in support of mandatory voting. He'd quit rubbing his forehead, and he was no longer grimacing in pain when he spoke. He was completely focused on the task at hand until the last few lines of his closing statement.

Other people watching might not have noticed the difference in his delivery. The way he leaned forward, his eyes landing on his parents and Wes in the front row, Beau and Lacy wiggling on their end seats next to them. The way his breath caught before he said his final words. The way the sound of it hung in the air like a whispered goodbye.

Other people might not have noticed, but I'm not other people.

He watched me, I watched him—that was our thing, after all. Something about keeping your friends close but your enemies closer.

The air felt tight like we were squeezing through some invisible and too-small space. Then everything subtly shifted, like a house settling back onto its foundation.

Wes Mitchell looked at his little brother and smiled. It was like he knew somehow, impossibly.

And then he faded away.

If I squinted, I could almost see the outline of his broad shoulders still seated there next to his parents. But he was gone.

Aiden gripped the podium tightly with his hands. He swallowed roughly and hung his head before slowly letting go, one finger at a time. He stood at the podium for a few seconds in total silence before the audience started to applaud. They looked a little uncertain and slightly confused, but still impressed nonetheless. Like they were collectively thinking, *"Wow, that Mitchell kid sure loves democracy!"* so they clapped along like they were in on it, and they pretended like they didn't notice the way the air had rippled around them, or how it had calmed like the sea after a storm.

One glance out the window showed me it was raining outside.

Wes was gone, and it was raining.

We were home.

Rose blinked heavily a few times and yawned the way she always did when she came to watch me debate—like she was trying her hardest not to fall asleep. Mom and Dad were still glancing around like they weren't sure how they'd got there in the first place. Cat was doodling on her sneakers but shot me a grin when she caught me looking at her.

Mr. and Mrs. Mitchell clapped the loudest, their faces shining proudly at their son. But once the judges quieted everyone down and motioned for the opposing team to begin their cross-examination, I noticed Betty Mitchell's eyes land on the empty seat between her and her husband, her forehead creasing as if she was wondering why they'd left that space there.

I didn't take any notes as Kyle attacked our opening arguments with all the gusto he had. I barely listened to his line of questioning; all I could think about was what Aiden had just done and how he must be feeling. I wanted to pause the debate, to use some of our prep time to take him off the stage and to let him be. Just for a moment.

But Aiden leaned into the podium, his posture more relaxed than it had been all morning as he easily worked his way through the cross, citing all of his references without any notes in hand (a fact that I knew must drive Kyle and Jared insane). Once he was finished, he sat down next to me, looking tired but a little relieved too.

My hand found his under the table as Jared droned on and on about uninformed voters and the dangers of tyranny. I laced my fingers through Aiden's and ran my thumb across his knuckles, hoping that my simple gesture would convey that I saw him—that I knew what he'd just done.

That letting go didn't have to mean forgetting. That moving on didn't mean he was leaving his brother behind.

There were so many things I wanted to say to him, but all I could do was squeeze his hand before rising to my feet when the timer signaled it was my turn to handle Jared.

"Wipe the floor with him," Aiden said softly as I brushed past him. His eyes were a little red around the edges, but he gave me his best Golden Boy grin and a flash of his dimple.

"Like there was ever any alternative," I said in his ear as I took the podium and began.

Thirty

I T DOESN'T NEED to be said, but I'll say it anyway: we won the tournament.

Ms. Torrence looked like she was ready to weep in relief as she hugged my teammates and jumped up and down (I could probably try to be a little nicer to her). Aiden and I barely got to speak as we were juggled back and forth between our exuberant team (who conveniently pretended they'd never outvoted me) and our families who weren't quite sure how to celebrate a big debate tournament win. It's not exactly like they could dump a cooler of Gatorade on us or anything.

My dad patted me awkwardly on the back, his eyes crinkling in the corners as he smiled at me. "So, what's next?" he asked.

"The regional tournament," I told him. "Then state." I was surprised he'd thought to ask—surprised, but pleased.

"You looked a little greasy under all those lights, Josephine," my mom said as she dabbed at my face with a tissue she'd pulled out of her purse. "Next time, let me do your makeup. I know all the brands that are sweat-proof, darling, I'll fix you right up." She didn't tell me I did a good job, or congratulate me on winning, but her implication that there would be a "next time" meant something, and we both knew that.

Rose snatched the tissue out of Mom's hand and balled it up in the pocket of her plaid bell bottoms. "Quit wiping Josephine down, Mom." She squealed and threw her arms around me. "You were amazing! I didn't understand half of what you said, but I loved every second of it." I didn't mention that I'd seen her nodding off I few times. Instead, I just squeezed her back.

Cat nudged me with her elbow until I ducked my head so she could whisper in my ear. "You two looked good together up there," she said meaningfully. "I was sensing a whole new vibe coming from your side of the stage. Care to explain?" She arched a black eyebrow at me.

"Nope," I said with a laugh as I smudged the "Go Josephine" still scrawled across her cheek in bright purple.

She pretended to pout until Aiden motioned to me and caught my eye, mouthing that he'd call me later as Beau and Lacy pulled on his arms and planned their celebratory dinner.

"I saw that!" Cat hissed. "*Vibes.* I told you."

I pointedly ignored her, but the blush that crept all the way to my hairline was a dead giveaway.

It felt strange to watch Aiden walking away after spending so much time together, but I guess that's what happens when life falls back into place—you keep going.

Back at home, I came out of my room to see Mom scooting over some of her old pageant awards, leaving a small space for my trophy on the top shelf. She set it down with a smile on her face—a soft and fragile wisp of a thing—as she went on dusting her crowns and straightening her sashes.

Dad said I could pick what to watch on TV in celebration. A true honor, coming from him.

"Dad," I asked as I sat on the couch next to his recliner. "Do you ever read comics?"

His eyes flicked away from the TV in surprise. "Yeah, I guess I do sometimes." He grinned sheepishly and shrugged. "I have since I was a kid," he said, tapping his foot on the floor. "You know there's this little shop in town that sells them; it's run by this kind of goofy guy..." He trailed off, suddenly looking unsure.

"Maybe we could go some time," I finished.

"Maybe we could." We blinked at each other a few times before he ran a hand through his unruly head of hair, the rusty gesture of a former Golden Boy. "Now how about you order us a victory pizza, hmm?" he said, patting my arm lightly. He snorted at *The Office* episode I'd chosen for us (mainly due to Rose's insistence). "This is a funny one."

Rose met me in the kitchen looking too sly for my own comfort. "Why is your face like that?" I asked, pinching my lips together at her shifty eyes and impish grin.

"Oh, it's nothing," she said idly right as my phone rang. She laughed and ran out of the kitchen, shooting me a significant look before hiding in her bedroom.

"Truth or Dare," Aiden said the moment I answered.

"Truth," I said with a laugh.

"You were supposed to say dare," he mumbled. "Fine. Time for your truth, and you have to answer honestly."

"I make no promises."

"Would you go to the homecoming dance with me tonight?"

I sagged into the chipped kitchen counter. "What did you just say?"

"You heard me. I dare you to go to the dance with me."

I scoffed. "You can't choose both truth *and* dare, that goes against the basic principles of the game—"

"Josephine! Will you please go with me?"

My stomach fell to my feet. "Yes," I whispered into the phone clutched against my cheek. "Yes, I'll go to the dance with you."

I could hear him smiling into his phone. "We'll be the talk of the school," he said in a voice that sounded like nothing could please him more.

"Or they'll bar us from entering because they're afraid we'll burn the place to the ground."

"But, Madame President, we're co-presidents; they have to let us in." I heard him shuffling around. I imagined him in his closet, rifling through his clothes and trying to find something to wear. "Go get ready. I'll meet you there."

I ended the call and stood frozen in the kitchen, staring at my wide-eyed reflection in the chrome surface of the microwave. Did I just agree to go to the homecoming dance with Aiden?

I could've convinced myself I was just doing it for the dare, but I knew that would be a lie.

Rose stuck her head out of her bedroom door. "Did he ask you?" She waggled her eyebrows at me.

"You *knew*?" I yelped.

"Of course I did. I know everything; I thought we'd already established that."

Our words from the fight we'd had at the homecoming game—the first homecoming game—came back to me in a rush, leaving my cheeks flushed and my heart lurching.

You think you know everything, but that couldn't be further from the truth, Josephine. Sometimes you're completely clueless.

"Look," I said, as I walked into her room and shut the door behind me. "I'm sorry for what I said at the game." I could barely choke the words out, but they needed to be said. "If you want to do a pageant, I'll be in the front row with an embarrassing sign covered in glitter, cheering louder than anyone else in the audience." Rose stared at me from the pile of dresses she was sitting in. "And you *are* smart," I continued, "definitely smarter than me."

She rolled her eyes and tugged on my arm until I fell into the heap of fabric next to her. "Oh, shut up. We both know you're the brain. I just wanted to look at some options for scholarships, that's all. And I thought it might be *fun*."

"Fun," I repeated in a deadpan. "I think I've heard that word before..."

She threw a pillow at me, right in the face.

"I'm letting you off the hook for now since we have to hurry and get ready for the dance. But you better believe that tomorrow Cat and I will spend the entire day grilling you for details about you and Aiden. First, let me just say... I *knew* it." She smiled smugly at me. I was beginning to miss the version of Rose who didn't have any commentary after finding me on the bleachers with mussed hair and Aiden's hand in mine.

Obviously, we didn't have time to go shopping (nor would I have gone willingly) to pick out a new dress for the dance. So we were forced to shop in Rose's closest, which was almost as bad as an entire thrift store. We settled on a vintage mid-length flowing gauzy-type thing (in black of course). I do have some limitations after all, and I wasn't keen on stretching my newfound "live a little" muscles so far that I pulled something.

I twirled around while Rose gave me a round of applause. "I look *good*," I said, placing my hands on my hips. The scattered sequins lining the fabric sparkled under the dim light of her closet.

I would just like to set the record straight: sequins are *not* glitter.

"I actually got this for you a while back," Rose admitted as she looked me over with approval.

"You did not."

"Do I ever wear black?" She put her hand on her chest in mock horror.

"Why would you get this for me?" I frowned at my reflection and her suddenly shy face.

"For this reason precisely," she said, wrapping an arm around my shoulders.

"You've been harboring a secret desire for me to go to the homecoming dance?" I asked skeptically.

"I haven't exactly kept that a secret," she said with a flip of her hand. "And not just homecoming. I wanted you to do something fun just because you wanted to, not because it looks good on your resume."

"Ah, more teenage lessons," I said. "You know, we could've just watched *Pretty in Pink*. Or any John Hughes movie, actually."

Rose sighed like I was a lost cause. "It's the actual act of *going* that matters. The experiences. The people. You're not going to be here much longer, you know. Don't you want something to remember us by?" She said it with a laugh, but her eyes avoided mine and stayed locked on the clothes-strewn floor instead.

"You know it's not you that I'm leaving."

"That doesn't really matter, does it? I'm still being left." She busied herself with straightening the straps of my dress, but she had that stiff chin she got when she was about two seconds away from crying. "I hate that I miss you already. Plus, who's going to microwave Dad's pizza when you're gone?"

We both burst out laughing at the same time, leaning into each other in our familiar way, both of us needing to be held.

"The dress is perfect," she said softly. "And Aiden's going to love it."

"I'm not wearing it for Aiden," I sniffed. "But yes, he will. I look divine."

Rose threw her head back and cackled, then started digging through the rest of her closet, looking for shoes to match. I stared at my reflection, surprised to see that I still looked like me, even in all the flouncy layers and over-the-top pageantry of it all. I flicked my hair over my shoulder and Rose whistled. I threw a shoe at her.

Cat showed up soon after with her makeup bag and thankfully no glitter. The three of us danced around to our '90s playlist while we got ready. Rose and Cat were romanticizing the night as much as possible, which was starting to make me sweat. Then they decided they didn't want to wait for tomorrow, they wanted answers about Aiden and they wanted them now.

I was glad when neither of them said, "But I thought you hated him?"

They just shared a knowing smile and went on applying eyeliner. It was annoying how smug they were, and part of me hated the attention, but the other part of me liked being known for something other than a good grade on a paper. I was just a girl, and he was just a boy, and somehow that was enough.

We planned on meeting the boys at the dance, considering our parents were home and they were bound to overreact. We'd snuck down the hall and nearly made it to the front door undetected when Cat stepped on one of the squeaky floorboards. "Sorry," she mouthed to Rose and me as we scurried down the rest of the hallway.

Dad's head whipped over to see the three of us wrapped in party dresses and carrying our shoes, Rose already halfway out the door. He opened and closed his mouth a few times, looking like a trout. Finally, he seemed to remember that he was the parent and the one who was actually in charge. "Jennifer?" he called out in a panicked voice. "Jenny, get out here!"

"What on earth are you hollering at me for," Mom said as she sauntered out of their bedroom. She froze when she locked eyes on us still hovering by the door, waiting to make our escape. As she slowly walked closer, she looked us up and down.

"You girls look—" she coughed, trying to clear her throat. "You look—" I could practically hear the war raging inside her. On one hand, her daughters finally looked the part—polished and primped, pressed and primed—ready to dazzle at the homecoming dance. But on the other hand, that meant dating and boys, staggered dreams, and harsh new realities.

She held out her hands in front of her as if asking for help with what to do next. It was a quiet gesture that said, *I'm still figuring this out, just like you.*

"They'll be fine, Jenny," Dad said, walking up behind her. "They'll be just fine. Be home by midnight," he added, trying to sound stern. It sounded weird on him. He must've thought so too because he slunk off back to his chair and switched the channel to ESPN.

Mom didn't say another word. She leaned against the wall that held the single photo from her wedding day and glanced at it as she watched us walk out. "Have a nice time," she whispered, just before the door shut behind us.

We hurried and ran to the old station wagon, too afraid to slow down just in case our parents changed their minds. Rose drove too fast as she always does, crooning along to the Shania Twain she had blasting from the speakers. The windows were down even though our hair was curled and hair-sprayed (very lightly in my case), and the first chill of autumn blew through the car as we pulled into the packed parking lot of Pearson High.

Aiden was waiting for me, leaning against his white Tacoma, dressed in his debate suit because that was probably the only suit he owned. Thankfully, Rose and Cat had already scattered to find their dates, leaving me and Aiden alone in the parking lot as his eyes slid over my dress, catching on my legs and the shoes that made me equal in height to him, maybe a smidge taller.

"You're literally speechless," I said smugly as I gave him a little twirl. "I win homecoming."

"Sure, fine, whatever. You win. I'll gladly take the loss if it means I get to see you in that dress." His eyes landed on mine, all lit up and happy under the terrible orange glow of the flickering street lights.

"Don't go all soft on me now, Aiden Christopher Mitchell III. Life will get very boring if you're putty in my hands the second you see me in a nice dress."

He scoffed as he slipped his arm around my shoulders and steered us toward the school. "Please. This is just for the night. We still have the battle royal; I hear valedictorian is up for grabs."

My chest expanded with warmth as I thought about going to class and fighting with him, layering new and exciting and terrifying complications into every word we said.

Now that was going to be fun.

"It's not up for grabs," I sniffed. "I bribed Mrs. Miller in the front office to show me your grades last week, and I've got to say, you're slacking."

He stared at me. "You did not."

"She loves those strawberry candies. You know, the ones that actually look like tiny little strawberries? She keeps them in a bowl on her desk." Aiden continued to stare at me in horror. "I'm disappointed in you, Mr. President. You should really work on your bribing skills if you're going to stay in politics."

The bribing part was true, but the part about his grades was a big fat lie. We were actually neck and neck, completely tied for the top GPA. Poor Mrs. Cartwright was going to keel over if she had to crown us co-valedictorians. She'd never recover.

Aiden frowned at me as he straitened his black tie and smoothed his golden waves back off his forehead. "Let's save the shoptalk for later. Temporary truce?"

"The truce expires at midnight. Until then, I'm all yours."

He grinned and tugged me past the front entrance where he flashed Katlyn our two tickets. She gaped after us, her eyes bulging out of her head when she saw Aiden's hand in mine. I winked at her and waved before the gym doors closed behind us.

I grimaced at the swarm of bodies packed together on the dance floor. A flash of auburn hair revealed Rose in the middle of the pandemonium with Jordan shyly shuffling alongside her. Cat and Ethan were over by the sad buffet tables ladened with bright red punch bowls and trays of stale-looking cookies.

"This looks terrible. Who was in charge of the decorations?"

"We were," Aiden said with a laugh.

For once I'd completely forgotten. For once I didn't care.

Aiden pulled me to the outskirts of the dancing crowd and placed his hands on my waist. I tried to think back to all the John Hughes movies and how I was supposed to dance with him, but I gave up and just slung my arms around his neck as we swayed to the music.

Carrie Underwood, of course.

"I haven't taken my meds yet," Aiden said near my ear as we danced. "My head hurts a little, but it's manageable for now."

I leaned back in surprise, trying to get a better look at his face, but his arms tightened around me. "I wanted to see if they would still be there—the cracks."

"And?" I asked, shifting my hands against the back of his neck so my fingers threaded through his hair.

He smiled but looked a little sad. "No cracks," he said. "But I could hear the whispers. I like to think that maybe they could be Wes's." His hands tightened on my waist. "I like to think about some version of him still existing out there."

I traced the shape of his jaw. "I like thinking about that too."

We danced to a few more songs in silence, not needing to say anything as the music swelled around us and our classmates got increasingly manic. Aiden dipped his head onto my shoulder as Tim Boren tried to crowd surf and fell behind us with a loud thud. "This is very lame. I'm so glad we came."

He wasn't being sarcastic (even though he should've been), but I knew what he meant. This was a moment I never wanted to forget, no matter how weird the gym smelled or how unflattering the flashing lights were.

It was mine to tuck away and revisit whenever I wanted to.

But right before they announced the homecoming court, Aiden asked if I wanted to leave.

"I thought you'd want to get your crown, your majesty," I said, offering him a slight curtsy.

"So you can mercilessly mock me for the rest of my life? I think not." He spun me out to the beat of the music before pulling me in tight to his chest. "Let's get out of here," he breathed.

I grinned as we ran out of the gym to the sound of his name being called over the speakers, the door slamming shut behind us before we could hear who was crowned queen.

We drove through Dairy Queen and picked up two Blizzards, and then we ended up at the airport without either of us deciding to. Sitting in the bed of his truck, we looked up at the stars with our legs tangled together, occasionally trading kisses that tasted like Oreos and vanilla ice cream.

"Can I ask you a question?" I asked after we'd both had a serious case of brain freeze.

"It's not midnight yet. Anything's fair game," he said.

"What do you really want?"

It was one of the most important questions I could think of, easy to dismiss and ever-changing in its answer. And I was only just beginning to understand the honesty it required from both of us.

He paused for a long moment. "I want to finish out this football season and then be done with the game. I want to apply to schools outside of Texas and see what else is out there even if it disappoints my dad. I don't want to be in the German Club or Chess Club—I'm actually pretty terrible—"

"But you're the president!"

"There are only two other people in the club, and they didn't know how to turn me down."

I snorted into my Blizzard.

"I want to write for the school paper more, not just their sports section, which is all they ever assign me. I want to get a job so I can actually save some money. I want to compete in more speech events because I'm good at it and I like the rush." He smirked. "Maybe even a poetry round or two."

I laughed and stole a bite of his ice cream since mine was empty.

"I want to read more comics and write more fan fiction because it's fun and kind of a waste of time, but I like that about it. But mostly, I just want you."

My breath caught in my chest.

"More time with you," he said. "That's what I want."

I didn't know where'd I'd end up next year, and neither did he. But I knew we had right now, this moment, and we could hold it close while we had it, however long that was.

"I want that too. Minus the fan fiction thing, of course."

He rolled his eyes and leaned in closer until our faces were hovering only an inch apart. "You know, it wasn't just about my brother, or me trying to live as much as possible because he didn't get to." His gaze burned into mine. "I like competing with you. You make me better. I have to think through things more clearly because I know you already have. Every argument needs to have just as many counters because you've already thought of them."

I opened my mouth to interrupt, but he pressed a finger to my lips. "And I thought that maybe if I beat you—*The* Josephine Crew—you'd really see me. Just Aiden."

My face was frozen in surprise, my mouth stilled under his light touch.

"Which is stupid, I know," he rushed on, "because sometimes that made me act like an idiot. Sometimes I'd forget that I wasn't just trying to beat you, but that I had a long game."

"I was your long game?" I whispered.

He dropped his finger and took my face in his hands. "Did I win?" he asked softly, pressing his lips to the ridge of my cheekbone.

I sighed and pulled his mouth to mine, kissing him long and hard. "Yes, Aiden. You won. Are you happy?"

"Supremely," he said with a hazy look on his face before he kissed me back.

Point to Mitchell.

I mentally gave him another tally, but with his hands on me, it still felt like I was in the lead.

And then I tossed out the scorecard and pulled him closer.

We could go back to keeping score tomorrow.

T HIS STORY CAME to me at a time when I wasn't sure if I had any more stories left to tell. But then in strolled Josephine and Aiden. Their words filled my head and my heart and changed me for the better. A gift; that's what this story is. And I know where every gift and good thing comes from. I thank my Heavenly Parents and my Savior Jesus Christ for offering me the opportunity to write again. It is the gift that keeps on giving, and one I am forever grateful for.

To Stewart, my wonderful husband and partner, thank you for always believing in me and for not caring that your laundry is never folded. I love you and this life we're building together. To my beautiful daughters, I am grateful every day to be your mom. I hope someday when you read my books, you'll feel all the love I have for you wrapped up in these words. Our time together is splashed all over the pages—you help me write every story.

To my amazing parents who taught me to work hard and who have a ridiculous amount of faith in me—thank you. Thank you for always telling me that I am limitless; I still lean on your belief in me on the hard days. To my siblings and their spouses, I love you. I'm so glad that you're mine. To all of my in-laws: thank you for helping me feel at home; I feel lucky to be part of your beautiful family.

I have so many incredible friends who have encouraged me and lifted me up that I could fill an entire book just with my acknowledgments, but I'll spare you and only list a few. Adri, you came into my life when I really needed a friend who understood what it's like to have a story hold you in its grip, and I will always be grateful for that. Here's to many more retreats and many more books together. To Maddie, for understanding this story (and me) at a level that few people do. Writing with you is truly one of my greatest joys. When they point to the pictures, please tell them my name. Thank you to Sheridan for being an early reader and for loving Josephine and Aiden just as much as I do. Your feedback and support gave me the courage to keep going. I'm so happy I found you.

To my talented beta readers: Kara, Shalee, Tammy, Marissa, and Maddie. Thank you for poking at plot holes and for asking the hard questions. This story is so much richer because of you. To the insanely talented writing community (aka the nicest people on the internet) who welcomed me with open arms and Gilmore Girls quotes, I could never thank you enough. You inspire me; your books will always be at the top of my TBR pile.

Many thanks to all the creative individuals who helped me make *Voted Most Likely*. Paige Poppe, your cover designs are what dreams are made of; I love collaborating with you. Thank you to my editor, Emily Klopfer, for her watchful eye and patient attention to detail. To Katherine Stephen and Phillip Gessert, my proofreader and formatter: your final touches turned this story into a book. I always have to give Jody Moore a shoutout because without her coaching and the tremendous work she's contributing to the world, I would be stuck in a place of indecision and doubt, never taking any forward action. So thank you, Jody.

To every reader who stuck with me after that ending in *A Tangle of Dreams*—thank you. Every review and every comment means more to me than I could ever express. Thank you for reading my words. I write my stories for myself, but I'm so glad I get to share them with you.

To Brooke, my best friend forever. Thank you for being with me every step along the way and for whispering which jokes to add to the book. I miss you so much, but I will never stop being grateful for every year of friendship with you.

Nicole Adair is the author of *A Tangle of Dreams*. She lives in Arizona with her husband and three daughters. Nicole studied Political Science at Brigham Young University but decided that writing teenage love stories is much more fun. When she's not writing, she spends her time reading, running, snuggling her girls, and avoiding doing laundry at all costs. You can find her on Instagram @writenicolewrite to get updates on her writing.

CPSIA information can be obtained
at www.ICGtesting.com
Printed in the USA
BVHW091640020822
643612BV00012B/1305